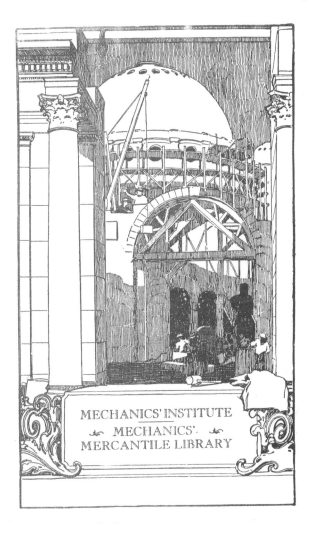

Fredericksburg

◆

KIRK MITCHELL

Fredericksburg

A NOVEL OF THE IRISH
AT MARYE'S HEIGHTS

ST. MARTIN'S PRESS ❧ NEW YORK

A THOMAS DUNNE BOOK.
An imprint of St. Martin's Press

Production Editor: David Stanford Burr

Design: Pei Loi Koay

Maps: Martie Holmer

Library of Congress Cataloging-in-Publication Data

Mitchell, Kirk.
    Fredericksburg : a novel of the Irish at Marye's
Heights / by Kirk Mitchell. —1st ed.
        p.   cm.
    "A Thomas Dunne book."
    ISBN 0-312-13974-8
    1. United States—History—Civil War, 1861–1865—
Participation, Irish American—Fiction.   2. Fredericks-
burg (Va.), Battle of, 1862— Fiction.   I. Title.
PS3563.I7675F74   1996
813'.54—dc20   95-41150
                                                    CIP

First Edition: March 1996

10 9 8 7 6 5 4 3 2 1

Acknowledgments

◆

I wish to thank the following with the understanding that any errors are entirely my own: George McMillan, for his generosity in sharing the memorabilia and oral history of his family; Donald C. Pfanz, Robert K. Krick, Mac Wyckoff, David Preston, and Frank O'Reilly of the Fredericksburg and Spotsylvania National Military Park; Lee Arnold and Lori E. Scherr of the Historical Society of Pennsylvania; Dr. Richard J. Sommers, Louise A. Arnold-Friend, and Michael J. Winey of the U.S. Army Military History Institute, Carlisle Barracks; Steven J. Wright of the Civil War Library and Museum, Philadelphia; Alice James of the Georgia Department of Archives and History; Wendy Schlereth of the Notre Dame University Archives; Padraic O'Farrell of County Westmeath, Ireland, for personal communication and his illuminating book, *How the Irish Speak English*; Keith S. Bohannon of Smyrna, Georgia; Jane E. Caldwell of the Kelly Library, Emory and Henry College; Pamela Liles of *The Post and Courier*, Charleston, South Carolina; David Morris of Brookhaven, Pennsylvania; Dr. Lawrence Kohl of the University of Alabama; Mary Wood of the City of Clarkesville, Georgia; the Clarkesville Methodist Church; the

Elbert County Library, Elberton, Georgia; the Hulett-Hargrett Library, University of Georgia; the Atwater Kent Museum of Philadelphia; the National Archives; and, of course, my researcher, Deborah Brackstone of Memphis State University.

For nothing can be sole or whole
That has not been rent.

— WILLIAM BUTLER YEATS

Washington, D.C., November 14, 1862

Maj. Gen. Ambrose E. Burnside,
Commanding Army of the Potomac:

The President has just assented to your plan. He thinks it will succeed if you move rapidly; otherwise not.

H. W. HALLECK
General-in-Chief

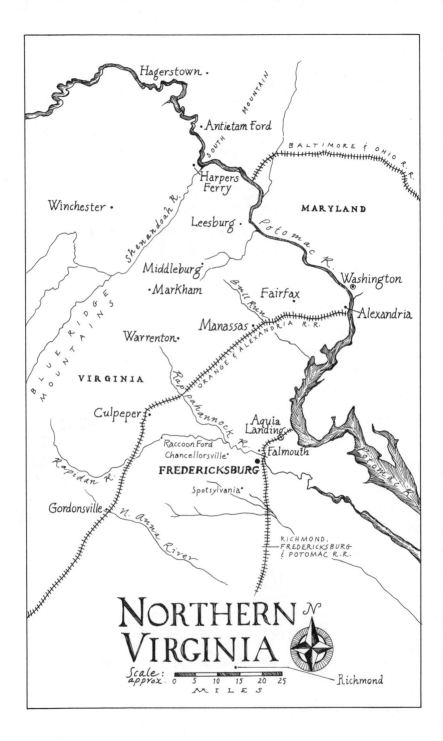

Hagerstown •

• Antietam Ford

Harpers
Ferry

SOUTH MOUNTAIN

BALTIMORE & OHIO R.R.

MARYLAND

Winchester •

Leesburg •

Shenandoah R.

Potomac R.

Washington

Middleburg •

• Markham

Fairfax

BLUE RIDGE MOUNTAINS

VIRGINIA

Bull Run

Manassas •

ORANGE & ALEXANDRIA R.R.

Alexandria

Warrenton •

Rappahannock R.

Culpeper •

Aquia
Landing

Raccoon Ford
Chancellorsville •

Falmouth

Rapidan R.

FREDERICKSBURG

Spotsylvania •

Potomac R.

Gordonsville •

N. Anna River

RICHMOND,
FREDERICKSBURG
& POTOMAC R.R.

NORTHERN
VIRGINIA

N

Richmond

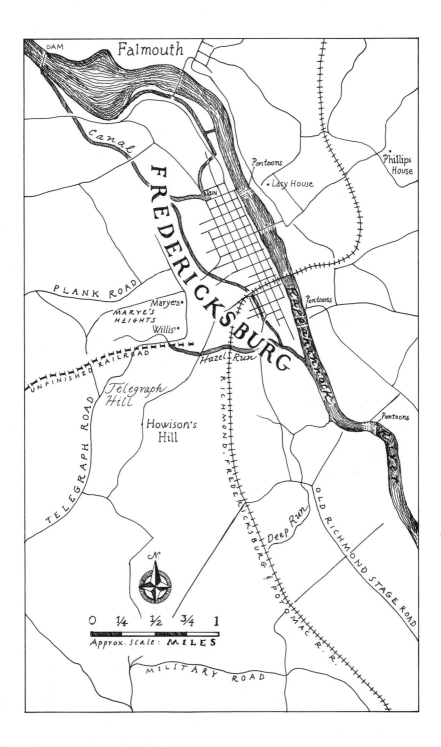

Fredericksburg

♦

*O*ne

◆

7:22 A.M., November 15, 1862
Near Warrenton, Virginia

"I like it no better than you, boys!" Thomas Meagher cried, then paused, his milk-white charger prancing beneath him. A raw wind shrilled down the ranks of the brigade, fluttering the blue overcoats and bullet-torn flags. Turning slightly in the saddle, Father Corby studied the faces of the recruits who'd just arrived from New York and Philadelphia. Those who'd never heard Meagher speak were surprised to hear that their brigadier—the greatest Irishman in America, the descendant of Irish kings—sounded so British. English Jesuits were to blame. They'd whipped his musical Munster accent out of him.

A teenage private of the 88th New York looked up in dismay at Corby. "Father, his chat ain't familiar. Where's Mr. Meagher from?"

The boy's sergeant whispered, "Shut your gob."

Meagher was gazing up into the morning sky. It was slate gray with the wind out of the northwest. He was a thickset man with good carriage. "The night the axe fell," he went on at last, his round and handsome face pained, "I could only pray that it wasn't so, that the schemers in Washington would never do this to us. That they'd never rob the Irish Brigade of its truest friend—General George McClellan!"

A defiant huzzah burst from the three New York regiments. It raised the hair on the back of the priest's neck, then echoed out across onto the misty plain teeming with dark masses of men—the 2d Corps of the Army of the Potomac, waiting for the order to lead the march. The roar startled the men of the 116th Pennsylvania, greenhorns who, other than for a brush with the enemy in the lower Shenandoah Valley, had never really fought for Little Mac. Their new overcoats stood out like blueberries in contrast to the faded, mud-stained uniforms of the veteran New Yorkers.

"To sack General McClellan at this time," Meagher shouted, "goes beyond the beyonds! It'll be remembered as the most unforgivable political crime of this war . . . !" Another roar broke from the formation. Several men in Father Corby's own regiment, the 88th New York, were shaking their muskets in the air. A few perched their caps on the tips of their bayonets to make their anger taller. "Just two months ago," Meagher went on, "George McClellan stopped the Rebels along Antietam Creek, then sent them limping back across the Potomac. Ah, you know that all too well. You were there with Mac in the grim cup of death. Hoist your own beloved green and show the world what it is to be McClellan men!"

Nothing that had gone before matched this thunderous cheer as the bearers waved the tattered flags. Of some, there was scarcely enough silk left to tack to the staffs. The color sergeant from the 116th Pennsylvania, a tall and swarthy young man with a somber expression, seemed ashamed to be holding such an unscathed banner. He wouldn't be embarrassed for long, Corby realized. The army was moving when it should have been settling into winter quarters. The schemers in Washington had plans.

Meagher had paused again, apparently taking a moment to control his own strong feelings.

Things had nearly gotten out of hand before McClellan had left for his New Jersey home. Celtic ardor. Meagher had ordered the color guards to throw down the green flags at the commanding general's feet. Little Mac had refused to go on until they were picked up. Had he given the slightest sign that he was for a revolution, the Irish Brigade would have been the first to march on Washington. "Careful now, Thomas Francis," Corby murmured. This was still the loyal army of the Republic, even if Lincoln—God help the poor baboon—had seen fit to put Ambrose Burnside at its head. An amiable and modest fellow, but no Little Mac.

"May the country forgive the connivers who sent George McClellan packing when they did. I'll be generous and call it ignorance. I'll say that these Black Republicans and abolitionist gadflies didn't know they were staying the wedge McClellan had so skillfully prepared to drive between the two wings of the enemy's army—and end this misguided rebellion once and for all!"

Fifes and drums could be heard from afar: the leading regiments were setting off down the pike that wound southeast. The march had begun. To where? Corby had no idea. Richmond, the priest supposed. The goal was always Richmond, and the enemy always found the means to stand in the way.

"Last week, there were officers in this very brigade who resigned rather than serve an administration so blind to the proper conduct of this war. I don't fault them—" A shout started up from the New Yorkers, but Meagher cut it short by holding up a gloved hand. "But neither do I applaud them!"

That silenced the men. Corby saw a few of them lower their heads. "Here comes the length of his tongue," somebody whispered.

"McClellan relied on you," Meagher went on, "as he did no others. When the Rebels outflanked the army that bloody twilight at Malvern Hill, it was you he sent to stop them. And stop them you did, braining them with the stocks of your muskets

when there was no time to fix bayonets. You chased them till
darkness fell . . ." He smiled, a sudden, radiant smile full of
warmth. The men grinned back at him. "And then, when the
army was saved, you politely bade the gray folk good-night, for
an Irishman is genial even to his foes."

The New Yorkers chuckled among themselves. "Devils in
battle," one of them said. "Angels after. That's us."

Then, as the laughter died, it seemed to hit the men—how
many fewer they were since that battle of early summer. Their
muster rolls were only a third of what they'd been when the
brigade had marched off to war, down Broadway with the band
thumping out "Garry Owen." Corby had lost count of all the
last anointings he'd given in field and hospital since leaving his
teaching post at Notre Dame. And he himself was a far different man from that young priest with soft hands. Harder and fit-
ter, for sure. He'd taken well to the marches and squalid camps,
unlike Father McKee of the 116th Pennsylvania, who now
slumped palely on his horse. He wouldn't last much longer.
That'd leave only Father Ouellette of the 69th New York and
himself to serve the entire brigade.

"Remember, boys—General McClellan asked you to serve his
old friend, General Burnside, with the same devotion you always
gave him . . ." There were a few grumbles, but Meagher stared
the offenders down. His usually heavy-lidded gaze could turn
piercing in a flash. "I think he'd be the first to warn us to hold
our greatest loyalty for the republic that sheltered us from
famine and oppression . . . because we are Irish. We, as a people, have erred again and again in our struggle for an indepen-
dent nation. How?" Then he suddenly barked like a stern father,
"How!"

There was no answer from the formation.

"I'll tell you then—by adhering blindly and passionately to in-
dividuals instead of the cause itself. All our efforts—however
heroic—have been feverish and spasmodic. All have failed. *Con-
sistency*. That's what we shall take from the army George Mc-

Clellan created . . . !" A kind of gloom settled over the men. It was obvious now that the fun was off. They weren't going to march up to Washington and throw the Black Republicans out. "Ah, boys," Meagher said chidingly, "why the long faces? We're not serving under strangers, are we now? We're part of the new Right Grand Division under General Sumner. Old Bull, who after those seven bloody days on the Peninsula swore he could whip the Rebel army with just the Irish Brigade and a field battery!"

"Ol' Bull was wrong," a voice sang out from the ranks of the 63d New York. "Who needs the bloody artillery?"

The men laughed again, and Meagher smiled. "Boys, I don't know where today's line of march will take us. But I do know that it will lead to another field where we'll prove once again that no race fights more valiantly than the Irish. And I promise this—the experience we gain here on American soil will be used to bring down the felon rag that flies over old Erin!"

That got the men going again, and their hurrah almost covered the sound of approaching hoofbeats. A courier galloped up from General Hancock, the division commander. He saluted and handed over a sealed envelope, which Meagher ripped open. Reading, he frowned, then said something to the rider, who tore off again into the mist.

"Well, boys," Meagher said, "General Hancock has a little job for us. One no less important than any other, so we'll case the colors and do what we're ordered."

Corby turned his ear on a new sound. He thought he could hear cattle lowing.

T w o

♦

It struck Robert McMillan how much they looked like boys. All of them inside the hospital tent. Even his fellow colonels of Cobb's Brigade. At fifty-seven, he felt like Methuselah. He had to swill precious coffee captured from the Yankees just to stay on top of the small talk, which was bright and happy and loud. Johnny Clark, General Cobb's wisp of a courier, was sure that the brigade would soon be sent back to Georgia. "I wrote my mama in Augusta," he was saying, "tellin' her to dust off her recipe for ginger cakes."

McMillan wasn't convinced that Lee would let go of Cobb's Brigade. But he held his tongue. It was good to see the men in such high spirits, especially after the losses at Crampton's Gap and Sharpsburg. On sick leave, he himself had missed the march into Maryland. The surgeon had blamed his disability on dropsy of the legs, but McMillan knew the cause: exhaustion. His body had just given out.

Clark wrinkled his nose at the bridge. "Col'nel, may I ask somethin' impertinent?"

McMillan almost smiled. Only a boy would beg to be impertinent. "If you must."

"How come you don't sound like the other Irishmen in your reg'ment?"

Garnett, McMillan's twenty-two-year-old son, sidled up to Clark and draped an arm around his shoulders. "Grandpa was a Scot, but Grandma Jane was a Montgomery. Her uncle was Richard Montgomery, the Irishman who joined Washington's army and died a Yankee general at Quebec, tryin' to help Benedict Arnold take Canada for the Continental Congress."

Clark asked, "Then you were born in this country, Col'nel?"

"No, son—County Antrim in the north of Ireland." McMillan frowned at his handsome son. Thick brown hair. Features so fine and smooth they almost seemed sculpted. "I wouldn't exactly call Richard Montgomery a *Yankee* general, Garnett."

His son winked at Clark. "Just wanted to make sure he was still awake."

"Oh, no pup of a lieutenant will ever find Colonel McMillan nappin'," Sullivan, his orderly sergeant, said. "Gentlemen, if you please . . ." He then begged them to stand aside so Jesse, General Cobb's Negro manservant, could make his way with the roasted turkey to the long table already spread with pickles, fried oysters, potatoes, and little cakes. A Tipperary man, Sullivan had dark curly hair and a wide face pitted by the smallpox he'd survived last spring during the siege of Yorktown. Before the war, he'd been a cook for the Central Railroad of Georgia, so McMillan had asked him to oversee the banquet.

Satisfied that all was ready, Sullivan drew near to Garnett and said, "I'll be watchin' your father's efforts. Lately, the flesh has been walkin' off him."

"I'll try to do justice, Michael," McMillan quietly said, "but there's no excuse for gluttony."

"You'll do more'n try, sir—Methodism or not." Then Sullivan ducked through the flaps on his way back out to the fire.

A gust of cold, dank air blew in behind the sergeant.

McMillan could feel the Virginia winter coming on. It made his arthritic fingers ache, and the hot tin mug was a comfort to

FREDERICKSBURG

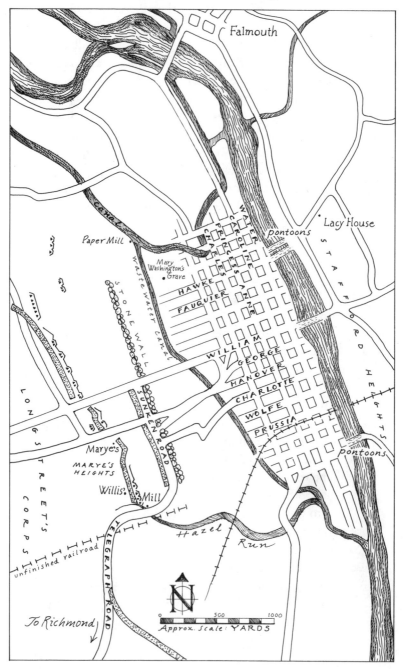

Falmouth

Lacy House

pontoons

Paper Mill

Mary Washington's Grave

WATER CAROLINE PRINCESS

HAWKE

FAUQUIER

STONE WALL

Waste water Canal

WILLIAM

GEORGE

HANOVER

CHARLOTTE

WOLFE

PRUSSIA

SUNKEN ROAD

LONGSTREET'S CORPS

Marye's

MARYE'S HEIGHTS

Willis Mill

STAFFORD HEIGHTS

Pontoons

unfinished railroad

TELEGRAPH ROAD

Hazel Run

To Richmond

N

0   500   1000

Approx. Scale: YARDS

his hands. A snowstorm a little over a week ago had given way to more autumn balminess, but now that was quickly fading. Some of the men still didn't have shoes or blankets, and only a few officers still had tents. McMillan was one of the fortunates.

A hush suddenly fell over everyone.

Boots could be heard slogging through the mud outside: Clark had slipped out and was now escorting the general to the banquet. The sound of Tom Cobb's voice drifted through the canvas. "Why the hospital tent?" he was demanding.

"Jesse says it's gonna rain," Clark said.

"Well, I can eat in my own tent. Does the surgeon know about this?"

"He knows, sir."

"I don't want—"

Sullivan threw back a flap for him, and Cobb gaped at the dress gray uniforms lined up on both sides of the table. Short of stature, he had a sharp nose and long brown hair that curled up at the back of his neck. He was as boyish-looking as all the others, despite having grown a beard in the last year. "What's this?" he finally managed to ask, stepping inside.

"Celebration, sir," Captain Brewster of McMillan's own regiment said. Good Scots lineage with a fine flow of language. He'd been asked to do the honors for the entire brigade. Garnett, another very junior officer, had been invited because the general was known to be fond of him.

"Celebration?" Cobb echoed after a moment.

"Yes sir—for Thomas Reade Rootes Cobb's long-overdue promotion to the rank of brigadier general. It's our humble opinion that Providence can be delayed, but never thwarted."

Cobb said nothing for another moment, visibly moved. He no doubt knew, deep down, that he wasn't so much admired as grudgingly preferred over his portly older brother, Howell, the former Georgia governor who'd proved himself a bungling commander up in Maryland while Cobb was on furlough. Before his already moist eyes got the better of him, he started down McMillan's side of the table toward his place at the head. He shook hands along the way, said this and that with an embarrassed smile to the men, joked something low with Reverend Porter, the brigade chaplain. Finally, he was pumping McMillan's hand. "And how are my Irishmen, Robert?"

"Fine, sir," McMillan said, although the 24th Georgia Volunteer Infantry was far more native Georgian than immigrant. Because he himself was Irish-born, it was somehow assumed the regiment was as well. "Congratulations."

"Thank you. Tell your boys more blankets are coming."

"I will, sir. Good news."

Cobb started to move on, but then turned back on McMillan in his quick, impulsive way. "How's young Rob?"

"The major's better, sir." A half-truth. The threat of amputation still hung over McMillan's eldest son, Robert Emmett, who lay in a Richmond hospital. He'd been hit in the right leg at Sharpsburg, losing enough bone to make full recovery doubtful.

"Glad to hear it. And here's that other McMillan rascal . . ." Cobb patted Garnett on the cheek, making him blush. He knew all the children from McMillan's and his days together in the state legislature. They'd worked together on the new constitution, and therein lay Cobb's genius. Law, not warfare. At last, he gave up trying to shake every hand and gestured for the men to sit. "Before that handsome bird gets cold, boys—come on, now . . ." McMillan eased down onto a camp stool. "I admit this gives me greater pleasure than the promotion itself. I just hope General Lee doesn't discover his dinner's missing before we have time to wolf it down." Cobb laughed louder than anyone. A month ago, the remark might've been rancorous—only recently had his opinion of Lee improved. He didn't think much of West Pointers. "Reverend, will you be so kind as to offer up grace?"

McMillan and the others bowed their heads. His mind refused to fix on Porter's words, and he found himself praying for his dead children. Emma, gone at seventeen almost a year ago now.

And James at age twenty-one before the war. Fevers with as many names as the number of physicians he and Ruth Ann had consulted.

"Amen," the chaplain concluded.

The officers took their linen napkins off the table—actually bandages from the surgeon's chest, but no one seemed to mind—and fell upon their food even before the turkey was sliced. They'd seen nothing like it for months, and McMillan had no idea how such delicacies had been scrounged up with half of Lee's army camped in the vicinity. Little was said except for some quick praise between mouthfuls for Jesse, who beamed as he carved the bird with a sharpened saber bayonet. "No, Sergeant—spread that around," Cobb protested as Sullivan dished a half pound of white meat onto his tin plate. "What're you fattening me for? The slaughter?"

"Brides and brigadiers ride better with plenty of flesh on 'em, sir."

McMillan was afraid for an instant that Cobb might take offense, but then the brigadier chuckled and filled his mouth with turkey.

"Gen'ral Cobb . . . ?" Clark asked.

"Yes, Johnny?"

"Are we still good for home, what with your promotion and all?"

Cobb's face darkened.

Recently, he'd won a concession from Lee. At the end of this campaign season, the brigade would be transferred to Georgia and mounted into two cavalry regiments. Christmas at home. McMillan was as eager as the others, but he'd also heard that Richmond didn't want to send one more general to that theater.

Cobb absentmindedly lit a cigar even though his plate was full. "I withheld my acceptance from President Davis till I could be assured nothing would interfere with our going home. We're bound for Georgia." He shook out his match. "Who's saying otherwise, Johnny?"

"Nobody, sir," the boy said, shamefaced at last, "it's just that I really didn't know one way or the other."

Cobb's expression softened. "I see. Then I'm sorry I didn't say something sooner."

McMillan hid his relief. He'd been as much on tenterhooks as the others. He noticed Sullivan start to slip outside, no doubt to spread the word to the troops, but the sergeant's exit was blocked by a captain. McMillan immediately recognized him to be one of General McLaws's aides. Sullivan stepped back, and the man from division strode for Cobb, holding his scabbard against his thigh to keep it from brushing against the backs of the officers. The cold was still clinging to his cape.

The table went silent.

The captain bent over to whisper in Cobb's ear. The general lowered his cigar, listened. McMillan saw the disappointment slowly take shape in his eyes.

Standing straight again, the captain waited for Cobb's reply.

"Kindly give General McLaws my compliments, and tell him we'll be ready."

The captain hungrily eyed the turkey, but declined Cobb's offer to have some. In a few seconds, he was on his way back to division headquarters.

No one was eating.

Cobb took a long pull off his cigar, then said, "Gentlemen, it seems the Army of the Potomac is stirring." He added nothing more. He didn't have to. Everyone, including Clark, had known that the transfer home hinged on something else too—the enemy going into winter quarters and staying there.

Three

♦

William Tyrrell looked around to make sure nobody was watching, then used the staff of the cased colors to prod one of the long-horned steers. It bolted ahead a few yards, spun around to snort at him, then finally turned and fell into the same lackadaisical walk as the rest of the herd. The little job General Hancock had given the brigade was to drive several hundred gaunt and half-wild cattle along the line of march. They were from the mountains of Texas, somebody had said. The New Yorkers had given up on hoots and whistles to goad them over the wooded ridges and were now using their bayonets. Every minute or so, one of the beasts would bellow, and the men would cheer, more out of frustration than meanness.

"I say we eat 'em here," somebody suggested.

"Sure, just knock the horns off and wipe their asses."

All four regiments of the brigade were so mixed up Tyrrell had lost track of Joe Hudson, who was carrying the regimental flag, and the rest of the color guard. One by one, they'd peeled off after wayward steers, and now there was no sign of them in the mob of men strung out behind the cattle. Nor were Colonel Heenan and Lieutenant Colonel Mulholland anywhere to be seen. No doubt, they were keeping to the pike instead of the herd, which flowed willy-nilly over the buckled countryside. The cattle dropped enormous amounts of shit, which now coated Tyrrell's brogans.

Another steer lowed, and a man shouted, "That's it—stick that bloody rickle of bones!"

Cresting a hill, Tyrrell looked back.

The church spires of Warrenton were still visible in the west, shining under a dark awning of cloud. Not so far for a day's march. One of Hancock's couriers had gone by an hour ago, and a sergeant from the 63d New York had asked for news. The rider had shouted that the leading regiments of the division had made fifteen miles and were still plunging deeper into Rebel territory. A record pace. But Tyrrell figured his own brigade had made only six or seven miles since setting out this morning.

A bayoneted steer charged through the middle of the herd, starting a small stampede. The brigade had to give chase, and Tyrrell picked up his tired feet. He leaped over a cedar brake and down a slope that still held a patch of snow. His soles made wet, slapping sounds against the whiteness, and the sweat-damp wool of his uniform tugged at his crotch and armpits.

"What'd you do to that poor Rebeller cow?" someone asked the sticker.

"Nothin' I wouldn't do on me weddin' night," he replied.

The cattle, as weary as the brigade, stopped running at the bottom of the hill and lumbered along again. Tyrrell had no idea how beef from Confederate Texas had made its way into the Federal army. His three months in uniform so far had taught him that countless little mysteries came and went without any hope of explanation. Somebody had said that the cattle were from Texas, and now it was gospel.

The sky suddenly changed.

The setting sun was reflecting off the undersides of the clouds, making them look like hammered silver. Beautiful. He thought of his tools, laying idle in a wooden chest at home. He'd been a silversmith back in Philadelphia.

"Will you look at those stupid c-c-cows?" a voice said off to Tyrrell's side. "Point 'em in one d-d-direction and off they go, come hell or high water."

Tyrrell smiled. "Like us, Mac." It was Bill McCarter, the regiment's mail agent when in camp. On the march, he was just another private in "A" Company, yet word had it he'd be General Meagher's clerk as soon as the army went into winter quarters. He had a stutter that grew worse the more fatigued he became, but his penmanship and spelling were the best in the brigade. Men often begged him to write their letters home, so elegant was his hand. He never charged for this service, which made him an odd Orangeman. Usually, Ulster Protestants were as money-grubbing as New England Yankees. Tyrrell himself had been born in Philadelphia of immigrant parents. Catholic. "Where d'you think we're headed?" he asked. While the brigade was camped just south of Warrenton, McCarter had clerked for the general. Clerks made copies of orders, and Tyrrell couldn't imagine how Meagher wouldn't know what Burnside had in mind. Even if he'd said he didn't. "Think we'd strike for Richmond this late in the year?"

McCarter shrugged.

A falling mist began to tickle Tyrrell's face. "I heard we're movin' closer to Washington before goin' into winter camp."

"Heard that t-too," McCarter said.

"And Hudson says we're goin' down to the Chesapeake to board boats. From there it's back to the Peninsula, the whole army."

McCarter averted his eyes. Maybe that was it then. The mist turned into a cold, steady drizzle, so cold Tyrrell wondered if it was sleet. He caught some drops in his palm—still liquid.

Lieutenant Foltz, of McCarter's company, bawled, "Keep your fire, boys!" Other officers took up the cry. The troops halted and shed their bedrolls. As color sergeant, Tyrrell carried no arms. He watched McCarter quickly peel his gum blanket from his two woolen ones and wrap it tightly around the lock and barrel of his musket. The 116th had learned from the New Yorkers to expect a Rebel ambush from every clump of woods, and a wet bedroll was to be preferred over wet powder.

"That a new potstick you have there, Mac?" Tyrrell asked.

"It is," McCarter said.

A fine musket with an unscarred stock. "Where'd you get it?"

A young steer started to lope away from the herd. McCarter lunged, breaking his bayonet over its backside. "Oh hell," he said over his shoulder to Tyrrell, but then laughed. "At least I s-stopped his highland fling."

Finally, the halt was called.

The rain was now so hard the cattle stopped dead and hung their heads. The order came down to corral the herd into a cove in the woods. A rope was strung around this clearing from tree to tree, and the steers driven in.

Tyrrell noticed Heenan's portly figure on horseback atop a small rise. He was shouting for the regiment to gather around him. Tyrrell approached. "Damn dreary country," the colonel said to no one in particular, his mount stamping the mud with a hoof. Then he told the company commanders, "This is it for the night. Remember—we're in enemy country, so have the men rest on their arms." Then he ordered the pickets out.

Squinting against the rain, Tyrrell gazed off toward the pike. He hoped to see the brigade's supply train. But after a few minutes only a solitary white-topped wagon appeared. General Meagher's. The man himself rode behind it on his now mud-splattered white charger. The bill of his cap was pulled low over his eyes, but he smiled and lofted a hand to acknowledge the men, who cheered him, as always. He dismounted—gingerly, Tyrrell thought—and climbed up into the wagon with the help of Joseph, his aged cook. Heenan rode over to him, and they talked in low tones through the rear parting in the canvas.

McCarter reappeared, and Tyrrell said, "Sad place for a color line, Mac."

"Ate up my day's rations this morning. No c-coffee left either."

Tyrrell handed him the flag and opened his haversack. He and the rest of the color guard were unburdened by ammunition, so he had salted beef and coffee to spare. He offered both to McCarter, then took back the colors and laid the pole across two musket stacks.

"Thanks, W-Will."

Foltz threaded his mount through the milling crowd, rain beading his clean-shaven face. Spotting some men of his company at last, the lieutenant said, "Light's going fast, boys. Get out in those trees and find some kindling and wood." McCarter went off with them. In single file, they crossed a muddy creek that seemed to have sprung instantly out of the soggy ground.

Tyrrell unfurled his bedroll and wrapped it around his shoulders with the gum blanket outward. The rain popped loudly against it. His overcoat was soaked, but he still felt warm from the march. That would quickly fade.

A lantern came on in Meagher's wagon, and he could see the general's profile limned darkly on the canvas. He was smoking a cigar.

"Here's Will." Hudson and the rest of the color guard came trooping in from the deep blue twilight, their uniforms covered with mud and bits of dead leaves.

"Where you been?" Tyrrell asked.

"Chasin' some goddamn cows what went off on their own hook." Hudson racked the regimental colors, then wiped his nose in the crook of his sleeve. "And next thing, we was lost from the whole brigade." He and the others flopped down on their knees and spread open their bedrolls. "Rations?" he asked hopefully.

"None," Tyrrell said.

"Bully."

"I've got a little salt horse left."

"Save it for mornin'." And with that the corporal crawled inside his blankets. Within minutes he was snoring. The others sat up a while, but then soon dropped off as well. Tyrrell, wide awake to the chill, began to envy them.

"S-sorry, Will," McCarter said, slipping in beside him again. He was shivering. "Snow laid too long on the twigs and leaves—too damp for proper kindling."

"That's all right, Mac," Tyrrell said. "You see the wagons from up there?"

"Nothing. Just rain."

The glow coming through the covering of Meagher's wagon had gone out. Tyrrell whipped his cape up over his head and sat down on a corner of his gum blanket. No tents. No supper, other than the bite of salt horse he'd save for breakfast. Worst of all, no fire to boil his coffee. At this hour, his wife Annie would be making supper for his mother and father, bustling prettily about the kitchen.

McCarter had sat and was bundled in his wet blankets, still trying to keep his powder dry. Dropping his voice, Tyrrell said, "I wasn't trying to slip any secrets from you, Mac."

McCarter brought his pipe to his mouth. He made quiet sucking sounds. Like most of the men, he was out of tobacco, but drawing on the empty bowl still seemed to give him comfort. "I know. And who can you trust if not your own color sergeant?"

That only made Tyrrell feel worse. He still didn't understand why of all the men in the regiment he'd been picked. The colonel had said something about his being a man without vices, stalwart and cool under fire. But the only fire they'd been under so far hadn't been much of a battle. Tyrrell figured his height had been the biggest reason. He was a foot taller than the average man in the 116th.

"I'll tell you something," McCarter said after a pause.

"You don't have to, Mac." Tyrrell listened to the rain rattle against the hundreds of gum blankets all around. Through the nightfall, the sitting men looked like rounded boulders in the shallows of a lake.

McCarter went on, "I'd like to." Then his tone turned plaintive. "It's been bothering me, I suppose."

Tyrrell said nothing.

"General Meagher gave me this smoothbore, Will."

Tyrrell took a moment so as not to sound too surprised. "He must think highly of you, Mac."

"No more than the rest of the boys, I'm sure." But then McCarter sighed. "Oh, I don't know."

"We can save this for later."

"No, I've opened the keg now." McCarter sucked hollowly on his pipe once more, then said, "Back in Warrenton, I drew guard duty at brigade headquarters. This was the time of that terrible cold, and it was lovely to have this great fire to pass by in the middle of my beat. You know, right in front of the general's tent. Well, I'm going back and forth—when who comes to the flaps but . . . well, you know."

"To speak to you, Mac?"

"No, that's the pity of it. He was too far gone to know that I was even on post there."

"Drunk, you mean?"

"Skuttered *blind.*"

"Oh Mary." Tyrrell sighed.

"So gone he had to hang on to the tent pole."

"How d'you know he wasn't just sick?"

"Oh, Will—you should've seen his eyes in that firelight. Full of demons. What a sight. He almost fell on his face once, then twice, and I was half out of my m-mind wondering what to do. He was only a couple feet from that fire. Should I call for the officers inside the tent? Would the general get angry if I did?"

"What'd you do?"

"Well, I—"

Suddenly, a cheer flew up from the huddled men, and they

started coming to their feet. Tyrrell asked what was happening, and a voice answered, "General Meagher's ordered a whiskey ration for us." Tyrrell decided not to join the line, even though a drop would have been a solace. Already, he could hear men bartering for the rations of others. And an argument had flared up between two men with what he believed to be Galway accents.

McCarter didn't get in line either. "So Will—I got as close to the general as I dared, and thank God I did. For then he went down like a sack of coal. I had to hold him back with the flat of my bayonet, otherwise the flames would've had him." Then McCarter fell silent.

Tyrrell finally said, "He wasn't drunk that day we drove the Rebels out of Charlestown. Never seen a man so sober. And brave. Made me feel better just lookin' at him." But it had troubled him to hear McCarter's story. A Republican newspaper in New York had hinted that it wasn't a shell that had sent Meagher reeling from the saddle at Antietam.

"That's right," McCarter said. "He's a great man, and it's a s-small failing for a great man. That's why I told nobody . . . till now."

"Well, I'll say nothin' of it, Mac. You won't find me repeatin' this."

"I knew you wouldn't. That's why I told you. But I just had to tell *somebody*."

Tyrrell said, "Sure, I know. I'm glad you did." He was the color sergeant. Men would come to him with things they'd never tell the chaplains, and for this burden, plus waving the flag from the center of the line in battle, Tyrrell would be excused from picket and other routine duties.

McCarter continued, "What gets me is this—how d-demonized he looked when he was holding on to that tent pole. I've never seen a man look like that before."

Tyrrell nodded in the darkness. He knew what his father would say. Annie wrote that the old man swelled his chest each time he told someone his son was serving under the Irish patriot who with O'Brien and Mitchel had led the Revolt of 1848. "The British did it to Thomas Meagher. They got ready to hang him for treason, let him make his speech. Then the bastards changed his sentence from death to bein' sent off to Australia or someplace far like that. You can't drag a man back from the gallows and expect him to be the same, can you, Mac?"

"No, of course not."

"You can't torture a man without leavin' a mark on him."

McCarter chuckled, and from that Tyrrell realized how much he'd been chafing under this load. "Why sure, you c-can't expect him to be a common fellow like us."

"No," Tyrrell said.

Then McCarter quickly said, "Not that you're common, Will. You're special. Anybody can see that."

Tyrrell doubted that. He only prayed that he wouldn't fail the regiment when the fighting started in earnest. And each time he made this prayer he recalled that, only two months ago, almost the entire color guard of the 69th New York had been wiped out at Antietam—God reminding him what a crushing obligation his was. And how mindlessly, perhaps, he'd undertaken it for pride's sake. "Mac, what's all this have to do with the general givin' you a musket?"

"Oh, I dropped my old one in the fire—you know, when I was struggling to hold him up. It went off, and out ran his staff. One of them told him I saved his life, and the n-n-next day he gave me this piece."

"Rightly so." Tyrrell wiped the rain off his chilled face with a hand. He was thinking of lying down when an angry shout from the "A" Company bivouac brought him to his feet. Dark blue silhouettes had formed a ring around the Galway men, who could be heard taunting each other.

"You'd drink whiskey outta the armpit of a corpse!"

"For the love of Jaysus—look who's talkin', boys! He'd bate his own mother for a gill!"

Amazingly, their words were slurred. They'd managed to finagle enough whiskey to get drunk in the twenty minutes since the ration had been offered. A ration of about only five tablespoons to each man. The taunts grew louder, less coherent, and then a punch could be heard landing against skull bone. A roar of approval went up. The circle of spectators broke in Tyrrell's direction, and one of the Galway men spilled out and fell dazed at Tyrrell's knees. "Who's that?" he snarled groggily. "Captain Pat Carrigan? Well, I'll bate the shoulder straps off you, Cap!" He blinked up into the dimness. "Who the bleedin' hell are you!"

"Your c-color sergeant," McCarter, a teetotaler, said contemptuously.

The Galway man's teeth shone in a grin. "Ah, Willie Tyree, darlin'," he said on a burst of sudden cheer. "They're handin' out grog—just like me old days in the Royal Navy. Didn't know it was the custom. God bless Amerikay!"

Four

♦

McMillan was still with the other colonels and Brigadier Cobb, chewing over the report that the blue people were on the move again. So Sullivan was at his leisure until tattoo, when the colonel would return to his tent to say his devotions. He strolled down the company streets, hands in his pockets. There were no stars, just cloud cover, but all the campfires on the surrounding meadows seemed to make up for it. Drizzle had come and gone a half dozen times, but now the wind had risen and the rain was done. He made his way to the "K" Company area, stopped and scanned the little groups of men. Their sun-darkened faces were shining in the firelight. One in particular caught his eye. It was long, droll-looking, and belonged to Thomas Dooley, who'd worked on the railroad with Sullivan. With him were his messmates, the Haddock brothers, Johnny and Billy. Unruly red hair on heads as round as cabbages. They were Protestants from County Antrim like Colonel McMillan—but loyal Fenians, through and through.

"Room for another, boys?" Sullivan asked, nearing their fire.

"We'll make room," Dooley said.

The three privates stood, but not because Sullivan was the

regimental orderly sergeant. It was no great post, even though he'd been elected by the men to serve the colonel. A glorified footman and muster roll checker—and thank God a priest in Savannah had taught him to read and cipher or he'd only be up to half the job. No, the three men stood because he was captain of their circle of the Fenian Brotherhood, a secret society pledged to the freeing of the homeland. Colonel McMillan tolerated its doings in his regiment as long as they remained hidden. General Cobb was more suspicious, realizing that most Fenians wore blue in this war. A fire-eating secessionist from the beginning, he felt that that was cause enough for a Rebel soldier.

"Are you a friend?" Dooley solemnly asked Sullivan.

"I am a friend."

"Then you're my friend."

Sullivan shook Dooley's hand, then repeated the ritual with the Haddock brothers. That out of the way, he reached inside his haversack and came out with the carcass of the turkey from Cobb's banquet. Enough meat was left on the bones, even after Jesse had had a go at it, to widen the eyes of the three men. But Dooley lamented, "Distressin'."

"What's that now?" Sullivan asked.

"They say it was stuffed with oysters."

"Have a look, Tommy . . ." Sullivan opened his mouth wide and pointed at his throat. "Go ahead and stare down the gob of this old gift horse."

Dooley chuckled as his fingers got busy with the carcass. The brothers tore into it as well, Billy Haddock pausing with eyes closed to savor the first taste.

"What're the Yanks doin'?" Dooley asked, chewing.

"Who knows?" Sullivan said. "Might be a trick, so be ready for a quick march and sore feet."

Johnny Haddock asked, "Which way they headed?"

"Cavalry says toward Falmouth."

"All of 'em?"

"Ah yes, that might be their trick. A couple divisions go on a lark to Falmouth and the rest of 'em cross the Rappahannock somewheres 'tween Ol' Jack and us." Sullivan had overheard McMillan and Cobb discussing, with some unease, the gap that lay between Longstreet's corps, of which they were part, and Stonewall Jackson's, which was still across the Blue Ridge in the Shenandoah. "We'll all know soon enough."

"Will we now . . . ?" Billy Haddock asked, sucking on a bone. "Or will Lee keep us knockin' round here just when we should be on our way home to Georgia?"

Sullivan had no answer to that.

"Mike," a voice called out to him from the darkness.

Turning, Sullivan saw that it was Dionicius Oliver, the regiment's quartermaster sergeant. Acting commissary sergeant too, now that Keenan Terrell had resigned after the Sharpsburg bloodbath, explaining only that he was available to shoot British soldiers, not American. Oliver was accompanied by a scrawny figure wearing a new kepi and carrying a musket at right shoulder arms. Leaving the stranger just outside the firelight, he came up to Sullivan. He eyed the dismembered bird on the flat rock that served as a hearth as he said, "Colonel just had a word with me."

"Where is he?"

"With Cobb, still." Oliver pointed at the bones, grasping a red bandanna in his hand. "Is there more of that, by chance?"

"Sorry, Dionicius. I think it was the last turkey left in Virginia."

Oliver grunted, then buried his bulbous nose in the bandanna and sneezed. "Here's the news . . ." A captain had returned from Georgia with a handful of recuits. "The examinin' surgeon did a fine job—two of 'em are sure to be underage. But the colonel don't want to be hasty, not as shorthanded as we are. So, the next officer to go home will get to the bottom of it."

"Why're you tellin' me this?" Sullivan asked.

Oliver showed his fleshy palms. "I'm gettin' to it, Mike. The colonel don't want the youngsters put in the companies yet. So, I got one to help me out and—"

"I got one." Sullivan rolled his eyes. "No thanks. Let the bandmaster teach both of 'em to play the drums and it won't matter how old they are."

"Just what I told the colonel."

"And what'd he say?"

"Kindly bear-r-r with the situation, Mr. Oliver-r-r," the quartermaster sergeant said, imitating McMillan's Scots burr.

That it was it, then. The orderly sergeant now had his own orderly, for the time being. "What's his name?"

"Didn't ask, and he didn't volunteer it," Oliver said, making his escape back out into the darkness. "Thanks for the turkey."

"Come forward there," Sullivan said.

The boy took three awkward steps into the light, but then halted again, his nervous eyes fixed on Sullivan's lips. All at once, the sergeant wanted to look away. But he couldn't, not for the moment at least, and the old grief ambushed him. *Is this what he would've looked like had the starvation fever not put him in the ground?* Same curly light brown hair and sharply upturned nose. "What's your name, lad?"

"O'Blivious," Dooley muttered, "by the looks of him."

"Quiet there," Sullivan warned. No use rattling the boy any more than he already was. It was a lonely thing to come into a blooded regiment a stranger. "Name, lad."

"Private Hugh Tully, sir."

"I'm Sullivan, Hugh. You just call me *sergeant.* Have you been to a camp of instruction?"

"Two weeks in Clarkesville," Tully said, scarcely able to contain his pride.

"Two weeks," Billy Haddock echoed, sifting through the bones with his greasy fingers for the last speck of flesh. "Why he's an old lag, Mike."

"He's a wean," Johnny Haddock said grimly. A child.

10:20 A.M., November 16
69th New York, Irish Brigade

The countryside—wheatfield in stubble crisscrossed by belts of thick timber—had begun to roll and dip toward the Valley of the Rappahannock. It was a bright morning, sunny yet soft around the edges from last night's rain, misty enough so that John Donovan couldn't see the river yet. He stood in the stirrups and peered southward. No glint of water was to be seen among the bare trees. Mostly bare, although the branches of the oaks were still holding their dead leaves. Nothing but a silvery graininess filled the distance, but he could sense the Rappahannock out there, smell it, a murky thing winding down its narrow channel toward the Chesapeake.

Donovan sank back into the saddle.

The 69th New York, marching four abreast, snaked along the pike through the hilly woods. It had led off this morning, the brigade going forward by regiments at an hour's interval between each. The cattle drive and then the night's fast under a steady downpour had left the men surly. But the supply wagons had finally caught up with them—so breakfast, hot coffee, and then some warming sunlight had bolstered their spirits. They'd even cheered when word came from General Hancock that the herd would be given over to some New Jersey brigade.

"Captain Donovan . . . ?"

Donovan startled a little. His young first sergeant, Hogan, had come on his blind side, the right. "Yes, Joe—what is it?"

"Captain McGee's hailin' you."

And so he was. Jimmy McGee was waving his hat for Donovan to join him farther forward in the column.

"Company's yours for a few minutes, Patrick," Donovan told Callaghan, his first lieutenant, then lightly dug in his spurs, putting his mount into a trot. The musket ball that had hit him at Malvern Hill had torn away part of his right ear, making hearing a chance thing sometimes, and then entered his skull to destroy the eye. Returning to the brigade in late September, he'd been told by McGee that the black patch made him look "piratical, dashing." He wasn't sure about that. But he did know that the mirror no longer gave him any vain pleasure. Not with much of his ear missing and a cleft in his temple almost as deep as the natural one in his chin. His collapsed eye socket reminded him of a raw oyster.

"Are you deaf now too?" McGee asked.

"No, Jimmy," Donovan said, falling in beside him, "but I'm as stiff as a salted cod from sleeping on that cold ground last night."

"Ah, you'll toughen up again. You'll see."

Malvern Hill had been a rearguard action, so Donovan had been left on the field like most of the Federal wounded. He'd been sent to a Richmond prison, then paroled by the Rebels, who had been sure he'd die of his wounds, only to finally recover at Bellevue Hospital in New York.

McGee glanced ahead at Colonel Nugent, as if to make sure he was out of earshot. Only then he said, "I've got it almost from the devil's own mouth—Bull Sumner's son-in-law."

"Oh?"

"We're bound for the coast."

"And from there?"

"We'll jump from river to river under the muzzles of our gunboats."

Donovan yawned. "Truly?"

"All the way to Petersburg, and then it's smartly up to Richmond."

"We don't go anywhere smartly."

"Well, this time we will."

Donovan mulled this over a moment, then said, "I don't think so, Jimmy. You've seen that tidewater country when it rains. We'd be up to our necks in mud the whole of the way."

McGee looked let down. In his late twenties, he was several years older than Donovan, but there was something boyishly tender in his nature that made him seem like the brigade's perennial younger brother. Not that he couldn't hold his own in a fray. At Antietam, he'd snatched up the 69th's green flag after eight color-bearers had already fallen, waving it until a ball broke the staff in two and another swatted his cap off his head. After that, he wrapped the colors around his waist like an emerald corset and screamed God only knew what at the Rebels in the sunken road. Latin verse, maybe. McGee had literary ambitions. He'd even written a book. No one in the brigade had read it. Or asked to. "Then how do *you* figure it, John?" he asked defensively. Tender, tender.

"I don't," Donovan said. "At least not to where I'd wager on it one way or another. One minute, I'm sure we'll take to our winter huts. The next, I expect us to turn and make a dash for Culpeper. You know, take on Lee's boys before the snow really flies."

"We could've done that from Warrenton."

"Perhaps," Donovan admitted. Whatever lay ahead, he'd feel easier about it if McClellan were still in command. Little Mac had hovered over his army like a guardian angel. So far, Burnside seemed nothing more than a tall hat and an empty smile. Those who'd fought up in Maryland at summer's end had nothing good to say about him. Then a corps commander, he'd dawdled before crossing Antietam Creek, wasting the army's only chance for a victory that day. A few tried to apologize for him, saying that getting 9th Corps across that narrow stone bridge had been like trying to squeeze an elephant through a mouse hole. Once across, some of Burnside's boys had nearly turned the feeble right side of Bobby Lee's line and ended the war that afternoon. But just nearly. The story of the Army of the Potomac.

"Captain McGee," a voice asked from the ranks. One of the privates, his trousers stained with reddish mud up to the shins.

Carried himself as if he were the mayor of New York's Lower East Side.

"Yes, soldier?"

"Sir, with your kind permission—can I ask Captain Donovan here a question?"

"Have a go at him," McGee said.

The private took a moment to compose himself, then said, "Cap, sir, me and the boys would like to know the truth of it. From your lips to our ears."

"The truth of what?" Donovan asked.

"You know, what you told Gen'ral Lee when they took you prisoner down there after Malvern."

Myth. Already it was clouding what had happened. He'd never realized what a yarn history was until he'd made a small bit of it himself. "Well—"

"Captain Donovan never met Lee," McGee butted in. "What he said was put to General Magruder, who came round to our officers in hospital, asking for their sidearms." He glanced, smirking, to Donovan.

"Go ahead, Captain McGee, by all means. I was only there."

"Magruder took one look at the captain here and remarked, 'I think from the nature of your wound, you won't have much need of your sword and revolver from now on.'" McGee had obviously earmarked the anecdote for some future literary effort.

"Is that how it was?" another private asked Donovan.

"Something like that," he said, trying to recall how things had precisely gone down. He'd been in an opium swoon.

"And what'd you answer, sir?"

After a few awkward moments in which Donovan said nothing, McGee volunteered for him, "The captain answered, 'I think differently, General Magruder. I think I have one good eye left yet and will risk it merrily—'"

"Happily, not merrily. You're making me sound like a simp."

"'*Happily* for the Union. Should I ever lose that, I'll go it blind!'"

The men laughed uproariously, and then one of them pressed, "And what'd the Rebeller say, sir?"

Donovan, grinning despite himself, replied, "He asked me what command I belonged to. Meagher's Irish Brigade, of course. His eyes got big and he said, 'Oh indeed,' as if that explained it all."

McGee added, "The old gentleman passed on without another word."

The men laughed again.

Colonel Nugent glanced back at the sound, frowning, and Donovan wheeled for his own place in the column. In truth, he couldn't recall what had been said, exactly. His memory refused to put too sharp an edge on that putrid hospital. If it could, he supposed that he wouldn't have come back to the brigade, even though he'd missed McGee and the others more than he'd ever missed anyone.

9:04 P.M.
24th Georgia
Culpeper

Garnett McMillan hesitated outside his father's candlelit tent. Through the part in the flaps, he could see the old man sitting on his cot, vigorously rubbing his lower legs. His long underwear had been pulled up above the knees, and the traceries of veins stood out like fat purple worms. Once, he'd complained to Rob that his extremities felt cold and dead, as if his heart had grown too weary to supply them with blood. Another time in camp, he'd suddenly gripped his left side as if he'd been stung by a spent bullet. On the sly, both Rob and Garnett had gone to the surgeon and reported these things. The sawbones had shrugged and said, "He's an old man, boys. I'm amazed he's lasted this long."

Garnett was about to announce himself when his father went stiffly to his knees and began praying.

Exhaling, Garnett waited again.

In his pocket was a letter from his mother. He'd been with-holding it from his father for more than twenty-four hours, ever since a captain returning from Habersham County had deliv-ered it to him. Ruth Ann Banks McMillan. Like most high-born women of South Carolina, she was indirect in everything she undertook, often infuriatingly so. She'd asked Garnett to broach a matter to his father only if he thought him capable of turning his mind on the loss at this time. On January 17—three months to the day, tomorrow—Emma would be gone a year. Her face flashed through Garnett's mind, leaving behind a brief pain, a hollowness. She'd made the house gay. His mother wanted to make some gift to the Clarkesville Methodist Church in her memory. As in all things, she deferred to the colonel's judgment.

Garnett shook his head.

His father had never discussed Emma's death with him. Nor James's before that. As a family, the McMillans didn't dwell on such things. And General Lee, who had himself just lost a daughter, was ready to move Longstreet's corps at any hour. His mother would understand a delay. The war came first.

As Garnett watched, his father rose and slumped on the cot again. His hands were still joined, his face twisted and wet. He was weeping, which astonished Garnett. He'd cried at neither funeral. He had never cried in the presence of his family. But now he sobbed, silently, as Garnett himself had that fall after going back to Emory and Henry without James, who'd sickened and died over the summer vacation. He'd lain at his second-story window for days, watching each Virginia and Tennessee train pull into the college station with the absurd hope that his brother would get off and come running up through the hot September fields, his suitcase in one hand and his coat in the other.

Garnett had no doubt his father's tears were for Emma. He

wanted to go to the old man, say something, but knew that wasn't possible. Instead, he turned back for his company, vowing not to needlessly expose himself in the next fight. Both Rob and he had been far too reckless at Sharpsburg, now that he thought of it.

Five

2:35 *P.M., November 17*
116th Pennsylvania
Nearing Falmouth

The brigade was ordered to halt in a clearing.

Skirmishers were sent out while the remaining troops stacked muskets and looked to making coffee fires, which Colonel Heenan quickly forbid. Most of the men then just unfurled their gum blankets and sprawled under the bright autumn sky. A footsore private limped into some nearby woods, crossed his forearms over his chest, closed his eyes and flopped down into a pile of wind-heaped leaves. He pretended to swim until his messmates noticed and laughed, then rolled on his back and shut his eyes. "Wake me in May," he said.

The colors were laid across stacked muskets, and the guard sank into the tufted pasture grass. But, after a minute, Tyrrell got up and set off for a slight rise. He wanted to see Falmouth. At the last rest stop, a sergeant from the 63d New York had said the village was now only a few miles to the southeast. The past three days were a blur of miles in Tyrrell's mind. The first, herding the cattle, had turned out to be the easiest. Yesterday they'd covered eighteen miles, when six or seven was all that McClellan had ever asked of them on the march from Harpers Ferry to Warrenton. That was one difference between Little Mac and

Burnside he would write Annie about. Today, with all four regiments and the division artillery in column together, they'd gone at least thirteen miles. And General Meagher had given no sign that they were ready to bivouac for the night.

Tyrrell stopped on the height, turned around.

The clearing on which the brigade was resting sloped gently toward the Rappahannock, although he couldn't see the river itself. Just the wooded bluff beyond. The leafless trees coated it like a smoky haze. There was nothing to be seen of Falmouth. The New York sergeant had said that the village was tucked down in a hollow below some rapids, so Tyrrell now figured that it was just over the first ridge to the east. But the New Yorker had also said that the spires of Fredericksburg, a mile south of Falmouth, loomed over the entire countryside. Tyrrell jumped up on a fallen log, but still couldn't spot them.

His spirits sank as he realized that they still might have several miles more to go. His legs felt thick, almost wooden, and his hands ached from grasping the flagstaff. Thank God there'd be no moon tonight, otherwise Burnside might keep up the march until the army reached the sea. Or Richmond, even. Just below, half-shielded from the rest of the brigade by a copse of cedars, several men from the regiment were tending to someone laid out on the ground. Tyrrell recognized the sergeant among them, Frank Missimer, of "C" Company. He was draping his overcoat over the downed man, who was already wearing his own.

Tyrrell stepped off the log and strolled down to them.

Missimer nodded hello—guardedly, for some reason.

Then Tyrrell recognized the sick man. Davey Major. He knew him from before the war in Philadelphia. They'd both been mustered into the regiment last August and, with some others from the old neighborhood, had gone to the theater together before leaving for Washington. His color was bad, and he gave no sign that he was aware of Tyrrell's approach until the shadow fell over him. "Davey . . . ?"

His glassy eyes slowly shifted as if it hurt to move them. And then came a wan smile. "Sergeant Willie?"

"Yes."

"Why aren't you with the colors?"

"Got more'n enough fellas to help me out with 'em," Tyrrell said. "How d'you feel?"

"Like a stewed chicken."

Missimer said, "He was complainin' of cramps earlier."

"They're gone now," Major said. Then he grinned. Or maybe it was just his parched lips sticking to his teeth.

Tyrrell knelt, felt the man's face. "But your fever ain't gone. It's off to the surgeon with you."

Major's hand came out from under Missimer's overcoat and took hold of Tyrrell by the wrist. "Please—don't blow on me. No blue pills. Not now. Somethin's gonna happen this afternoon. Don't wanna miss it. All last night, I knew somethin' big was gonna come today."

Tyrrell looked to Missimer. "When'd this start?"

"He was as fit as the rest of us at breakfast."

Tyrrell hesitated. He knew he might force the issue, but then decided that Major's own messmates would take better care of him than some drunk of a hospital steward. "Well," he finally said, "as long as he can march."

"I can march fine," Major insisted.

Tyrrell patted him on the shoulder, then said, "I'll come round tonight, Davey, and see how you're doin'."

"Sure, you do that, Will. Lookin' forward to it."

Tyrrell was slipping through cedars, heading back to the guard color—when bugle notes rose above the murmurous voices of the resting men. He began jogging. He hopped briefly on his left foot to scrape a mud cake off the sole of his other brogan. Virginia mud. It was either as slick as whale oil or clung like mussel shells. A horse galloped close behind, its legs rustling through the dry grass. Tyrrell didn't recognize the rider, a captain with braid and piping all over his uniform. He'd just delivered a sealed envelope to Meagher, who was ripping it open. The men were coming to their feet, getting into column again.

Tyrrell reached Hudson. "What is it?"

The regimental flag was wrapped around its staff, and the corporal untangled it. "Order from Sumner. That's all I heard."

Tyrrell slid the heel of his own flagstaff into the socket on his flag belt. He wished that this, whatever it was, had come earlier in the day. He was tired, woolly-headed.

Meagher, the opened message in his left hand, rode over to Colonel Heenan, had a quick word with him, then trotted toward Nugent of the 69th New York. Heenan, in turn, had a brief conference with Mulholland. The lieutenant colonel offered a pulpy smile up into the sky, a prayer maybe, then dismounted and walked his horse by the bridle over to the color guard. His pale blue eyes were shining under the brim of his slouch hat as he said, "Get yourselves ready, boys."

"For what, sir?" Hudson blurted.

"We're going to take some enemy guns across the river. If we do it, Fredericksburg will be ours by nightfall."

A city. They were going to seize a city. Charlestown all over again. Instantly, Tyrrell's weariness was gone. Yet, his knees felt strange, as if the bones coming together there had turned to custard. He hoped that he wasn't as pasty-faced as Mulholland.

The lieutenant colonel gave the color guard a self-deprecating wink. "Let's see if we can *all* stand steady this time."

The men chuckled knowingly.

At Charlestown, while supporting a battery, the regiment had come under fire for the first time. Everyone flinched as the shells hissed overhead, landing among the artillerymen, killing two and wounding another two. "Steady, men, steady," Mulholland had said in a cool singsong—until a near miss made him jerk his head down into his shoulders, turtlelike. At least he'd laughed at himself that afternoon. Nothing pompous about St. Clair Mulholland.

He now moved down the line, halted in front of McCarter. "My God, Mac—what happened to your bayonet?"

"C-c-cow, sir."

"A *cow?*"

"Broke it over his b-backside."

The laughter from the ranks was cut short by the sounds of the artillery taking off, the horses being lashed and the caissons bouncing over the hummocky pasture. The Pennsylvanians keenly watched this movement, while the New Yorkers ignored it, chatting and joking among themselves. The battery reached the road and continued down the plain toward the river. It stopped much sooner than expected, a bald knoll less than a quarter mile away, and the cannoneers began unlimbering their twelve-pounders.

"Johnnies that close?" Hudson asked uneasily.

The thought disquieted Tyrrell as well, although he made sure to hide it. At Charlestown, he'd seen what shot and shell could do to flesh and bone. A cannoneer, while sponging his barrel to douse any lingering sparks, had had both legs ripped off by a round shot. No sooner had he died than another crewman was decapitated. Then a fellow spun around, gripping the wrist from which his hand had just been lopped off. Finally, in the furious confusion of answering the enemy battery fire, a man was run over by a gun carriage wheel. All in a single skirmish the New Yorkers refused to count as a worthy brush with enemy. It had seemed impossible for even a cautious man to remain whole in such a situation.

"Excuse me, boys," some wag suddenly said from the ranks, "but I got a pain in me stomach."

Tyrrell laughed as loudly as the others. He felt better by the time he'd sobered again. Some awful inward pressure had been relieved a little.

"And where's the gallant Lieutenant Squirt this afternoon?" somebody asked facetiously.

"Got himself posted as a spittoon in Gen'ral Halleck's office."

The man under discussion had been the most hated officer in the regiment. If Mulholland got his boots muddy, he'd wipe them himself, lieutenant colonel or not. Squirt would order a private to do it for him. He played the parade-ground soldier to the hilt, but when the shelling had turned hot at Charlestown he fell on his wide ass, blanched and pardoned himself from the field with: "I don't like them sparkly-tailed things so near me. I got a pain in my stomach, boys, so I'll get out of the way for a while and lay down."

Tyrrell glanced along the line. There stood Davey Major, face ashen, his coat buttoned to the top, bracing himself with both hands around the barrel of his musket—but still standing there.

General Meagher cantered to the front of the brigade and drew rein. He took a long moment and stared up and down the length of his regiments. It was reassuring just to look at him, sitting on his charger, his gaze clear and steady as it swept the line. "Men of the Irish Brigade," he began almost in a hush, yet Tyrrell was sure that even the farthest men could hear him. "You've been chosen by the chief officer of this grand division to ford that river . . ." He pointed toward the wooded gorge at the foot of the pasture. ". . . and capture the Confederate artillery on the opposite shore. Two full batteries . . ." Like everyone else, Tyrrell strained for a glimpse of the guns but saw nothing except barren woods and rocky natural terraces across the Rappahannock. Then Meagher smiled warmly, intimately, and Tyrrell felt as if the brigadier was looking just at him. "Follow me. I lead the way. Be brave—and victory's ours."

Then the brigade was marched by the flank down the road through the pasture, drummers marking the cadence. Stretching back along the pike toward Warrenton, at least two other brigades were lounging under the trees, waiting for Meagher to open the ford before springing forward in support. Their overcoats looked black, like lumps of coal, against the patches of snow.

Fredericksburg by nightfall.

The last two days, he'd been led to believe that Falmouth was the goal. Nobody had ever said anything about Fredericksburg.

He realized once again, now that the first jolt of nerves had worn off, how tired he was. Too tired for a battle that might well last until after nightfall. The sun was already declining through the skeletonlike branches of the dogwoods. Another man was thinking the same thing, for he said, "Look at us—leppin' into the thick of it at vespers."

"Ah what harm," another brogue asked philosophically, "if it's all for the poor Old *Dairt?*"

Tyrrell fixed his eyes ahead on the neck of a teenage soldier in the 63d New York. Strangely, the sight reminded him of the smooth, white back of Annie's neck, of padding down the rickety stairs at home in his stocking feet, creeping across the kitchen floor to sneak up on her from behind. Cover her eyes with his fingers. She squealed in delighted surprise just as the brigade was halted, then began deploying into a double line of battle.

Waiting the 116th's turn, Tyrrell gazed across the gorge. Still no sign of the guns. But any instant, as at Charlestown, he expected to see white smoke squirt out of those distant woods, followed by that evil hissing of a fuse coming toward him. Him, personally. Did every man feel the same about that? He could see the brigade's skirmishers crouched in the tall grass at the lower end of the pasture. Really just their caps, like blue blossoms dotting the field.

Finally, Colonel Heenan put the regiment into motion again, filling in the last quarter of the brigade line. "Steady, boys," Mulholland said, winking again, as the color guard passed before him. "We'll all do fine . . . steady."

The river came into view. It was narrower at this point than Tyrrell had expected, a squiggle of tarnished silver between steep, winding banks. Still, no guns. He rested his forehead against the staff for a few seconds.

"You all right?" Hudson asked.

"Sleepy," Tyrrell murmured.

The corporal gave him a peculiar look.

Tyrrell couldn't believe how drowsy he was. He wished now that he'd napped during the halt instead of trying to get a view of Falmouth. His sleepiness made him feel as if he were stumbling along in a dream. He hoped the river water wouldn't be too cold. Too deep. Colonel Heenan might not let the regiment light fires after the fight, and then he'd be miserable all night.

Hudson frowned. "How can you be sleepy at time like this?"

"Just am."

The line was complete.

Meagher galloped to the center front once more and cried, "Attention!" And then with a calm smile: "Forward!" As usual, almost a minute elapsed—time standing still in that minute—before he roared, "March!"

Tyrrell couldn't feel his feet, just the colors in his grasp. As if the stars and stripes were a sail, and he were floating along behind them. With a quick, sideward glance, he checked the brigade's alignment. The pasture was uneven, but the line was beautifully straight. His fellow Pennsylvanians were grimly silent, unsmiling, but beyond them the New Yorkers were still chatting among themselves. Little flurries of laughter came and went.

The skirmishers were falling back to rejoin the brigade. Beyond them, across the Rappahannock, Tyrrell thought he saw a jeweled glint. A gun, maybe. Or rainwater pooled on a flat rock. The river looked translucently green from this angle. Shallows. This was a ford, then, and he was relieved to see that he'd get soaked no higher than his knees.

He began to wake up.

The muted fall leaves struck him as being very nice—tans and russets and soft grays. New spikes of green were poking up through a mat of brown grass that had already been flattened by the first hard frost. It was getting cold. The steamy breath of Meagher's horse was rolling back over the general.

Tyrrell wanted to run now, down the slope, through the shoreline belt of woods, across the river and onto the opposing bluff. He was sure that the order to double-quick was coming momentarily when a rider streaked across the front of the brigade and handed another sealed envelope to General Meagher.

He read the message, then scowled and called a halt.

Tyrrell stood with his eyes riveted on the far bluff, trying not to look perplexed. But before he understood what had happened, the brigade was starting back up the pasture toward the pike. What had gone wrong? He tried to recall if that distant glint had been a Confederate cannon, but he wasn't sure. "Did we scare the Rebels off?" a voice asked from the withdrawing line.

$\mathcal{S}$ i x

3:13 P.M.
24th Georgia
Culpeper

"Colonel . . . ?"

McMillan startled to a touch on his arm, yet his eyes seemed to be sealed shut. He struggled to open them to slits. A human shape was bending over him, backdropped by tent canvas. It was still day.

"Sir, Generals Longstreet and McLaws are with Brigadier Cobb, so I'll wake you like you asked."

Then McMillan remembered.

He'd sent Sullivan to watch Cobb's headquarters for this eventuality. He wanted time to prepare himself before the general sent Johnny Clark to fetch him. Last night had passed without sleep. He'd been unable to shake off the fear that Rob would die unless he could get him home to his mother. She alone would know how to save him. Yet, shortly before reveille, it came over McMillan that Providence didn't want the brigade to return to Georgia at this time. God had some further test for it here in Virginia, and Robert McMillan had no right to wish otherwise. *Thy will, not mine.* With that, he began to feel drowsy. But then a new worry cropped up as the drums roused the camp—would his old man's body, his swollen legs and aching chest, stand up to an-

44 ◆ *Kirk Mitchell*

other test of fire so soon? He'd counted on a long winter's rest before the next big fight. So had the surgeons.

He sat up, cradled his face in his hands. "What time is it, Michael?"

"After three some. Here, sir—drink."

McMillan gulped the coffee down, but it scarcely put a dent in his weariness. Coffee captured in September along with more than ten thousand Yankees when their garrison at Harpers Ferry had capitulated. Soon it'd all be gone. He gave back the empty cup to Sullivan, then stood and threaded his suspender straps over his shoulders. He'd dozed off in full uniform, except for his shell jacket and sword, and the sergeant now helped him with these. "Does something seem imminent, Michael?"

"It does indeed, sir."

Good, thought McMillan, *at least I got a wee sleep in, should we set off at once.*

Sullivan brought him a tin full of bracingly cold water, and McMillan washed his face. Like most everything else, the towel had been packed away, so he made do with his jacket sleeve.

"Sorry, sir," Sullivan said. "I shoulda taken out your kit again."

"Don't bother, Michael. No wit in loading for the march twice." Then McMillan stepped through the flaps. The air was mild. A band of high, wispy clouds had been turned golden by the declining sun. Across the plain, most of the tents had been struck. Not that there'd been many of them in the first place.

As expected, Clark rode up, beaming as always. "Gen'ral Cobb's compliments, sir."

"Afternoon, Johnny."

"The gen'ral asks to see the col'nels at his tent."

"On my way, lad."

The boy nodded, gratified that one name could be scratched off his mental list, then trotted off toward the color line of the 15th North Carolina, the only non-Georgians in the brigade.

"Well, Michael," McMillan said, "have a rest while I'm gone, if you please. Did me wonders."

"I might at that, sir." Sullivan reached out and smoothed down McMillan's jacket collar. It'd been standing up.

"Thank you." McMillan started off for Cobb's headquarters, some feeling coming into his heavy legs as he walked. The motion began to clear his mind as well. The warning order to march had been acted upon. The wagons were loaded. Three days' rations had been cooked. But Lee had yet to give the final word that would send 1st Corps, Longstreet's, chasing after the Federals streaming southeast out of Warrenton. The other half of the Army of Northern Virginia, Jackson's 2d Corps, was still on the west side of the Blue Ridge, in place to blunt a Union sweep up the Shenandoah Valley, should that be Lincoln's true plan. Yesterday, Lee had rushed an infantry regiment and some light artillery to reinforce the small garrison at Fredericksburg, a handsome little town from colonial days just below the falls of the Rappahannock. McClellan might mean to occupy it once again.

Burnside, McMillan corrected himself.

Hard to think of anybody but McClellan in charge of their side. Those Confederate officers who'd known Burnside at West Point or in the Regular Army before the war said that he was personable and smart enough. He'd invented an excellent carbine, but then gone bankrupt trying to fulfill his contract to the government. So he had his limitations. Admitted them, even.

McMillan glanced up.

Two generals were coming toward him from the direction of Cobb's tent. Both were in their early forties. One was bearishly large with a bear's small eyes. He was wearing an Austrian-style tunic and a plain black felt halt. A private from the 16th Georgia tried to hail him, maybe to trade some banter. But James Longstreet ignored the soldier, his sloe-eyed gaze turned inward, his sluggish intellect apparently pulverizing some question. Riding beside him was McMillan's division commander, Lafayette McLaws, who was as rotund as Longstreet, although the fleshiness around his eyes seemed more affable than his superior's, more sentimental. McLaws raked back his gray cape so he could wave to the Georgians who were now lining the dirt lane, hoping for news.

"Yankees got the jump on us this time, Gen'ral?" one of them asked.

McLaws laughed as he reined up. "Never, boys."

Longstreet rode on ahead, hunched slightly over the pommel. At close range, McMillan found his face vaguely worried. It was now widely suspected that if Richmond was Burnside's immediate goal he had a two-day jump on Lee. And yet, the commanding general insisted on waiting for Jeb Stuart to come back from a cavalry spree north of the Rappahannock before giving chase with Longstreet's corps. Lately, especially since the promise of the brigade's transfer back to Georgia, Cobb's opinion of Lee had gone up. But, in guarded moments, he still maintained that the "Old Tycoon" was the epitome of "West Pointism"—pushing textbook tactics to an extreme, treating officers of the volunteers as if they were naughty children.

"Why, Robert," McLaws said as McMillan stepped up to him and saluted, "you certainly look spry this afternoon."

That lifted McMillan's spirits. He'd been afraid he looked haggard. "Thank you, sir."

McLaws lowered his voice. "Stuart's back. Get yourself a good night's sleep." Then he lightly spurred his mount to catch up with Longstreet.

McMillan stood in the middle of the lane a moment longer, then contined on his way.

He was the first of the colonels to arrive, and an excited Cobb immediately ushered him inside the tent and invited him to sit. McMillan remained standing. He couldn't tell if the brigadier was pleased or anxious. When he spoke, his words came even more rapid-fire than usual. "It's Edwin Sumner's Right Grand Division. Strung out all along the pike from Warrenton to Falmouth. Well, almost to Falmouth at last word, but some of them should be there by now."

"Right Grand Division?" McMillan asked. He'd never heard the term before.

"I suppose it's still a secret we know such things, Robert." Then Cobb's eyes flared mischievously as he added, "It's from one of our spies up in Fauquier County. Burnside's reorganized his army into three big divisions. Reduced the number of West Pointers between himself and his men. Might have something there, you know . . . ?"

Burnside was pouring into Falmouth. He was now across the river from Fredericksburg, poised on a straight line to Richmond and largely unopposed. And last week, some other spy reported that Yankee gunboats had sailed into Aquia Creek just north of Falmouth. A big wharf and railroad terminus there made it an obvious resupply point for a sudden drive on Richmond, sixty miles south.

"Then we march, sir?" McMillan asked.

Cobb tried to smile but failed. Despite his animation, he was clearly disappointed. There would be no winter hiatus this year. No transfer back home. "That's right," he said, his hands shaking somewhat as he lit a cigar, "first thing in the morning. Our division and Bob Ransom's. We'll be supported by some cavalry and Lane's battery. Longstreet made himself *more* than plain to Lafayette and me—we're not to let Sumner cross the Rappahannock. He'll be right behind us with the rest of the corps by a day or two."

It would be a footrace and then, with no rest, a battle. At last, McMillan sank onto a camp stool.

3:59 P.M.
Stafford Heights, opposite Fredericksburg

Meagher and Hancock's aide stopped on a grassy rise a half mile southeast of Falmouth. The slender lieutenant pointed with a riding crop. "See the house now, sir?"

"Ah, yes." Clearly. A Georgian brick mansion.

"General Hancock's out front of it."

"A good view of Fredericksburg from there?" Meagher asked, slipping his flask from the top of his riding boot.

"Excellent, sir. And the opposite's true—so mind the sharp-shooters. General Hancock's been warned. But, as usual, it don't mean a thing to him."

Meagher chuckled, offered the lieutenant a swallow, which he waved off with a smile. Other messages to deliver. Other brigade commanders to summon from rough bivouacs in the timber around Falmouth. The young man touched his fingers to the bill of his cap and galloped back toward the brooding woods in which he'd found the Irish Brigade, resting on its arms, mysti-fied that the order to cross the river had been countermanded at the last minute.

Meagher drank.

Tucking the flask back in his boot, he then dug in his spurs and put his white charger into an extended gallop toward the big house. He felt like a boy, studies neglected and out free on a crisp autumn afternoon. Yet, there was sadness in the thought. His own boy was an ocean away, living with his grandfather in the old ancestral mansion. County Waterford. Soft, gray Irish mornings.

Off toward the river, cannon began barking again after a pause of some minutes.

Meagher turned in the saddle toward the sound.

White smoke rose from a grove of pines, bumped along the ground in the light breeze. Federal twelve-pounders were hav-ing a go at a bluff just across the Rappahannock from Falmouth. He could see a thin pillar of black smoke rising from the woods over there. He turned toward the pines and trotted in behind the battery. Their familiar flag made him smile: the 1st New York Light Artillery. His own division's guns. Mostly Irish, too. Stripped to their shirtsleeves even though the day was quickly turning cool, the men sponged, loaded, yanked their lanyards, watched and waited, then shrugged indifferently, only to start the entire dance all over again several seconds later.

Meagher asked a sergeant, "What're you firing at?"

"One of their batteries, sir," the man shouted over the desultory cannonade. "It drove our boys back 'cross Falmouth ford a while ago. Infantry almost got over and captivated their guns." But then he added with a satisfied wink, "We still shelled 'em off that knoll you see down there, General Meagher—and we're hammerin' the woods where they skedaddled. We'll get 'em yet."

"Happy thought," Meagher said. But he also realized that two chances to cross the Rappahannock, which had been drawn down by summer to a broad but shallow stream, had been lost this afternoon. Did Burnside want Fredericksburg or not? Perhaps not, judging from that second message Meagher had got earlier this afternoon, ordering all forces to remain on the north side of the river.

He urged his horse on.

A deep, brushy ravine between the mansion and Meagher forced him away from the river. Approaching the house from the north, he could see a church spire in town, as sharp as a lance, jutting into the sky.

Hancock, as promised by his aide, was on the lawn facing Fredericksburg. He was standing apart from his staff, glassing the town. Tall, erect, his uniform and famous starched white shirt looking as fresh as the morning he'd left Warrenton. He seemed preoccupied, so Meagher decided to put off reporting for the moment.

The division engineer was sitting on the steps of a double-decked veranda, a large map spread over his lap. Two younger aides were on the deck itself, leaning against the brick wall in dining hall chairs and smoking their pipes.

Meagher dismounted, gritting his teeth as he straightened his injured left knee. It was getting worse, not better. An abscess was gradually filling the joint with pus. But he masked his limp as he went up to the engineer. "Good afternoon," he said, somewhat embarrassed that he'd forgotten the man's name. Hancock knew the name of nearly every officer under his command.

"General . . ." The engineer started to rise, but Meagher put a hand on his shoulder. "Care to see the map, sir?"

"Kind of you, Major." He eased down beside the man, grinning to keep the pain off his face. "Where are we now?"

"Here, sir." The major's charcoal-stained finger tapped a dot on a long series of ink billows labeled Stafford Heights. They fell away in two terraces. The mansion crowned the first. A lower one, overgrown with scrub, leveled off just above the river. At this point, a mile below its first falls near Falmouth, the Rappahannock sheeted past Fredericksburg like green glass. "And this is Mr. Lacy's house."

"And where's the lord of the manor?" Meagher asked.

"In Confederate service."

"You must remind me to wipe my boots, then."

The major gave a fleeting smile, then lifted his chin at a ruined bridge that had once connected Stafford Heights to the lower end of town. Only its stone columns remained. "The old railway bridge. Destroyed by the Rebels. As was the span up at Falmouth."

Meagher began absently rubbing his knee. "This war's been hard on bridges."

"Sir?"

"I suppose everyone's out to prove that there's no going back." Meagher let go of his kneecap. "In any event, I'm sure we can just wade across."

"Yes, sir—till the first heavy rain."

Meagher studied Fredericksburg itself. The quaintest town in old Virginia, he'd been told. And it did have a certain colonial charm. The forest of chimneys—at least two to a house—reminded him of Ireland. He could peer straight up one of the east-west streets onto an open plain that rose to a long broken hill about a half mile behind town. "What's that ridge immediately back there?"

The engineer had to consult the map. "Uh, Marye's and Willis' hills, sir . . . known jointly as Marye's Heights. The northern end of Fredericksburg Heights, which extend about three miles south down to Hamilton's Crossing."

"Goddammit, Tom," Hancock's voice boomed, "how long you been sitting there?"

"Just arrived, sir."

The division commander strode up the gravel walk and sat down beside him. The major excused himself, leaving his map with Meagher.

"Well, what d'you think so far?" Hancock asked.

"I'm thankful we're sitting on Stafford Heights. Has to be the best ground around."

Hancock jerked his thumb toward the south. "Unfortunately, Richmond's across the river that way."

Meagher nodded. "What do they have waiting for us over there?"

"Not much at the second. Some cavalry. Maybe four or five companies of infantry. A light battery smart enough to keep moving from place to place." Hancock gave Meagher his field glasses and slipped the map from his fingers. Studying it, he fluffed up his chin tuft with a knuckle. Always primping. Himself. His command. Tirelessly efficient, forever dissatisfied.

Meagher brought the glasses to his eyes—and immediately picked up some brisk movement on the north end of town. A troop of gray cavalry was trotting along between the well-spaced houses there, seemingly confident that the Federal batteries wouldn't open up on them. He trusted that the artillery wouldn't. It was an inhabited city, after all.

He lowered the glasses and stole a sideward glance at Hancock's face. It was mobile, intently expressive; each thought seemed to register on it. Meagher often wondered if that comic opera of a fight at the village of Ballingarry would have ended differently—had he and the other Irish insurgents of 1848 been led by a man like Winfield Scott Hancock. When he took over the division after poor old General Richardson received his mortal wound at Antietam, Hancock immediately struck Meagher as the sort of man he himself must become, if Erin was ever to be free. But then something made Meagher smile faintly to himself. Was this sort of thinking simply out of habit now? Was Ireland behind him forever and his fate here in Amerikay? Sometimes he wondered.

Hancock stared off at Fredericksburg Heights. "We've beaten him here, Tom. Two full days, maybe more."

"Beaten whom, sir?"

"Lee," Hancock said quietly. "And now we'll sit on our asses while he races down from Culpeper." He folded the map in disgust and tossed it aside. "Just once, why the hell can't we grab time by the forelock and get on with it? If Burnside wants Richmond, the goddamned door is open!" Then he calmed himself with a bitter laugh and looked around the grounds. Horse hooves had played havoc with the turf, and much of the shrubbery was trampled. When he spoke again, a surprising softness had come into his voice. "He courted his wife in this garden."

"Burnside?" Meagher asked, confused.

Hancock shook his head. "Lee. I believe this house once belonged to his wife's family." He took out his own metal flask, offered Meagher a nip, which he decided to decline. Hancock, no doubt, had heard about that night back in Warrenton. "He kept me in the army, you know."

"I didn't."

"Yes," Hancock went on. "Allie wasn't sure if she wanted to go out to California with me. Lee told her that her post was at my side. Said no good would come to our marriage if such a small thing made us live apart. We'd *cease to be essential to each other.* He says things like that . . ." He paused, his eyes far away, almost moist, but then sprang to his feet and took back his glasses. "Go ahead, Tom, and have your boys bivouac for the night where they are now."

He started for the door, but Meagher stopped him. "Sir . . . ?"

"What?"

"If another crossing's in the cards, I want my brigade to lead it."

"Damn your Irish impudence!" But then Hancock laughed as he went inside. Admiringly, Meagher felt sure.

8:50 P.M.
116th Pennsylvania
Bivouac of the Irish Brigade

Tyrrell stared into the flames of the color guard's fire. Through them he saw Annie. At this hour, she was letting down her hair for bed. Her hair shone in the lamplight as it slowly uncoiled around her thin shoulders. Smiling, she turned to look back at him. He shot up from his gum blanket to stop the sweet torture. His loneliness was suffocating him. And all at once, he hated the army, everything about it. Annie was waiting for his pay. Months overdue. He'd signed the payroll in camp near Harpers Ferry, but the money had yet to catch up with the regiment. Now, she'd gone and applied for state aid, but that hadn't come through either. What kind of government would do this to a man's family?

He gazed up into the overhanging branches. Stars were showing through this black latticework, which had begun in the last few minutes to creak and quiver from a rising breeze. A change in the weather on the way.

Hudson sprawled on the other side of the fire ring, holding a month-old copy of the *Philadelphia Hibernian* into the guttering light. He was smiling as he read.

Tyrrell felt like chatting, but not about today's near brush with the enemy batteries he'd never really seen. He wanted no one to know how relieved he'd felt as the brigade marched back up that pasture toward safety. Floating. Lieutenant Colonel Mulholland said Burnside hadn't wanted one grand division stretched out across the river like a chicken's neck.

Hudson finally winked over at Tyrrell. "Listen to this, Will . . ." He began reading out loud an article about an actress named Charlotte Thompson, who was appearing at the Walnut Street Theater. Tyrrell had never seen Miss Thompson, but he'd been to the Walnut many times. A bunch of them from the regiment had gone, including Davey Major, before boarding the train for Washington. " '. . . Miss Thompson will play three different women in the same performance. Victorine, an embroideress. Madame St. Victor . . .' " Hudson glanced up. "No occupation given. Somebody famous?"

Tyrrell hiked his shoulders. He knew so little. The regiment would do better with an educated man for color sergeant, not a tradesman.

"And another lady named Victorine, the keeper of a board-inghouse. Imagine, *three*. And if that ain't enough for one night—'Mr. Brian Borihme, esquire' . . . what's *esquire* mean, Will?"

"Don't know. Sounds like a fella puttin' on airs."

" 'Mr. Brian Borihme will do *The Last of the Irish Kings.*' "

Tyrrell said, "Let me take that over 'C' Company way."

"Why?"

"Davey Major's feelin' poorly. It'd cheer him up to hear about the Walnut, just like it did us, Joe."

Hudson hesitated, but then gave up the newspaper. "I want it back."

Tyrrell headed for where Major's company had settled in for the night. He'd last checked on Davey at sundown. Sergeant Missimer and the boys had laid him close to the fire. He cracked a smile when Tyrrell asked how he was doing, licked his dry lips and said, "You see them New Yorkers this afternoon?"

"I did."

"It's daft how they go into a scrap."

"It is."

A sad, haunted look came over Major's pale face as he said, "Don't you ever get that crazy for blood, Will." Then he'd shut his feverish eyes and slept.

Now, through the trees, Tyrrell could see the dying fires of the 88th New York. As he watched, the drums could be heard beating out tattoo. The paddies seemed to take this not as the call to get ready for their bedrolls, but rather as an invitation to get up and dance, if they weren't already. Their fiddles and tin whistles had been echoing throughout the entire bivouac all evening. He supposed that he didn't understand them. Not really. They went into battle as if it were a wedding feast. And no matter what happened, however bad, their answer was, "What harm if it's for the poor Old *Dairt*." He knew from his father that a *dairt* was a clod of earth. The Old Sod. Maybe that was it—they were more like his Irish-born father than himself. Patrick Tyrrell was a tough old man, full of memories from the homeland so terrible he couldn't talk about them. Maybe that's why the paddies had to get up and dance before trying to sleep. The old country.

Slowing his pace, Tyrrell reached where he'd last seen Davey Major and the others. Their camp was darkened, their fire glowing only when the breeze stirred it. Several silhouettes were seated around the almost dead embers. "Frank?" he called out for Missimer.

"Who's that?"

"Tyrrell. Come to see how Davey's doin'."

Missimer said nothing for a few moments, then: "Throw some pine needles on the coals, and let Will have a look."

Someone did this, and a bright orange flame shot up through the smoke. Davey Major was where Tyrrell had last seen him, beside the fire, but now he was wrapped from head to toe in his gum blanket.

"Oh no." Then Tyrrell remembered to cross himself.

"Just after you went back to the color line, he got worse," Missimer said. "Burnin' up. Out of his head with his talk."

The needles were consumed, and the darkness came down again.

"You send for the surgeon?" Tyrrell asked.

"Sure, Will. But it was camp fever, and you know there's nothin' to be done for that."

"He was good-hearted," a middle-aged brogue said from the farthest reach of the circle. "And he woulda made a fine old man."

Missimer went on, "His mind cleared right before the end, didn't it though? He wanted us to have his money and such."

"That goes home to his people," Tyrrell said.

"Sure, we all agreed to that . . ." Then Missimer added that Lieutenant Willauer of their company had been told. They were waiting for him to come back with instructions.

The entire bivouac was quieting down.

Tyrrell stooped, pressed his knees against the cold, soft ground. Davey wasn't the first to die in the regiment. A case of camp fever near Harpers Ferry. Another private was killed when his loaded musket fell to the ground and went off. But Tyrrell hadn't known those men well.

"Don't care what the colonel decides," a sullen voice said, "I won't see Davey buried in the same country what spawned them Warrenton whores."

Tyrrell could see the men nodding.

Leading the brigade into Warrenton, the regiment had been greeted by the town's women, dressed in black as if in mourning. It started with hisses from the doorways and windows, then cries of: "There go the damned abolitionists—kill 'em!" Suddenly, a hail of coal, rocks, firewood, and even tools came from the rooftops. Heenan's mount was struck with a shoemaker's hammer and nearly threw him, but the colonel shouted, "Calm, boys, easy now!" Tyrrell recalled one old biddy in particular, leaning over a board fence, screaming at him, "You with that striped rag—go back to your whorin' mother and leave us be!"

"Missimer . . . ?" a new voice asked from the dark.

"Here, sir."

More pine needles were tossed atop the embers, and Seneca Willauer came into view, the lieutenant's overcoat unbuttoned, revealing a soiled linen shirt beneath. "Well, I talked to the adjutant—colonel's with General Meagher. Looks like we march first thing in the mornin'."

"Where to—?"

"We'll have to bury Davey tonight," the lieutenant interrupted.

Silence.

At last, a corporal stirred and said, "Why can't we use the company fund to ship him home, Seneca?" Tyrrell realized that it was Sam Willauer, the lieutenant's younger brother.

"Because that's not what the fund's for, *Corporal*," he replied.

And the regiment hadn't been paid in three months, so passing a cap around the fire would be fruitless. Besides, Tyrrell had no idea how much it'd cost to ship a body back to Philadelphia. He knew that it involved embalming, another expense neither Davey's mother nor his friends could afford.

"See here, boys," the lieutenant went on, "we marched by a nice little church comin' in today. Can't be more'n a mile back up the pike. I think it'd suit Davey's ma fine if he was put in a churchyard."

"What if the gentry don't want him in their cemetery, Lieutenant?" It was the man who'd first said he didn't want Major buried in Virginia.

"We don't ask," Lieutenant Willauer said curtly. Then he paused. Nobody had anything to add, so he said, "I'll see to the musicians and Father McKee. The rest of you cut some pine-knot torches." With that, he walked off.

A few of the wagons belonging to the 88th New York had rolled into the bivouac after nightfall, so Missimer ran over to borrow an ax. The rest of the men gathered bunches of needles, lit them off the fire coals and went out into the encircling woods in search of pine branches.

Tyrrell was left alone with the corpse.

After a while, he built the fire back up, using the wood the men had laid aside to cook breakfast. He figured they wouldn't mind, and the priest would need light for his work.

Tyrrell stared at the body in its India rubber shroud.

Davey had known that something big would happen to him today. It seemed a cruel joke that this was it. He was gone, and he'd never even been in a real battle. Leaving Philadelphia, every man had probably half-expected to die. But not like this.

A racking cough could be heard approaching through the woods. It belonged to Father McKee, who had a woolen muffler wrapped around his throat. "There, Father . . ." Not knowing what more to say, Tyrrell simply gestured at the body. The priest's rheumy eyes settled on it, but showed no emotion. Then, stiffly, he knelt over Davey and began mumbling.

Lieutenant Willauer returned with a drummer and two fife players, who were toting a stretcher between them. He asked Tyrrell if he'd carry the company guidon for the procession. He said yes, gladly. The men came back in and lit their crude torches. Willauer had them fall in, and they started through the bivouac toward the pike, his brother and Missimer bearing Davey on the stretcher. The priest led the company, and then Tyrrell with the small, swallow-tailed flag. The muffled drum and fifes played the "Dead March," which made Tyrrell realize again—as if for the first time—that Davey Major was gone. He'd never go to the Walnut Street Theater again.

They were passing the darkened camp of the 88th New York when a harsh voice sang out, "Bah!"

The fifes and drum went on playing, but then left off when something rattled across the ground in front of the procession. A cooking pot, Tyrrell saw when the torches got near to it.

When the music continued, another New Yorker bawled, "Will you shut the bloody hell up!"

The fife players quit, but the drummer went on marking time with bleak little clicks.

"Bah . . . bah!"

It finally got to Sam Willauer, who shouted indignantly, "We're settin' out for a burial here!"

Silence for a moment, then: "How many, Pennsylvania?"

Like Tyrrell, the corporal had no idea what the New Yorker meant. "What?"

"How many you buryin' tonight with that grand parade?"

"One . . . we're burying one man."

And then something incredible broke from the 88th New York—laughter, howling laughter.

$\mathscr{S}$even

◆

At first, Sullivan thought that his arms and legs were simply growing stiff from the long miles, maybe twenty of them since leaving Culpeper at dawn. But then he realized that his wet clothes were slowly freezing, delicate white crystals forming a web over the fabric. He chuckled.

"What, Sarn't?" young Hugh Tully asked, slogging alongside.

"We're turnin' into ice."

The boy, shivering, looked down at himself. "Are we?"

"Are we, he asks. Next thing, Old Pete—"

"Who?"

"General Longstreet to you. Old Pete'll come ridin' back along the column, wrapped up in his warm gray shawl—and find the whole of Lafayette's division frozed solid in line of march. Why, he'd have to wait till spring for his corps to thaw, what if the Yankees don't find us first. Cart us all north like statues . . ." Sullivan shook the sleet off his haversack cover. "Wouldn't that be a fine message for Jeff Davis to get from the Original Gorilla up there in Washington?—*Got your Army of Northern Virginia packed away in sawdust. Surrender and I'll thaw 'em for transport home.*"

Tully eyed him suspiciously.

Sullivan tried to wipe his face inside the bend of his arm, but it did no good. The cloth there was yet unfrozen, but still sopping. "Of course," he went on, "Old Jeff'd fire a telegram right back at Abe: *No surrender. I got ice in me veins and it's never slowed this fella down in the least.*" He'd been drenched to the skin long before the column had waded across the Rapidan at Raccoon Ford. It had been either raining or sleeting since mid-morning, and now the stuff was slanting down in spongy little pellets that refused to melt once they hit the ground. A thin, crackling crust was forming on the Orange Turnpike, but he and the men still broke through with every step, sinking in up to their ankles in reddish mud.

He looked at the boy. "Where's your father, Hugh?—if I might ask."

"Dead."

"In the war?"

"No, when I was little."

"How little?"

"Just after him and my ma come over from Ireland."

"And where were you baptized?"

"Not sure."

Craftier than he looked, Sullivan decided: nobody was going to use church records against his staying in the army. "But you were baptized . . . right?"

" 'Course."

"Episcopalian?" the sergeant asked, poker-faced.

Tully spat, and Sullivan chuckled again, giving the boy's skinny neck a squeeze.

"Ma's gonna get a letter from the travelin' priest who done it for her," Tully said hotly.

"A letter from the travelin' people?" an eavesdropper in the ranks asked, snorting. "Never met a tinker who could even write his own name."

"Travelin' *priest*," Sullivan clarified. Then he glanced over at the colonel. McMillan was walking to spare his horse, a mangy plug now that most of the decent mounts had been given over to Jeb Stuart's cavalry. The man's lips had turned lavender, and he kept staring northward as he plodded along, off into the gray half-light of the storm.

"Colonel," Sullivan called to him.

McMillan's eyes, squeezed nearly shut against the cold, widened. "Yes, Michael?"

"What do you say, sir? Up in the saddle now."

"Soon," McMillan promised, as he had an hour ago, "soon."

"That's an Ulsterman for you, Hugh," Sullivan said under his breath. "Walkin' on a day wet enough to kill a smolt—all to save a two-guinea horse."

But Tully was off in his own thoughts. "Sarn't . . . ?"

"Aye."

"We was ordered to cook three days' rations, right?"

"That we were."

"Then why'd we eat 'em all this mornin'?"

"Easier to carry 'em in your belly than in your haversack."

Tully tried to fasten his topmost coat button, but then his grimy, tremulous fingers seemed to recall that it was missing. He wiped his nose instead. "Private Dooley says you was a cook before the war."

"Among other things."

"You a good cook?"

Sullivan answered, "A dog would roll in my stew. And I couldn't even boil stirabout without burnin' it. See, I was hired by the railroad, not some fancy hotel."

"Stirabout?"

Sullivan tried to think of the word. The cold was starting to numb his brain. It was well past time to call a halt, but he suspected Longstreet might keep them going all night. At Raccoon Ford, while watching McLaws's division cross over, the burly corps commander had had the look of a groom late for his own wedding. And for all anybody knew, at this very moment Ambrose Burnside was having supper in Richmond—with Jefferson Davis waiting on him. "Porridge," Sullivan said at last. "Ye gods, you never heard of stirabout?"

Tully said nothing for a few paces, and then asked, "What other work you do back then?"

"Stevedorin'."

"You good at that?"

"No."

"Why not?"

"I drank too much in those Savannah days. So much, I came off the mother of hard nights and who but Father Jeremiah O'Neill was workin' me hand to sign the pledge."

"But everybody says you drink spirits."

"What d'you expect, boy?" Sullivan said, irked with the regimental gossips. "Didn't I just tell you I was drunk when I took the pledge?" Then it pained him to see the look that came over the boy's face. "What's that for now?"

"Sometimes I don't know if you're coddin' me or not."

Sullivan said, "Well, there's a bit of gab from the Old *Dairt* still in you." Then he glanced downward, frowned. There were traces of blood in the slush. Some poor fellow's bare feet had started bleeding. Returning from Georgia, Cobb had raised hell to get most of the brigade shod before winter set in, but there were those still going without.

Bad memories came to Sullivan with the cold. "You know, Hugh," he said quietly after a while, "sometimes I wonder if God's coddin' all of us. . . ." He shut his eyes and for a sickening instant saw the three of them—their eyes made enormous by the hunger, their hair falling out by the handfuls—huddling together under a tattered horsecloth. He shoved the image back into the darkness. "So you're not alone. We all wonder on that. And if you're askin' what I'm good at, which is an insult after our association of these past days, I'll tell you outright—I'm good at deliverin' the likes of you and the colonel there in one piece to wherever Bob Lee wants you to stand. After that, you're in the Lord's hands."

At long last, Johnny Clark came splashing down the line. Muddy icicles were hanging off his horse's belly. "That one lepped from his mother's teat right into the saddle," Sullivan said. Clark rode up to McMillan, gave a jaunty salute and loudly relayed the general's order to bivouac for the night. Fires would be allowed.

McMillan nodded, and Clark dashed happily off again. The colonel looked after him—enviously, Sullivan thought—then climbed laboriously into the saddle and said, "I'll be seeing to the pickets, Michael."

There was no reason for the old man to do this himself. But Sullivan knew that McMillan felt the need to keep moving. "Very good, sir. I'll get us situated."

"Thank you."

Sullivan peered roundabout.

It was a dismal place, with scrubby woods on one side of the pike, too thick and brambly to shelter in, and a swale on the other. He'd lay claim to the slushy depression before the other regiments left the 24th Georgia with the ravine that emptied it. The daylight was going fast. "Come on," Sullivan said to Tully, leading him into the low trees. They rolled over a dead log and Sullivan cobbed out the crumbly, termite-eaten pulp with the boy's bayonet. It was damp but would quickly dry when laid over the wood shavings Sullivan had packed in the bottom of his haversack. "Now, lad," he said, protecting the pulp by tucking it up one end of his bedroll oilskin, "find me plenty of limb wood. Nothin' bigger, for we have no axe. Pine if you can get it."

Crossing the pike again, Sullivan looked westward, hoping for a glimpse of the colonel's wagon. But he knew there was small chance of that. It began to snow big, wet flakes.

He was crouching over his kindling pile, struggling with his flint and steel, when Tully came in from the woods a third time, dragging a long branch. "I got lucifers, Sarn't," the boy said.

Sullivan looked up hopefully.

Tully eagerly threw off his knapsack, but upon opening it found that his matches and most everything else were wet.

"No matter," Sullivan said, going back to striking his flint. Finally, a fragile flame licked up out of the shavings. He told Tully to kneel to help him shield it from the wind and snow.

"Where we pitch the col'nel's tent, Sarn't?"

"We won't. It's miles behind. He'll sleep with us. More wood, boy, and we'll have a snug rest." Sullivan watched him lope back out to the trees, gawky, loose-jointed. He couldn't be more than sixteen. When he returned with another branch, Sullivan told him to have a look inside his haversack. There, Tully discovered a Yankee hardtack biscuit.

"You want this, Sarn't?"

"No, it's for you. Go to it." And the boy did, greedily, his mouth wide open as he chewed. Sullivan watched, his dark eyes sad, then opened his palms to the growing fire. Night had fallen, and the snow sizzled as it hit the flames. He felt a gaze on the back of his neck. Turning, he noticed a wraith standing out at the edge of the light. "What regiment?" he asked.

"Eighteenth Mississippi." One of Colonel Barksdale's boys. And an Irishman. "Just admirin' your fire."

"Well, admire it closer, if you please. The Twenty-fourth Georgia always has room for another."

The man padded up to the fire in his bare feet. They were livid from the cold. Sullivan had the manners not to stare, but Tully gaped at the naked, purplish toes. The Mississippian also had no blanket roll. It was amazing how hardened everyone had become to the cold, but that didn't end the suffering. He shuddered as the heat came through his sopping uniform, then slowly smiled as he took his long-stemmed clay pipe from the pocket of his jacket. His tobacco was probably wet, but he sucked on the bit all the same and watched the flames curl up into the shimmering veils of snow. "Lovely," he muttered, "just lovely."

Sullivan studied his face a moment, then asked, "Are you a friend?"

Plucking his pipe from his mouth, the Mississippian quickly said, "I am a friend."

"Then you're my friend." They shook hands. "I'm Mike Sullivan, and this here's Hugh Tully."

"*Captain* Sullivan?" the man asked.

Sullivan nodded.

"Then this is more than a pleasure, sir. It's an honor. My name's Mooney. County Kilkenny. An honor."

From the corner of his eye, Sullivan saw Tully pitch his eyes back and forth in confusion.

"Well," Sullivan said, "whenever we get settled in for the winter, I'll call a meetin'."

"Fine, sir." Mooney's often-patched clothes had begun to steam. "I'll pass the word along to the lads in the Sixteenth Mississippi over in Anderson's division. They just said to me they were ready for a gatherin' of the circle."

"Sharpsburg set us back on our heels. Almost afraid to see who's gone."

"Aye," Mooney said. He stood on one chapped foot and held the other out to the heat. But the fire was quickly dying. Then, reluctantly, he said, "Back to me regiment. Thank you, sir."

"Anytime."

As soon as the Mississippian had gone, Tully asked, his forehead in wrinkles, "You told me never to call you *sir*."

"That's right. I'm a lowly sergeant in the Provisional Army of the Confederate States. Did they teach you nothin' down there in Clarkesville?"

"They taught me plenty." Defiant, suddenly. "What're you captain of, then?"

"Tomorrow, Hugh. I'll explain it all on the march. Let's get some sleep."

Still pouting, Tully began to spread his oilcloth on the icy mud, but Sullivan told him to wait. "Stand on the other side of this bed of coals . . ." Then he passed one end of a limb he'd saved to the boy. "Rake, Hugh." Stopping, they began skimming the coals out into the ooze, which swiftly swallowed them, the red sparkles winking out with sharp little hisses. Tully and he made several passes until the fire-baked ground was swept clean of ashes. "Now, toss down your roll, oilcloth first, and open it flat." He spread his own blanket and oilcloth over Tully's, and they crawled in together, as did all the other men in pairs to weather the night. Sullivan burrowed down so that his head was covered, then listened to the snow pelting his oilcloth. The heat of the fired earth radiated up through the bottom blanket. It took the chill out of his damp clothes, and with that came a sweet drowsiness.

Garnett McMillan slogged past, checking on his father, no doubt. The old man's only adult offspring left unscathed. Sullivan had thought Major Rob would be dead by now, his leg had looked so bent and gashed the night after Sharpsburg. But he had his father's toughness. Garnett was gentle. Like his mother, perhaps. He'd seen Mrs. McMillan only once, a proud little woman who'd lifted her chin and smiled as she presented the colors to Fred Satterfield.

As soon as the lieutenant was gone again, a small and troubled voice came from the other side of the makeshift bed. "You're a Rebel, aren't you?"

Sullivan sighed. "And what're you—a Lincoln Republican?"

"No, I mean an *Irish* Rebel."

Sullivan opened his eyes under the covers. "And what'd be wrong with that?"

"Ma says they're the biggest knaves in the world."

Sullivan sat up. Plodding hoofbeats were approaching. That would be the colonel. He rose and shouted for the horse orderly, who left his own bed to take the bridle for McMillan. "We've got everythin' ready for you, sir," Sullivan said.

The colonel was too exhausted to talk. Sullivan led him by the arm to the bed, laid him down, and then slipped under the covers beside Tully. The snow had turned to sleet again and was chattering against the oilcloth. He wanted that curtain of sudden black which turned mud to goosedown and stony ground to clouds. But he was all awake now.

And he was still wide-eyed an hour later when the colonel groaned, "Rob . . . Robbie . . ." The old man woke Tully with his nightmare, but Sullivan clamped a hand over the boy's mouth before he could say anything. After a few moments, he let go, and the boy whispered, "Is he awake?"

"Just his heart. Quiet now."

He'd almost drifted off when hooves plashed heavily along the pike. He could hear the poor beast breathing explosively. Terrible to use an animal up like that, whatever the need. "Col'nel McMillan!" came the cry from the mounted figure.

But the old man didn't stir until Sullivan tapped his arm. Then he bolted upright. *"Yes?"*

"Clark with a message, sir." Sullivan stood and hollered, "Here!" Clark rode over. "Sir, Gen'ral Cobb's compli—"

"Yes?" McMillan interrupted, hunched against the sting of the sleet.

"Fredericksburg, sir. We know now. That's where they're headed with everythin' they got. Gen'ral Longstreet says we gotta beat 'em there, or Richmond's gone."

"When do we march again?"

"Right now, sir. That's what Brigadier Cobb sent me to tell you."

8:45 P.M.
Irish Brigade
Falmouth Encampment

"Father Corby!" Meagher exclaimed, rising clumsily and waving for the priest to take the last empty stool at the table. "Just in time for supper. Wine first?"

The priest wiped his face with a linen napkin. It'd been drizzling since dusk. "Well, sir—"

"Claret for the good father, please," Meagher told an orderly. "Uncork my best bottle." His color was up and his eyes bright. As they always were on the eve of battle. He gestured at his regimental commanders seated all around. "I'm trying to get a row going. But since the Twenty-ninth Massachusetts left us, we're all of the same mind . . ." After Antietam, this regiment of Yankee Protestants had been reassigned to another corps. "So the evening's been a bore." Life sometimes seemed a race against boredom for Thomas Francis. He'd no sooner set himself up in New York than he traipsed off to Central America, looking to build a railroad across the isthmus. "Bob," he said coyly, turning to Colonel Nugent of the 69th New York at his elbow. "My dear Bob."

"Sir?"

"You must be our devil's advocate."

"I decline the honor."

"No, you don't."

"Why pick on me, sir?"

"Because you're the only Presbyterian here," the brigadier said, winking at Corby. "What's the use of having an Orangeman in the brigade if he won't play the devil's advocate?"

Corby said, "I've heard that your Orangeman here is a prominent Fenian leader."

"Don't believe a word of it," Meagher said. "Everyone thinks that because Bob's from Antrim, and people from Antrim are naturally quarrelsome. The weather up there." Meagher clapped Nugent around the shoulders. "Isn't that so, Bob?"

"It's also said Waterford men are natural agitators. It comes from blowing all that glass."

Meagher feigned shock. "Are you calling me a blowhard?"

The men laughed quietly.

Corby's glass of wine arrived, followed in short order by supper itself. He said grace for the table, then just sat a moment, admiring the baked ham that Joseph, Meagher's old Irish cook, was carving for them. The brigade had marched from its overnight bivouac to this site a mile northeast of Falmouth only this morning, yet the floor to the general's tent was already boarded. His bed was covered by a rich brown buffalo robe. A tin fireplace was pouring out soft yellow light and oceans of heat. Close by, fifteen-year-old Johnny Flaherty and his father, Meagher's personal musicians, were quietly playing violin and pipes.

"Where's Father Ouellette?" Meagher asked.

"Seeing to Father McKee, sir."

"Still down with that awful ague?"

Dennis Heenan, the fleshy colonel of the 116th Pennsylvania, answered for Corby, "And getting worse, sir. I'm afraid Father McKee should be sent home. For his own sake."

"By all means," Meagher said. He'd made up his mind that quickly. "Arrange it first thing in the morning, Dennis. Home till he's on his feet again." Then, on an afterthought, he asked Corby, "But can you and Father Ouellette take over one more load of sin?"

Corby nodded without comment. It'd be easier than nursing the priest, whose health had been utterly broken by his three months of service. A funeral detail in last night's chill had finally prostrated him.

"Done," Meagher said. Then he glanced slyly at Nugent. "Bob . . . ?"

The dapper colonel was holding up his plate so Joseph could pile thick slices of ham on it. "Father, you might be wondering why our brigadier is spoiling for a fight."

"He does seem to be beating the long roll tonight," Corby said.

Meagher shrugged, eating. "Nonsense."

"*The Cork Examiner*," Nugent went on, "the same paper that

once sang the praises of 'Young Meagher of the Sword,' has just cut the socks off him."

"Oh?" Corby realized that he was famished. "Why?"

"For taking up the Union side over here. Oh enough, Joseph—looks divine. General Meagher can't get back at those cowardly rascals, not with the Atlantic in between, so the local Orangeman will have to do."

"Rot, Bob," Meagher said. "I simply enjoy lively discussion. The mustard, please."

"Well," Patrick Kelly of the 88th New York, Corby's own colonel, said, "Cork should mind the affairs at home . . ." The Galway man had a full beard and mild eyes, which had just heated up. "*The Examiner* has no right to give the general the length of its tongue. Where were those scribblers in 'forty-eight?"

"Why—thank you, Pat," Meagher said. "Take a smile with me." Both men hoisted their glasses and drank. Corby shook his head to himself. Thomas Francis was such a child in how swiftly he could be warmed by praise. But that, the priest supposed, could be forgiven. He'd been flayed by critics nearly all his adult life.

As tattoo sounded over the camp, Meagher folded his hands under his chin and said, "We're waiting, Bob."

The colonel stopped chewing, then gave up with a sigh and said, "Oh all right . . ." He set his fork on the edge of his plate and thought a moment. "How can we say Ireland has the right to separate from the British Empire if we deny the same right to the Southern Confederacy?"

"*What?*" Joe O'Neill of the 63d New York went off like a fire-cracker. "How can you say such a ludicrous thing, especially in front of the clergy?" Nugent threw up his hands, and Meagher chuckled happily. "Why," O'Neill went on, "there's no com-paring this unlawful rebellion to the right of the Irish people to throw off the yoke of foreign rule. You astonish me, Bob!"

"Satisfied, sir?" Nugent asked Meagher. "Now you've got one more Cork man riled. Joe thinks I'm a Copperhead."

"What d'you expect?" O'Neill snapped. "Talking rubbish like that. And you a brother Fenian."

"You didn't hear that, Father," Meagher said.

Nugent took a breath and faced O'Neill. "All I'm saying is this, Joe—the right of separation is a universal thing. Didn't Thomas Jefferson say just that? We Irish insist on consenting to our own government. Is the South wrong for wanting any less?"

"Damn them, yes!"

"Respectfully, there is a difference," Heenan said good-naturedly. A politician before the war, he knew how to keep his temper in an argument. Also, he'd served in the British army in his youth and liked this kind of mess banter. "Ireland never consented to crown rule. It was imposed upon us. Laws passed with one purpose—to keep us a subjugated race. The Southern states freely submitted to the Union—"

"But not the Union defined by the Republicans," Nugent said. "In the gentry's view, it was never to be a Union with full sway over the rights of each state. So don't you see? The vile Republicans, their political antecedents, why they twisted the definition of the basic agreement on which the Union was founded."

Meagher innocently asked, "Are there any vile Republicans present to defend themselves?"

Laughter followed.

Every man in the brigade was a Democrat. And if a recruit wasn't one upon enlisting, he was soon persuaded otherwise.

"I'm over my head in this company," O'Neill said low but earnestly, finally holding his quick temper down. "But what I know is this—the last, best hope for a free Ireland are the United States of America. Whole and undivided. When it's all said and done, the Confederacy won't lift a finger to help us Irish.

They're all Anglicans down here, or close to it, and they'd sell their own mothers to be recognized by John Bull. Why, they'd—"

O'Neill quieted himself at a sudden sound.

Corby thought that Joseph, just outside, was boiling water to do the dishes. But then he realized that a heavy rain was falling. The Flahertys stopped playing. As the roar and patter went on, the priest glimpsed the colonels exchanging relieved glances. The river would rise, and that would end the campaigning season. Meagher must have caught their looks too, for he said, "I don't think we're going into winter quarters yet."

"Sir?" Kelly said.

Meagher shoved his plate aside and filled his glass from a decanter of whiskey. "The pontoon bridges we used to cross the upper Potomac this summer—Burnside's ordered them barged down to Aquia Creek. From there, they'll be hauled overland here." He paused. "For a crossing somewhere in this vicinity."

Nugent asked, "As soon as they arrive, General?"

"Yes. Any day now, unless there's been some delay. The engineers started them down the Potomac three mornings ago."

"Sir," O'Neill said, "I'm down to less than one hundred and seventy men. Not one of us is much better off, except maybe Dennis here. Won't Washington even give us the chance for some recruiting?"

"No," Meagher said somberly, "and that's not the worst of the news . . ." As the colonels grimly watched, he took a newspaper clipping from his vest pocket and slowly unfolded it. "An open letter, boys, to Horace Greeley of the *New York Herald*. Dated two weeks after Antietam. 'Sir, I recently attended a gala performance in one of Washington's finest theaters to celebrate the victory of our army in Maryland. Unfortunately, this event was marred by the behavior of one officer among the hundreds in attendance. After Mrs. Wood, that superb actress, finished her rousing rendition of "The Bold Soldier Boys," a young gallant in blue stood in his box and bowed deeply to the woman, his right hand over his heart. Had he ended his expression of gratitude at that, no one would have thought any less of him, for his left arm hung in a sling—' "

"Oh no," Nugent said with rising alarm, "oh he would, wouldn't he?"

Meagher shushed him, then read on. " 'However, our officer then spied a bouquet in the grasp of an old Washingtonian sitting directly below. He drew his sword, slipped the nosegay from the aged hand and neatly flipped it onto the stage at Mrs. Wood's feet.' "

While the New Yorkers laughed, Heenan turned in smiling confusion to Corby and whispered, "Who is it, Father? Who's he talking about?"

"You'll see," Corby said, laughing too. The suspected culprit was Meagher's former aide-de-camp, who'd had two horses shot out from under him at Antietam, leaving him with a broken left clavicle.

" 'The old man spun around,' " Meagher continued, " 'and, shaking his fist, demanded to know the identity of his tormenter. "Shut up, you," our officer replied, "or I'll leap down your gullet—boots, spurs and all, by ____!" ' " The general glanced up. "Expletive omitted. 'The old Washingtonian grew faint, and the house was rocked by a mix of cheers, laughter, and cries of "Shame!" The latter only further emboldened our young gallant, who quieted the crowd with a long stare, then drew himself tall and announced, "I am a member of the famous Irish Brigade—" ' "

"Oh God help us," Kelly said, covering his eyes with a hand.

" ' "Captain Jack Gosson of General's Meagher's staff. If my heartfelt appreciation of this fine woman's talents has given offense to any gentleman present, I'll be pleased to give him satisfaction. I may be found tomorrow morning at Willard's Hotel." ' "

"Did anyone?" Nugent asked, wiping away tears with his napkin.

"I think we would've heard by now." Meagher grinned. "So far so good, but I remind you that Jack's now loose in New York." Then he stood with glass raised. "Boys, to the brigade."

$\mathcal{E}$ight

◆

Donovan gripped the rein with one hand and a gum blanket around his shoulders with the other. Still, he was getting drenched by the squall. The wind was gusting the rain from every which way, sometimes seemingly up from the flooded ground itself. His horse, wrenching its head down and to the side, sneezed violently, then started to buck. Donovan halted. He patted the gelding's sopping neck before the beast panicked and bolted.

McGee rode up beside him, water pouring off the front of his hat brim, and asked, nearly shouting, "Don't think we went and somehow crossed the Rappahannock, d'you?"

"No matter, Jimmy," Donovan said. "If this keeps up, we could ride all the way to Florida and not be challenged." He lifted the eyepatch out of his empty socket and gave the black felt a squeeze. Uncomfortably wet. Like the compress the Rebel surgeon on the Peninsula had stuffed there until the bleeding stopped.

"Should we go back?" McGee asked.

"Back where . . . ?" Donovan gestured at the gray curtains of falling water all around, more impenetrable than fog. He wasn't sure that he could find the brigade camp again until it eased up. He had only vague directions to Lacy House but figured that it was either right or left when they reached the river. "Let's push ahead."

McGee theatrically crossed himself, and they splashed on.

Meagher's aide-de-camp, Rich Emmet, was down again with the shakes, so the adjutant had ordered Donovan to carry dispatches to the riverside mansion, where Sumner might be sheltering with every other general in the Army of the Potomac until the storm let up. Handing over the packet, the adjutant glanced out his tent front at the rain and then at Donovan's eyepatch. "Take McGee with you," he'd added.

Setting off from camp, both captains had been eager to see Fredericksburg. Despite the weather. They'd had only glimpses of its spires on the march in. But they soon realized that they'd be fortunate enough to find Lacy House.

"There, John!" McGee cried.

Dimly, across a broad plain, Donovan thought he could see chimneys through the murk. "Has to be it." Wheeling their mounts that way, the men crossed a swale that looked like a pond but for the snake-rail fence running through it. The dimpled water lapped over the fetlocks of the horses. "And when are those pontoon bridges due now?" McGee asked.

"I don't know . . . why?"

"We may bloody well need one to get back!"

Somehow, they'd wound up downriver of the mansion. Near them stood a cow barn with hay doors facing the town, which was scarcely visible through the deluge.

McGee said, "You take the mounts inside there, and I'll run the dispatches up to the house."

"Agreed." Donovan tossed him the packet, and McGee jumped down to continue on foot toward Lacy House. Grooms and orderlies were crowded on the lower porch, having abandoned a bonfire on the lawn to the rain.

Donovan opened the main barn door. For a second, he

thought that he'd found a field hospital. Men were lying atop the heaps of cornstalks on the earthen floor, motionless in the light of a wall lantern. But then one of them stirred, the stalks rustling beneath him, and grumbled, "Leave them goddamn horses outside and close that pneumonie hole!"

"Watch your mouth," Donovan said.

Squinting, the man at last noticed the shoulder straps. "Sorry, sir." He scratched lamely at his undershirt.

Donovan tied both his and McGee's reins to a hitching post, covered the saddles with his gum blanket, then went back inside the barn. It stank of damp wool. The men had draped their muddy uniforms from the rafters to dry. Signal Corps, Regular Army. Donovan told them to stay down, that he was only there to have a peek at Fredericksburg.

"Meant no disrespect, sir . . ." The signalman who'd barked at him went on to explain that they were dead-tired, having spent most of the night pushing their wagon and team through the bottomless mud between here and Hartwood Church. "Would you care to view the town through our telescope?"

"I might."

"Go into the loft first, sir—and I'll hand it up."

Donovan climbed up and took the four-foot-long piece from the signalman. It was as heavy as a small howitzer.

"And here comes the tripod, sir."

"Thanks." Donovan opened only one of two hay doors to keep down the draft. He knelt there a long moment. The town looked dreamlike through the rain. Only the houses hugging the riverbank were clearly visible, their kitchen gardens browned by the hard frosts of the past two weeks. The dominating churches faded in and out of the rain.

McGee could be heard coming into the barn. "Is there a Captain—?"

"In the loft, sir," the same signalman said obligingly.

McGee hurried up the ladder and stooped beside Donovan.

"Let's make it fast, John. The manor's crawling with brass collars—even Burnside's about somewhere."

"Help me with this blunderbuss."

They fitted the telescope on the tripod, and McGee motioned for Donovan to have the first look. "What d'you see?"

"Nothing," Donovan said, screwing his patch up to the eyepiece. "Absolutely nothing."

"Get on with it," McGee said, swatting him with his wet hat.

Laughing, Donovan switched eyes and focused on the ruined railroad bridge. The tracks on both sides leaped off charred timbers into thin air. In town, they ran beside a gristmill, and in a window above the waterwheel Donovan could see a gray sentry clasping his musket around the muzzle. He waved at some Union pickets hugging a small fire near the opposite buttress of the bridge. They waved back. At that moment, the rain hardened into sleet again. It thundered against the roof shingles for a minute, whitening out the visibility, then stopped, leaving the lower sky clearer than before. The entire city sprang into view, and Donovan grunted, "Grand old burg. Streets look like fellas in powdered wigs oughta be strolling about."

"See any of their boys?"

"One."

"*One?*" McGee asked in surprise. "We're sitting over here, blowing on our coffee—and there's only one graycoat in the entire city?"

"Hold on." Donovan aimed the telescope higher. Behind town, a series of ancient river terraces rose up in a half circle to a crest. Much of it was thickly wooded, but on the more open northern end he could see a brick mansion the equal of Lacy House. It had a colonnaded portico, grounds with birch trees and a sweeping lawn that fell away toward Fredericksburg. Near it was a depression, a road cut, and through this shallow gap he could see gray infantry coming on in column of fours. Donovan felt an odd thrill to see them again after so many months.

"What d'you see, John?"

Donovan just backed away from the scope.

"Holy God," McGee said after a moment's scan, "that's a power of Rebellers."

"Back, Jimmy."

"What?"

Donovan whispered, "Get back!"

But it was too late. A cavalry escort came trotting under the hay doors toward the house. Immaculate troopers on spanking bays. The commanding general was right behind them. Burnside must have seen Donovan reaching for the telescope, for he turned around in the saddle and glanced up. He reacted as most did to the eyepatch and mutilated ear: his eyes widened a little, but then he quickly smiled and drew rein.

"We're in for it now," Donovan said.

"Why?" McGee asked. Such an innocent for a man in his thirties.

"We're on courier duty, Jimmy. Who said we could help ourselves to the signal station for a gander?"

"Just tell him we're with Zook's brigade."

"With this brogue?"

"Afternoon, boys," Burnside said, his bobtailed gray sidestepping beneath him. A hearty voice. He touched the brim of his rain-soaked hat in answer to their salutes. He was a larger man than Donovan recalled, although he was seeing him at closer range than he had at a review in Warrenton. His face was agreeable, especially given those flamboyant side-whiskers that joined together at his mustache, and there was something in his eyes that said he liked to please. But there were dark circles under the lower lids, and his smile seemed mournful. "What regiment are you with?"

"Sir, Sixty-sixth New York," Donovan said.

"Oh, Sam Zook's brigade," Burnside said, his staff catching up, gathering round him like seabirds drawn to a speck of land.

"Well, thank you for getting down here as quickly as you did, boys. I'll never forget it."

The earnest way he said this made Donovan ashamed of the lie about his brigade, ashamed of the things he'd muttered these past weeks at mess about Ambrose Burnside. By all accounts, the man had no more wanted McClellan's job than Little Mac wanted to give it up.

"We'll do our best, General," McGee said, obviously moved as well by this cordial man with the sad smile. But then something made him add, "No matter what."

Burnside nodded gratefully and rode on toward the house.

"You know," Donovan said, "I liked it better hating him."

"Me too," McGee added.

4:13 P.M.
24th Georgia
Approaching Fredericksburg

McMillan began to believe that the division was being marched directly into a fight. Signs of it everywhere. Couriers had been dashing up and down the pike as fast as the mud would allow. Then the roadway had been cleared of infantry by the cavalry so that Lane's artillery could be rushed ahead. Just after, McLaws and his aides had swept by Cobb's Brigade. And then something breathtaking happened, something so powerful it could only be an omen. McMillan had been walking his horse and fallen some distance behind Color Sergeant Satterfield—when suddenly a ray of sun slanted down through the clouds and rested on the red battle flag, its starry St. Andrew's cross. The light held fast on the flag until all the men had noticed and were pointing or murmuring, then it dimmed.

All this convinced him to save what little energy he had left for the coming hour. He struggled up into the saddle again. He nearly couldn't do it, but a sudden panic that the men would see him floundering in the stirrup helped swing his right leg over the horse's croup.

Late.

It was late in the day. The rain had let up, but the light would be gone soon. Twilight was brief this time of year. So even if things started now, the firing would be cut short or even forestalled by darkness. A godsend, maybe. His mind wasn't clear, as it'd been on the Peninsula. Inhumanly so. Driving son and stranger forward with the same ruthless determination. *Dear God, how spent am I?* Sometime today, he'd looked back from the head of the regiment and seen Rob riding along its flank, grinning despite his bandaged leg. McMillan had almost galloped back, feeling a mix of joy to see his eldest son and anger that Robbie was returning to duty too soon—before he realized that the rider was young Captain Brewster, his white knee sticking out of a rent in his trouser leg.

McMillan now halted a moment, listening over the shuffle of tired feet.

He heard no long drumroll, no sputter of skirmish fire, but up ahead on a hill he could see Lane's guns being trundled into place. McLaws and his staff were standing nearby, talking strenuously under some birch trees on one side of a large brick house. Cobb had just left their company and was cantering down the slope toward the pike. He gestured for McMillan to meet him, and the colonel lightly spurred his horse.

"Well, Robert," the brigadier said, taking a sodden cigar from the corner of his mouth, "we may've made it in time."

"Have the Federals already crossed?"

"No, but they can force the issue whenever they please. Cavalry says the river's not rising enough to cover the fords, believe it or not." Cobb paused and looked over his shoulder. "We're on what's called Marye's Hill. That's Marye's House there. We're to extend south of the hill for as far as we reasonably can . . ." He gestured southeast with the flat of his hand as if pushing back some invisible force. "Out about a mile, I should think.

I want your Irishmen on a line between Telegraph and Howison's Hills."

"Where—?"

"Cavalryman from the Fifteenth Virginia will guide you. He's waiting for you on the sunken road just around the corner here."

"Thank you, sir."

As McMillan started to catch up with the regiment, Cobb half-shouted, "And don't be afraid to let the Yankees know that Georgia has arrived. Big fires tonight, Robert."

McMillan waved without turning. His blood was still racing, but he felt relieved. No fight. Rest tonight. He thanked God, and for the first time that day allowed himself the luxury of secretly checking on his son. He was marching with his company. No horse, none to be spared for second lieutenants. McMillan wondered if Garnett, who had a strong romantic bent, would grow disillusioned with this ragtag struggle, this life of filth and privation. He and almost the entire senior class of Emory and Henry had foregone their diplomas to enlist. It had disappointed McMillan—and filled him with pride.

A teenage captain of cavalry came up on his side. "Colonel McMillan . . . ?"

"Yes, lad."

"If you'll follow me please, sir." Both he and his mount were coated with different-hued patches of mud. His eyes were inflamed from sleeplessness. He and McMillan turned the regiment right, down a sunken road that ran along the base of the hill. It was flanked by two fieldstone walls, both about four feet high. One had been built into the hillside as a retaining wall. The freestanding one separated the road from a long plain that sloped down toward a creek or ditch a quarter mile distant. Just beyond that, the outskirts of Fredericksburg began.

"What lane is this, Captain?" McMillan asked.

"Telegraph Road, sir."

They passed two small frame houses, both showing lamplight through the windows. An elderly woman stood outside at the well, drawing water. Her homely face was framed by an old-fashioned coal scuttle bonnet. "Bless you," she cried, stopping midturn on the windlass. "Welcome to Spotsylvania County!"

McMillan doffed his hat, as did all his men within earshot. Sullivan jogged over and helped her wheel her bucket the rest of the way up. Then he carried it inside for her. McMillan smiled to himself. At first, he'd been concerned by the election of the Savannah man as orderly sergeant. Sullivan was a known tippler, although the rest of his past was largely a mystery. But he'd proved to be a rock on the battle line, and if he drank it was always away from the regiment. Now, he came running back into the column from the old woman's house, clenching a hot biscuit in his mouth.

McMillan gazed north through the twilight, past a two-story brick house standing alone with an outbuilding on the plain—and fixed his eyes on the misty bluffs across the river. Fires everywhere. Why hadn't those men crossed? What was keeping them? Strange. Disconcerting.

The cavalryman wound the regiment around the southern end of the hill and to a small bridge. They crossed the sluggish creek and continued out into an open pasture, the wet grass swishing around the legs of the men. "What stream was that?" McMillan asked, forcing his brain to learn this countryside while there was still time.

"Hazel Run, sir."

McMillan pointed at a long scar in the earth across the field from them. "And that?"

"Fredericksburg and Gordonsville Railroad Line, sir."

"Unfinished?"

"Yes, the war."

Glancing below, McMillan could see where the railroad builders had left a deep cut in the sloping plain, a perfect trench. *Mustn't forget it's there,* he thought, *if they come at us that way. Mustn't let the enemy reveal these features to us tomorrow morning through surprise.*

The captain led them past a substantial home, newly built by the looks of it, and up into some tall trees. McMillan thought it'd started to rain again, but then realized that it was just a steady dripping off the branches. He turned for a glance behind. The tan and yellow tints of the plain showed through the trunks. A light had come on in the house below. "Whose place is that?"

"Uh, the Howisons', sir. This is all their land, their timber. The menfolk are away in Confederate service."

"Then we'll safeguard everything in their absence."

The young man gestured through the swiftly darkening forest. "That rise there is Howison's Hill, sir." Then he swiveled and indicated the highest promontory in the entire area. "And that's Telegraph Hill." Fires were already dotting its flanks down to the edge of the trees. "Led your Sixteenth Georgia there about a half hour ago. Or was it Cobb's Legion?" He shook his head as if trying to clear it. "Will you require anything else, Colonel McMillan?"

"No—thank you, son."

The captain galloped back toward Marye's Hill, and the regiment stood quietly in formation. After the hoofbeats faded, there was no sound except the dripping out of the trees into the autumn leaves. A milky strand of cloud, foglike, slid down into the wooded hollow between the two hills in which they stood, then dissipated as suddenly as it had appeared. Still mounted, McMillan called for his captains to gather round him. His voice beginning to fail, he told them that he wanted a strong picket line at the edge of the trees. He wanted all the men to rest on their arms tonight, ready for anything. Privately, he still couldn't believe that the Federals had failed to cross the river. They might be lurking somewhere downriver, hidden in the woods. It made no sense—rush headlong from Warrenton to Falmouth, then halt and let the Army of Northern Virginia fortify these heights.

McMillan closed his burning eyes for a moment, seeing the endless muddy Orange Pike before him. Just as he'd dreamed of the rolling wastes of the Atlantic for weeks after crossing over from Belfast.

Behind him, the order was shouted, "Break rank, march!"

He opened his eyes.

Those men not on the first picket tour began looking to their comforts. Some just flopped down as soon as they were shown their company areas, many not even bothering to open their bedrolls. Fatigue instantly froze one man as if he'd been shot. He lay flat on his back, one forearm upright with hand bent slightly at the wrist. Another was vomiting.

McMillan turned his face from this sight. *Must find some way to thank them for this march.*

He started to dismount, but the joints in his legs and feet locked. When he tried to will them into motion, they just buzzed with raw pain. He swayed in the saddle, blinking, gripping the pommel with both hands. Inside the left side of his chest, a tiny iron ball seemed to be bouncing around, making his heart flutter. Seeing a flat rock ledge nearby, he rode over to it, sidestepped his horse as close as he could. Finally, he managed to swing his left leg around, then braced both boots on the rock. After another long moment, he stood, gasping.

"Colonel . . . ?" Sullivan asked, his face worried.

Quickly, McMillan reached into a saddlebag and brought out his field glasses as if he'd meant to use the boulder as a perch, not a crutch. "Yes," he said, trying to hide his breathlessness.

"Would you care for some coffee?" Then, miraculously, Sullivan handed up a cup. It was chicory and only tepid, but McMillan had never tasted anything so delicious. He offered his glasses to Sullivan. The man's younger eyes would do better with the fading light. "Tell me what you see across the river."

Sullivan took at least a minute, then said, "Campfires. Miles of 'em spreadin' north."

"Yes, I can see that."

"Ah, here we go—must be the pike to Warrenton. Why, sir, they're flowin' down it like water. Wagons and artillery too."

"What batteries already in place?"

Sullivan softly grunted. "Cannon along those heights across from town." Another pause, then he added, "*All* along it."

McMillan finished the last bit of coffee. He wanted more but suspected that Sullivan had given him all there was until the wagons could catch up. "Thank you," he said, exchanging the empty cup for his glasses.

"My pleasure, Colonel."

Leading McMillan's horse by the reins, Sullivan went back to his smudgy fire. He gave the mount over to the waiflike boy who'd just come up from Clarkesville. Hopefully, his true age would be discovered before the regiment was engaged. But until then, they were too shorthanded for McMillan to do anything but trust him at his word. The horse orderly ran up, relieved the boy of the saddle before he fell under its weight.

McMillan sat on the cold ledge. The rain was coming down again, hard. Yet, for the first time in two days, he felt a glimmer of warmth inside his chest. He realized that it was pride in his regiment, McLaws's entire division. The countless fires on those distant heights told that the Army of the Potomac was stacking up behind the barrier of the river. Longstreet's approach had kept Burnside from immediately using Fredericksburg as the gateway to Richmond. If he tried tomorrow, he'd be facing at least two divisions, for Ransom was close behind with his North Carolinians. Then, by Friday at the latest, the rest of Longstreet's corps would fan out along this long ridge above the plain.

McMillan glanced to both sides of him. It was very decent ground, he quickly decided. If the four undersized brigades of his division could hold it until Friday morning.

$\mathcal{N}$ine

$\bullet$

1:55 A.M., November 20
Headquarters, Irish Brigade

Near midnight, Meagher had been in the middle of a long letter to Elizabeth when he was interrupted by Joseph. The cook burst through the flaps and said urgently, "Sir, young *Leftenant* Emmet's shakes are killin' him for sure this time." Immediately, Meagher ordered his aide-de-camp carried to his tent and Surgeon Reynolds sent for. Emmet was put in Meagher's own bed and covered with the buffalo robe. His eyes were open, but he didn't appear to know where he was. By questioning Joseph, who slept in the tent next to Emmet's, Dr. Reynolds determined the timing of the lieutenant's paroxysms and told Meagher to give him bitters, a mixture of whiskey and quinine, every two hours until dawn, when the next violent episode was expected. If at any time Emmet complained of ringing ears, no more was to be given to him. "I've got it, Larry," Meagher said. "Go back to bed before you bring out the leeches."

"And you get some sleep, Thomas Francis," the gray-bearded brigade surgeon said. "For all we know, Old Burn will point us across the river right after breakfast, and I prefer to operate on rested men." Reynolds and the cook then withdrew, leaving

Meagher to look after Emmet, who'd slept soundly until awakened for his second dose of bitters.

"Rich . . . ?" the general now whispered to him. Favoring his left knee, he sat on a camp stool beside the bed. "Richard . . . ?"

Emmet's eyelids twitched, but he seemed too weak to part them. He licked his lips and croaked, "Grandpa?"

"A couple years more." Smiling, Meagher took a cloth from a basin of water, wrung it out and wiped his aide's forehead. He had a marble-pale complexion, aquiline nose and a slightly disdainful set to his mouth—almost the same face as his granduncle's, Robert Emmet, the great martyr of 1803. A Protestant who'd given his life for Ireland. Bloodline of a martyr, Meagher thought, cleansing young Emmet's eyes of the sleep that sealed them shut. He tossed the cloth back into the basin.

Thomas Francis Meagher, the great martyr of 1848. How close it'd come to that. How desperately close.

He reached for the bottle and spoon Reynolds had left on his writing table.

"Here, Rich . . ." Robert Emmet had died at twenty-five, the same age Meagher had been when sentenced by the lord chief justice to be hanged, drawn and quartered. But Emmet's sentence had not been commuted to penal servitude for life, and now his name was sacrosanct. *The Cork Examiner* didn't make light of Robert Emmet.

Meagher closed his eyes. *But what a price for reverence.*

Emmet had mounted the scaffold, arms tied behind him, and said, "My friends, I die in peace and with sentiments of universal love and kindness towards all men." That was all. No bombast, no politics. He then strode onto a plank which the executioner tilted off the edge of the scaffold. Emmet dropped, writhed at the end of the rope and finally convulsed into stillness. His body was taken down, and the head struck from the body. Some witnesses said there was a great flow of blood as this was done—the rope hadn't finished him. The executioner seized the crown's trophy by the hair, paraded it before the crowd and proclaimed, "This is the head of a traitor, Robert Emmet!"

Meagher opened his eyes, then lifted Richard Emmet's head off the sweaty pillowcase. "Help me lad. Can't do this by myself."

The lieutenant finally looked up at him. "General . . . ?"

"Yes, my dear boy. Swallow this down now."

Emmet did so, but then fainted.

"Stay with me, Richard," Meagher begged. "Don't make me break your father's heart again." He put aside the bottle and spoon, pulled the robe back up under Emmet's slack chin. He brushed the damp, unruly hair into place with his fingers, then rose and limped across the tent floor to add more wood to the fire. The boy's brother, Temple, had also been one of Meagher's aides. He'd contracted the same dogged fever on the Peninsula and then died at home in New York this August.

From the tin fireplace, Meagher looked back at the bed.

There was now a calm beauty to the boy's face. As some of the witnesses said there had been to Robert Emmet's as his blood ran over the square. The faithful had tried to dip their handkerchiefs in it but were pushed back by the soldiers.

Still, a grisly end.

Yet, what was the alternative? Meagher knew it all too well. Worries over dwindling prospects. Trying to pump life into a flagging career as a circuit lecturer, rattling on and on about the Irish question. Living under the roof of a wealthy American father-in-law who calls you "a professional Irishman" behind your back, who watches every forkful go into your mouth.

Meagher went back to his table, sat. He scanned his words to Elizabeth. Lovely, elegant Elizabeth Townsend who'd charmed the entire brigade as she presented the colors on behalf of the ladies of New York. She'd called the 88th New York her own, and they in turn had taken her into their hearts. Yet, Meagher had overheard one soldier telling another, "She has a power of money—the general's done right well."

"Yes," he whispered, "right well." There was a saying back home. *If you want praise, die. If you want blame, marry.*

He listened.

The rain had stopped. Or perhaps it'd begun snowing. He saw snow falling silently on Catherine Bennett's grave. The artless Irish girl he'd taken as his first wife while in Tasmanian exile. He loved Elizabeth dearly, yet lately he thought of his days with Catherine, the cottage he'd built for her on a mountain lake ringed by eucalyptus. It was unnerving. Always a man of great energy, he now found it bizarre for the past to intrude so powerfully on the present. Yet, he knew what this meant. The question was being put to him on the eve of each battle—did he still believe, as he had so completely as a young man, that violent death and salvation were one and the same?

"Grandpa," Rich Emmet called from the bed.

4:06 P.M.
24th Georgia
Camp Jeannie

"What d'you want, Sullivan?" Banks, the regimental adjutant, asked without looking up from his papers. The baggage wagons had arrived this morning, and he'd set up his field desk under a tent fly.

"A two-hour pass from the grounds, sir."

"Purpose?"

"Edificational."

Dropping his pen, the adjutant glanced up sharply. "What?"

"I want to visit the grave of Mary Washington."

"Mary Washington."

"Yes, sir—the mother of all rebels."

"Nonsense. You're off to some *shebeen* in town for a snootful." But Banks didn't go back to work, so hope was still alive. "You ask the colonel about this?"

"No, sir. I had no wish to bother him with trifles."

"I don't know, Sullivan. There's ax work to be done all along the line. You might help keep the men at it."

"That I've been, sir. By me own example." Sullivan opened his palms and showed Banks the fresh blisters. "As for drinkin', swearin', and violatin' the sabbath—I'll go back to 'em gladly. After the war. When I'm no longer under General Cobb's rules."

The adjutant smirked, sighed, but finally began scratching out a pass. "Return drunk, and I'll have the colonel put you back in the ranks."

"On my honor, sir." Sullivan took the slip of paper and hurried to the fire outside McMillan's tent. The old man was inside, napping. Tully, worn out from a day of building field fortifications from fallen trees, was stirring the embers with a charred stick. "Now, Hugh lad—you stay here to answer the colonel's call," Sullivan said, putting on his jacket, which he'd left all day to dry on a tent rope.

"Where you goin'?"

"Never mind. Just don't go off on your own hook, you hear me?"

"But if Col'nel McMillan asks for you?"

"Tell him I'm on an errand for the adjutant."

Sullivan started off across the smoky, wooded hollow. The entire brigade was now encamped here, the other regiments driven down off crowns of the hills by rain squalls that moved through every few hours. Cobb had christened it "Camp Jeannie" in honor of Chaplain Porter's wife, but it looked more like an Indian village than a military installation. Cornstalks were plentiful in the nearby fields, so the men had used them and evergreen brush to weave arbors over their bedrolls.

He broke from the trees, and a voice rang out, "Sullivan." It was Billy Haddock on camp sentry duty. The main picket line now ran along the riverbank and through town—almost a mile distant, so he had little to do except yawn. "You off, then?"

"I am."

"If you get the chance, ask about a fella named Hart. Sergeant in the Sixty-third New York. I heard he was kilt at Sharpsburg by one of our shells. But that can't be true. Not Matty Hart."

"I'll ask."

The sprawling plain drew Sullivan on, the light agreeable after the gloom of the timber. It felt good to be out in the open. The wet grass wrapped around his shins and dusted his trouser legs with tiny seeds. Off to his right lay the tracks of the Richmond, Fredericksburg and Potomac Railroad, the slick rails gleaming like gunmetal. Southward, they curved along the foot of the heights. To the north, they threaded back into the lower part of town, where a train was just pulling out for Richmond. Filled with civilians and soldiers who'd taken sick along the march. It should've been gone hours ago.

"She riz," Sullivan said to himself, chuckling, remembering what a backwoods Georgia private had said on the train trip to Richmond in '61. His first ride ever. The train passed over a chasm on a high trestle, and the trees fell away with a rush. The Rabun County lad cried in horror, "She riz! We're flyin'! I knowed she couldn't stick to the ground and go like this!"

Suddenly, Sullivan saw a tiny puff of smoke rise from the bluff across the river. "No . . ." And then came the plunging scream, banshee-shrill. He went down on a knee, then flat on his chest as the shell burst in the swampy ravine that lay between himself and the tracks. The yellow flash sent up a huge gout of muddy water. For an instant, he thought that the big rifled gun was after him, which seemed a ridiculous waste of ammunition. But then, through a screen of sedges, he saw two more shells plow into the fields around the locomotive.

The engineer quickly laid on his brakes, and the squeal gave Sullivan a chill.

He rose, flabbergasted to think that the Yankees would fire on a train like this. Maybe the shots had just been in warning, but at least one of them had been close enough to crack the windows in some of the coaches. He waited for more, but the heights across the Rappahannock stayed silent as the engineer backed his train into Fredericksburg. He stopped it and leaped from his cab for the safety of a nearby house. His passengers—women, children, and the walking wounded—streamed out of the doors a moment behind.

Quickly now, Sullivan made his way across Hazel Run to Telegraph Road. Barksdale's Mississippians were strung out thinly behind the stone wall. Some were lounging wearily in rifle pits they'd dug into the hillside above the road. "You see that Yankee madness?" he asked one of their sergeants.

The Mississippian drawled, "We'll make 'em screech for quarter. All'n good time."

"Hey, Paddy," a teasing voice said from one of the pits, "is Ireland heaven?"

"Heaven on earth," Sullivan replied.

"Then why'd you leave?"

"Because I'd still be hidin' in a bog up to me eyes from the goddamn British."

"Hah!" the man chortled, then clamped his smoldering pipe between his teeth again.

Barksdale's men had spent the day improving this already handsome defensive position. Fresh earth was heaped mostly outside the downslope wall, but inside it as well. "It's a fine dig you have here, Grandfather," Sullivan said to a grayhaired man leaning on the handle of his spade. "I may rent it for me and the rest of Cobb's boys if things get hot over our way."

"Hell, Georgia—y'all can stand in front of our wall for free."

Sullivan laughed, picking up his pace. The light would soon go in a rush when the half-shrouded sun finally set.

He vaulted over the wall and strode through a fallow field. A brick house stood by itself just below, a forge glowing through the open door of a nearby shed. Blacksmith's shop, perhaps. He turned down a road to cross a swift millrace on a plank bridge.

A small frame house lay nearby, darkened. A mule-drawn cart had been backed up to the door, although no one was in sight. Furniture was heaped in the bed of the cart, plus a round little pile cloaked by a tablecloth. Sullivan pulled up a corner of the covering and found twin girls beneath. No more than five years old. Clouds of red hair. They looked frightened to death, so he whispered, "It's just me, darlin's—General Lee."

That got their eyes big. "*You're* General Lee?" one of them gasped. She immediately covered a missing front tooth with a hand, just as his own girl had.

"I am. But keep it quiet. Everybody invites me to supper, and I've already had three tonight. Your poor mother has enough to do."

"Mama's dead," the other one said.

"Help you?" a voice demanded from the stoop.

Sullivan turned. The man had a square, humorless face, burned russet by the sun and wind. Calloused hands and pinched eyes blinking against the drizzle that had just begun to fall. He was holding a framed mirror.

"Never like seein' kids and the furniture loaded in a cart," Sullivan said. "Left me own place like this, and never made it back."

The man had no comment.

"I'd ask your girls for a kiss, but not with this pig's bristle on me cheeks."

The man took the mirror to the cart. "You're Irish," he said. Not exactly pleased.

Sullivan hesitated, then nodded. He caught a glimpse of himself in the mirror—frightful. "So you farm this land?"

"For Colonel Marye. But he's gone to war now." A tenant farmer then, just as Sullivan himself had been until his absentee landlord in London jacked the rent through the roof and sent his family and him packing.

The farmer gestured at the fields between his own dooryard and the stone wall. "This all went to the Irish."

"What did, sir?"

"The crops. In 'forty-eight, it was all sent to feed the starvin' in Ireland. Every last bushel."

Gazing out across the dim fields, Sullivan said, "I see." He and his family had gotten none of it, yet he felt a sudden urge to give the man and his children something, anything. But he had nothing, least of all money. He'd been destitute all these months, but hadn't realized it until this minute. He almost laughed out loud. He'd fancied himself one of Georgia's most worthy men, orderly sergeant to Colonel Robert McMillan, attorney, formerly of the state legislature. In truth, here he stood unshaved, in dirty rags, without a cent to his name—and wanting to offer alms to a fellow who at least had some furniture. And his children. "God bless these fields, sir," he finally said, "keep you and the girls safe."

"And you drive them Yankees off, you hear?"

Sullivan moved on, memories of Sharpsburg keeping him from promising anything. Those had been hard men across that bloody pasture just west of the sunken lane. Eventually, they'd forced Cobb's Brigade back into the West Woods.

Skirting Fredericksburg, where he'd have to show his pass at every turn, he stayed to the plain. A great white pillar loomed ahead. Artillerymen were resting on the backside of the knoll on which it stood. Their guns were limbered up, ready to roll at a moment's notice. "Would this be the grave of Mary Washington?" Sullivan asked.

A blond corporal rolled on his side and stared, chewing on a twig. "That it is."

Sullivan doffed his cap.

"Don't get too worked up about it, Sarn't."

"Pardon?"

"I'm grew up over here on Hanover Street," the corporal went on, "and the old folks say she wasn't no saint. Woman was a Tory, she was. Wrote George to come home and tend to business before the Britishers hanged him. She was damn cruel to her Negroes too. You can ask anybody round here."

"I won't," Sullivan said angrily. "And with all your subtractin', she's still a grand lady. If only for the fruit of her womb!"

The corporal spat out the twig and grinned insolently. "So . . . ?"

"So maybe it's time I give you a lip."

"A lip?"

"One a pig could trip over." Sullivan stepped toward him, rolling up his jacket sleeves, but the entire crew stood as one, and the corporal armed himself with a sponge staff. "All right then, who's first?"

"No one," their lieutenant said, rising from beneath a caisson, where he'd been resting unseen. "Kindly accept our apologies. You're quite right to defend the honor of Mrs. Washington, Sergeant, and I'm sure the corporal here applauds your patriotism as much as I do."

"Yes, sir," the blond man said sullenly.

"Apologies accepted." Sullivan saluted and hurried on—before McMillan got wind of this. Still, it rankled him, how men had to find a way to knock down their heroes. It'd been that way with Thomas Meagher. Sullivan had gone with thousands of other admiring Irish to Augusta to hear him speak before the war. The man thrilled the crowd, especially when he admitted a streak of sympathy for the South in the growing troubles. But then, after Fort Sumter, Meagher had thrown in lots with the Union, and from that time on he was a fool and a coward to the same paddies who'd worshiped him. A fool for not having had the brains to pull off a revolution with a starving population and no weapons. And a coward for having violated his word of honor to the governor of Tasmania by escaping. It had mystified Sullivan, Irish worrying about a promise made to an English governor.

He would still serve Meagher when the hour of liberation came. Gladly, for the willingness the man had shown to stand alone and die for his country.

The rain was getting harder.

He slowed as he neared the river, making some noise as he walked so as not to spook the pickets. One of them came back to him through some tall corn that had gone unharvested, a clerkish-looking man wearing spectacles. "Yes . . . ?"

"Much talk back and forth with the other side?"

"None. If you ask me, they're gettin' ready to come across. We got a willow-stick stuck out in the shallows. You know, see how fast the water's risin'. Well, it ain't."

"Any Irishmen on their line over there?"

"No," the man said flatly.

"How can you be so sure?"

"No offense—but you Irish'll gab away even if I got nothin' to say back." Smiling, he took off his spectacles and wiped them on his shirttail. "It's kinda fun to go on picket against 'em. I don't think they know there's a war."

"Oh, they know," Sullivan said. "It's just that they see no beginnin' and no end to it. Thanks."

He ambled downriver, toward town. A trifling haze lay over the dark waters. Among the trees on the other side he thought he could see an occasional human figure, but the nightfall was now complete. He asked the men along the way if they knew whether Meagher's brigade had manned the opposite picket line over the past two days. No one could say. A few seemed suspicious that he'd inquire about such a thing.

"And I don't care to see that damn green flag of theirs anytime soon," a South Carolinian said bitterly.

Sullivan asked, "Why's that?"

"Them wild men gave us a sickenin' dose up at Sharpsburg with their bayonets."

The rain came in sheets. It left bands of luminous foam on the Rappahannock that marked the eddies. On the crest beyond, the lights of a mansion shone. Torches sparkled on the grounds, reflecting off the wet coats of the horses, the India rubber blankets the Yankee grooms had wrapped around themselves.

Finally, running out of time, Sullivan shouted, his voice echoing across the river, "Are you a friend . . . ?"

Nothing.

He tried again, louder.

Then, on the far bank, a gunlock clicked.

Frowning, Sullivan turned back for Howison's Hill.

T e n
.

Meagher sat on the front steps of Phillips House, tapping his boot to the mess call being bugled for some regiment camped in the muddy pasture behind the place. It was the choicest mansion in the area. Four chimneys. But it sat on a hilltop a mile north of the river and lacked Lacy House's close view of Fredericksburg. He got up and limped along the porch, his hands clasped behind his back. He'd received an invitation to dine with General Sumner here, apparently a common headquarters for both Burnside and Old Bull until the commanding general revealed what he meant to do.

Nothing was happening. Only tonight would the brigade be sent out on picket along the Rappahannock for the first time. It felt like being exiled on Tasmania again, given the run of the island but with nothing worthwhile to do. Pacing was the best sedative, yet his knee was killing him. The abscessed joint grew more inflamed each day, but Surgeon Reynolds said that a premature lancing would bring on only more pain and stiffness. He wanted to wait.

Wait.

Meagher peered westward. He could just see the heights beyond town. They were filling up with graybacks, the woods there alive with them. The smoke of their fires left a brownish haze that clung to the entire ridge from the falls of the Rappahannock all the way down to Hamilton's Crossing, five miles to the southwest. Brass cannon glinted like gold nuggets. Through field glasses, their infantry could be seen entrenching, building earthen fortifications.

All the more reason to get moving. Now.

Early this morning the hardest rain of the entire week had fallen. But then about two hours ago it quit. The clouds broke, and patches of sunshine drifted over the steamy fields. This godsend might be the last spell of decent weather before spring, but Burnside was apparently still waiting on the pontoons.

Meagher hid his limp as he went through the front door.

He laid his hat, overcoat, sword, and gloves on a table already cluttered with them. Elizabeth would be completely at home here, although she'd be quick to add her own touches. A strange thought—what would poor Catherine, the Tasmanian nanny, have thought of Phillips House? She would've been overawed, of course, as she'd been by his father's estate in Waterford, where he sent her to have their second son while Meagher went to California on a lecture tour. She died there a few weeks after Thomas Francis Junior was born. He could see her spinning round in this corridor, peeking through doors, gasping at the paintings, the furniture. "Oh, Tom . . . *look!*" She'd been infectiously girlish, embarrassingly so at times. Even the loss of their first son in infancy had failed to darken her spirit. He'd dreamed of her last night, smiling across from him in the sailboat, her bonnet ruffling against a screen of eucalyptus trees.

Boots drummed down the staircase.

It was Bill Teall, Sumner's son-in-law and aide. The loyal son-in-law. The other one had gone with the South. "Ah, good morning, sir—the general apologizes . . ." He'd been an attorney before the war and had that curious lawyer's habit of smiling when he didn't mean it. "Dinner will be delayed a few minutes. He's upstairs with some dispatches that just came in. Care to join General Pleasonton in the morning room?"

"Yes, thank you. Has General Hooker arrived?"

"Not yet, sir."

Teall went back up the stairs, and Meagher continued his hobbling progress down the hallway. A shrew-faced mulatto woman was setting the table in the dining room. At the sound of his footfalls, she glanced up, her light brown eyes full of spite. The Phillips family had abandoned the place for Fredericksburg as soon as the Union army reached Falmouth, although they'd left their housekeeper behind to keep the Yankees from muddying the Belgian carpets.

"Alfred, how are you?"

Pleasonton was standing at the small fireplace in the morning room, a mug cupped in his hands. "Damned if I can get warm. I'd take the North Pole over Virginia this time of year. The wet chill goes through you like canister." The cavalry brigadier flicked his chin at the tea service on a tripod table. "Care for some beef tea?"

"No, thanks. It's close to noon, and I'm looking for ardent."

"Good luck—our little darkey has the keys to the cellar, and Burnside won't let us bash in the door," Pleasonton grumbled. "In fact, I don't think we're even supposed to sit on the goddamned furniture."

"I'll keep any pillaging to a minimum." Meagher lowered his voice. "Crossing in the works yet?"

"I suppose."

"Dependent on the pontoons?"

"Naturally. Rappahannock's still fordable at least three places within spitting distance of town . . ." Pleasonton paused when Meagher looked surprised. "Oh yes, despite the rains. But we're waiting for bridges. Might as well send for a key to open an unlocked door."

Meagher couldn't help but to ask, "Any idea who's going over first when they finally arrive?"

Pleasonton started to answer when Sumner's voice came booming in from the hallway. "Anybody for dinner?"

"Coming, General," Pleasonton said, leaving his mug on the mantle. Meagher let him go out first. He was afraid that his lameness could no longer be concealed. Sumner and the others were already seated by the time he reached the dining room. Flanking the old man were Sam, his dandyish son, and Teall.

"Where's Hooker, Tom?" Sumner asked.

"No idea, sir. Haven't seen him in days."

"Count your blessings," Sam Sumner muttered.

The old man shot his son a hard glance. It didn't last long. At Antietam, Sumner had ordered Sam on a perilous courier ride. The young man hadn't gone far when Old Bull called him back, kissed him, then sent him on again.

Sumner closed his eyes, lips moving silently, then looked around the table and said, "Eat, everyone." His gray eyebrows looked like smoke. He asked Meagher if his brigade was settled in all right.

"Fine sir. Excellent location . . . for a short wait."

"Glad to hear it."

The front door could be heard slamming shut, and a sudden draft flattened the steam rising from the soup tureen. A few seconds later, Joe Hooker came into the room. The commander of the Center Grand Division had his own limp to deal with— he'd taken a bullet in the foot at Antietam.

"Joseph," Sumner coolly greeted him, his fork stopping halfway to his mouth.

Hooker nodded, his ruddy face in a frustrated scowl, his eyes blazing. But then, noticing Meagher, he winked at him.

Sumner asked, "What'd you find?"

"Rode all the way to Aquia Creek," Hooker said, "and then a mile up along the Potomac. Nary a pontoon in sight." He turned to the mulatto housekeeper, who, astonishingly, gave him a grudging smile. "Missy, my darling woman—get me a great big whiskey from massa's stores, will you? And an even bigger one for Thomas Francis here. He's fighting a lingering wound, as I am. Anybody else fighting anything?"

"Just the cold," Pleasonton said, but like the others he declined.

"Who all do they have over there now?" Hooker asked the cavalryman.

"McLaws's and Anderson's divisions."

Sam Sumner piped up, "I'm sorry, sir—McLaws is there, but it's Ransom with him, not Anderson."

Pleasonton looked chagrined that a mere major, even if he was Sumner's son, would dare correct him. "Sorry, the source of my intelligence is unassailable. A freedman who crossed over in a rowboat just last night." Then he asked, brushing his mustaches with a knuckle, "And your source, if I might ask?"

"Our own Signal Corps, sir," Sam said, scarcely able to hold back his glee. "We have a telescope at Lacy House, and . . ." He paused to make sure that the servant had left the room. ". . . we've been reading their signal flags."

Pleasonton said nothing more, and Sumner clearly was embarrassed for the cavalryman. "Anderson's division may have arrived by now, Alfred."

"Hell, no doubt Longstreet's whole goddamn corps has shown up by now. He's there himself, isn't he? What're you all quibbling about?" Hooker turned to Meagher, then grinned. "Thomas Francis," he said as their whiskeys arrived on a tray. "Thanks, Missy. I've just heard the most outrageous thing about your brigade . . ."

Catching on to the man's playful tone at once, Meagher puffed himself up. "General Hooker?"

"I've heard that on the eve of battle at Antietam, an officer on your staff kicked General Richardson."

"No rumor, sir."

"Oh . . . ?"

"And the officer, Jack Gosson, was entirely within his rights as a soldier."

"To kick Old Dick?" Sumner asked, trying not to smile.

"Exactly, sir," Meagher went on. "If you'll recall, it was raining that night. Captain Gosson was fortunate enough to find a nice dry haystack, so he crawled in. He'd no sooner drifted off than he felt someone joining him. He told the intruder to find his own haystack. This was ignored . . ." Meagher took a sip of whiskey. Delicious. "So he did what any self-respecting Irishman would do—he kicked the trespasser as hard as he could on the backside."

Hooker asked, straightfaced, "So Gosson had no idea it was his division commander?"

"That, sir, is between him and his Maker," Meagher said.

"Did your captain apologize when he realized who it was?" Teall asked.

"No, sir. He was laughing too hard. But he did offer General Richardson his flask."

When the chuckling had faded, Sam Sumner asked, "And what'd Old Dick do . . . ?"

Meagher said, "Why, he drank."

"And the next day took his death wound," Sumner said quietly. All at once, he looked old, deflated.

Hooker wasn't about to turn maudlin. He leaned over and clapped his arm around Meagher's shoulders. "You brighten a dark day, Thomas—that's why I had Edwin send for you. I need some good Irish company before the idiocy around here drives me mad."

Meagher had to mask his disappointment. He'd thought that Sumner had wanted him, intending perhaps for the brigade to spearhead an advance across the river.

Suddenly, the windowpanes rattled in their frames and the silverware jingled on the table.

"What the devil . . . ?" Sumner asked, rising. "Who ordered that fire?" He started outside, his napkin still tucked in the waistband of his trousers. Hooker was right behind him, skipping to keep the weight off his injured foot, and then the rest of the party. Some junior officers were crowding the porch, but they jumped down at Sumner's approach.

The old general had guessed it right—smoke was rising from at least two of the Union batteries along Stafford Heights.

Teall shouted at the grooms for his horse, and Pleasonton ordered his escort to go with the lieutenant colonel. Within a minute, Sumner's son-in-law and four cavalrymen were galloping off to find out what was happening.

Shaking his head, Hooker said, "Just like that old man to come at us first." Lee, he no doubt meant.

Yesterday, Burnside had sent his provost marshal over with a written demand for the town to be surrendered by five that afternoon. If not, Fredericksburg would be bombarded. Longstreet refused. He wouldn't let it be occupied without a fight. Yet, his return message came so late in the day that Burnside decided to extend the deadline, for fear of shelling women and children, and promised to let evacuation trains run unmolested along the Richmond line until eleven in the morning on Sunday. Tomorrow.

Meagher listened for more cannon fire. But the minutes trickled away, and the silence held. Hooker had had the foresight to bring his glass with him out on the porch.

Teall and the cavalry escort came back sooner than expected, accompanied by an artillery major whose face was as red as his hat cords. He begged to report and started stammering that he'd already been on his way to headquarters—when Sumner roared at him, "What in thunder were you people shooting at!"

"Sir, a train," came the weak reply.

"*Another* train!"

"Yes, sir—it was an accident."

Sumner was speechless.

Hooker caught the old man's look and snorted.

"It isn't believed the train was damaged," Teall said. "But we can expect an immediate response from the Rebel guns. Lacy House is being evacuated."

"Where's Hunt?" Sumner demanded.

No one knew where the artillery chief was.

Sumner explained that he was going to sort the mess out himself. He was sick and tired of batteries popping at trains without orders. He was soon off for Stafford Heights, taking nearly everyone at Phillips House with him in a long cavalcade. Meagher and Hooker were left alone on the porch, listening, watching the sky to the south for bursts.

"Back in a moment," Hooker said.

Off to the east was the most gorgeous bank of clouds Meagher could ever remember seeing, creamy billows of white, gray, and yellow. He could hear a dripping sound. It was coming off the eaves, a seeping from the waterlogged shingles. After a rain in Tasmania, the eucalyptus trees dripping. Catherine and he scooping the water out of the bottom of the sailboat with tin cups, flinging it on each other.

Then Hooker was handing him his glass. "Here. Look who's coming." He pointed with a freshly lit cigar.

Burnside, trailed by his staff, was riding up the drive on the north side of the hill. His eyes seemed to be fixed on his mount's neck. He held the rein slack, almost letting the horse pick his own way. The grooms came out from the stable to meet him, and he dismounted. "Rubdown, please," he ordered, then started up the steps.

Only then did he notice Meagher and Hooker above him on the porch. His mouth formed something that was more grimace than smile.

"Burn," Hooker said.

The commanding general began fumbling in his various pockets. At last he found it—a telegram. "This came after you left this morning, Joe."

Hooker held out his hand for the yellow flimsy, but Burnside suddenly balled it up, flung it over the railing. "Five miles a day. That's all the faster my bridges are coming." Then he hurried through the front door.

Hooker drank, pursed his wet lips and finally said when the last of Burnside's staff had filed past, "I would've thought of that, Old Burn, before I made any fantastic promises to Lincoln."

7:17 P.M.
Cobb's Brigade
Camp Jeannie

"Col'nel McMillan . . . ?" Johnny Clark said breathlessly. "Gen'ral Cobb wants to see you right away. *Right* away, sir."

McMillan felt a spasm of pain in his heart. Like a squirt of liquid fire. His immediate thought was that things had come to a head with his son Rob. A turn for the worse. The long-expected amputation. The unthinkable, even.

"Is there anythin' I can do, Colonel?" Sullivan asked.

"No, no—stay by the fire, Michael." McMillan then rushed up the company streets as fast as his legs would carry him. The light of the fires shone redly on the trunks of the trees around him. The men were laughing, singing, smoking their pipes under the stars. Apparently, Cobb had received the news first. It often happened this way: one letter from Georgia beating another to the regiment, so that a friend of the bereaved learned of the tragedy before the man himself did.

Cobb was sitting at his own fire, a sheet of paper in his hands. A letter from Clarkesville or the Richmond hospital?

The crushing weight of the other deaths came back to McMillan in an instant, a frozen blast of grief. *Return home at once. Your daughter Emma is dying. . . .*

Cobb shot up from his camp stool and insisted that McMillan take it. "Listen to this, Robert . . ."

McMillan sank onto the stool. From a distance, in the half-light, it didn't look like Ruth Ann's hand. "Something from home, sir?"

"No," the brigadier said impatiently.

"The medical service?"

"No, no."

McMillan clenched his eyes tightly shut, then opened them and sat straighter. He felt that if he didn't grip the legs of the stool he might float up into the treetops. All his surviving children were still his, for the time being.

"My dear General Lee . . ." Cobb began, tilting the page into the firelight, eyes electrified. The commanding general had now arrived and pitched his headquarters down near Hamilton's Crossing, where the enemy attack was most expected. "Today, I witnessed hellish malignity beyond the reckoning of Christians . . ." He went on to describe the outrages that had been perpetrated against the population of Fredericksburg by the Federal army, women and children forced out of their homes by the threat of bombardment, the attempted shelling of trains filled with civilians. Gradually, McMillan's heart began to calm down. He, like the entire army, had been angered by the Yankee ultimatum to lay waste to Fredericksburg—but this was vintage Tom Cobb. The fire-eater. War had done nothing to tame him. Before it, he'd boasted, ironically perhaps, that he would drink all the blood that would be shed because of secession. His brother Howell had tried to best him, promising that he'd eat the bodies of all the dead that would be slain. Well, there was plenty to drink and eat now, especially after that murderous day at Sharpsburg. Yet, Tom Cobb refused to step back from his old zealotry. In this, there was something oddly remote about the man. Seemingly, it had dawned on everyone but him how much this war might cost.

"Therefore," Cobb concluded, "it is my opinion that our army ought to raise the black flag and give no quarter to any scoundrel who crosses the river." He lowered the page and looked to McMillan. "Well, what do you think, Robert?"

McMillan took a breath, then asked, "Is that a copy, sir?"

"What do you mean?"

"Have you already sent it to General Lee?"

Eleven

4:07 P.M., *November 23*
Irish Brigade
On Picket

Mr. Turner's house stood on a bluff overlooking the village of Falmouth. A stiff wind had being blowing since dawn out of the northwest, churning the river into whitecaps and making the shrubbery in the old man's garden tremble. Tyrrell sat on a stone bench among the azaleas, his cape turned up and his hands inside his pockets. Mr. Turner had just shuffled outside after sharing his sabbath dinner with General Meagher and the colonels. He found Captain McGee enjoying a smoke on the porch and insisted on showing him the grounds.

Tyrrell knew McGee at a glance—all the color-bearers did. For what he'd done at Antietam, taking up the green flag when it meant almost certain death. Even McClellan had commented on his valor that day. Strange that McGee looked more like a professor than a soldier.

"Oh, will you see this, my boy," Mr. Turner exclaimed, his bald pate shining in the sunlight. "See my rhododendrons now—leaves are curling toward the centers. Means it's already below freezing. I fear for your poor lads tonight."

"Fortunately, our brigade goes off picket at nine o'clock," McGee said. "We've almost done our twenty-four hours."

"Oh, but those who follow you."

"Indeed, sir. It'll be miserable. Last night was bad enough."

Mr. Turner was a Virginian, had lived here all his life, but was still strong for the Union, according to Lieutenant Colonel Mulholland. He'd offered his house to the Federal army as a picket headquarters.

"Well, I know what I must do," the old man went on, using his ebony cane to point to some scarlet orange fruits hanging on the leafless branches of a nearby tree. "Must have my girls get the last of the persimmons in before dark. They can take a light frost. Sweetens them, a nip of frost. But nothing like what's coming. Will you excuse me?"

"Of course, sir," McGee said.

Passing Tyrrell on his way to the kitchen house, Mr. Turner smiled, his ruddy cheeks crinkling, and said, "Go inside and find a place by the cookstove, my boy. Let my girls brew you something hot."

"Thank you, sir."

Captain McGee had taken his field glasses from a coat pocket and was training them on the river. "Ah ha," he said. Peering that way, Tyrrell thought he could see something in the water close to the southern shore.

McGee waved him over. "Have a look."

Tyrrell took the glasses from him, saw that a large brown horse, saddled and bridled, was wading northward. Rebel pickets had come out to the riverbank, trying to call the stallion back, but he was already halfway across. So clearly, the river still could be forded. Why then did Mulholland say that Burnside was waiting for pontoons?

McGee said, "Seems the poor beast wants to take the oath and join the Union again."

"I suppose so, sir." Tyrrell gave back the glasses.

"You're color sergeant for the One-sixteenth, aren't you?"

"Sir, Sergeant Tyrrell." He stood taller.

"Relax, man. What're you doing here?"

"Captain?"

"What's the use of being a color-bearer if you can't lounge around camp when your regiment goes on picket?"

"I volunteered, sir."

"You what?"

"I'm to replace any sergeant of the guard who gets sick or can't take the cold. So far, I've just waited around."

The captain smiled, but Tyrrell could tell that he approved. Still, McGee said with mild reproach, "Seize all the time you can for yourself, Tyrrell. Every second."

"Sir . . . ?"

The captain's eyes were watering. It might have been from the cold wind, but Tyrrell wasn't sure. McGee sighed, then looked off as if trying to think of something to say, his jaw muscles working under the skin. At last, he asked, "Who'd you bury the night we reached Falmouth?"

"David Major was his name."

"Know him before the war?"

Tyrrell nodded.

"You're angry," McGee softly said, "aren't you?"

"Sir?"

"At my boys, the other New Yorkers for carrying on the way they did that night. I hear that some of you Pennsylvanians are spoiling for a fight over it."

True, but Tyrrell said nothing.

"Well, let the hare lie, Sergeant."

Tyrrell shrugged, not understanding.

"Let it go," McGee said. "You'll all see your mistake soon enough."

"And that, sir?" Piqued now.

"Don't confuse death at home with death here. They're worlds apart." Then McGee changed the subject. "What d'you think of the news?"

"News, sir?"

"The Twenty-eighth Massachusetts being assigned to the brigade."

Tyrrell had heard nothing about it. Yet, it explained a rather haughty-looking colonel calling on General Meagher this morning. The Twenty-eighth was almost entirely Irish-born and blooded by a half dozen battles—unlike the 116th Pennsylvania. "The boys'll be glad to hear it, sir."

The sound of female voices turned them both toward the kitchen house. Three Negro women were coming down the steps, carrying among them a bushel basket and two straw brooms.

"Ah," McGee said, "here comes the old man's property."

Tyrrell was thunderstruck. "You mean . . . ?" He didn't know how to finish. He'd assumed the women were just servants of some sort. "But Colonel Mulholland said Mr. Turner's a Union man."

"Welcome to Virginia." McGee pocketed his field glasses. "Well, I'm off. I've got the second relief. Good luck, Sergeant Tyrrell."

"Thank you, sir."

Tyrrell watched the women. He'd seldom seen Negroes in his part of Philadelphia. The oldest of the three was in her sixties, maybe even older. She had hair like lamb's wool and a broad, flat nose. The other two, possibly sisters, were closer to his own age. The persimmons left on the tree were beyond the reach of their hands, and the two younger women were trying to gently knock them down with the brooms—with little success. After a few minutes, they stopped and turned toward him, their breaths misting away.

"Can I help?" he asked, dropping his cape back around his shoulders.

"Ce'tainly, honey," the old woman said. The other two cheerfully said something, but Tyrrell didn't understand a word they said. The old woman saw his confusion. "They just come from Louisiana, and sometimes even I don't know what they sayin'."

Tyrrell approached the threesome, feeling awkward. But he was also fascinated to see them so close-up. The paler skin of their palms and the rims of their eyelids made him wonder if their blackness was indelible. Or had it rubbed off from labor and tears? He wanted to remember everything about them for his next letter to Annie. He wanted to learn about their lives. But chitchat came hard. He didn't know what to say to a Negro, let alone a slave. Finally, he managed to ask the old woman, "Are you from here?"

"No, honey—Georgia. I was sold to the first Massa Turner when I was just a girl. You know, this massa's daddy." Then she added, "I'm one of the fam'ly now."

Tyrrell nodded, made himself quit staring, then climbed up into the wind-tossed tree. The bigger branches were groaning like the timbers of a ship and the smaller ones tapping against one another.

"Got a mighty lot of growth," the old woman said from below. "That ol' tree needs a prunin', but nobody left to do it."

"Yes, ma'am."

His answer, mysteriously, made them all titter.

Tyrrell grabbed a persimmon. It was icy cold, the texture both leathery and soft. He tossed it down to one of the young women and reached for another. He could see the sun dropping behind a roundish hill just to the west, the last rays flaming golden. He knew what Annie would want to know, but was afraid to ask. The younger women passed the fruits to the old one, who gathered them in a fold of her apron before rolling them into the basket. "You happy here?" It seemed to have just burst from his mouth.

They said nothing for the longest time, and Tyrrell didn't want to glance down at them.

But then the old woman finally said, "I guess. The Good Lord give me all I want."

"Would you like to be free?"

"Why, honey," the old woman went on with a hoarse laugh, "what you mean free? *Free?* I couldn't be freer than I am. Got all I want. All I need. Take this broom, now—and whack them tall ones. Not too hard." She told the other two to be ready to catch the persimmons before they split against the ground.

Tyrrell batted the last of them off the high branches, then climbed down. The old woman invited him inside the kitchen for some coffee.

There, she ordered the other two to go to the main house with fresh pots for the officers, and then poured Tyrrell a cup. Alone with him, she lowered her voice and said, "But I was only tellin' you 'bout myself, honey. You all go on with what you doin' down here." Her eyes had turned hard.

"What d'you mean?"

She whispered, "Go on with Mr. Lincoln's business."

At that moment, Lieutenant Colonel Mulholland stepped inside the kitchen, blowing on his bare hands. "We need you for post one, Tyrrell . . ." It was down near the burned Falmouth bridge. "We've got a wagon waiting for the second relief."

"Yes, sir." He started to rise.

"But finish your coffee."

"Lord yes," the old woman said happily, her eyes nothing like they'd been the moment before, "he earned it helpin' with the chores."

The wagon was an omnibus with wooden benches along the sides. Junior officers were piling in, headed to their outposts down along the river. They'd been resting in a cluster of shacks in a wooded ravine behind the house. Slave shacks, Tyrrell realized now. He had just talked to an actual slave. This all made Virginia feel like a different country to him, more so even than the violent reception the secesh women of Warrenton had given the brigade. The flag. The Union it represented. That was why he was in Virginia. The flag he'd carry into the next battle. He took his place on the bench, and the driver clucked his tongue, setting off down an icy road that sloped away to the river. No one talked. It was too cold. And it got worse the nearer the wagon got to the Rappahannock. The air burned like fire on his face. It found the slits between his gloves and coatsleeves, and he clamped his hands in his armpits.

10:00 A.M., November 24
Falmouth Encampment

Corby sat astride his mount near the 116th Pennsylvania. He'd tried to stay as close as possible to them since the departure of Father McKee for home. The ailing priest had made him promise to look after his boys. Last evening on picket had nearly frozen a few of them to death.

Meagher was patting his stallion on the neck, the brigade drawn up before him. Slightly to his rear were General Hancock and his staff, all looking impatient.

"The reputation of the Irish Brigade," Meagher began at last, "is identified with the race it represents. The three original regiments left New York City two thousand, two hundred and fifty strong . . ." He paused, as if to let everyone feel the missing hundreds. "After Fair Oaks, we were reinforced by the Twenty-ninth Massachusetts, a brave American regiment which saw us through the defense of Maryland. It was replaced by the Irish sons of the Pennsylvania . . . well, mostly Irish . . ." He smiled at the 116th, whose men chuckled. Finally, the old enthusiasm was beginning to show in his eyes. He'd been unusually pensive these past few days. "But let me tell you, boys—there was another plan before the political generals stepped in, perhaps hoping that by toadying to the British they could woo them from their incestuous affection for the Confederacy. Well, we all know you can't woo the British!"

The men roared their agreement.

Meagher went on, "That original plan was to have an all-Irish brigade. One that would start the ball in Richmond and dance the last waltz in Dublin!"

The brigade cheered again; even the Pennsylvanians joined in.

"Today . . ." Meagher had to wait for them to calm down. "Today, that plan is met . . ." He then read an order reassigning the 28th Massachusetts from the 9th Corps to the 2d, and then another from General Darius Couch, corps commander, bringing the Bostonians into the brigade. "Will you welcome the Twenty-eighth, boys?" An obvious cue, for the band broke into "Garry Owen," and the regiment marched from the pines into the clearing.

The showing of the Bostonians this way was no great surprise to the brigade. They'd camped last night next to the 88th New York. Corby realized that it was the sudden appearance of their Irish flag that got the men cheering. It, unlike those of the New York regiments, was still in decent shape. A miracle, considering the number of battles the 28th Massachusetts had been through. The green flag streamed vividly against the clear morning sky as their colonel saluted and reported in. His manner was stiff, aloof.

"I'm delighted to receive the regiment, Colonel Byrnes," Meagher replied. "We're in front of the enemy. A narrow river divides us. Whether we go forward or stand here in the defense of Washington, we welcome your help in saving the last safe asylum for so many of our race . . ." Corby noticed the unease among the men of the 116th Pennsylvania. It was unsettling some of them, not knowing whether a forced crossing or going into winter quarters was Burnside's plan. "Like the Fenians of old who guarded our ancient kings—"

Another raucous cry from the ranks.

"Like the Fenians of old, we of the Irish Brigade are a guardian circle that will not be broken. Colonel Byrnes, take your place in the circle."

As the 28th Massachusetts joined the formation beside the 116th Pennsylvania, Meagher called out James McGee of the 69th New York. The hero of Antietam looked terrified. He gripped his rein with both hands. "Captain McGee," the general continued, reading from an order, "you, who so honorably distinguished yourself defending your regiment's green flag at Antietam, are deputed to deliver the Irish colors of the Sixty-ninth, Eighty-eighth, and Sixty-third New York regiments to the executive committee of our brigade in Manhattan, and then to receive in turn a new set of flags." He smiled up from the order at McGee. "Being made as I speak by Tiffany's. So, Captain, we rely on you to assure the citizens of New York that no banner from this brigade has ever fallen into the hands of the enemy." Then he looked out over the formation and cried, "Nor shall any, as long as there's one of us left!"

The ranks remained silent. Maybe after Antietam, this sort of thing no longer sounded far-fetched. One man left.

McGee said something to Meagher, but Corby couldn't hear what.

As last, General Hancock dismounted to inspect the brigade. He breezed through the 28th Massachusetts, finding everything in order—except for two "dusty overcoats"—and then turned to the 116th Pennsylvania. The greenhorns tensed as he waded among them. Muskets were presented to him. Questions humbly answered. Suddenly, Hancock seemed to rise up on his toes, and he shouted at the top of his lungs, "What in the name of Christ are *you* doing here!"

Corby couldn't see the offending private, but he did glimpse the color sergeant, who dropped his head as he clasped the stars and stripes, mortified for the entire regiment. Meagher, fortunately, was out of earshot, at the other end of the line inspecting the 69th New York.

"Are you supposed to be a soldier in the goddamned American army!" Hancock brayed.

The private mumbled something in answer, but it obviously failed to satisfy the division commander. Hancock seized him by the coat collar as if taking hold of a dog and dragged him out in front of the regiment. "Get back to your tent, you filthy shit-heel!" He sent the man stumbling in that direction with a ferocious kick to the buttocks, which nearly sent him sprawling. "If ever I find you in this shit-ass condition during drill, parade, or inspection—why, I'll string you up by the thumbs for a week! No, by Jesus, I'll have you shot right between your feeble-looking crossed eyes!" The private started running. "Neither food nor water for him for twenty-four hours! D'you hear me, Colonel Heenan?" Corby nudged his horse forward slightly so the infuriated general might spot his Roman collar before venting any more blasphemies. But Hancock was too far gone to take notice. "I just get you ignorant bastards to stop shooting sheep—and now you put a chimney sweep in the uniform of the Republic!" He was referring to an inexplicable sport the men had taken up in the Shenandoah: shooting every ewe they saw, often just letting the carcasses lie. "Goddamn you Irish!"

"That was a Welshman you just kicked, General," a salty voice said from down the line.

Colonel Heenan ordered the man who'd said that to step forward. But he didn't, of course. Hancock had come to Corby. His face was livid above his white shirt, and the priest expected him to explode over this latest transgression, but he took a deep breath and let it go before saying mildly, "Good morning, Father."

Corby whispered, "You're a fine general, sir, but you'll burn in hell for that tongue of yours."

"Gladly," Hancock whispered back, almost smiling, "if it makes soldiers of these Philadelphia street arabs."

Then one of the general's aides called for him. Hancock turned, and the major pointed at the pike to Aquia Creek, which ran along the far side of the meadow. Struggling through the mud was a dray pulled by an exhausted-looking team of horses.

On it was a pontoon.

"I'll be damned," Hancock said. "Finally."

*T*welve

♦

6:30 P.M., November 26
Cobb's Brigade
On Picket

McMillan was half-convinced that he was seeing things.

Ghosts were streaming up out of town along the edges of the road. They glided past in the moonless evening, misshapen for the bundles they carried on their backs, silent. Eventually, the bonfire at a provost guard post showed him these phantasms for what they were: the women, children, and old men of Fredericksburg. They were fleeing out of the range of the enemy artillery, which might open up at any second. He was almost past the firelight when an elderly woman in furs grabbed his stirrup with both hands. He was forced to rein up.

"Drive them off," she insisted. "You drive those people away!" Her aged Negro servant, in butler's livery, quietly begged her to keep moving. It was too cold to dawdle, he said, reminding her of the guns pointed down on them by sweeping a bony arm toward Stafford Heights. She stared at him as if she weren't quite right in the head, her thin mouth crumpled, and then together they slipped into the darkness.

McMillan urged his horse on again, trotted to the head of the regiment.

He had no idea what to say to these people. The truth would

be little comfort to them. Under no circumstances was the town to be surrendered.

Those who had friends and relatives to the south had already left by train. Lee had offered the use of army wagons and ambulances to carry furniture and heirlooms to the far side of Fredericksburg Heights, where a half-shabby and half-elegant camp was taking shape along the pike to Richmond, sofas and pendulum clocks mixed with brush lean-tos and smoky fires. Cold. Unseasonably cold, a Virginia colonel had told McMillan last night. How long could these people stand it out in the open? But Lee apparently had no desire to assault the massed Union batteries across the river. Cobb's Brigade was simply going on picket duty in town—and in support at that, backing up the videttes, or mounted sentinels, strung out along the waterfront. If the enemy tried to cross, Cobb was to stall it until the troops on Marye's Heights could reach Fredericksburg. Stall it "at all hazards," the orders had read.

The Rappahannock was rising, but now pontoon boats had been spotted in the Federal camps behind Falmouth. So Burnside was going to bridge the river, probably sooner than later if he knew anything at all about the capricious winter of northern Virginia.

Ahead, someone was wagging a candle lantern for McMillan's attention. Jesse, Cobb's manservant. The brigadier himself had dismounted and was standing before a darkened mansion. "Federal Hill, Robert," he said, turning. He looked quite happy.

"Sir?"

"My grandfather's house."

"Really."

"Yes. Named after the old Federalist party. Grandpa was a staunch member."

"Are your family gone?"

"Oh, for years now." Cobb paused, smiling. "Mother and Father were married here. Must show it to you in the daylight. Splendid house." He climbed back into the saddle and motioned for McMillan to ride alongside him. "Familiar with town?" he asked, raising his voice over the clop of hooves, the tramp of shoes on the street.

"No, sir," McMillan said. Most of the houses they passed were tightly shuttered, as had been Federal Hill, but lights shone from a few. He squinted through the darkness. "Ah, the Methodist Church . . . isn't it?"

"Northern Methodist," Cobb noted. "Our Methodist South no longer meets there. . . ." The church had split almost twenty years ago over slavery. McMillan eyed the front stained glass window, but it was hard to make sense of the unlit design. He wanted to come back and see it in the morning, the facets of colored light coming together to re-create scripture. Emma had been fond of stained glass. Fond of anything beautiful.

"This is Princess Anne Street," Cobb went on, obviously enjoying himself. "Most are named after the House of Hanover . . ." King George III's Germanic lineage. "Frederick Street, Princess Elizabeth, George, Wolfe . . . well, it goes on and on. But we've come to Caroline, Robert, where we'll form our line."

A provost detail turned the regiment right onto this street.

Cobb rose in the stirrups. "What's this now . . . ?"

McMillan looked the same direction. Huge fires could be seen burning.

"We're to keep our fires small," Cobb fumed, "so they can be kicked out if the shelling starts!"

"Beg your pardon, sir," a cavalry officer said from the shadows. "Those you see belong to the Yankee picket posts across the river."

"Don't tell me," Cobb said, sinking into the saddle again.

McMillan was surprised as well. They looked so close. The level of the river was thirty feet below them at this point, down two steep terraces, and for that reason the enemy fires appeared to be dotting the same bank on which town stood.

"My videttes have no comforts," the cavalryman further explained. "They're just over these houses from you. On Water

Street, along the riverfront. Excuse me, General." Then he melted into the dimness of an alleyway between two brick shops, the hoofbeats of his mount echoing away.

When the last regiment, Cobb's Legion, had turned the corner, the brigadier halted the column. Within minutes, the captains had their instructions and were busy setting the picket line the length of Caroline Street.

McMillan went to see where "K" Company, Garnett's, would spend the night. He hoped his son, who'd suffered from weak lungs as a child, would go inside some building after midnight, when the temperatures would sharply plunge. But Garnett wasn't one to take hold of his privileges. He was inspecting the muskets of his men. He looked self-confident. Last night, he'd seemed less so when he dropped by McMillan's tent, hemming and hawing until he finally got to the point of his visit: his mother wanted to give a gift to the Clarkesville church in Emma's memory. McMillan felt as if he'd been waylaid. Something carefully suppressed all these months suddenly welled up, and he'd barely made it outside the tent. When he returned moments later to his chagrined son, the only words McMillan could manage were: "Let's talk about this some other time."

He now wheeled his horse, wondering where he might sleep tonight. Sullivan wasn't along to find a place for him. The sergeant had remained in Camp Jeannie to head a detail guarding the regiment's belongings. This precaution hadn't been taken at Culpeper. All the men had gone out to battle with snowballs against Hood's division, only to return and find the camp looted, most of their cooking utensils stolen.

"Robert." Cobb again.

"Sir."

"Ride with me a while longer?"

"My pleasure."

"Thought we might check on our neighbors."

Cobb led them down a half-frozen mud lane to Water Street.

McMillan began picking out mounted figures. They loomed in the gardens and along the boardwalks, reins held slack, keeping watch northward. The Rappahannock came into view between the houses. It shone like tar, striped with the gold of the enemy fires. McMillan could see a big house on the brow of Stafford Heights, windows glowing.

"Chatham," Cobb said, seeing that the mansion had caught McMillan's eye. "At least, that's what Grandpa used to call it. Family named Lacy owns it now. Washington used to ride over from Mount Vernon to visit."

McMillan said nothing. He was thinking of his mother's granduncle, Richard Montgomery, who'd gone to Canada for Washington. And died there under English guns. He felt close to the dead tonight. Maybe it was the deep clarity of the sky. The stars.

The two men moved on, and Cobb hunched over the pommel to light a cigar. "Did I tell you Lee asked me how we're faring?"

"No, sir."

"I told him our brigade has the best position on the line. Up on Howison's Hill," he clarified. "Why, we can whip ten thousand of them attacking us in front. Although they won't come at us like that, I'm sure. They'll make a feint someplace near town, then cross lower down the river." He shook out the match.

"And what did the general say, sir—if I might ask?"

"He doesn't want to give battle here."

That astonished McMillan, especially with Jackson's corps due to start arriving in two days, concentrating the entire army in and around Fredericksburg. "But *why?*"

"Stafford Heights. They'd give a safe retreat to Burnside even if we beat him. I heard this from McLaws, not the old man himself—but Lee's thinking of delaying the Yankees here, then falling back behind the North Anna. If we whip Burnside down there, our cavalry can chase him over open country. End this once and for all."

McMillan held his tongue.

He was no professional soldier like Lee or McLaws, but he'd had a solid military education by British officers as a young man in Ulster. He saw advantages to standing pat, not the least of which was the food that was beginning to pour in from the fields and orchards between here and the North Anna River. That provender would be lost if they gave up Fredericksburg. Not to mention the women, children, and old men he'd just seen tonight, heading for the woods. He felt as if he should say something for their sake, to add their welfare into this reckoning. But who was he? One colonel among many. An immigrant dependent on the graces of the native-born. But still he knew that he should speak. Cobb was listened to, despite his occasional outbursts. "I believe Fredericksburg's civilians . . . how many, sir?"

"Five thousand," Cobb said. An encyclopedic memory. Knew the Code Napoleon by heart.

"These people are relying on us to save their homes from occupation, don't you think?"

"Precisely what I told . . ." Then Cobb halted and fell silent. Strains of martial band music were drifting across the river from the enemy-held side. Cobb wrapped the rein tighter around his gloved fist. His eyes began glistening with anger, and he tossed away his almost whole cigar. "How it makes my blood boil to hear a foreign army making music in *my* country." Then he shouted across the black water, "To a righteous God I look for protection—and vengeance!"

12:01 A.M., November 27
Irish Brigade Colors Detail
On a Train to New York

"Where are we, Jim?" Rich Emmet asked, having awakened from a sweaty nap just as the conductor came through the train, snuffing out the lamps.

"Still Maryland," McGee said, "I think."

Emmet nodded, shut his eyes, and then darkness fell over the car. The windows were steamed up, not that there was much to see outside. McGee wasn't sleepy. He thought of checking in on the ravaged flags in the baggage car, but they were already under a sergeant's guard.

The gaslights on a station platform flickered past, falling briefly over the faces of the thirty or more officers crowded into the coach. Some were northbound on recruiting duty to fill up their regiments with fresh meat after Antietam. These were to be envied, for the others were going home on sick leave to slowly die of fever or wounds that refused to heal. That was probably the case with Emmet, as General Meagher had assigned him to the colors detail at the last minute. McGee had a few suspicions, none of them generous, why he himself had been picked to lead it.

Emmet began shaking again.

"More medicine, Rich?" McGee asked. Surgeon Reynolds had entrusted him a bottle for Emmet.

"No, not yet. This is nothing. Comes and goes."

McGee took his overcoat from under the seat and spread it over Meagher's aide-de-camp like a blanket. Paper made a crinkling sound from one of the deep pockets—letters from the general for McGee to deliver to various people in New York, including the last of the widows of 69th men killed at Antietam.

"Rich . . . ?"

"Yes." A sleepy murmur. He'd stopped shivering.

McGee hesitated, but then went ahead and asked, "Has there been any talk of my brother, d'Arcy, around headquarters?"

"None I've heard. Why?"

"Just wondering," McGee said. But it'd gone beyond that. Meagher played favorites when handing out promotions and honors. So it'd flabbergasted McGee to find himself the general's choice to lead the detail, he the younger brother of d'Arcy McGee, who criticized "Young Meagher of the Sword" at every turn. The two men had been fellow revolutionaries in '48, as thick as thieves. But then d'Arcy had taken the high road, siding with the Church against violent struggle, and Meagher saw guns as the only solution. McGee knew from his days as a junior editor with the *American Celt* that the liberation of the homeland figured first in everything Meagher did. And by sending James McGee to New York to exchange the colors, he might be holding out an olive branch to d'Arcy, who was now living in Canada and said that Irish involvement in an American war of rebellion was lunacy.

All this took the luster off the honor for McGee.

He shut his eyes, determined to sleep. But he'd begun to fear the dreams. They'd started up in the last week, fitful things full of carnage.

The train slowed. A small station came into view, and a jerky stop followed. Several men got off, one of them limping with the aid of a cane. Suddenly, he tried to break into a run, but stumbled and then fell into the arms of his wife, who'd been rushing forward to greet him. McGee glanced away. The moment seemed too private to watch. He thought of his own wife and children. And he wanted to see Jack Gosson again, the over-aged wild colonial boy, who was recovering from a broken collarbone. But he found himself missing Donovan as much as the family and friends awaiting him.

As the train pulled out again, he began having trouble keeping his eyes open. Last night had been spent even more uncomfortably in a horsedrawn omnibus from Falmouth to Washington, with Emmet suffering terribly from his fever. Always a disappointment, the capital, so muddy and squalid.

2:17 A.M.
"K" Company, 24th Georgia

Garnett McMillan didn't realize that he'd dozed off until the sergeant of the third relief shook him. "Sir, the boys hear horses across the river."

Immediately, Garnett threw off the blanket in which he'd wrapped himself. His small fire had burned out. "How many?"

"Several."

He stood, rubbed his face. It was stiff from the cold, and his ears were completely numb, even though the board fence enclosing the garden had kept the slight breeze off him. He passed through the gate toward Water Street, the sergeant trailing him. Most of the Yankee fires had gone out too, except for one which continued to blaze up at Lacy House. It showed him the purled surface of the Rappahannock. The videttes had sent for their officers too, and Garnett joined a pair of them in the middle of the riverfront street.

They listened a few moments, but heard nothing but the waters lapping the shoreline.

"I'm sure it was horses," Garnett's sergeant said.

"We caught it too," a vidette added.

One of the cavalry officers asked, "What about trace chains?"

Silence from the men.

The enemy would need horses to draw their pontoon boats down to the river. But if nobody had heard chains rattling or wagons creaking it was probably a false alarm. "No matter," Garnett said, "you men were right to report it." He turned back for the garden on Caroline Street. There, he was surprised to find General Cobb, alone, tossing wood on the fire he'd just left.

"Sir."

"Something stirring, Garnett?" he asked, pulling his woolen muffler down from his mouth and under his chin.

"The men heard horses, but I don't think it had anything to do with hauling pontoons."

Cobb nodded, opened his hands to the heat. "I slept all right for a while. But then I had the feeling something's not right out here on the line." He smiled. "What do you think, Garn—am I just getting old?"

"No, sir. I keep waiting for them to cross too." The setting felt so familiar, chatting with Tom Cobb in the light of a fire, Garnett asked, "Is Pa resting?"

"Yes. We're sharing the same house."

Garnett saw that Cobb wasn't using the cracker box he himself had squatted on prior to being roused by the sergeant. "Sir, why don't you sit down?"

"I'd be taking your place."

"The steps over here will suit me just fine."

"Thanks, Garn." Cobb sat, stared into the flames. Garnett half-reclined on the back stairs of the house. An awkward quiet between general and second lieutenant ended when Cobb cleared his throat and said, "Your father tells me you might go into the ministry."

"Yes, sir. That or the law."

"Oh, take it from an old country lawyer—follow God's calling."

Georgia's best legal mind was hardly a country lawyer, but Garnett said that he'd think hard before he made any decision. He rested his hand on the wrought iron porch railing, then quickly withdrew it as if he'd been burned. His flesh had begun to stick to the frigid metal.

Cobb was looking deeply into the fire again. He began twirling a strand of his beard between his fingers. "It'd please your father to no end if you served the church. He's a Christian by instinct. Perhaps the only one I know."

"I don't understand, sir."

"I myself must work at it. Constant work and prayer." Cobb paused. "Tonight, he asked me if I thought expressions of grief were a sign of faithlessness."

"Are they?" Garnett softly asked.

Cobb seemed not to have heard. "I thought I knew all there is to know about loss after my sweet Lucy . . ." His teenage daughter had died some years before of scarlet fever. "Well, I do know that loss can be a strange mercy. For a time, I was sure

132 ◆ Kirk Mitchell

it was the end of everything meaningful in my life. But it wasn't.
God would never do that. It was the beginning of seeing the
world at its true value. Fame, wealth, society—God strikes, and
how puerile these things suddenly seem." He looked across the
fire at Garnett. "Yet, your father taught me something new
about loss tonight. With a simple question." He turned his ear
toward the river for a moment. "And he's right, of course. We
shouldn't grieve for our Christian dead. We should envy them."
He stood. "Good-night, Garn."

Thirteen

♦

"Let me show you how that's done," Sullivan said, shedding his jacket before the threadbare armpits ripped out. "You're diggin' a redoubt for a gun, Hugh, not bustin' out of the stockade ten minutes before the hangman shows." He jumped down into the pit, spat into his hands, then slipped the pick from Tully's grasp. "Go sit up on the bank a spell," he told him, then swung into a slow, steady rhythm. The blade thudded against the harder, drier layer of earth beneath the six inches of mud that were freezing each night and only partially thawing out during the day. Soon, winter would have its way, and there'd be no more digging until spring. Thank God.

Tully sat cross-legged in the parapet dirt, smudging his sweaty face by wiping it on his filthy coatsleeve. "What kinda gun's goin' here, Sarn't?"

"Thirty-pound Parrott."

"Big?"

"Aye, turn a regiment . . ." Thud. ". . . into a company . . ." Thud. ". . . 'fore the blue people know what's thunder and what's not." General Pendleton, Lee's grizzled chief of artillery, had ridden up a few hours after the brigade returned from picket

duty in town. Cobb had given the men breakfast and a prayer—
but no rest—before getting them busy on the earthen defenses.
Pendleton found the progress so admirable he decided to place
the Parrott rifle here, as well as five twelve-pounders to the rear
of the Howisons' house, which meant digging five more redoubts on the slope.

"I heard we're leavin'," Tully said, trying to pull a hangnail
out with his teeth. "Headin' down to the North Anna, gonna
fight the Yanks there."

"Makes fine military sense," Sullivan said. Thud. "After raisin'
a crop of blisters on this ground, find some new heights to fortify." Leaning on the handle, he stared up at Tully. The boy had
stretched out and was clasping his grimy hands behind his neck.
"Don't get too comfortable. This is just edificational on me
part." He paused, shook his head. "Here I am, the regimental
orderly sergeant, diggin' a potato pit for the glory of Georgia.
If I was with some flush outfit, why I'd have a horse and maybe
even a sword. Where's the spade?"

"Ain't but two of 'em for the whole reg'ment."

"That's not what I asked." But Sullivan went back to work. It
felt good in the cold. It brought summer to the body again, got
out the poisons that built up with the idleness of camp life in
chilly weather.

"You think we're pullin' out?" Tully asked, by and by.

Sullivan buried the pick-head in the ground and crawled up
beside him. "No," he said, sitting, "we're not."

"How you know?"

At that hour, General Hood's division was hacking a military
road through the trees and brush behind the entire line, so when
the battle came Lee wouldn't have to shuttle troops back and
forth on meandering country lanes. But that isn't why Sullivan
felt the army would stick here. Roads had been cut and then
abandoned before. It was something else, a sense he'd honed by
seeing wholesale death in Ireland, from passing through a living village in Tipperary one month and finding it starved out

the next. He'd carried that sense with him to America. And if he got to these out-of-the-way places in Maryland or Virginia before the shooting started, as he had at Sharpsburg, he believed that he could feel a deep stillness hovering over the countryside. He wouldn't know it to be stillness until suddenly bugs chirred or a woodpecker thumped a hollow snag. Some ground where the regiment had fought didn't give off this quality, as if the land itself were caught unawares by the colliding of two blind armies. That's how it had been at Crampton's Gap. But here, as at Sharpsburg, it seemed that the rolling hills had known what was coming since the waters of the Great Flood ebbed.

"Sarn't . . . ?"

So still this afternoon. And clear. Sullivan half-believed he could reach down and wrap his hands around Fredericksburg's spires, feel them hum with that queer stillness.

A courier rode past on the lane.

"From McLaws's headquarters," Tully observed. Good, he was picking up a few things.

The courier halted in front of Cobb's tent and dismounted. After a moment, he went inside.

Sullivan and the boy stood. "Is this it?" Tully asked, but the sergeant frowned for him to be quiet.

Across the river there was no visible scurrying around the batteries, no blue rectangles of troops in column on the road stretching northward from Falmouth.

Yet, over these past days, Sullivan had seen the Yankees going about their business in that slow, deliberate Northern way. Senior staff officers carefully glassed the Confederate-held shore while their aides took pages of notes. A party of engineers had ignored the threat of sharpshooter fire as they stood on the buttress of the ruined railroad bridge and peered down an imaginary line along the stone piers toward the town shore.

They were coming. Not as Southerners would come, with dash and hot blood. They'd come slowly, ponderously, grinding down everything in their path. He feared their icy weight more than anything. He'd felt it at Crampton's Gap, the mass of that great blue army crawling over South Mountain toward him. The brigade hadn't done well that day. They'd run. Of course, they'd been under Howell Cobb then, Tom's brother, a fat buffoon, who missed the chance to form the regiment behind a stone wall. But still—the weight of all those Yankees had struck terror in the men. And only Sharpsburg, three days later, had renewed their faith in themselves.

The courier came out of Cobb's tent, mounted, then trotted back the way he'd come. Trotted, not galloped. That meant something.

Cobb came through the flaps, hat in his hand. His chest heaved as he took in a breath and stared off toward the 15th North Carolina's camp. Then he strode through the trees to the Tarheels. Their colonel met him at the color line. Cobb did all the talking. It took only a minute for him to finish, then he clasped the colonel's hand before turning back for his tent.

"What's it mean?" Tully asked.

"We're losin' the Tarheels."

"How?"

Sullivan said, "Wait and see."

A North Carolinia drummer boy began tapping out the assembly call. The Tarheels formed up, and their colonel had a few words with them. Sullivan went back to work so as not to listen. It felt like eavesdropping. Within minutes of being dismissed, the men of the 15th were dousing their fires, rolling up their blankets, and gathering their scant gear.

At last, Sullivan slogged down parapet, followed by Tully, and went over to them. He found a raw-boned corporal he knew well enough, one of the few Irish in the regiment, and put out his right hand.

"Well, Mike," the Tarheel said, squeezing back hard, "Cobb's gonna have more Fenians than he'll know what to do with."

"How's that?"

"You'll be gettin' Phillips's Legion and the Eighteenth Georgia."

"What about you fellas?"

"Ah, we're off to Ransom's division. Cooke's brigade."

Sullivan nodded, not sure how to take all this. He was fond of the North Carolinians, trusted them in a fight. "They give any reason for the trade?"

"No," the corporal said. "But I think some clerk in Richmond just wanted to tidy things up. Now Cobb's Brigade is all Georgian and Cooke's all Tarheel. Too bad that inkslinger don't divvy things up by religion, or we might have ourselves a papal brigade."

Sullivan chuckled. "Well," he said quietly, "we'll miss you."

"Won't be far, Mike. Just over the hill at Marye's House."

Within the hour they were on their way. There was no fanfare, just Cobb and the Georgians lining the boggy lane, nodding farewell to friends, trading good-natured barbs over the sucking noise of shoes churning the mud. A handful of Fenians were among them, and each in passing gave Sullivan a sign—a wink or a nod. One called over his shoulder, "The devil a thing, I been bought and sold like a darkey."

"No, Paddy," another brogue answered, "Johnny Cooke would never buy an Irishman. I hear he's got a pretty wife and a great stock of wines."

Tully said somberly, "Dooley told me it ain't lucky to bust up what's got you by so far."

Maybe, Sullivan thought. Time would tell. "Well, back to the diggin'."

Just after mess call was sounded, the 18th Georgia marched in. A ragged mass of tired-looking men, lean as wolves. Many were shoeless even though they had a reputation for picking the countryside clean of anything they found useful. Minutes later, Phillips's Legion followed. Sullivan hurried over to greet this regiment. The companies were marching in order of the seniority of their captains, so he had to ask, "Would this be 'F' Company?"

"No, they're staggerin' behind us a spell."

Sullivan waited a moment. " 'F' Company?"

"Hell, do I look Irish?"

"No," Sullivan said, "God wasn't so kind."

At last, a voice answered, "Who's askin' for the Lochrane Guards?" Sullivan recognized the face. Their first sergeant, a bruin of a man. His uniform was thickly patched, but he was wearing a beaver top hat with the dignity of a grand duke. His eyes got wide. "Mike Sullivan?"

"Who else? Have supper with me after fallin' out?"

The man nodded deeply.

"Me orderly will fetch you," Sullivan said, turning for his fire.

There, he tossed dried sticks on the coals, then sent Tully off to Phillips's Legion, saying, "Lead him back like he's an angel in disguise." Now that he'd had a moment to think about it, Sullivan realized what the attaching of this regiment to the brigade meant. Macon's Lochrane Guards were all Irish. His host of Fenians had just been increased tenfold. Still, his mind kept running over all the times, the fights, he'd shared with the North Carolinians. Maybe Dooley was right, and it was unlucky to split up the old brigade.

Tully and the Lochrane sergeant appeared through the darkening woods. The man doffed his top hat and asked, "Are you a friend?"

"I am a friend," Sullivan replied.

"Then you're my friend."

They shook hands, then Sullivan motioned for him to sit on the log he and Tully had dragged over for a fireside bench. "I can trot out no better than ramrod bread," he apologized. "It was back there at Culpeper. We all went out to toss snowballs at Hood's boys, and some bastards came into camp and gobbled me fryin' pan."

"Gobbled?" Tully asked.

"Snatched away," the Lochrane sergeant explained, giving him a quick wink.

The boy had already mixed some hoecake dough, and Sullivan now told him to swirl it in bacon grease, as he'd been taught.

"That's a rare colonel you have," the sergeant said, "givin' you an orderly to help with the Brotherhood's business."

Sullivan decided not to correct him. "Aye, Colonel McMillan's a good man. And yours?"

"Colonel Phillips is home sick now."

"Who commands then?"

"Tom Cook. Just promoted to lieutenant colonel. Gallant man."

Tully handed him a bent ramrod, around which the dough was snaked. "Thank you, lad—and are you a friend?"

The boy looked questioningly to Sullivan, who hedged, "He's gettin' his instructions still."

The Lochrane sergeant nodded, then slanted the rod on end over the heat. "We hear tell Cobb's a holy wreaker on drinkin' and swearin'."

"And violatin' the sabbath," Sullivan added.

"Is he a man you can warm to, then?"

Sullivan hesitated. Neither Cobb brother had won the love of the brigade, and he'd seen Old Tom refuse to let the ranks break for water on a murderously hot day. The colonel had even posted an aide at the spring to keep the troops away, who then watched as the lieutenant's horse slopped up water by the gallons. "I'll say this much about him," Sullivan finally said. "I've seen him come within an inch of takin' the flat of his sword to a captain for beratin' a private with profanity. If there's shoes to be had, he'll make sure his boys get 'em. And he was ready to turn down his stars if it meant the brigade couldn't go home to become cavalry. But no—nobody warms to Tom Cobb."

The Lochrane sergeant gave the rod a half-spin to brown the

other side of the dough. "Is the brigade still bound home for Georgia?"

"Maybe not now. But it was a close thing for a time."

Nothing was said for several minutes. The Lochrane sergeant looked disappointed. But finally he grinned and tossed the first bread to Tully.

"You're our guest," Sullivan protested.

"That's a boy with a boy's hunger."

"Thank the man, Hugh," Sullivan said.

"Thanks, Sarn't," Tully said, already chewing.

The Lochrane sergeant's eyes had locked on something above. Twisting around on the log, Sullivan tracked the man's gaze to the open summit of Telegraph Hill. "Why, is that him?" he asked.

"Sure it is," the Lochrane sergeant said.

"Who?" Tully asked, standing for a better look at the mounted figure atop the hill. "General Lee?"

Both men laughed. "Not even after a hard night," Sullivan said.

"It'd be a thing for the boy to write home about, Mike."

"I doubt he can write anywheres."

"Take him up for a gander anyhow. A thing to remember, it'd be."

Sullivan frowned but eventually rose. "Ah, what harm?" He stretched his back, then curled a finger for Tully to follow. They started up the slope through the trees, climbing out of the smoke shrouding Camp Jeannie. The cold made Sullivan burrow his hands inside his jacket pockets. It bit at his cheeks and the tip of his nose. They worked their way up a game trail on the south side of the hill, shoes thrashing through the dead leaves. The view from a small clearing made Sullivan stop for a moment. To the distant west lay the Blue Ridge, invisible but marked by a fan of sunlight glancing up behind it. Just below the clearing a long, almost straight rent in the timber revealed where Hood's military road was taking shape. Beyond that lay

Telegraph Road, and through the branches of the oaks lining it he could see regiment after regiment marching toward him.

"Who's that?" Tully asked, fingering a large red pimple on his chin.

"Second Corps, comin' in from the Shenandoah."

"Ours?"

Sullivan rolled his eyes. "D'you think we'd be dallyin' over supper if it was *their* Second Corps behind us?"

"Don't know," the boy confessed.

"Then you'll make a fine general." Sullivan pointed along the heights to the south of them. "We're strengthenin' and extendin' the right side of the line." In truth, its thinness had worried him these past days. When the enemy crossed, it might well be downriver of town.

As they set off again, Tully said, hurt, "I can read."

"Have I said otherwise?"

"You did."

"Then I apologize."

"I can read most anythin'."

"Ye gods," Sullivan said, "you got the skin of a peach, Hugh Tully."

They broke onto some level ground and passed through an artillery camp, the cannoneers finishing their supper to the squawk of badly played fiddle. A slight breeze was flowing over the summit, making the air feel even colder. Within a few strides, Sullivan saw that they were almost on him—a tall, gaunt fellow on an undersized sorrel. The sergeant halted. Tully kept moving forward as if to introduce himself, and Sullivan had to grab him by the scruff. "We're long outta camp with no pass," he whispered, "in case you don't know."

The man wore the three collar stars that marked all generals, but that was as far as he went with any special insignia. His rumpled forage cap was snugged low over his eyes, and Sullivan could tell from the utter stillness of his head that he was taken with the topography below. First, the man studied the brushy, facing slopes of Stafford Heights, the Yankee batteries crowning them. From this vantage, much of Fredericksburg was blocked from view by Willis' Hill, so he slowly turned his face toward the plain downstream of town and scanned its grassy, golden broadening toward the dark line of trees that marked Massaponax Creek, the end of the crest on the right. He lowered his head until his beard touched his breastbone, then sat straight again and said something to one of his aides. Sullivan couldn't hear the words, but the murmurous, slightly disgruntled tone gave him a grim satisfaction. His intuition had been right. They were staying, and the general wasn't entirely pleased by it.

Tully finally asked, "Who is it?"

"Thomas Jackson."

"*That's* Stonewall?"

Sullivan fought a smile. He'd had the same reaction when he'd first seen the man. Definitely not a leader in the Irish mold. No flamboyance. No gushes of fine language. And if a romantic gesture ever occurred to Jackson, his strict Calvinism would never let him carry it out. "That is Stonewall."

"But he looks so plain and sour."

"That's what Presbyterianism will do to you, Hugh," Sullivan said low.

Fourteen

♦

The chimneys of Lacy House were spreading fans of smoke against the stars. All the windowpanes were frosted around the edges, but through their clear centers Meagher could see officers crowding the chambers, uniforms accented with gold, faces rosy in the lamplight. At an upper-story window stood Bull Sumner, staring off toward town, glooming. His white hair and beard matched the sheen of ice on the glass, making an onyx cameo of the window.

Meagher eased down out of the saddle into six inches of snow. He was close to ordering Surgeon Reynolds to lance his left knee, medical wisdom be damned.

A groom appeared and led his horse away.

Meagher turned and, taking a long puff from his cigar, looked out over Fredericksburg. Its roofs and gardens shone a ghostly white under a rising moon that was just a sliver off full. Picket fires glowed on the frozen streets.

He started for the entryway. The trampled snow was frozen so hard it squeaked under his boots. He'd suspended drill lately on Reynolds's recommendation. Just too cold. It'd been relatively mild this morning, but now winter was back with a vengeance.

Pausing on the steps to rest his knee, he glanced up. Sumner was no longer at the high window.

The assigning of the various Stafford County mansions as headquarters had finally been worked out. Naturally, Phillips House, the largest and most elegant, had been taken over by Burnside, although in a fit of self-deprecation the commander insisted that Sumner have it. His reason for wanting this was never made clear, unless it was because Old Bull had been soldiering when Burnside was in diapers. In the end, Sumner moved here into Lacy House, which had the better view of town and the now heavily fortified heights beyond.

Inside the first hall, Meagher was stripping off his gloves and coat when he noticed the officer beside him, doing the same. Darius Couch, his corps commander. "Evening, sir."

Couch had been in the mercantile business between stints in the army, so he could usually be counted on to exchange a few pleasantries. But not tonight. "Damned if it isn't off now," he snapped, throwing his coat atop those already heaped over the wooden tree.

"Sir?"

"The crossing down at Skinkers Neck. It's just been put off. Supposedly not enough pontoon boats yet to bridge that stretch of river." Couch blew into his hands, then used them to sweep some thinning strands of hair off his massive brow. "We have enough goddamn boats to bridge the Atlantic."

"I thought it was settled," Meagher said, dismayed.

"So'd I." Then Couch went on alone into the reception room.

The crossing was to have been made nine miles downstream from Fredericksburg at Skinkers Neck. Everyone, especially the engineers, had agreed this was the best place for it, a big oxbow bend in the river. So it went with Burnside. Another flip-flop. Meagher had written Elizabeth that the new commanding general would make a splendid fellow passenger on a steamship, but his abilities as captain were still in doubt. The troops were busy building log huts for winter quarters. Perhaps they knew better than their generals.

Meagher drifted into the adjoining dining room, tossed the stub of his cigar into the fireplace.

A buffet of cold meats, cheese, and bread had been laid out on the table. Yet, after a few moment's temptation, he decided against a second supper. Elizabeth said that she liked him a tad portly, that she found flesh on her fellow manly. But he knew that a uniform looked better on a lean frame, such as Hancock's. He'd been boyishly thin when he married Catherine. He recalled her eyes on him as they sailed the lake. Their son was still in Ireland. Did he have her eyes? Meagher had never seen him. The boy was eight now, as thoroughly Irish as he'd ever be. That had been the purpose of leaving him in his grandfather's care, hadn't it? Making him an Irishman first, an American later . . . if necessary?

"What will you have, sir?" asked the orderly manning the assortment of bottles at the far end of the table.

Something smooth to douse these remembrances of Catherine. They were beginning to unsettle him. "Brandy, please."

"Very good, sir." A deft pourer.

"Thank you, lad." He let the delicious warmth trickle down his throat. "Can you take a smile with me?"

"General?"

"Would you care to have a drink with me?"

"Afraid I can't, sir."

Meagher nodded. He'd known that. It was the gesture that mattered.

At last, he went into the reception room. Modest in size, as were even the formal rooms in most Virginia mansions. Chairs from all over the house had been crammed inside, and seated on them were all Sumner's division and brigade commanders, eating, drinking, chatting. The fireplace was going at full roar. The only empty chair in sight was next to Bill French, the squinty-eyed commander of the 3d Division. Meagher said hello to him, but the man decided to play his usual game. He enjoyed putting on a gruff front, even though rumor had it that he'd wept over his casualties at Antietam. "Been meaning to ask you," he drawled, "how the devil do you pronounce your last name?"

Meagher carefully ennunciated. *Ma-har.*

"For God's sake," French grunted, "I been calling you *Meeger.*"

"Apology accepted . . . for the third time, sir."

French took a gulp from his glass, then stared off, smiling faintly.

Hancock, who was two chairs away, winked. He looked cool, crisp, perfectly alert. Meagher went to him, knelt on his good knee and whispered, "What's happened to Skinkers Neck?"

"Franklin scotched it," Hancock said, referring to the commander of the Left Grand Division. He didn't bother to lower his voice. "He's worried about their *strong* defensive positions down there."

That nearly convulsed all the officers within earshot, men who'd watched Lee fortify the crest behind town day after day. The Signal Corps telescope now counted thirty batteries along their front between the river above Fredericksburg and Massaponax Creek. French snorted and said, "What's Franklin think they have up here? And where's he suggest we cross?"

"Harpers Ferry," some wag said.

Then Sumner came in, and the officers rose. He said, "Please, boys—sit down." He looked his age tonight.

Meagher went back to his chair and massaged his knee until he realized that Hancock was watching.

Sumner stood on the slight elevation offered by the hearth, the flames curling up behind his legs. Meagher was reminded of a lithograph in a religious book of his youth, a hoary-bearded saint being burned at the stake. The old man took a moment to smile around the room, but no one seemed to take reassurance from this. In fact, it seemed to disquiet them. "This afternoon," he said at last, "I met with General Burnside up at Phillips House . . ." The smile went out. "He told me, Generals Hooker and Franklin, of his determination to cross the Rappahannock at daybreak two days from now. Thursday, the eleventh of December . . ."

Behind Meagher, somebody sighed loudly. A die-hard believer that the army would go into winter quarters. Somehow, the notion seemed ridiculous now. Lincoln had anointed Burnside to do something—and do it swiftly. The newspapers had only added to this chorus, clamoring that unless Richmond fell by the greening of the leaves Jefferson Davis had himself a permanent job.

"We, the Right Grand Division," Sumner went on, putting his hands behind him, as one was trembling slightly, "will take the advance. We'll cross on three bridges directly opposite town, under more than one hundred and fifty guns on our bank. Hooker's Center Grand Division will follow immediately after us, using our lower bridge. He'll wait in reserve just below town. Franklin's Left Grand Division will cross a mile, maybe somewhat more, downriver of us on two bridges. So there you have it—our army will cross both at and below Fredericksburg, simultaneously driving at the enemy with a frontal assault, our job, and curling his right flank backward, Franklin's job."

"And the expected result, sir?" Couch asked.

The old man looked as if he'd been slapped, but he then forced another weak smile. "Why, Darius, the surprise crossing alone will catch the enemy with half his forces a dozen miles away."

Hancock asked, clearly not trying to sound confrontational, "At Skinkers Neck, you mean, General?"

"Yes."

"Are we to make a substantial feint down there then?"

"No, I don't believe so." Sumner said. "Regardless, if we move with all speed over the next two days the Confederates will find themselves in a weakened situation on the bluffs above town. We can drive between the two halves of their army. Defeat them in detail." He paused, searching the faces for encouragement. There was none. "That, gentlemen, is General Burnside's plan of operations. Any further questions?"

No one said a thing.

The silence seemed to press all the officers back in their chairs, immobilizing them like the hot, steamy air of the Peninsula in summer. Not one man could find his tongue, and Meagher could hear the aides and couriers laughing about something in a far room. Hancock was grinning, but in shock—for his eyes were glazed as they held steady on Sumner's as if waiting for the old man to suddenly explain that this plan had been mulled over at Phillips House and tabled in light of its glaring stupidity. Then he shook his head, once, as if trying to clear it, and when he stared back at Sumner it was with disgust. Meagher recalled that there was some old bad blood between the two men, something about Sumner reassigning Hancock's family quarters before he and his wife were done with them.

He saw that Couch had come to his feet.

"General Sumner," the 2d Corps chief said, "with all due respect to our commander, that's the most likely recipe for military disaster since the Light Brigade had its day at Balaklava . . ." The men murmured their approval, and Sumner's lips tightened. "I see no chance for surprise," Couch continued, "when Lee's had nearly three weeks to fortify his side of the river."

"Thank you, Darius," Sumner said, "but Lee will be more than surprised if we strike where he least expects it."

"Sir," Hancock said, "the expectations of an opponent are best gauged by his preparations. I hope everyone can agree on that. Robert Lee . . ." The name alone seemed to draw a shadow over his face, some brief sadness. ". . . has concentrated all of Longstreet's corps just where General Burnside would have us go."

French grabbed Meagher's knee, almost making him jump

out of his chair. "Old Bull isn't fooling me," he said under his breath. "This plan is mostly his, I'm sure. He was against the Skinkers Neck crossing from the beginning."

"What do you think of it?" Meagher asked.

Mercifully, French let go. "It doesn't mean a thing, like any other goddamn plan as soon as the shooting starts. I still like crossing below. More room to maneuver."

"Sir," Hancock was going on, almost begging now, "we can plainly see their massed batteries—"

"Ah, Winfield, a battery seen is a battery lost," Sumner said cheerfully, falling back on the old artillery maxim.

Hancock gave up and sat down again. His agitated fingers began whirling the rowel on one of his spurs.

Couch took over. "Sir, this is a decent enough plan. Bold but well grounded in the fundamentals. It might even be brilliant..." Sumner was starting to look hopeful when Couch added, "But its time has come and gone. We should've carried it out a fortnight ago, when Longstreet had but a couple of divisions over there, and Jackson was still in the valley. Let me quote Nelson: 'Time is everything; five minutes makes the difference between victory and defeat.' Sir, we are now talking about weeks, not minutes!"

The men applauded, and Sumner gazed off, flustered, weary, unable to carry on the argument. He looked as if he wanted to go to bed very badly.

Meagher saw his moment. He set his snifter on the floor and stood, enjoying the feel of all the eyes in the room on him. "My dear General Sumner, I find myself in the uncomfortable position of agreeing with Lord Nelson. And the Duke of Wellington, who said that time is everything in military operations. *And* Oliver Cromwell. He warned us to forebear waste of time, precious time. The British take time to task in all matters except the freeing of my native land."

As hoped, the laughter cut the tension, and even Sumner smiled.

"I believe our concern here is a common one," Meagher went on, "but in no way should it be construed as disrespect for your person, General Burnside's person, and your positions at the head of this army."

"Well said," someone murmured.

"Still, we *are* concerned," Meagher said. "I shrink before the military experience in this room. I can't argue the merits and faults of this plan, not with lifelong practitioners of the arts of war. All I know is this—I must go back to my boys and explain to them how we intend to win in this instance. Make no mistake, sir, they will cross over to Fredericksburg whether I explain or not, for that is their duty as American soldiers . . ." Sumner nodded, gratefully it seemed. "But I must understand this plan in such a way as to satisfy my own conscience that we can throw the enemy off those heights. That's all I ask."

Meagher sat to warm applause.

French squeezed his knee again. "No wonder those English didn't find the grit to hang you."

"I'm in your debt, General Meagher," Sumner said. "As usual, your keen tongue has put the problem in a nutshell. Greater detail. That's what you're all asking for, and that's what you'll get, shortly." With that, Sumner left the room.

Hancock, still quietly smoldering, invited Meagher to ride with him, as the Irish Brigade's camp and division headquarters lay in the same direction. They said their farewells and left, their horses moving at a northward walk, Hancock's aides trailing them at a distance.

The snow was glistening in the moonlight.

Meagher found that his gloves were no match for the chill, and he tucked his hands under the saddle blanket at the pommel. A glint drew his eye toward Hancock, who was uplifting his flask to drink. He grunted, then passed over his flask. Meagher hated losing contact with the warm horseflesh, but he accepted it and took a nip. They'd broken from a skirt of trees into a pasture which was serving as park for the pontoon boats.

The wind had risen. It felt like flame on Meagher's face. "Any idea what sort of detail Sumner will bring to us?"

"Yes," Hancock said, taking back his flask, "the Napoleonic argument."

"Sir?"

"They'll resurrect Bonaparte, say he'd go with a frontal assault precisely where the Johnnies least expect him to come simply because they believe too much in their own defenses."

"But that kind of assault always depends on surprise . . . doesn't it?" Meagher asked.

"No, not always. Helpful but not essential. You throw attack after attack against one narrow part of your enemy's front. Line after line at the double-quick, like wave after wave hitting a beach. Keep throwing in the attacks no matter what. Shock after shock after shock. And eventually he'll break, so the argument goes. *Attaque à outrance.* Attack excessively."

"But *could* it work, sir?" Damn, but suddenly it sounded reasonable.

Hancock stared at him a moment, then peeled off at a gallop toward the house in which he made his headquarters. "Goodnight, Tom." The hooves of his mount raised a fine icy spray, and his aides followed in the wake of this little blizzard.

Fifteen

◆

The hod carrier set down his wheelbarrow and pointed. "You'll have to go straightway through there, Gen'ral, to be reachin' it." McGee thanked the laborer, then crossed the busy street and entered the alley. It passed between two factories, then angled into a compound enclosed by tenements, small taverns, and livery stables. A blacksmith stopped hammering at his forge long enough to sneer at McGee's blue uniform before turning back to his ringing work. The tenements here were of the kind thrown up to house the big crush of immigrants from the Famine—wooden structures so rickety they couldn't stand free but had to be leaned against others. Pigs grunted at him from a muddy sty in an alcove.

He found the tenement Jack Gosson had described to him at the flag ceremony, two stories built over a stable. The smell of horse urine followed him up the steps. The dim stairway was so narrow his shoulders brushed the walls, leaving black smears of mold on his uniform he noticed only when he reached the sunlight of the first landing. While brushing himself off, he heard a man and woman arguing bitterly behind one of the doors down the corridor. Crockery shattered, and the woman screamed. Thankfully, he was bound for the top floor.

The door to the single room was already open, so he found himself looking at the dirty floor and knocking on the outside wall.

"What is it?" a tired voice asked.

He glanced up. The woman was about his own age, stoutly built, with unruly billows of auburn hair and sleepy-looking eyes. She was kneeling before two small boys, putting shoes on their stockingless feet. A girl and another boy, slightly older, were playing with clay marbles in a corner. At least all of them had shoes. Three were redheaded, as their father had been. His cap had fallen off, or been shot off, and McGee remembered his red hair. And the smell of his blood, which was everywhere—on the ground, the silk of the colors, the staff. "Forgive me for intruding like this . . . I'm James McGee."

She stared back him, blankly.

"From the Sixty-ninth, you see." Still no reaction. What to say next? He'd not known the man, not really. He'd just watched him let go of the colors and die. "I've been in New York on business for the brigade—"

"What sort of business?" she interrupted, her eyes keen for the first time.

"Well, there was this affair concerning the flags. I helped deliver the old ones and receive the new . . ." During the ceremony, he'd been more jittery than he'd been that day in Maryland. He'd nearly forgotten to kiss the archbishop's ring, then had slapped Judge O'Connor in the shin with his scabbard when he turned too abruptly. "They're beautiful. The new ones, I mean. Made by Tiffany's. I'm off in a few hours to take them back to Virginia. To General Meagher." That reminded him of the letter, the last one, although other officers from the brigade in New York had delivered most of them for him. "He asked me to give you something."

"Come in," she said at last.

Stepping over the threshold, he whisked off his hat and said, "Bless all who dwell here." The woman had but one chair, and he feared lice if he sat on the unmade bed. "I'm on my way back, having spent some time with my own family," he prattled on, "and I just couldn't go without . . . without . . ." He realized that he'd already stated his reason for coming. "Members of the brigade's executive committee will be going along with me. To present the new colors." Rich Emmet had already slipped out of Manhattan, presumably to return to the brigade before some surgeon prevented it.

She offered him the chair before sending the children out onto the landing.

"It's warmed up nicely since that cold snap," McGee said.

"It has," she said listlessly, easing down onto a corner of the bed, smoothing her hair with a slow hand. "What do you have for me?"

"Oh yes." He took the envelope from his pocket. It and the letter itself bore a fine script by Meagher's new clerk, a private from the 116th with a ferocious stutter.

She nearly snatched it from McGee's grasp, tore it open and dumped the letter on the coverlet. Unfolding the paper, she frowned, then checked the envelope once again. "Is this all?"

"It's a letter from *Thomas Meagher.*" Could she read? He didn't know how to ask. "He's a very famous man. He's concerned about how you are."

"Tell him I got a pain on me face from laughin'," she said somberly. "Did you know me man?"

"No, not well. Your husband wasn't in my company." McGee looked out the window. A brick wall view. "But I was with him when he died." Again, no reaction. He'd prepared himself for anguished curiosity. Not this. "He refused to let go of the colors . . ." McGee took a breath, blanked his mind with a vision of Carlingford Lough near his boyhood home, green but white-capped. A misty breeze. ". . . till they were safely given over . . . to me."

She rubbed her scalp, then her hand trailed down the side of her face. "What of the money then?"

"I'm sorry?"

"The money's what's owed me from the army. His pay 'fore he died. Not a whisper of it in six months."

McGee paused. "This call's entirely social, ma'am. I came only to pay my respects, those of Brigadier—"

"Then you're not here to settle it out?"

"I can make an inquiry. See my adjutant when I return to the brigade. I'm sorry, but these things are usually far more complicated than—"

"No," she said, "don't promise what you don't mean to do." She sighed. "Me brother's right. You're all fools, dyin' for the uptown Republicans and their precious niggurs."

McGee felt lightheaded. The room faded, and he saw only the redheaded man giving up the colors. "I'd be glad to bring this matter to the attention of Mr. Devlin. He's the chairman of the committee. The brigade's committee I just spoke of."

But she seemed not to have heard him. "I told him not to go. But he said he was ready for a spree. Some spree. He got the shakes terrible down there in Virginia. And now shot dead for what? I'll tell you what—you see it on every corner, a black face. They run north for the work, and the Republicans give it to 'em." She made a hissing sound between her teeth. In disgust. "I had me a position in a house, cookin', but they let me go and took on a niggur woman. For the good of the country, the master said, like it's patriotic to let me go. Well, it was for the good of his purse that the old man done it, for these niggurs don't know money from spit."

"I'm sure Mr. Devlin can—"

"Go," she said, "you've paid everythin' you come to pay, Mr. McGee. Just go."

9:11 P.M.
Lacy House

"I understand," Ambrose Burnside said, "that all of you, in some general way, are opposed to my plans. . . ." Meagher, as much as anyone, was disturbed by the commanding general's appearance. Burnside had always been a large and jovial man, but this evening he seemed shrunken by fatigue. His eyelids drooped, and his whiskers were peppered with gray that hadn't been noticed before. He stood at the hearth, where Sumner had the night before, and gazed dully upon the general officers of the Right Grand Division, whom he'd summoned here to hear him out. "Before you throw cold water on these plans," he went on, "I ask only that you listen to my arguments. Fairly and without prejudice." He began to scratch some sort of skin eruption on his neck, but then seemed to think better of it. "In short, it's my aim to attack both Marye's Heights and the enemy's right below town. I've given this an enormous amount of thought, at the price of two nights' sleep now . . ." He gave a meaningless grin. "And I believe that we can successfully do this before Jackson's corps can shift to reinforce Longstreet's. Is that much clear, Win?"

After a moment, Hancock said, "It is, sir." He seemed surprised at being singled out, as Couch had done most of the griping last night. Darius was seated at the back, quietly smoking a cigar. French, who'd also made his views strongly known, was nowhere to be seen.

"Now," Burnside said, "I've never claimed to have the experience of some in this brotherhood . . ." The emphasis he put on the word made it sound anything but fraternal. "Five years out west chasing the Apaches, and all I got for my exertions was an arrow in the neck . . ." Meagher couldn't see the scar, only the unsightly rash. "And I believe you all know that I didn't want this command. The fact is—my old friend, George McClellan, insisted I take it, and I did so only to further his policies, which had served this army so well . . ." Burnside's face was now taking on heat. "So here I am, with all my faults, commanding *you*, the men who will determine whether or not the Republic's assault on Marye's Heights triumphs or fails. Know *this*," he said, "I have formulated my plans, and we will go ahead with them." He paused.

Meagher hadn't thought that Burnside had a dramatic flair, but through the silence came the creak and rumble of artillery trains on the roll, dozens more of them moving into position along Stafford Heights.

Hancock shut his eyes, exhaled. Couch put his hand to his head.

Burnside then said, "This is my argument. You can take it or leave it. The enemy expects a flanking movement. Jackson prepares to be engaged, and Longstreet—no matter how many guns he digs in—waits to have a ringside view on Jackson's fight. Rest assured, the Rebels do not anticipate an audacious attack on their front." His voice turned raw, and he motioned for his aide-de-camp to bring him an already poured glass of water. He drank, nearly gulping, then wiped his mouth with a handkerchief. "Now, for the sake of debate, let's say that I'm wrong. That Longstreet rightfully expects his corps to take the brunt of our assault. Allegedly, it's foolish in war to do what your enemy anticipates. But, gentlemen, does it necessarily follow in all cases that you must do what he least expects? Even if it means missing the chance to break his line where it can be broken and defeating him in detail?"

Meagher nodded. A neat turn.

"So now, Winfield," Burnside said acidly, "tell me where I'm wrong, as you did behind my back last night." If he expected Hancock to be caught off-guard, he was disappointed.

It was Couch who shifted uncomfortably in his chair while Hancock came coolly to his feet and said, "Whatever was said, sir, I meant no personal discourtesy to you."

"Then what was your point?" Burnside snapped.

"Only that there's a considerable line of fortified heights over there, and that it'll be fairly difficult for us to go over and take them."

"But not impossible."

Hancock paused as long as he dared without appearing insubordinate. "No, sir—not impossible."

"That's it, Win," Sumner muttered, seemingly to himself but loudly enough to be heard throughout the room. "All together on this."

Hancock sat, and Couch immediately stood. Meagher was sure that the corps commander was going to get Hancock off the hook about what had been said by whom last night, but instead he drew himself up to attention and said, "General Burnside, I wish only to serve you loyally, to make the Second Corps instrumental in the defeat of the enemy. And if I've ever done anything in any battle, in this one I intend to do twice as much."

Hancock looked miffed, but Burnside smiled. "Thank you, Darius."

It was then that French swept in, chafing his pale hands together, and boomed, "What the hell is this? A Methodist camp meeting?"

Most everyone laughed. Burnside, especially, who appeared to take it as the collapse of the conspiracy against him. Yet, Hancock and several others remained stone-faced, and the jovial mood quickly sputtered and died. Meagher had chuckled, but only out of politeness.

Then, one by one, the officers rose and expressed their fealty to Burnside and his plan. There was something strangely medieval about it, knights repledging themselves to their king after some quarrel. Burnside and Sumner were visibly moved by each declaration, but they were out of tune with the undercurrent of sadness in the room. Meagher's turn came, and he rose, careful not to favor his throbbing knee. Once standing, he felt as if he were floating a foot or so above the floor, the same sensation he'd had in docket while being sentenced to death. Putting on a slight brogue, he said, "At home we have a sayin' . . ." He was interrupted by a good-natured groan from the officers. ". . . a gentleman always leaves the finest situations in his wake, and so it is that the Irish Brigade trusts

Ambrose Burnside to be a gentleman. God bless you, General."

Outside, after they were dismissed, he found Hancock leaning against the barrel of a Napoleon, brooding. His greatcoat was unbuttoned, and his white shirt shone in the moonlight.

"Then that's it?" Meagher asked.

"That's it," Hancock said with chilling finality. But then he sucked in a deep breath and let it out with a yawn. "Oh great Christ—who knows? Maybe Burn's right. Maybe we'll find a gap in their line two hundred yards wide. Maybe—" He fell silent.

Couch was approaching. Meagher stepped back two paces.

"Win . . . ?" the corps commander asked, tentatively.

"Yes, sir."

A moment dragged on in which neither man said a word, just stared at each other. "Win," Couch finally went on, "we'll need two infantry regiments. You know, to cover the engineers as they throw across the bridges tonight."

"All right," Hancock said, holding up a hand for Meagher to keep quiet when he started to volunteer two of his own for the detail. "I'll detach a couple from Zook's brigade."

"Which?" Couch added. "Sumner will want to know."

"How about the Fifty-seventh, Sixty-sixth New York?"

"Choice is yours."

"Why, thank you," Hancock said, his voice flat.

Couch opened his mouth, closed it again, then finally said, "Have them here in the yard before midnight." He hurried back inside.

Hancock said, "Sorry, Tom, but there's worse ahead than the crossing, and I'll need your boys more for that. Promise to keep you informed. Loan me a rider, if you don't mind—that way I'm sure I can get word to you. I'll run short of couriers before this goddamned night's through."

"I'll send you my best man." Then Meagher shouted for his horse.

10:45 P.M.
Camp Jeannie

Two riders were coming down from the summit of Telegraph Hill, becoming visible as they passed over the moonlit patches of snow and then vanishing as they wound through the dark thickets and woods. McMillan turned back toward the bonfire Sullivan had built for him. Cobb had found it intolerable waiting inside his tent for couriers, going to the flaps every few minutes, so he'd finally thrown on his coat and gone outside to Sullivan's fire, the brightest in the entire camp.

Sullivan was less garrulous than usual. Cobb had refused to let the brigade partake of a gift. The remaining citizens of Fredericksburg had sent casks of Madeira wine up to the heights rather than see the vintage go down Yankee gullets, should the enemy cross the Rappahannock.

And they would cross. That was now held to be a certainty by the Army of Northern Virginia. Except by Cobb, who still didn't think Burnside would give battle now. Yet, in the last few hours, Barksdale's pickets in town had reported a stirring on the far shore. New batteries were being drawn in position along Stafford Heights. Occasionally, a heavy creaking could be heard coming from the roads beyond the bluff. More and more fires were flickering in the broad swale behind the Lacy mansion. Earlier, McMillan had given Sullivan his glasses and sent him partway up Telegraph Hill. The sergeant returned and reported, "Those are warmin' fires, sirs, not cookin'."

"Did you see tents?" Cobb had asked, his voice muffled, the lower part of his face buried in the neck of a new coat that had just arrived from his wife.

"No, sir. That's what made me think."

Now, slow hoofbeats approached from behind, then stopped. A horse snorted.

McMillan turned, his left side giving him a sharp pain.

Two men waited in the saddle at the edge of the firelight, a lieutenant from Lee's staff and a civilian in a long tweed coat. A leather crop was clenched in his left fist. His thick coat looked of good quality, but the man was shivering, the tip of his crop shaking like a pole with a fish on it. The lieutenant said, "General Cobb, gentlemen—General's Lee's compliments. He saw your fire from above and wonders if you'd be so kind as to share its warmth with Mr. Lawley here."

"If you'd be so kind," Lawley repeated, the chattering of his teeth exaggerating his British accent. "Charles Lawley, London *Times*. Afraid this weather has left me with a touch of the ague."

McMillan tried to catch another glimpse of Lee, but the summit was in moon shadow. The commanding general was now making repeated trips to Telegraph Hill to observe the enemy. This morning, McMillan had watched him for over ten minutes, a contemplative gray figure glassing the blue forces. Reportedly, Lee's hands had been injured some weeks ago by a sudden rearing of his horse while he held the reins. But McMillan had seen no sign of it in the way he handled the glasses.

"Please do join us, Mr. Lawley. I'm Thomas Cobb."

"Oh yes," Lawley said as he climbed stiffly out of the saddle. "General Cobb. Georgia. Delighted."

The lieutenant took his leave, and a glowering Sullivan led away the Englishman's horse. Cobb introduced McMillan.

"Colonel." Lawley took off his gloves with his teeth and began warming his hands over the flames. "Well, things seem to be afoot tonight. This will be the place, ha . . . ?" And then he hinted at his recent intimacy with Lee and his staff, although neither Cobb nor McMillan showed any displeasure. Everyone was eager to learn what was going on inside the old man's head, why he'd decided to fight here and not withdraw to the North Anna. "Only last Thursday General Lee was quite fearful the Federals were collecting south of the James River," Lawley said with a confiding tone. "Doesn't seem to be the case now, does it?"

It distressed McMillan to imagine that even part of the Army of the Potomac lay between them and Georgia, let alone investing Richmond. So he was glad when Cobb asked, "But was there ever any truth to those reports, Mr. Lawley?"

"No, their whole army's here—and growing restless. Don't imagine you chaps will be seeing much of their advance, though."

"Why's that, sir?" McMillan said.

"Scotsman?" Lawley asked.

"Scots-Irish."

"Ah, very good. Well, I heard the most marvelous anecdote last night. Seems General Longstreet was giving his artillery chief . . . ah, name escapes me . . ."

"General Alexander," Cobb prompted.

"Yes, splendid man. Is he Jewish?"

"I don't believe so."

"Well, in any event," Lawley went on, "Longstreet found this lone cannon not being utilized on Marye's Hill. Became quite irate about it. He's overly meticulous about matters of defense, ha?" Neither Cobb nor McMillan replied. "Well, he lit into poor Alexander about it, and the artilleryman replied, 'General, we cover that ground now so well that we will comb it as with a fine-toothed comb. A chicken could not live on that field when we open on it!' " Lawley's barking laugh was cut short by a paroxysm of his shoulders. "Devilish, this cold."

"Yes," Cobb said, "the other night I washed up only to have my beard freeze solid."

"Dreadful," Lawley said, chuckling. "You know, General Jackson was quite opposed to staying here along the Rappahannock." McMillan had heard something to that effect, but like Cobb he now said nothing about it, afraid the newspaperman only wanted confirmation. "But Lee was quite correct in his final view. This is the place."

"Mr. Lawley," Cobb said, "perhaps you can clear something up for me."

"I shall try, General."

"I've heard a rumor that Louis Napoléon has issued a proclamation acknowledging the Confederacy."

"Yes, I too. Frankly don't know what to think of it yet."

"The report might be credible, though?"

"Perhaps."

Cobb fastened his topmost button. "If it is, set me down as a friend of France. I'd like to say the same of Earl Russell, but some of his recent published correspondence troubles me. I don't mean to put a guest on the spot, but sir—are we or are we not to be recognized by Her Majesty's government?"

"Well, General—I can't speak for Whitehall, but I do hear things, you know. And all the signs are there. Don't give up hope. . . ." Lawley was gazing northeast. McMillan looked that way too. Lower Stafford County reminded him of a Georgian pine forest being consumed by flames at night, the same bleary haze of smoke. Or was a fog gathering? "Oh, how I'd love to know what their side is up to."

Cobb smirked at Lawley's slip of the tongue. Their side. "So would General Lee, Mr. Lawley."

"Ha!"

Suddenly, a dot of red wobbled up into the sky over Fredericksburg and burst into a cascading shower of sparks. Another signal rocket followed before the first had extinguished itself, and the countryside was lit up for a few moments. Nothing as bright as day, but even McMillan could see boats in a line on the road that wound down off Stafford Heights onto the riverbank.

"Rockets' red glare, ha?" Lawley said, grinning.

$\mathcal{S}$ixteen

◆

The red sparks from the rockets winked out as they fell toward the river. The meadow behind Lacy House seemed to go completely dark until Donovan's remaining eye adjusted again to the light of the warming fires. They were scattered over the fields and throughout the woods. Troops in the thousands stood on the frozen ground around these blazes, waiting to cross as soon as the bridges were ready. They'd cheered the rocket bursts over Fredericksburg, even though they were enemy signals telling the likes of Lee and Longstreet that the Army of the Potomac was on the way. It was pressing up to its bank of the Rappahannock, collecting in the hollows and on the plains near the mansion. On the trot in, Donovan had found most of the camps of 2d Corps already abandoned, the fires dying.

Tapping his mount's flanks with his spurs, he galloped around six horses struggling to pull a heavy siege gun.

He'd been up before reveille, dashing off letters by candlelight. All day seeing that his company was ready to march at a moment's notice. They'd struck camp, except for taking down the shelter-halves that formed the roofs of the log huts the men had just finished. Then, this evening, he'd made one last trip to the adjutant's tent to see if there was any word of the paymaster's coming. The families of his men were in bad straits at this point, and Donovan wanted them to go into tomorrow's fight with at least the hope that they'd be paid soon. This jaunt across camp had been his undoing. Had he not gone, he'd be under his blankets and overcoat right now, perhaps wide awake but at least warm. General Meagher, coming back from a big meeting of all the brass collars, had spotted him and ordered him to report to Hancock for courier duty.

Donovan galloped into the garden on the east side of Lacy House. Most of the trees had been cut down, but a hedge poked through the snow, and he jumped it as if he were in a steeplechase. A sentry applauded. Donovan asked him where Hancock could be found. "Kitchen, sir," the soldier answered, finishing his rifle salute by dipping his bayonet toward the small wooden structure that had been added on to the south side of the mansion.

There was a horse-line at the garden's edge, but it was busy with couriers coming and going. Dismounting, Donovan walked his mount over to the kitchen, looped the rein over the railing, and went up the steps.

Hancock was seated alone at the table inside, scribbling orders, checking a large map between furious scratchings of his pen. He didn't glance up at Donovan, but frowned. He'd obviously come here for some quiet in which to work. *"What?"*

"Captain Donovan reporting, sir, with General Meagher's compliments."

The general was stripped down to his white shirt, trousers, and stockinged feet. "Oh yes, Donovan," he said, finally glancing up. "Heard about you." Who hadn't? Blow off to one Rebel general and your reputation was made in this army. "At least Tom's come through." But then Hancock tossed down his pen. "Now where the devil are Zook's regiments!"

"The Fifty-seventh and Sixty-sixth New York, sir?"

Icy control suddenly. "Yes."

"Passed them drawn up in column on the ride in. They'll be here in minutes."

Hancock seemed to relax a little. "Coffee's ready," he said. "Help yourself."

"Obliged, sir." The cookstove was going with a popping roar, and Donovan was drawn to its heat like a moth to flame. This would be a lovely place to idle away the night. Bless General Meagher.

All at once, Hancock rose and padded to the door. He threw it open, letting in a gust of cold air, looked out with a scowl, then slammed it shut. "Shit." He stared questioningly at Donovan's eyepatch as he went back to the table. "How's your sight?—be honest."

"Keen, sir."

"Then come here." Hancock tapped three places along the river on his map with his forefinger. "Bridges will be thrown across at the upper and lower ends of town. And then about a mile downriver, for Franklin's people. I've got one of the town crossings covered by an aide—everything hinges on those goddamned bridges. But I need somebody to . . ." Donovan gave an unexpected shudder. "You ill, Donovan?"

"No, sir. Just chilled."

"There's whiskey on the sideboard. Put a splash in your coffee."

"Many thanks, sir." Donovan did as ordered, then wasted no time getting back to the map.

"I need you to keep watch on the progress here . . ." Hancock pointed at the end of town opposite Lacy House, where the upper bridge would be built. He went on to explain how the pontoon trains would roll the last yards down to the river about three o'clock in the morning. Boats and planks would be offloaded from the drays, construction swiftly undertaken by the 17th and 20th New York Engineers. The two infantry regiments from Zook's brigade would cover them, as would the massed cannon on Stafford Heights, if the need arose. "I should be down to check on things myself in a couple of hours. But we're going into conference with Sumner any minute, so I may be delayed. Stay there, Donovan. Observe . . ." He glanced at the eyepatch once more. "I'll grab somebody else to ride for your brigade if I must. Report to me right away if the bridging effort either suddenly fails or succeeds. Go." Hancock picked up his pen again.

"Yes, sir," Donovan said, starting for the door. He had yet to touch his coffee, so he bolted it down. Thunderously hot. But it filled his belly with warmth. He left the cup on a butter churn and went out.

After the warmth of the kitchen, the night's cold seemed even sharper. He got in the saddle, but paused, exploring the roof of his mouth with his tongue. The coffee had raised a puffy blister. *Well, something to keep me company all night.* He rode around to the front of the house, and Fredericksburg came into view. No enemy picket fires tonight. The streets were empty and still. The gibbous moon was directly overhead, its weak light reflecting off the tops of the church spires. Slowly, he moved behind the long line of batteries, cannon resting almost hub to hub. Like the enemy, the Federal troops this close to the river had no fires, so Donovan had to wend his way through darkened clusters of men to the lane he'd memorized off Hancock's map. It dipped down through a gully to the riverside. There, in this ravine, he found the pontoon train, parked, wheels chocked. The engineers were trying to nap beneath the drays.

A Negro teamster was dancing around, beating himself with his arms. "Jesus," he kept saying, "sweet Lord Jesus."

The wind had come up. It cut through Donovan's coat and found the warmth in his stomach left by the coffee and whiskey, blew it out like a match. He turned his horse off the lane and took refuge in some cedars on the upslope side of the bottom terrace. He dropped out of the saddle and held the bridle. The town was throwing a shadow halfway across the river, which had a faint glint from that point to the near shore. He couldn't hear the water running. Now and again, a mist scudded by, hugging the Rappahannock.

At least this bridge would be shielded from their artillery fire by the town itself.

Beyond, stretching for miles along the heights, was a string of enemy campfires, bleared by the vapors of the night. Burning late. One more sign that the Rebels weren't in their bedrolls tonight. The upper half of that line would be Longstreet's corps, the lower half Jackson's.

Torture to have to stand up in this kind of cold.

Donovan thought to unsaddle his mount and use the coarse blanket to huddle on the ground. But what if he had to rush back to Lacy House? Or worse yet—Hancock found him bivouacked for the night, wearing his horse's blanket like a shawl?

The town's shadow was now touching the Stafford shore. A stroll down to the river finally seemed safe enough. He wanted to get his blood going. He tied his horse to a sapling, then set out on foot. He followed the steep, icy lane down the slope, slipping once but catching himself by grasping a shrub. He'd been reassured to see several officers mixed among the pickets along the bank, their scabbards shining. They were murmuring among themselves. The engineers had been roused from under the drays. In pairs, they were carrying the planks down to the water's edge, stacking them in piles as quietly as they could.

Donovan still couldn't hear the river flowing.

Stooping, he picked up a pebble and tossed it a few feet out. It rattled and clicked against ice.

"About an inch thick," a voice whispered to his side. A bay rum scent, strong enough to penetrate the chill. The figure carried himself like a senior officer. "And getting thicker all the time."

"Will that stop the crossing, sir?" Donovan asked, equally hushed.

"No. Who're you?"

"Sir, Captain John Donovan, Sixty-ninth New York."

"What're Meagher's boys doing here?"

"Just me, sir—in General Hancock's service tonight."

"Well, that makes two of us, Donovan," the voice answered. "Colonel Bull, Sixty-sixth New York." One of the two regiments tasked to cover the crossing.

"Do you require anything, sir?"

"Yes. A warmer night and a narrower river."

Donovan chuckled. "How wide is it at this point, Colonel?" Hard to gauge with just one eye.

"More than four hundred feet. Look out there, Captain—" He pulled Donovan aside to make way for two engineers lugging a tool chest.

Donovan realized that his blind side made him a nuisance here. "Sir, I'll be up the bank a little, standing by my horse. If there's any difficulty, General Hancock would like to know at once."

"Oh," Bull griped, "he can count on difficulty. As soon as we open the ball."

Ascending the lane, Donovan kept to its edge where the ice was rougher for traction. His gelding had put its rump to the wind and lowered its head. He stepped around the croup to use the animal as a windbreak. It helped, but his toes were growing numb. Stamping his feet only made them ache. It'd be a long day tomorrow, and now he'd go into it sleepless, exhausted by the cold.

Below, metal rang against stone. Someone had dropped a tool. Donovan bit his underlip. The racket had probably gotten Lee out of bed. Why hadn't the sharpshooters over there opened up? Certainly, their rockets had showed them what was gathering to come over.

He gazed up, started tracking the North Star through the leafless branches of a tree to mark time. No hope of reading his pocket watch.

A dog barked over in Fredericksburg. Lonely sound. Made him think of his boyhood in Ireland, somehow.

He wondered where the brigade's part in the coming fight would be played out. Certainly not under the guns on the crest right above town. He glanced downriver at the black, slanting woods where Jackson's men were lurking. A big brush with the Johnnies seemed more likely there, yet these engineers were getting ready to float a bridge here, into town, and 2d Corps was stacked up, waiting to use it.

Jimmy McGee.

He would miss this battle. Just as well, what with his eagerness to snatch up the colors precisely when the bullets were turning them into confetti. He was expected back Friday night or Saturday morning with the new flags. For an instant, Donovan wondered if he himself would still be alive to greet Jimmy. But then the thought was shrugged off. Of course he'd be there, and McGee and he would go arm-in-arm to the banquet General Meagher had planned to receive the colors.

Time passed. Two or more hours. Donovan began asking himself if Hancock had forgotten him. He was tempted to go back up to the house, that toasty kitchen, but then recalled the general's orders to stay and observe. The moon was another thirty or so minutes from setting, but it seemed small, its light weak and powdery. Even with two eyes, he would've seen little. Still, he hadn't liked the way Hancock had looked at his eyepatch.

Finally, something began moving in the ravine.

Boat by boat, the engineers had started easing the pontoon train to the shore. Soft groans and creaks came from wood under pressure, like an old house in a windstorm. Each pontoon was wheeled along by hand. On the frozen mud flats below, a team of dim figures disengaged the arriving boat from its dray. Then, shuffling along like pallbearers, they laid it in an ever-lengthening row, prow dropped into the water with a crack of ice and a splash. Donovan was sure the enemy pickets could hear all this. He waited with gritted teeth for muzzle flashes to erupt along the waterfront. He'd seen their rifle pits in daylight, musket barrels sticking out of cellar windows.

BRIDGING EFFORTS,
EARLY A.M., DEC. 11

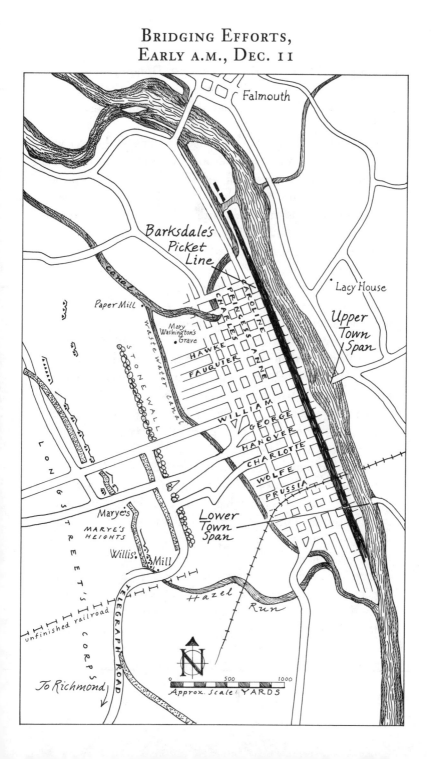

Falmouth

Barksdale's
Picket
Line

Paper Mill

Mary
Washington's
Grave

HAWKE

FAUGUIER

Lacy House

Upper
Town
Span

STONE WALL

Wastewater Canal

WILLIAM

GEORGE

HANOVER

CHARLOTTE

WOLFE

PRUSSIA

Lower
Town
Span

L O N G S T R E E T ' S   C O R P S

Marye's

MARYE'S
HEIGHTS

Willis' Mill

unfinished railroad

TELEGRAPH ROAD

Hazel Run

To Richmond

N

0   500   1000

Approx. scale: YARDS

But the readying of the pontoons went on unmolested. Twenty minutes. Then an hour, at least. Donovan snapped off some cedar branches, made a small pile of them and stood on it. Still, the cold burned through the soles of his boots.

Another hour.

He watched for the first inkling of dawn. Nothing. Just a gathering mist. Actually, a proper fog by now. Dank and swirling. A file of infantrymen—Zook's New Yorkers—formed a skirmish line along the slope below him. They thrashed through the growth, mess tins rattling, halted, then settled in to wait. A man with the air of a sergeant came up to Donovan. He hunched his shoulders and asked, "Lieutenant?"

"Not recently."

"Sorry, sir." The man withdrew.

Donovan got back in the saddle. Things were going to get hot soon, he decided. He rode up to the highest terrace, looked for something more solid than brush to hide behind. He found a pile of firewood that had been left to dry on the airy lip of the ravine. He fell in behind it, but remained mounted. Easier on his feet that way. He didn't know why he hadn't thought of it sooner. Yet, eight feet off the ground, his face had less protection from the wind. His cheeks felt as if they were being scalded.

Where the hell was Hancock?

Then a sloshing sound made him look below.

He could just make out a boat being launched, the dark shape gliding out into the Rappahannock, crunching and tinkling through the skin of ice. Another left shore. And then another. These were quickly lashed together, and then hammerblows echoed off the bluff as the pontoniers began laying down the planks. Soon the bridge stretched at least fifty feet out into the fog, with more boats being poled into position all the while. Once delivered, their crews jogged back along one side of the span to ferry another pontoon while a second antlike stream of engineers carried out more planks.

Donovan watched, fascinated. And afraid for them. Each

plank brought them closer to the enemy's muskets, but they worked on, unarmed. They were now dissolving into the last few yards of visibility, shadows of men, laying down their planks and swinging their mallets.

Then a musket barked.

The work stopped all along the bridge, and everyone looked out to its end. Donovan saw no movement but heard a splash. "Don't go for him!" a voice out in the fog warned. "You'll freeze to death, tryin'!"

Donovan finally glimpsed the body floating away—head, hands, and knees breaking the surface. It collided with a shelf of ice, flipped over and went under. At that instant, a volley came from the far bank. The balls thudded against the boats and chirped into the open water around the bridge.

Donovan dismounted, drew his revolver.

Someone, Colonel Bull maybe, hollered for the 66th to hold its fire. The pontoniers were still out there. They weren't fleeing. They simply crouched as they went on with the job. Another man was pitched dead over the side. Two more in quick succession.

"I see their flashes!" an infantryman cried. "Can I fire?"

He was refused.

In the midst of all this, two reports had rumbled over the valley like thunder. At first, Donovan believed they marked the Union artillery opening up on the waterfront. But no. He soon realized that they'd come from the direction of Marye's Heights. Heavy ordnance. He held his breath and waited for the massive shells to come plunging down on the bridge, on himself perhaps. But the seconds ticked away and no detonations followed.

A signal, then.

The Confederate muskets now sounded like green reeds thrown on a fire. Engineers were sprawling against the planking, others were floating away. Those who could were coming back to shore, dragging wounded friends, crawling, duckwalking, even wading the frigid shallows.

A ball clipped a branch over Donovan's head, spooking his horse. "It's all right, fella. Just a light shower." But he could hear lead pelting the slope all around him. A man in the skirmish line went down, dropping his musket as he tumbled headlong through the brush.

At last, Bull freed the 66th to return fire.

It went on for some minutes. At nothing, really. Donovan saw an occasional flash over there, but as soon as it went out he had no idea where it'd been in the murk. The New Yorkers' fire had no effect on the enemy sharpshooters, for balls from that side continued to prune the trees or spark off the river rocks along the bank. And the bridge was empty, except for the dead and wounded. One engineer was scuttling toward shore on his elbows and knees, moaning deliriously that he'd been gut-shot.

A bugle ordered the skirmishers to cease fire.

In the silence that followed, a whisper could be heard passing from man to man up the line toward Donovan. When it came close enough, he heard that Colonel Bull was dead. Bay rum. He could still smell it. *That makes two of us, Donovan.* He supposed that he should ride back to Lacy House and report to Hancock.

But then another message was whispered along the skirmish line: the engineers were going to try again. Hold fire. Donovan could see them gathering near the bridgehead, shouldering planks like muskets. Others were pushing off from shore in the boats.

He was praying when the next volley came out of the fog. More sickening splashes. He realized that the Rebels were aiming at the sounds of the hammers.

$\mathscr{S}$ e v e n t e e n

◆

4:49 A.M., December 11
Camp Jeannie

Sullivan snapped awake.

He looked around, wondering if he'd slept at all. Perhaps not. Just drowsed a little. He was sitting up, his arms folded atop his knees, blanket and oilcloth tucked around him. He was facing the fire, which was almost dead. There was a low band of light in the east, gray from a mist that had set in. He steeled himself, threw off his covers and fumbled to rekindle the fire. Murdering cold. He'd have a cup of chicory coffee, then check on the colonel. After that, the pickets in the fields below. A man in just a shell jacket and threadbare trousers could freeze to death out there on a morning like this.

Squatting, he blew on the coals, adding twigs and straw and even acorns to them. He realized that he had slept, some. He'd been dreaming of rain, a hard rain on a tin roof. It had turned to hail, pounded whitely, frosted a dreamscape that might have been the Slieveardagh Hills of home.

A small blue flame rose from the tinder. He was about to fan it with his hat when, off to the left, a cannon boomed, sending echoes up and down the valley. The entire camp stirred. The men threw off their blankets and came to their feet. Those who had shoes put them on.

Tully stumbled over to Sullivan. "That a Yankee gun?" he asked, his hair up in cowlicks.

Sullivan shushed him.

And then a second shot was fired, also from somewhere on Marye's Heights. The signal that the enemy was getting ready to bridge the river. "They're comin' over," Sullivan said quietly, then held his breath to listen. He could pick up a distant rattle like the hail he'd been dreaming of. Musket fire, and a good deal of it. Just guessing, he thought the gunfire was about a mile off, coming from the direction of town. Yet fog could play tricks with noises. The shots could even be from Jackson's pickets far downriver.

Tully spun around and rushed back for his bedroll. He began folding it up. The long drumroll broke from a neighboring camp. Then another brigade took it up. The boy dropped his bedding and staggered off for his stacked musket as if the Yankees were already running through the camp.

"Hugh, come here." Before he charged down the slope on his own hook.

"Sarn't?"

"What d'you hear below us?"

"Muskets."

Sullivan gripped Tully's arm, trying to squeeze some sense into him. "Other'n muskets."

"Bugle."

"Cavalry trumpet," Sullivan said. "D'you know that call?" Tully shook his head. "Boots and saddles. That's what it is. So our cavalry's goin' out to see what the blue people are up to. Not to mention our own picket line keepin' watch down in the grass. I think that gives us time enough for breakfast." He made the boy sit on the log, then let go of his arm and added a few sticks of green pine to the flames. "One thing about these frays—once they start, nobody has the sense to stop 'em. You know, so a fella can answer his own needs. My canteen and haversack, quick now."

Cobb was up, his face puffy around the eyes. He was waiting beside his own fire for the courier who'd no doubt show up from McLaws's headquarters any second. The brigadier looked snug in a new greatcoat, and Jesse, his Negro, was sporting his old one, collar stars and all. The men had started saluting the manservant, which made him laugh, self-consciously.

Tully handed over Sullivan's haversack and canteen, then sat again, shivering, wrapping himself in his skinny arms. "What's gonna happen, Sarn't . . . ?"

Sullivan narrowed his eyes against the smoke.

"Sarn't?"

Maybe it all loomed worse in anticipation. But then remembering Sharpsburg made Sullivan think again—no, it was worse in the living. Nothing prepared you for it. The satanic confusion. "God only knows. But come what may, it'll look better on a full stomach." Sullivan added water to some cornmeal, began kneading it into dough for hoecakes. "By the tree—grab the old ramrod. And curse the bastard who gobbled me fryin' pan."

But Tully had bigger worries than breakfast. He remained seated. "Will the Yanks just kinda squirt across all at once?"

"The ramrod, lad."

The boy hurried for it while Sullivan went on working the dough with his hands. It was cold from the ice water in his half-frozen canteen.

Tully came back and knelt, his jaw muscles fluttering under the skin.

"I don't recollect the Yanks *squirtin'* anywheres," Sullivan explained. "Their army's more like molasses. It oozes, dark and heavy. Now start bakin' dough before Tom Cobb has us all standin' in formation, pissin' down our legs."

Tully snorted, then held the ramrod over the flames.

Sullivan paused. He couldn't recall having seen the boy laugh before. It made him look ridiculously young. That other face had been in the ground many years now. Destroyed by worms. Yet, was God showing him what it would've looked like had the potato crop not failed?

"Sarn't . . . ?"

"Aye."

"When can I become a friend?"

"What?"

"A Fenian."

Sullivan thought a moment. "After this fight. Maybe then we'll send for you." He plucked the first hoecake off the rod and passed it from hand to hand as he rushed for the colonel's tent.

McMillan was still lying on his cot.

Sullivan lit the candle lantern and saw at once that the man was awake, a glassy softness in his eyes. "Michael, you'll have to help up this morning," he said, his voice small and gravelly.

"It's just the cold, sir. Awful cold since midnight."

"I don't know if I can get my boots on."

"They'll go on fine."

McMillan nodded but looked unconvinced. He hung his arm around Sullivan's shoulders and hobbled upright. Several moments passed before he could stand on his own, and then he pressed his fist against the left side of his chest.

"Pain, sir?" Sullivan asked.

"It'll go soon enough."

"I brought a cake for you, fresh baked." When McMillan started to decline, Sullivan added, "I believe Burnside's truly comin' this mornin'. Don't know when I can find you somethin' more to eat."

The colonel finally started chewing, then sat so Sullivan could help pull his boots on. "Is General Cobb up, Michael?"

"He is."

"Tell him I'll join him shortly."

Sullivan ducked through the flaps and ran for Cobb's fire. Nearing it, he could tell from the brigadier's restless hands that he knew no more than anyone else. "Sir, the colonel—"

And then a string of popping noises came out of the east.

Sullivan and Cobb pivoted toward it. The light was growing, but fog was banked all along the Rappahannock, a second river of moisture winding fluffily down toward the Chesapeake. Above this, Sullivan could see cannon muzzles flashing along Stafford Heights.

"Field pieces," Cobb noted. "They've got a lot more than that."

He was right. Their heavier guns hadn't opened up. The mist over the river was streaked with sparkling fuses. And then the shells began landing, jaundiced lights peppering the fog all along the waterfront.

Sullivan heard hooves thudding above and behind him.

A courier was plunging straight down the south face of Telegraph Hill. One of McLaws's riders. Cobb and then McMillan, who'd come limping from his tent, met him out in the trees.

Sullivan could hear none of what was said over the bombardment, so he went back to his own fire. Tully tossed him a hoecake. It was half charred and half raw dough, but he winked and said, "You've done fine."

Cobb's adjutant then bawled for the brigade to fall in.

6:45 A.M.
116th Pennsylvania
Camp of the Irish Brigade

The roof came off with a final tug, and Tyrrell packed his shelter-half. The canvas had an admirable patina now, a dull gray from woodsmoke underlain with a faint redness from Virginia dirt and mud. The hut looked forlorn without its roof. For some reason the man couldn't explain, Hudson had wanted to bash in the wattle chimney with the butt of his musket, tear down the logs. But Tyrrell wouldn't let him, and the corporal had gone off grumbling to the sinks to relieve himself.

The little hovel still had use. If not for themselves, for somebody else, even the Virginians after the war. A henhouse or whatever. He didn't care for destruction. His first real memory was of the riots in his Philadelphia neighborhood, the native-born Americans trying to drive out the Irish. He could still re-call broken glass on the sidewalks, fires everywhere, and the militia out in force. Some of the neighbors had flown the stars and stripes from their upper-story windows to show that they weren't Irish. The same flag he would carry today.

"Five minutes, Tyrrell," Lieutenant Colonel Mulholland said as he rode past.

"Yes, sir."

The brigade's fifes and drums were going. "The Girl I Left Behind Me." Last night, he'd written Annie, tried not to make it sound like a voice from the grave. Nothing to frighten her. He hadn't even told her that the brigade would be striking camp this morning, each man drawing eighty rounds of ammunition. His last letter to her, sent north over a week ago, had reported that they were building huts, going into winter quarters. Now this.

A dry, acrid fog was sifting through camp. It'd seemed moist and sweet before the long artillery barrage that had just let up about thirty minutes ago.

The men began cheering.

Meagher swept by, his horse kicking up dirty snow. The two priests, Corby and Ouellette, were right behind him, and then his staff, all in their best uniforms, bright-cheeked, ready for anything. Tyrrell himself felt groggy, floundering through a waking dream. He'd just fallen off at long last when the twin thumps of the enemy's signal guns made him stumble outside the hut, closely followed by the rest of the color guard. They'd listened to the first artillery barrage until the cold drove them back inside.

"S-s-sergeant."

Turning, Tyrrell was surprised to see McCarter with a blan-ket roll and his new musket. He was now brigade clerk and ex-pected to stay out of the battle. "Mac, what're you doin'?"

The private shrugged. "Marching with my company."

"Does General Meagher know about this?"

"No."

"Well, he'll see you for sure in formation."

"I'll catch up later, when he's at the head of the column."

Tyrrell frowned.

"Don't b-blow on me, please," McCarter begged, then melted into the skirt of woods beside the meadow where the brigade was forming, the regiments collecting into blue rectangles. Tyrrell looked one last time at his roofless hut, then called for Hudson and the others to hurry.

7:41 A.M.
Howison's Hill

Garnett McMillan lay on a pile of dead oak leaves in the shallow trench the brigade had dug around the base of the hill. The men of his company were resting on their muskets to both sides of him. A few slept, but most were watching the crest off to the east, quiet-faced. There, the fog was constantly aswirl, scattering off Stafford Heights, then closing in on them again. The same was true of the plain just below the trench, grottoes and rifts being dipped out of the gray bank by the breeze. But the town itself and the river had remained hidden from sight since dawn.

Now and again, the musket fire along the riverfront would get hot, and Garnett's men would raise up on their elbows, hoping to glimpse the three pontoon bridges General Cobb had said the Yankees were building across the Rappahannock. They never saw them, but the enemy batteries could be spotted by their flashes. After each musket volley, they arced shells into town, hoping to silence Barksdale's sharpshooters. Yellowish twinklings in the fog. The Federals were also slinging solid shot against the waterfront. Garnett couldn't see these, for the big iron balls didn't explode, but he could hear them crunching into wooden houses, knocking over chimneys. The Mississippians were shelled each time they fired at the bridge-builders. Yet, in the pause after each cannonade, they opened up again.

"Barksdale's boys never have a tittle of luck," a private said. He had an Ulster accent not unlike Garnett's father's—Billy Haddock, who was sprawling between his brother, Johnny, and Thomas Dooley. Strange, Garnett thought, that that accent had embarrassed him when he was younger. An immigrant father with odd words for obvious things. "Cursed, the lot of 'em."

"That's true," Dooley said, "and a poor brigade too. I hear they was ordered to pile up their equipment before goin' into it at Sharpsburg. Eight blankets, that was all there was of it."

"Eight blankets," Johnny Haddock repeated, commiserating.

Barksdale's Mississippians had gone on picket in town last night and now couldn't be withdrawn, with Yankee cannon pounding their rifle pits and hiding places, and the enemy's long-range guns covering the streets where they emerged from the fog onto the plain below Marye's Hill. Barksdale was trapped until night, while Cobb's Brigade watched helplessly in reserve.

Billy Haddock said, "More lashin's of artillery like that earlier—well, there won't be eight Mississippians left."

"Then we must pray for them," a voice said from the woods behind the trench. Cobb, checking on the line by horseback. His face was like stone.

The men said nothing.

Then the Yankee artillery started up a slow, plodding barrage. It went on and on. Spindles of smoke rose through the fog.

10:29 A.M.
Lacy House

"How much do you know about old Larry here, Father Corby?" Meagher asked. He was sitting on the bed with his left trouser leg rolled up over the abscessed knee, which had swollen to twice its normal size and turned an ugly purple.

Corby knew full well that Surgeon Reynolds was the leading Fenian in the Army of the Potomac, but decided to play it coy. "He comes from your hometown of Waterford—doesn't he, sir?"

"Prescient of you, Father," Meagher said, "for I was about to remark that a Waterford physician will send you home with your brain in a sling if you complain of a headache. He'll leave you in crutches after treating a bunion—"

"Careful," Reynolds growled, rattling among the metal tools in his kit.

"Look how he picks his instrument with such maniacal care."

At nine o'clock, the brigade had been halted by Hancock near the mansion. Dismounting, Meagher faltered on his bad leg and kept from collapsing to the ground only by grabbing a stirrup. He laughed it off, saying, "I have yet to walk into a battle, boys, and I'm not about to start now." But at long last Reynolds declared that a lancing was in order. Meagher insisted on walking under his own power and then on climbing upstairs to a small bedroom, where none of the other officers milling around the headquarters would see. Hancock, especially. Along the way, Corby learned from Sumner's son-in-law, Teall, that the crossing planned for early this morning had been put off. Enemy musket fire had decimated the engineers, and it'd proved impossible to depress the barrels of most of the Federal cannon on Stafford Heights enough to bring them to bear on the waterfront steeply below.

"Merciful God," Meagher said as Reynolds now knelt before him with something sharp-looking in hand. "What's that devilish-looking implement called, Larry?"

"Doesn't matter. I'm finally going to try to relieve the pressure of all that tainted blood and pus."

"*Try?*"

"Hold still before I put the priest on you."

"Oh, I always hold still, no matter what. Came within a hairbreadth of becoming a martyr, and I held still all the while."

Meagher smiled across the room at Corby. "A race has fallen on sad times when martyrdom's the highest thing to which its sons can aspire . . . don't you think, Father?"

"I have no idea," Corby said. "I'm from Detroit."

The general chuckled, then braced.

Corby didn't want to watch. He went through the open door and out into the corridor. It was lined with windows facing the Rappahannock. A pale sun kept breaking through, but the fog held fast to the river, and the half-completed bridge was invisible. Neither musket nor cannon fire broke the smoky calm of the moment. Two catalpa trees lay just beyond the glass, their cigarlike seedpods hanging limply off the bare branches. At the edge of the lawn, Father Ouellette was lecturing an artillery sergeant, probably telling him how to position his guns so they'd reach town. Small and wiry, frenetically energetic, the French-Canadian Jesuit had gone to war probably because his bishop had told him to.

"Father Corby . . . ?"

"Yes, Doctor?" He stepped back inside the room.

"Kindly bring me that bowl and towel. And there's a bottle of medicine in my bag."

"Yes, hurry with that medicine," Meagher said. He'd summoned Ouellette and Corby first thing this morning and not let them go since. His good cheer was spasmodic, punctuated by silences and distant looks.

"I find just a bottle of brandy, Doctor," Corby said. "Is your medicine somewhere else?

"No, that's it," Reynolds said, "best medicine in the world."

"Finally," Meagher said, "something out of Larry's mouth worth agreement." He accepted the bottle and a water glass from Corby, poured, then took a sip as Reynolds began gently probing the inflamed knee with his finger. "Father, have I ever told you how I lost my Munster accent?"

"He was riding in a London hack," the surgeon said, still probing. "The driver hit a bump in the street, and Thomas

Francis's accent fell out. A noblewoman was on a stroll and picked it up. Within the week she was transported to Van Diemen's Land. Twenty years' hard labor. Rule Britannia."

"Not quite," Meagher said, then took a bigger quaff. "I was at school in England—"

"Then I was close."

"Yes, Larry—close. It was Christmas . . ." Meagher paused as Reynolds pressed the instrument to his knee. There was a click as the surgeon touched off some sort of trigger, and then he quickly brought up the bowl to catch the trickle of effluent. The general had stiffened at the instant of penetration, but now went on as casually as before, ". . . and at Christmas Father Johnson, school of rhetoric, let us do theatricals. Ordinarily very gentle, very kind. But ears like sails . . ." Reynolds dabbed the fresh wound with the towel, then began probing for another place to stab. "He gave me the part of the Earl of Kent, *Lear,* but then took me aside and said, 'Meagher, that's a horrible brogue you have.' I tried to please him, of course, but the night of the full rehearsal I was still very much Munster—'Fare thee well, King; since thus thou wilt appear—!' "

" 'Freedom lives hence,' " Reynolds finished for him, " 'and banishment is here!' " Then he cut another opening in Meagher's knee.

The general took a long swallow. His gaze, watery and tremulous now, drifted out the east-facing window. Corby followed it, noticed a vast park of canvas-topped wagons and ambulances just beyond a row of trees. More ambulances than he'd ever seen in one place.

"Well," Meagher went on at last, "I no sooner got that out than Father Johnson whacked me on the back of the head with a big copy of the play and shouted, 'It'll never do, Meagher— that frightful brogue of yours will never do for Shakespeare!' " The general chuckled softly. "I was reduced in rank from earl to common soldier. On opening night, I wore a fool's cap instead of a helmet. And God help me, I cried to Cordelia in the grandest brogue I could muster, 'The British powers were marchin' thitherward!' "

Corby smiled.

"I vowed then and there never to lose my brogue, no matter what. Never would I sound like one of those mincing Dublin dandies . . ." Meagher's face tightened. "But a constant dripping wears away even the hardest stone. And when I eventually got home to Ireland—"

"You found that the driver had hit a bump in the street," Reynolds said, taking a bandage roll from his pocket. He began wrapping the knee.

"Finished, you barbarous old Fenian?" Meagher asked, setting the empty glass on the floor.

"For the time being." Almost imperceptibly, Reynolds jerked his head toward Corby.

"Oh relax, Larry," Meagher said, "he's an American priest. He won't excommunicate you for a little patriotic feeling. No doubt a dues-paying member of the Brotherhood himself."

Corby said, "Not quite, sir."

Meagher lowered his voice. "Larry presides—" He cut himself short at another long eruption of musket fire from across the river, then continued, "He presides over a secret meeting in his hospital tent the first Sunday of every month. Punch included, but bring your own pike and bombs."

Reynolds shook his head. "You're delirious. You should be in bed."

"We should all be in bed." Meagher winked at Corby. "The clergy excepted, of course."

The door flew open, and a breathless aide stood at the threshold. "It starts again, General. Hunt's going to make them pay for it." The chief of artillery. "There's room to watch on the upper porch."

Meagher let down his trouser leg to hide the bandage, then stood, balancing himself by resting a hand on Reynolds's shoulder. "Thank you, Lieutenant." He waited until the young man had gone down the hallway before testing his knee with his full weight. He pressed his lips together but managed to go through the door with only a trifling limp. "Boys, it starts again!" he said, mimicking his aide's excitement. Then his grin faded and his expression turned remote as he led Corby and Reynolds out onto the elevated porch.

"I really think you should sit inside a while," the surgeon recommended.

Meagher ignored him, lit a cigar.

The breeze had died. The fog mostly clung to the river, but still covered Fredericksburg over the rooftops. It left only the steeples and a few of the tallest chimneys visible. Movement drew Corby's eye to the upper bridge. Engineers were sprinting down it toward the near shore to escape another flurry of sharpshooter fire. Their dead were laid out in a row on the bank.

Voices drifted up from the porch below. One of them broke above the others, saying, "Let's get it over with."

Reynolds must have seen Corby's questioning look, for he whispered, "General Burnside."

The priest checked his pocket watch. Eleven o'clock. He'd lost count of all the barrages since five this morning. The order to fire went out to the batteries, and Corby felt the first thumps in the middle of his chest. Felt them before he heard them, he believed. The fuses of the shells could be seen streaking across the river, and then—above the mist and the vaulting spires— ragged little clouds burst into view.

Corby laid a hand on Meagher's forearm. He almost had to shout. "Are all the women and children gone, sir?"

"Oh yes, Father. Days ago."

Timber and bricks soared up out of some of the flashes.

Suddenly, a shell burst early, dimpling the river within yards of the crouching engineers. They shouted and waved their arms. The battery responsible ceased fire, and the cannoneers began loading solid shot.

Corby was tracing the flights of balls into town when he realized that houses and shops were materializing out of the fog. He saw the tumbling of a wall, shingles flying when a roof was stitched from side to side. A cupola somersaulted and crashed against the street below. He asked Meagher if the batteries knew where the sharpshooters were hiding. But it was no good. The general couldn't hear him. Smoke rolled off the batteries and over the porch. Nostrils stinging, Corby fumbled for his handkerchief. In between the suffocating gusts he could see signs of the growing destruction. Every wall was blackened by shell or pocked by shot. A red flame flickered up out of the hole in a roof. The entire town looked to be quaking, giving off dust. So many guns were now firing the porch seemed to lurch beneath his feet, making him feel queasy. He was afraid of being deafened, but was powerless to go inside. He had to see how long it went on. How long the crews could go on sponging, loading, and jerking lanyards. A column of black smoke rose through the shellbursts, fed by smaller strands, each a building engulfed by fire. This pall rose straight up for at least a thousand feet before its top found breeze and spread into the shape of an anvil.

Eighteen

◆

McMillan swept his field glasses over Fredericksburg. The fog was finally gone, but now a cowl of black smoke hid most of town. The enemy cannon were keeping up a rapid fire. He could see the massed batteries as a line of white gossamer rising and dipping in keeping with the lay of the Stafford Hills. Faintly, the shrieks of the shells and the crumps of their detonations came to him across the long, sloping plain.

"Sir," Captain Brewster said, "I believe they mean to burn the town down around Barksdale's ears."

"So do I, Walter," McMillan added, handing the glasses to him. "What's that in the middle of upper Hanover Street?"

Brewster studied the scene a moment, then said, "A burst caught three Mississippians out in the open."

McMillan had thought so.

The captain gestured with the glasses toward Hazel Run, tracing its winding course to where it met the Rappahannock at the lower edge of town. "Sir, I'm nobody to say, but it seems to me we could get a couple of companies down that way to town and give Barksdale a hand. What might General Cobb say to such a thing?"

McMillan didn't reply. And a moment later an odd sound cocked his head toward the left side of his own line. "What's that?"

Brewster listened briefly, brow wrinkled. "Cheering."

"On Telegraph Hill?"

"No, farther along, sir. The boys over on Marye's Hill are shouting for something." Brewster began to scan the plain just above town, then froze. "Ah, here we go . . ."

"What is it?"

"Don't know, Colonel . . ." A pause. "Two of our horsemen are riding up the old pike. One's flying a white flag from his carbine. Somebody's walking between them . . . some . . ." And then he paused. "My God, they're bringing out a woman."

"A *woman?*"

"Yes, with a baby at her breast."

"Lunacy. She should've gone when Lee ordered."

"Yes, sir," Brewster said. McMillan could tell that the young man was moved, but his eyes remained dry. To his credit. Walter Scott Brewster, born in New York of Scots parents but reared solidly by them in Charleston. He'd make a good senior officer, if the war went on. "But they don't like being run out, sir. These are first-rate people." Brewster gave back the glasses. "Aren't they though?"

"Aye," McMillan said, then continued his restless stroll behind the line.

Where possible, the men were keeping away from the trees to take full advantage of the sunshine that was finally pouring down on the heights. Despite the thumping of the enemy cannon, there was a sleepy, basking stillness to the hillside that made McMillan want to find a mound of sun-warmed leaves and burrow in. No sleep last night and probably none tonight. He prayed in every spare moment that his body wouldn't fail him. Upslope, Cobb was sitting before a fire ring filled with ashes, reading his Bible. McMillan decided not to bother him, but then the brigadier waved him over. "Robert," he asked, "why don't you lie down a while?"

"I may do that, sir. Any word?"

"Yes," Cobb said, expressionless. "Their bridge a mile below town is finished. They're coming across."

McMillan mulled this over, puzzled. Barksdale's brigade, plus some Floridians, was fighting tooth and nail to halt work on the two spans creeping across the Rappahannock toward town, while Jackson's entire corps had let Burnside's left come over with scarcely a fight. Maybe Lee meant only to delay the crossings, bloody the Union advance as much as he could before withdrawing every last man to the safety of these heights.

A courier rode up. Cobb snapped shut his Bible and stood. "Here!" he cried, and the man came over at a trot. He had a cut above his right eye, but it'd stopped bleeding. "Shrapnel?" Cobb asked.

"Yes, sir," the courier said, flashing a quick smile, "the stuff does make a trip to town lively." Then he turned dutiful. "General McLaws's compliments, sir. He asks you send one regiment down Deep Run with all haste to support Colonel Barksdale below town on the picket line."

Cobb hesitated a few seconds, his eyes on McMillan, then said, "Please tell the general it'll be my Sixteenth Georgia."

The courier rode off, and Cobb said, "Well, Robert—will you see to it the brigade does some stretching? No breaks in the line."

"At once, sir."

As the 16th Georgia streamed back from the trench and fell in for the march down to the river, McMillan found Sullivan napping in camp and awakened him with a nudge. Like most railroad laborers, he could lie down and sleep at once. "Go to each of the regimental commanders, Michael," he explained. "The Sixteenth has been sent down to support the picket line. General Cobb orders the rest of us to extend the line to cover the gap."

Sullivan repeated the message, dried spittle crackling in the corners of his mouth, then shambled off.

The 16th Georgia marched from camp in column of fours, the brigade sending them off with a cheer. The men hoisted their hats in reply. They reached Deep Run, but kept atop the right bank of the stream.

After a while, McMillan gravitated toward Brewster, who sat on a stump with an air of quiet dejection, watching Fredericksburg burn. "General Cobb has done what you suggested," he said to the captain, gesturing at the 16th Georgia, which now looked like a gray and butternut worm inching down the plain.

"Did he really, sir?"

Brewster looked so pleased McMillan found himself trapped by the fib.

Suddenly, sharp cracking sounds broke through the low thunder of the Union bombardment. Long-range rifled guns. McMillan brought the glasses up to his eyes just as the first shells fell on the 16th Georgia. The column disintegrated as the men broke ranks and leaped down into the brambly ravine. Several men were left prostrated on the bank. McMillan frowned. He was relieved that it wasn't his own regiment under fire down there. But then he realized something. Had Cobb looked across those dead coals and seen youth and vigor in Robert McMillan, the 24th and not the 16th would have been sent down to the river. His hand tried to find the source of the pain in his chest and rub it out of existence.

Brewster noticed. "Are you all right, sir?" he asked.

2:28 P.M.
Lacy House

The door to the master bedroom was open, and Meagher could see General Sumner slumped in a large armchair. His eyes were shut while he listened to Hancock, who was standing at the window, going on about something. For a moment Meagher thought that the old man had dozed off, but then he raised his hand and interrupted, "Are the pontoniers below us across or not?"

Hancock claimed not to know. "I've sent a courier to find out, sir . . ." His voice was drowned out by a twenty-pounder going off in the yard. The bass rumble made an empty wineglass skitter a few inches across the windowsill. ". . . he's not come back from Franklin yet."

Sumner's eyes opened to glazed slits. "Damn."

Then the batteries fell silent.

Turning from the window, Hancock noticed Meagher for the first time. "Tom," he said impatiently, "ride with me."

"Yes, that's it," Sumner said, sitting up, "take Meagher. He'll see if it can work. But it's all out of my hands, boys. Hunt and Burn have agreed."

Before Meagher could ask what the artillery chief and Burnside had cooked up, Hancock whisked past him, out into the narrow, sunny corridor. He said over his shoulder as he started down the stairs, "You hear that? Out of his hands. Birds of a feather, Old Bull and Pontius Pilate." Meagher followed as quickly as he could, his knee giving him flashes of white-hot agony. But he made sure to step jauntily off the porch, as Hancock was watching closely once again. "Leg seems better," the general said as they waited for the groom to bring around their horses.

"It is, sir." Meagher lied.

Some of Hancock's aides came running up, but he ordered them to stay at the house, adding that one of them was bound to get hit if he brought along a cavalcade. Then, swinging into the saddle, he said to Meagher, "We're going to cross infantry over in some boats. Should've been tried this morning in the fog."

"Are volunteers needed?"

"Got them. Hall's brigade."

"Hall," Meagher echoed flatly.

"Some problem with Norman?"

"No, no. Fine fellow. He was at Fort Sumter when it all started, wasn't he?"

"Right."

"Is that why he's getting the nod now?"

Hancock set off without answering, and Meagher had to dig in his spurs to catch up.

Hall's brigade was part of Oliver Howard's division, but Hancock—if persuaded—might still go to Sumner and ask that the Irish Brigade lead the assault across the river. Too precious an opportunity to lose. The eyes of the world—*Harper's Weekly*, the New York papers, and even the London *Times*—would be riveted on this crossing, while later actions, no matter how daring, might go unnoticed in the chaos of the greater battle.

"Look, Tom!" Hancock said, pointing.

Floating above the field behind the mansion were two immense balloons, straining against their tethers. A man could be seen in each of the wicker baskets hanging beneath the globes. Hancock grinned at Meagher's surprise. "We found a way to put all that goddamned hot air at headquarters to use."

"Are they out of range of the enemy's guns?" Meagher asked.

"Those poor fools in the baskets will be the first to find out." Hancock slowed his horse's gait, then both men reined up on the edge of the bluff. They were almost directly above the unfinished bridge. The upper neighborhoods of town spread smokily before them. Several houses were engulfed by flames. As the two men watched, one began to collapse in on itself, wall by wall. Below, at the foot of the plunging slope, were ten pontoon boats, their prows dipping into the stream.

Meagher's heart sank. Hall's brigade was concealed in a nearby ravine, ready to shove off. His own men were just over the brow of the hill, but it was too late. A signal gun near Lacy House pealed, and all the batteries opened up once again. Transfixed, Meagher watched the shells swarm over the river like a meteor shower. Black dots—solid shot—were added to the mix, and chimneys began tumbling, leaving fans of brick rubble in the gardens. One iron ball skipped up a street and out onto the frozen plain beyond. It almost reached the foot of Marye's Hill before burying itself like a porpoise diving into the waves.

Meagher heard something whir past his left ear. But he stayed in the saddle.

Hancock remarked, "I believe we're taking some fire, Tom."

"Yes, that may be, sir, but I don't think it's terribly accurate fire."

Hancock chuckled. They both dismounted and walked their horses back from the brink to the breastwork thrown up before a Parrott rifle. "This'll be something to write home about," Hancock said, taking his field glasses from his saddle valise.

"Yes, I'll write Catherine tonight." A moment later, he realized. Elizabeth. Catherine was long dead. But he'd been thinking of her again. Standing on the porch of Lacy House this morning in the fragile winter warmth, he'd remembered her bursting from their Tasmanian cottage to exclaim prettily at snow on the surrounding mountains. It'd been that rare to her. Snow. The eucalyptus trees looked as if they'd been dipped in sugar.

"Christ," Hancock said after some minutes, "I can't see a damned thing from here." On foot, he led Meagher out to the edge of the bluff again. They knelt in a patch of wet snow and, passing Hancock's glasses back and forth, watched the slow, methodical crumbling of the town. During one of Meagher's turns, he saw a house blown nearly to dust. Yet two men writhed out of the debris and sprinted down the street, dodging a second shell before ducking down a cellar door. He smiled at their luck, but then quietly sobered. That was it, he supposed, the reason for his mood of these past weeks. He had no luck left. The arithmetic of Antietam had finally sunk in. No officer survived three battles of that size. Somehow, Catherine had come back to ease his way. He didn't fear going, but he just had to make it count. The world had to take notice, London especially, or he had lived for nothing. *Ireland, Ireland.*

"Hall's crossing might have a chance," Hancock said over the barrage, "as long as he heads for that stretch . . ." He pointed at the shelving bank almost directly across from them. ". . . which I hope is Hunt's plan." Meagher saw that all the muzzle flashes along this section of the Confederate skirmish line were well above the shore. Being so high left them only a partial view of the river. "But he'll still take plenty of lead from the rest of their rifle pits."

"Is there any chance my boys can support Hall's?"

"No, goddammit!" But then Hancock smiled, stroking his mustaches. "Who does your thinking for you?"

"Sir?" Meagher felt heat rise to his face.

"Oh, don't take offense, for chrissake. That was meant more for me than you."

"I don't understand."

Hancock glanced away. The cannonade had begun to taper off. For the first time since it'd started, Meagher realized that the air was humming with sharpshooters' bullets. "It doesn't matter what we think," Hancock sighed. "When all's said and done, Tom, we'll do a fool's bidding."

The artillery ceased fire.

Hancock stood. "Here we go." A dozen blue figures, carrying oars, broke from the overgrown bank and ran for the boats. "Engineers," he explained. "They'll ferry Hall's people over." Rebel muskets starting popping. Two engineers stumbled and went facedown on the icy beach, stayed down. Three more fell as they approached the boats, spinning, clutching their wounds. Bullets pecked the shallows all around the survivors. They crouched among the hulls, heads low. Only one engineer managed to set his oars. An instant later, he was pitched dead over the side. The men hiding among the boats visibly weighed their chances, argued among themselves. It'd been a long day for these New Yorkers. Fifty of them had been killed so far.

Finally, they turned back and melted into the brush, losing one more man along the way.

"Shit," Hancock hissed, kneeling again. "Now what?"

Meagher said, "Well, we'll get across, sir—one way or another."

"So what," Hancock said angrily. "Lee knows that. The old fox is using this time to concentrate his forces on those damned heights over there. It's twilight, for godsake, and we should be up there—" He stabbed a finger toward the distant band of low hills. "—proving that Burn's a bloody genius!"

"*Huzzah!*" The cheer from below almost made Meagher bite his tongue.

Hall's infantry rushed out of the ravine, a mob streaming down to the boats, bayonets glinting. The sudden dash so excited Hancock he rose again and bawled, "Yes, Michigan! Do it your goddamned selves!" He then turned to Meagher, laughing. "Lord only knows if they can row and steer!" Meagher eased up, his knee almost locking. The 7th Michigan, he took it, was going to cross with or without the help of the engineers. Behind Hancock and himself, another regiment from Hall's brigade was stringing out along the terrace to cover the Michiganders. "Nineteenth Massachusetts," Hancock said, gesturing for Meagher to join him in getting out of their line of fire. They ran. After the first three strides, Meagher hobbled. Thankfully, Hancock didn't see.

The 19th Massachusetts started pouring a brisk masking fire across the river. Meagher could see nothing through the clouds of white smoke. Except Catherine, holding her hands out to him from those far heights.

3:51 P.M.
Stafford Heights

Tyrrell realized that something was happening when the artillerymen of a heavy battery on the crest above suddenly rose from the grass where they'd been lounging. He was afraid that they'd start firing their big guns again. His jaw muscles were sore from grinding his teeth together against the noise. Seven hours of it since the brigade had been halted here on the back slope of Stafford Heights. But the cannoneers didn't reach for their lanyards. Instead, standing half-crouched, they began gesturing toward a point on the river below them.

He glanced at the colors. They were cased, resting atop stacked muskets, and Hudson was napping nearby.

Tyrrell decided to follow the men who, in small groups, were hiking up the bluff. They were backlit by the sunset, blood and copper swirled together in dazzling bands above the south-western horizon. As he neared the crest, he heard muskets, hundreds of them, snapping. Something whizzed overhead, and he flopped down between two men in the trampled grass. It was wet with snowmelt, and he didn't want the moisture to work through his coat—but the view transfixed him. Both shores of the river were steeped in musket smoke, but the channel itself was visible through the fading light. There, a little flotilla was gliding across. One by one, men were dropping inside the pontoon boats. Others tumbled over the gunwales. It didn't seem real, men dying like that before his very eyes. He didn't want to see it, so he lifted his eyes to the town beyond. Black smoke was rising from several big fires. It had gusted over Stafford Heights earlier, the smoldery stink of a city and all its contents slowly melting, shriveling, drizzling into rank heaps.

The boats had reached the town shore. The men jumped out, gathered under the protection of an embankment and started forming a skirmish line. Tyrrell thought he saw gray figures dart across a street above, but it happened so quickly he was left wondering if he'd just imagined it.

"They're advancin'," the man on Tyrrell's left whispered.

The blue line crested the embankment, driving toward the first street paralleling the waterfront. He saw more men fall. But most kept moving, pausing only to fire and reload. Then their smoke enveloped them. Yet, on its fringes, he glimpsed something that made his breath catch in his throat—squads of enemy infantry hurrying down the boardwalks to reinforce their pickets.

"You see them Rebs?" another man lying in the grass asked. "By God, this is somethin'."

A second swarm of boats was crossing over when Tyrrell felt hoofbeats pass from the ground into his chest. Mulholland was a few yards below them, his horse prancing. The lieutenant colonel ordered the men of the 116th back to their bivouac area, but then rode up to the crest and lingered, watching the growing fight in town as the Pennsylvanians began trooping down the slope.

"We goin' into Fredericksburg, sir?" somebody asked.

Mulholland said, "Sooner or later."

"Tonight, sir?"

"Don't know."

7:01 P.M.
Camp Jeannie

Sullivan was enjoying his fire when the order came from McLaws's headquarters. It made him stand up in surprise.

He'd expected to fight on the wooded slopes of Howison's Hill. The brigade had occupied this part of the line for three weeks now, had dug the fortifications that could be dug in the icy ground. On picket, the men had scouted the plain the enemy would have to come up if they advanced here. The 24th Georgia had memorized every curve and swale along Hazel Run, every rocky or overgrown place behind which the enemy skirmishers might lie down to fire. The brigade had felt confident on Howison's Hill.

But that had changed a minute ago with a rider galloping in out of the night, whipping his mount with the ends of his reins. Cobb was to leave a single regiment, Cobb's Legion, to support the batteries on Howison's Hill and then, with the rest of the brigade, relieve Barksdale's men at the foot of Marye's Hill.

Immediately.

Sullivan hadn't known that the Mississippians were safely out of town. He asked McMillan, who was on his way to talk to the captains, and the colonel answered, "Yes, Michael— Longstreet's ordered Barksdale to withdraw . . ." His brigade was now coming back through the darkness to the sunken road. Sullivan was wondering where the 16th Georgia might be. With Barksdale, he supposed. But before he could ask, McMillan turned and added, "Tell Oliver I want a cooking detail to stay with him here in camp. They'll bring our rations to Marye's Heights. Use the weans."

"Yes, sir." Tully wouldn't care for that.

And he didn't. "Why?" the boy demanded, returning from Dooley's fire.

"Because the colonel said so," Sullivan said.

"But—"

"It's called an order, in case they didn't mention such things down in Clarkesville."

Tully's eyes had gone damp.

"For the love of Mary—count your blessin's. You could be with the Sixteenth right now, cut off maybe." Sullivan began rolling up his bedding. "The blue people are comin' across on three bridges, and there's no time to do anythin' but what we're told."

"I won't be seein' you again," the boy said with a chilling finality.

"Happy thought," Sullivan snapped. But then he added, "Of course you'll see me again. At breakfast tomorrow, when you bring me and Dooley and the Haddock brothers hoecakes."

But Tully was digging in his heels. "If I don't see you again, how'll I get to be a Fenian? Go with y'all to fight in Ireland?"

Sullivan tossed down his haversack, which he'd been stuffing with his few articles of spare clothing, and faced the boy. "Raise your right hand."

Tully did so, but snuffling under his breath.

Cobb's bugler was playing for the brigade to fall in, so Sullivan hurried. " 'I, Hugh Tully, in the presence of Almighty God, do solemnly swear allegiance to the Irish Republic, now virtually established, and I will do my very utmost, at every risk while life lasts, to defend its independence and integrity; and, finally, that I will yield *obedience* in all things, not contrary to the laws or morality, to the commands of my superior officers. So help me God.' Now repeat the last there."

"So help me God."

Sullivan kissed him on his pimply brow. "You are now a friend. Don't put too much water in the dough." Then he rushed to find Quartermaster Sergeant Oliver. Men were running everywhere. Little teepees of stacked arms were torn apart in the blink of an eye, canvas lean-tos struck. He found Oliver near the small wagon park, gave him the colonel's orders concerning Tully and the other boy of suspect age, whom the quartermaster sergeant had been wet-nursing. "And don't send 'em over with rations, Dionicius, what if the firin' gets hot."

"I'll send 'em over when the food's ready to go," Oliver said indifferently.

"Do it and I'll lep through you with a bayonet."

"The devil you say."

"Try me." Then Sullivan had to run again to catch up with the colonel, his canteen thunking against his hip. The brigade had started off through a wooded draw toward the military road Hood's men had hacked behind the length of the line. Cobb had already turned the head of the column onto it. The darkness was nearly total, except for the stars. They seemed to be hanging low from the cold. The rising of the moon was hours away. He glimpsed McMillan riding ahead. But then the officers had to dismount and lead their horses by the bridles—the crude road was studded with tree stumps. Sullivan lost sight of the colonel. The troops stumbled along as best they could, cursing each time toes were jammed or an ankle barked on a stump. The campfires on Telegraph Hill threw their light too high to be of

Cobb's Brigade Moves into Sunken Road, Evening, Dec. 11

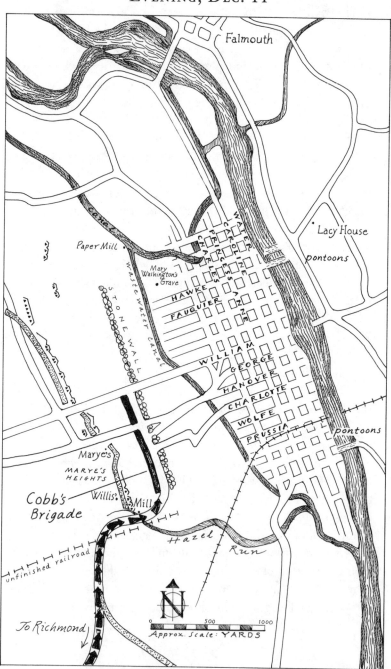

Falmouth

Lacy House

pontoons

Paper Mill

Mary Washington's Grave

WALL

CAROLINE

PRINCESS ANNE

CHARLES

SOPHIA

ELIZABETH

LIBERTY

HAWKE

FAUQUIER

Waste water Canal

STONEWALL

WILLIAM

GEORGE

HANOVER

CHARLOTTE

WOLFE

PRUSSIA

pontoons

Marye's

MARYE'S HEIGHTS

Cobb's Brigade

Willis. Mill

Hazel Run

unfinished railroad

To Richmond

N

0   500   1000

Approx. Scale: YARDS

any use down in the trees. Somebody ran up on Sullivan's heels and demanded with no hint of apology, "Who's that there?"

"Colonel *Mac*-Millan," Sullivan imitated.

Silence.

Then Sullivan laughed when the man began sputtering how sorry he was.

"Damn you—Sullivan, ain't it? Damn you to hell."

"Been ordered on holier authority than yours."

The column passed into a hollow that still reeked of cannon smoke. At nightfall, Alexander's artillery had opened on the Federal regiments pouring into town. The enemy's rifled batteries quickly answered, shells screeching across the valley and plunging willy-nilly into Fredericksburg Heights. Nothing had fallen close to Cobb's Brigade, and soon both sides decided to call it a day. As the column rounded the north slope of Telegraph Hill, a glow filtered through the branches of the pines. The fires in town. They seemed worse in the dark than they had earlier, entire blocks seemingly given up to the flames.

But good for Barksdale's men.

They'd survived all that, coming out only when Longstreet said and not a minute before. Now, if the 16th was safe too, Sullivan would rest easier. But not too easy. The whole Union army would cross tonight and attack tomorrow. They'd use the fog, if it set in again tonight. A mortal, tough fight in the morning. Must get the men up early. With dawn, however wan the light, blue sharpshooters and skirmishers would be popping away from behind every fence and house corner.

A provost guard was stationed where Hood's road met Telegraph Road. He waved the column north with his lantern, his breath misting in the candlelight. The man also had a warming fire, and Sullivan didn't realize how chilled he himself was until the regiment went past its intoxicating heat and his body leaned toward the flames, begging him to break ranks and rush over, hoard the warmth inside his thin jacket. No fires would be allowed along the sunken road, he was sure of it. Too close to town. And the pickets sent out tonight would have to brave both the cold and the Yankees, who'd try to creep as near as they could before dawn. They might even keep up a pesky musket fire all night.

"There's a pretty sight now," someone said.

Sullivan noticed the brass glints of massed cannon atop Marye's Heights. It was indeed.

"Michael?" McMillan's voice called out from ahead.

Sullivan ran ahead to him, no longer fearful of tripping over stumps. The road was muddy but smooth. "Sir?"

McMillan was badly winded. "You'll . . . so dark . . . where are . . . ?"

"Back in the saddle, sir. Your horse won't balk now." Sullivan helped him up, hearing the man's brittle joints creak.

"Thank you," McMillan said, sitting stooped. "I'm trying to remember—how long's this stretch of road?"

"About a thousand feet, sir." Sullivan paused, visualizing it in daylight. "No, less than that. Eight hundred feet, maybe."

"Is Marye's House situated behind the middle of it?"

"No. More to the left. And about forty feet in elevation above us."

Sullivan began to see troops lounging against the low shelf of dirt that had been heaped up against the inside of the stone wall. They smelled strongly of char and sweat. "What regiment is this?" McMillan asked, and when one of them drawled, "Eighteenth Mississippi," the Georgians reached out to clasp hands, congratulating Barksdale's men.

"Keep marching," McMillan said. But then he added, "God bless you, Mississippi."

Sullivan asked about the 16th Georgia, and a voice answered that it was already in bivouac somewhere behind the heights.

"Were they chewed up bad?"

"No, not bad."

Word came down the line for the column to halt, and then Captain Herring, Cobb's adjutant, could be heard calling in a fishmonger's singsong for the regimental commanders. McMillan rode ahead, and Sullivan squatted, hoping to get out of the slight breeze that was putting a knife's edge on the cold.

A Mississippian lit his pipe and, in the flaring of the match, Sullivan saw that he was wearing muddy carpet slippers. He must've caught the sergeant looking at his footwear, for his grimy, drawn face tightened around a wink before the darkness closed on him again. "Found 'em in a cellar," he said, a smile in his voice. "Figured nobody was usin' 'em if they was down there, so I he'pped myself."

"Just don't let Longstreet see 'em," Sullivan said. "I hear Old Pete's partial to slippers."

The Mississippian chuckled. But it quickly sputtered into coughing. "Smoky in town," he explained when he could. "And foggy too. Nothin' like round shot comin' down on your head outta fog."

"Sure," Sullivan said. "It ain't danger I mind. It's sudden danger."

Another chuckle. But weaker. "Well, they mean to come on," the Mississippian said with conviction.

"Press you, did they?"

"More'n we liked. We caught 'em in one crossfire. A whole platoon out in the open where two streets come together. Caught 'em bad. Kilt most every third man with just one volley. And then put the rest down pretty quick. They had 'emselves an officer, though. He stood in the middle of all them dead and said over his shoulder as cool as springwater, 'Second platoon—forward.' Those were hard men. And they finally pushed us back too."

The weight, Sullivan thought to himself again. The great weight of that blue army. "Were you up against a division?"

"No, just a brigade, I think." And then the Mississippian repeated, his weary stupefaction becoming evident for the first time: "They mean to come on, you know."

Rumor had it that Lee still didn't know what Burnside had in mind. A quick crossing downriver after a feint at town was still a possibility. But this Mississippian was saying that he hadn't come up against men just out to create a diversion.

McMillan rode back and quietly asked Sullivan to gather his captains for him on the slope behind the wall. The cold was making him small. It was shrinking everyone as it grew more biting by the minute. Setting out, Sullivan found Dooley stamping his feet on the hump between the ruts in the lane. "It's a night for a snug turf fire—what, Tommy?"

"I'd take a mound of the curly turf too," Dooley quipped.

Chuckling, Sullivan moved on. He summoned all the captains, then trailed them back to McMillan. The colonel explained that, as soon as Barksdale's brigade went into bivouac, the regiment was to take the center of the line along the wall, with Phillips's Legion on the left and the 18th Georgia on the right.

A bugle brought the Mississippians to their feet. Sullivan had to pull the man in the carpet slippers up. He said, "I was damn near frozed to the ground."

"I'd check for the seat of your trousers before the next review," Sullivan said.

But the man was too fatigued to recognize a joke.

The Mississippians formed a loose, ragged column of fours and, carrying their muskets at right shoulder, started up the slope past McMillan. The colonel doffed his hat. On the crown of the hill, the artillerymen stepped out in front of the guns to cheer the passing of Barksdale's brigade. The sound moved off into the woods with the Mississippians, and then faded.

Cobb trotted by, ordered the regiment shifted to the right slightly, and then moved on to see to the 18th.

The pickets went out, swaddled in their blankets. Sullivan swung his legs over the side of the stone wall, and sat watching the myriad Yankee fires in Stafford County. He was listening to the humming, the vibrant expectation hovering over this ground, when Dooley came up and knelt on the banked earth behind the wall. "Hear it too?" he asked, taking Sullivan aback.

"What?"

"That ungodly rumble. Somebody says it's their artillery trains comin' over the pontoon bridges."

The great, bloody weight. Sullivan slid his hands under the buttoned front of his jacket.

$\mathcal{N}$ineteen

◆

Meagher hoped to find Hancock at breakfast, but instead Sumner, his son and son-in-law were at the table in the dining room. To make matters worse, the threesome were obviously arguing over some family matter, for Sumner suddenly tossed down his toast and said to son Sam, "Then she didn't mean what she said, did she?" At that point Teall, the son-in-law, noticed Meagher out in the entry hall. The colonel cleared his throat to alert the old man, and a quick escape became impossible.

"Come in, come in," Sumner boomed. "Willie," he said to Teall, although a dozen chairs around the long table were vacant, "make room for Tom."

"Please," Teall said graciously, "do join us, sir."

And that was that. Meagher entered, walking as if on eggshells to keep from limping, and took a seat opposite Sumner. An orderly appeared at his elbow. He asked for tea.

"Nothing else?" Sumner said, picking up his toast again. "Eat something, man. Something substantial."

"No thank you, sir."

"What brings you to the madhouse this early?"

The mansion was unusually quiet. Meagher wondered if all

the other brigade commanders were taking greater pains than
he to avoid Sumner and especially Burnside, should he drop by
from Phillips House. "I was looking for General Hancock, sir."

"Haven't seen him this morning," Sumner said. "Where's
Win, boys?"

"Out and about," Sam Sumner said with a shrug.

The old man repeated, "Out and about."

Meagher stared through the window. The fog beyond was so
deep it seemed more like an abyss than a curtain. He'd gotten
up at three this morning, expecting the order to cross at any
time. It never came. He finished his toilet, dressed, and rode
through the murk down to the bluff, where his ears quickly told
him that the bridges were empty. As far as the captain of engineers at the bridgehead knew, only a brigade from 9th Corps
and Howard's division from 2d Corps were occupying town.
Meagher had then turned for Lacy House.

"Tom?" Sumner now asked, looking grandfatherly-worried.
"Is something wrong?"

"Wrong, sir . . . ?" Meagher sat up, tried to clear his head with
a gulp of strong tea. "Why, no." Of course something was
wrong—it was slipping away: the sense of acceptance, of in-
evitability, the state of grace he'd almost achieved yesterday
evening. With Catherine's help. And now pouring in to fill the
void was the same old restless confusion. The bitter aftertaste
of chances lost. Of battles turned into burlesques. "Our can-
nonades yesterday . . ." His voice trailed off as he reminded himself—mustn't appear insubordinate. A careless word might cost
the brigade its rightful place in the attack, if one was yet planned.
But still, the whole of the grand division should have crossed last
night and the assault already been under way by this hour. "Sir,
I was wondering . . . all that shellfire for—"

"Yes," Sumner interrupted, "poor Burn regretted having to
punish the town like that. Didn't he, Sam?"

"Quite, Father," his son said, wiping his neat little mustaches
with his napkin.

Then Meagher saw an innocent-sounding way to find out what had gone wrong. "Sir, what time did the crossings stop?"

"Oh . . . when was it, Willie? Eight or nine?"

"Thereabouts, sir."

"Eight or nine," Sumner said conclusively to Meagher, as if things discussed between family members were inaudible to guests. A peculiar Americanism. "Burn was worried about crowding large columns into the city under darkness. The muddle of it all. And who knows? Lee might've been tempted to counterattack." The old man used his fork to stab a slab of ham off the platter. For an instant, the cross-section of pink flesh and bone reminded Meagher of an amputation he'd foolishly witnessed at Antietam. More and more, these awful pictures sprang to mind. "Damned smart of him, really."

"Of whom, sir?" Meagher asked, coming back to the conversation.

Sumner swallowed his mouthful before going on. "Burn, of course. Keeping Lee at a loss over our intentions. Putting across little more than a division can be interpreted only one way—yesterday's effort up here was a diversion."

"Was it, sir?"

Sumner smiled as he chewed, then gestured with his fork for his son to eat more ham. "Come on, Sammy—getting cold."

Meagher wanted to groan. The advance was grinding so fitfully toward that distant crest he was now sure Burnside would call it quits and take the army back into winter quarters. The notion that this operation had any hope of surprise was ludicrous. Winter inactivity. He feared it, how low his spirits might sink before the trees budded and the army moved again. This was becoming Tasmania all over.

"I just don't know, Tom," Sumner abruptly said. "It's a clever diversion, if that's what Burn wants. But I'm awaiting orders, just like everybody else."

"Looks like some of Howard's men have exceeded theirs," Teall said drolly.

"How's that?" Sam asked.

"Reports of looting in town last night."

"Oh, don't believe a word of it," Sumner said. "Oliver Howard wouldn't allow that. He'd take a looter by the scruff and give him a thrashing he'd never forget."

"Sir, General Howard has but one arm," Teall said.

Sumner regarded his son-in-law a moment, then reached over, guffawing, and slapped his knee. "Good wheeze, Willie."

Meagher wanted to get up and leave. But where to go? He knew that he'd feel even more agitated in his own bivouac, fog-bound, cut off from news. Burnside simply had to do something today. He stared out the window again. Catherine had detested fog. He wondered how she felt, now, when it sifted in off the Celtic Sea, pressed coolly against the grass covering her grave. He threw off the thought. "Sir," he then asked Sumner, again trying to find out if the crossing into town was only a diversion, "if I might inquire about something . . . it may be none of my business . . ." The old man motioned with his knife for him to go on. "Was General Franklin also ordered to keep most of his troops on this side of the river?" If not, the main action would be down there, and the Irish Brigade, Sumner's entire Right Grand Division, would do nothing more than demonstrate in front of Longstreet.

"He was, Tom," Sumner said, then held out his hand to some-one who'd come into the dining room behind Meagher. He saw that it was one of Burnside's aides, who gave the old man a mes-sage. Sumner scanned it, then, smiling, passed the slip of paper to Meagher.

In Burnside's own hand. The kind of message one had come to expect from him, telling Sumner to move as he thought best.

Meagher looked to the old man, questioningly.

"What the devil, boys," he said, dropping his napkin onto his plate. "Let's get over into Fredericksburg. But I'm sure Lee won't stand up to us. Burn's got to figure out some way to cut off his retreat." Sumner paused, and Meagher had to hide his

212 ◆ Kirk Mitchell

astonishment at the notion that the enemy would withdraw from their fortified heights. "Tom, do you mind sending a rider to Washington House to find out where the hell Win is?" Hancock's headquarters.

"Not at all, sir," Meagher said, already rising. He walked carefully out, but once in the entry hall he broke into a lumbering run, grabbing his hat, coat, and gloves as he rushed past the table there. If Sumner crossed most of his grand division into town, Burnside might find his hand forced. He'd have to attack.

Outside, Meagher shouted for his horse, then put his spurs to the animal and charged blindly into the fog.

8:30 A.M.
69th New York

Donovan, waiting sleepily on horseback, watched the blue columns of four crossing the two upper bridges, vanishing mid-river into the mist. Once no longer raked by enemy sharp-shooter fire yesterday evening, the engineers had quickly finished the first span and then added a second alongside it. The brigade was waiting to use the lower of these.

A light rain before dawn had left the men in damp uniforms, but they seemed cheerful enough. A band—the 9th New York's, Brooklyn's own—was thumping out national airs just back from the edge of the bluff. The music sounded tinny in the dank stillness, but the men were tapping their brogans to the beat, chatting and laughing among themselves. How quickly they recovered from gloom. Just yesterday morning, they'd been surly and morose when ordered to abandon the huts they had expected to while away the winter in. Some had even razed their little dwellings to the ground. But now they joked and gossiped.

Colonel Nugent rode past, saying, "Double-quick down the slope, John. Fog or no fog, their gunners have the range."

"Yes, sir."

The band of the 9th New York struck up "The Star Spangled Banner," and the men came to attention of their own accord. Donovan drew his sword, steel blade rasping, and saluted the colors. Everything would turn out well. He now felt surer of that. Last night, a rumor had circulated through the wet, fireless bivouac. At last, the Union was going to throw its full might against the Confederacy in a single, orchestrated blow. General Banks and his army out of Fortress Monroe would march on Richmond through Petersburg. General Sigel had already forded the Rappahannock upstream of Fredericksburg and, along with Franklin's Left Grand Division below town, would cut off Lee's skedaddle—after Bull Sumner bloodied his nose on Marye's Heights.

The band paused after the anthem, and through the fog came faint strains of music in answer. It took Donovan a moment to realize that it was "The Bonnie Blue Flag."

A man asked in surprise, "What're the Rebellers playin' 'The Irish Jauntin' Car' at us for?"

"Shut your stupid gob," another voice said. "Don't you know they took it for a patriotic tune?"

"Do they have no songs of their own?"

" 'Dixie,' " somebody else suggested.

"Bah, that was written by a Northern fella."

"The hell you say. It's an ol' niggur song."

Finally, the order came. Donovan repeated it—attention, shoulder arms, right face . . . forward, march. The men hurrahed, and the brigade was off. As soon as the 69th, the leading regiment, reached the open slope, Nugent shouted, "Doublequick!," and from there it was a sprint down to the bridgehead, bayonets rattling in their scabbards, shoes beating the mud. The 9th New York's band must have noticed the 28th Massachusetts' green flag in the middle of the column, for it broke out with "Garry Owen." Plunging down the bank, Donovan's horse braced its front legs to keep from sliding. "Easy, boy." He could see the gray waters getting closer. He remembered the dead engineers floating away on them. Where were they now? Out to sea?

Ahead, all the officers were dismounting as soon as they'd gone a few yards onto the bridge. The rocking and pitching of the span. Donovan decided to climb out of the saddle early. He was surprised to see two civilians standing at the bridgehead, lank men in dark suits and derbies, grins like butterflies pinned to a board. They were thrusting cards into the hands of the running men. Donovan took one, read it, then pulled his balking horse along by the rein. A moment later, he laughed.

"Bloodsuckin' spawn!" a private cried.

"Into the drink with 'em, boys!"

The captains of the other companies had to keep their men from going back and tossing the civilians into the Rappahannock. But Donovan's men just grinned as he laughed helplessly, almost deliriously. He'd never read anything as funny. They were embalmers, and their card guaranteed prompt delivery "as fresh as a nut" to loved ones anywhere in the Union. "Fresh as a nut," Donovan repeated, his laughter giving him the hiccups.

He'd save the card for Jimmy McGee.

9:55 A.M.
The Sunken Road

McMillan was awakened by the ping of a bullet against the face of the fieldstone wall. It'd come so close he could smell the rock dust from the impact. He started to rise for a look, but a hand held him down. "Not so hasty, sir," Sullivan said, "there's a Yank sharpshooter in a garden down there. Company K's havin' a go at him, but it'll take a bit of patience, I think. He's bold."

McMillan's eyes began watering from the strong sunlight. The fog had been warmed off, then. He'd catnapped, even though Garnett was down there with his company, trying to slow the push of enemy skirmishers up from town as long as possible. McMillan shook his head in shame, although he hadn't slept a wink last night. The present was losing its sharpness, its immediacy. It seemed a momentary blur between past and future. The day was turning warm and cloudless. A good winter's morning for riding to church in the open carriage with his family, all his children, even Emma and James. Clarkesville Methodist. The white building glided into view through the oaks. He strolled inside with Ruth Ann on his arm. The pews and woodwork had been left their natural color, so how would a new stained glass window for Emma appear against these plain touches?

No time to think about that.

McMillan rolled on his back and peered down the line. A few of his men had found some precious spades and were throwing more dirt over the wall. The twin wagon ruts along the road had become a single broad furrow, thanks to this digging. Longstreet wanted the work on the field fortifications to continue until the very moment the blue lines appeared on the plain below, even though in most places the earth was frozen a foot deep. The troops lying in support on the heights were having a harder time yet, chopping more and more rifle pits out of the ground with axes and shoveling the soil with tin plates.

"Here, sir." Incredibly, Sullivan once again was handing him a cup of coffee, this time served in china.

"How'd you ever—?"

"General Cobb's compliments, sir. He sent Jesse over from headquarters with it a while ago, pipin' hot." Sullivan looked apologetic. "Didn't want to wake you after such a wretched night."

Unbelievably wretched. One picket in the division had frozen to death. "Thank you, Michael," McMillan said. The coffee was tepid but refreshing.

Cobb had made his headquarters in a small frame house along

the wall. It belonged to a Mrs. Stevens. Sullivan had helped her draw water the night the brigade had arrived. Having refused to leave, she waited on Cobb's staff hand and foot, vowed to nurse the wounded when the time came.

The coffee was gone all too soon. McMillan turned the china cup in his hand. Reminded him of home, of Ruth Ann. She'd be sewing in the morning room at this hour.

A spattering of musket fire, quick and intense, was followed by a telling silence. "Well, sir," Sullivan said, inching on his belly across the soggy embankment to the stone lip, "let's see if it's safe for a gander." He peeked over.

A minute passed, and no more bullets bounced off the wall.

McMillan carefully set down the cup and crept up beside Sullivan. He was struck by the clarity of the scene. A few houses were languidly smoldering in town, but the big fires had burned themselves out. Fredericksburg almost looked normal from this side, facing away from the enemy batteries. Then something confounded his tired gaze. Stafford Heights seemed to be covered with a crawling, ripply blue, which made absolutely no sense to him until he picked out the flags and the spangles off the bayonets. "God help us, Michael," he said, "that's all infantry, isn't it?"

"It is," Sullivan said quietly.

And there was more of it in the countryside beyond, a midnight blue flood spilling down between the Falmouth Hills, pooling on the river's far shore behind the bridgeheads. Artillery, too, was on the move, light batteries being pulled down the banks at madcap speeds, guns bouncing and horses rearing. Trains of black-topped ordnance and white-topped supply wagons were winding along the roads like striped snakes.

McMillan fumbled in his coat pocket for his field glasses.

More men were waiting in the ravines to cross. Men whichever way he swept the binoculars. More men than he'd ever seen in one view. "How long since the fog lifted, Michael?"

"Just minutes, sir."

As if answering McMillan's curiosity, the long-range guns behind him on the heights opened up. The sparking fuses were lost in the sunshine, but he could trace the thin smoke trails of the shells as they dipped over the church steeples and exploded along the waterfront.

"That'll slow 'em," Sullivan said.

But only slow them, McMillan thought to himself. Ammunition. Did Alexander's batteries have enough to stop a host that vast? He didn't believe so. Not if Burnside's brigades kept swarming up the plain like locusts.

"Oh no."

"Michael . . . ?"

The sergeant pointed. "Poor Mary Washington's monument, sir—they went and blew it down."

"Colonel," Captain Brewster said from behind.

McMillan turned. The man was stooping, his knees and the front of his coat caked with mud. "Yes, Walter?"

"We have some prisoners. Brought in by our scouts."

"When?"

"Just now. They came back by way of Hazel Run. Because of the sharpshooters."

"Let me see." Then, keeping his head down, McMillan followed Brewster along the sunken road. The sun felt good on his chest, but the muscles were still tight and aching from the night's cold. Some of the men were eating roasted beets. Pilfered from a local garden, no doubt. Must look into it, if there was time.

Brewster said offhandedly, "We tried to find out where their point of attack's being developed."

"Officers among them?"

"No, sir—just a sergeant."

"I'm sure they admitted nothing," McMillan said, "and we shouldn't unduly press them if they wish to keep faith."

"They said they knew nothing, sir. Nobody down there knows what Burnside means to do."

"Whose division?"

"Howard's. Second Corps."

They rounded a slight bend in the road, and there the prisoners squatted in a row. McMillan had expected a handful, not fifteen. Some were without their caps. One was missing a boot. Two were slightly wounded. But they looked well fed, even well groomed. Disregarding their blue overcoats, he could imagine them to be friends of Rob's or Garnett's before the war, filling the parlor with bright talk, munching on Ruth Ann's ginger cakes.

A bullet whizzed several feet overhead, thudded into the hillside.

McMillan knelt, then said to Brewster, quietly so as not to seem to gloat before the prisoners, "Tell our boys they did well."

"Sir—" A blue-coated sergeant started to rise, but one of the guards told him to stay down for his own good.

"Your sharpshooters ain't as sharp as they fancy," the Georgian added.

"Sir," the sergeant went on, his face haggard, "we're not sharpshooters. I'll admit we got a company of 'em in our brigade. But we're just infantry . . . like you."

"Why are you telling me this?" McMillan asked.

"Well . . ." The man dropped his eyes. ". . . we hear you hang captured sharpshooters."

McMillan said nothing for a moment, then: "What state are you men from?"

"Minnesota mostly, sir," the sergeant said, hugging himself in his arms. He wore a red flannel shirt under his blouse.

Minnesota. Prairie and wild Indians. McMillan said over the continuing cannon fire, "That's a long way from here."

The sergeant kept looking down between his boots. "Yes, sir—I reckon it is."

"You've taken great pains to invade us." The rest of the prisoners began avoiding McMillan's glare. All except one boy who looked quietly back at him, a private with spectacles and hair so blond it was almost white. He was sitting with his back to the hill, a small book open in his lap. "Well," McMillan went on, "we're all Christians in the Twenty-fourth Georgia. We don't hang our prisoners, even if they've tried to murder us from hiding. . . ." He paused, feeling his temper flare. He wanted them to understand that they'd invaded his country, that God will not wink at it—just as He'd never countenance Georgians marching into Minnesota, shelling its towns. But something in the blond private's face made McMillan's anger shrink. "You'll be taken to the rear shortly," he finally said. "May Providence see you all safely united with your families again. God bless you."

"Thank you, sir," the sergeant muttered.

McMillan turned to Brewster and ordered the prisoners rested a few minutes more, then given over to the provost guard. He started toward the towheaded private, to have a word with him. But he stopped halfway across the road, hesitated. This boy could have killed Garnett. Perhaps he or another of his company already had, and McMillan had yet to hear of his son's death on the picket line. Yet this was the near impossibility Jesus demanded of his flock. Loving one's enemy. He made himself go on and sit beside the soldier. "What are you reading, son?" The private flashed the cover. McMillan had seen one before, a small Bible given to Yankee soldiers by some Christian organization. Text so tiny it was fit only for young eyes. "And which book is giving you comfort this morning?"

"Job, sir." A German accent and a steady, honest gaze.

"Yes, I believe I too would read Job in your circumstances. But if all goes well, you'll be home soon enough, your trials behind you."

The private nodded. A big gun thundered atop the ridge, and he flinched.

"What did you do before the war?" McMillan asked.

"I was a divinity student."

"Which . . ." Another cannon roared. ". . . which denomination?"

"Lutheran."

McMillan hadn't known many Lutherans. Northeastern Georgia had a number of German immigrants, but they'd kept to themselves. "I myself am a Methodist." The private took this in without comment, and the battery smoke rolled down over them. Then McMillan's curiosity got the better of him. "Why did you choose to fight?"

The boy thought a moment, using his gunpowder-stained forefinger as a bookmark. "I am new to this country," he said at last. "I could not stay home in good conscience."

At first, McMillan didn't think much of his answer. Then it struck him—he'd said much the same thing to Ruth Ann. He too had felt compelled to fight, if only because he was an immigrant. Staying in Georgia, reaping the bounty of his adopted country while the native sons of Habersham County fought and bled would've been unconscionable. He stood. "When paroled, I hope you'll go back to your studies."

The boy nodded again.

McMillan started back up the road. The smoke from the batteries came and went, giving him glimpses of the plain below. He was just above the two-story brick house and its outbuilding. The western boundary of this estate was marked by a high wooden fence. The artillerymen had torn away most of the boards to make platforms for their gun carriages on the muddy earth, and only the rails and posts remained along much of the border. Yet, it might be a good idea to leave the remaining sections standing. To break up the alignments of the onrushing Federal lines.

A long scream came at him out of the sky. He was fighting

Irish Brigade River Crossing
Morning, Dec. 12

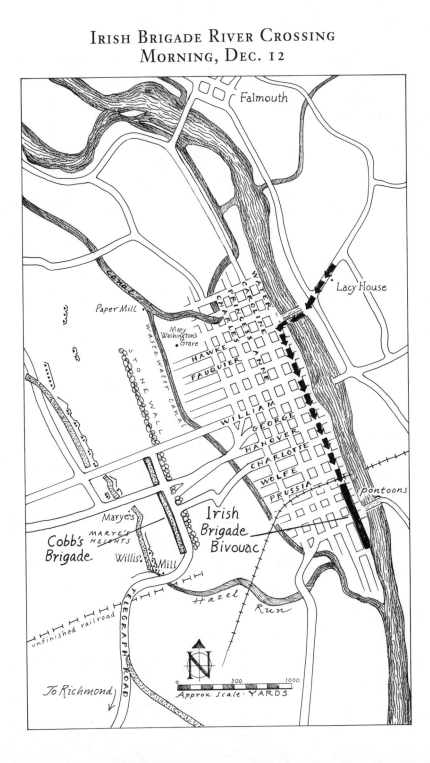

Falmouth

Lacy House

Paper Mill

CANAL

WATER

CAROLINE

PRINCESS ANNE

Mary
Washington's
Grave

Waste Water Canal

STONE WALL

HAWKE

FAUQUIER

WILLIAM

GEORGE

HANOVER

CHARLOTTE

WOLFE

PRUSSIA

Pontoons

Marye's

Cobb's
Brigade

MARYE'S
HEIGHTS

Willis
Mill

Irish
Brigade
Bivouac

Hazel   Run

unfinished railroad

TELEGRAPH ROAD

To Richmond

N

0   500   1000
Approx. Scale: YARDS

the urge to cringe when the shell struck a plowed field below and sent up a fountain of clods. The men were closely watching him. "I'll have no stealing from the gardens in the neighborhood," he said. Beets began disappearing. "God will never give victory to an army of thieves."

$\mathcal{T}$wenty

◆

12:15 P.M.
116th Pennsylvania
Fredericksburg

Tyrrell was first to see it as the regiment stood on the wharf in town, awaiting orders. His mistake, he quickly realized, was to point out the shadow in the green shallows a few yards off the bank. A sunken barge. It meant nothing to him, just a derelict like many he'd seen rotting in the Delaware at home. But a man who'd lived in the South before the war said that it was the kind of craft that hauled tobacco down to the tidewater ports. At that moment, a big sodden leaf floated lazily to the surface.

"Don't," Tyrrell warned.

But immediately, a half dozen tobacco-starved men chucked off their overcoats and waded out through icy water up to their waists. They were soon standing on the barge's deck, immersed to the knees, fishing bundles of leaves out of the hatches.

"Make it quick," Tyrrell said, keeping an eye out for officers. None was in sight. They'd gone inside houses along the riverfront after waiting to no avail for a rider from Hancock to show up with orders. Three hours ago now, the brigade had come over a wobbly bridge, passed down the west bank and crossed the railroad tracks into the lower city. Here, Meagher had halted the column in ankle-deep mud like porridge. Tyrrell was surprised to see that few of the streets in the aristocratic old town were cobbled. Hudson said that Southerners were lazy and backward; slaves doing all the work for generations had made them that way. The brigade stood waiting another ten minutes, then Meagher had the men stack arms and fall out, leaving a long row of muskets along the steamboat wharf. Still no word from division about what to do. Even some of the veteran New Yorkers got fidgety, having expected to go right into line of battle.

"Another barge!" one of the men cried, diving headlong for it. He then broke the surface like a whale, sputtering for air.

Tyrrell called out, "You'll never get dry now!"

"Oh Sergeant," a middle-aged private said, holding his empty pipe in his hand, "we can burn the whole damn town to dry our clothes."

"No, we can't."

"Why not? It's a cruel folk who'd sink all this just to deprive us of a little smoke."

Some of the men were coming ashore again, their blouses bulging with tobacco. "Break out your rubber blankets before you get camp fever," Tyrrell said, remembering Davey Major. "You won't think much of a little smoke if you wind up dyin' for it."

One man, dripping, smirked. "Don't indulge, d'you?"

Tyrrell was about to answer when Hudson grabbed his arm and said, "You gotta see these ones, Will." A strange look in his eyes, soft and sticky.

"Already seen," Tyrrell said, having no wish to gawk over another shapeless chunk of flesh and bone, some poor Johnny mangled by a shell.

"You seen nothin' like these," Hudson insisted.

"We should stay near the colors."

"The rest of the guard's doin' fine. And we won't go far. *Please*, Will."

Tyrrell realized that the men were staring at him, faintly amused. Somehow, his grit was being questioned. He saw no way out but to go. "All right," he said, then followed Hudson up a rocky lane to the street that ran along the waterfront.

"It's somethin' you won't forget," Hudson promised.

That was what Tyrrell dreaded most, knowing that these sights would stay with him forever.

They went past a big house with an entire wall sheared off by an explosion. Troops of another brigade—Zook's, Tyrrell believed—could be seen on the next street up, building small coffee fires. He said, "Let's be stayin' in our own brigade area."

"We will. Ain't far."

They slowed to pick their way over a mound of brick that had been a chimney, then began elbowing through the men of the 69th. The New Yorkers were milling about with their hands in their trouser pockets, examining household things that had been dragged out into the street by Howard's troops. Second Division had made a night of it—oil paintings slashed with bayonets, furniture and mirrors hurled from upper-story windows, mattresses ripped open. Broken crockery everywhere. Feathers were drifting along like snow. A dog lay in a pile of them, dead from a gaping wound that looked as if a sharp-toothed beast had taken a bite out of its back.

"That's what solid shot does," Hudson said convincingly. Turning toward the Rappahannock again, he led Tyrrell between two houses. They climbed over a shattered trellis, the thorns of the creeping rose clawing at their trousers. Finally, the corporal whispered, "This here's it." A gate was hanging askew on the lower hinge, and he wrenched it aside before gesturing for Tyrrell to go first.

He stepped inside the small garden.

It was in shadow this time of year and held last night's cold. A foot of snow was still banked against the house. The far border of the kitchen garden was set by a chest-high board fence, whitewashed, splintered in several places by bullets. Lying among some frost-blackened bean vines at the foot of the boards were three men. They were dressed in odds and ends of uniforms, most of the articles a dirty, yellowish gray. For an instant, Tyrrell thought that Hudson had stumbled on some Rebel pickets so exhausted they couldn't be roused. He'd heard of such things, of men collapsing after several sleepless nights, awakening to find themselves prisoners.

Stepping closer, Tyrrell hunted for wounds, but saw none. No blood either. "What got 'em?" he asked in dismay. He was sure that the Rebels were dead but had an eerie feeling that they were only sleeping and might spring for their muskets at any second.

Hudson hesitated, then went ahead and straddled one of the pickets, turned him over. He immediately backed away in shock. The Rebel was frozen solid. Wide-eyed, he peered up at Hudson, his open palms seemingly pushing against the sky. Tyrrell was struck by the peace in the boyishly handsome face. He'd never seen such flawless male beauty, except in statues, and that made him wonder if the effect was some trick of the cold. His fingers shaking, Hudson pointed at the bullet wound right over the heart. Death so swift the Rebel had scarcely bled a drop.

"How'd you find 'em?" Tyrrell finally asked.

"I don't know. Just lookin' round."

"You weren't lootin', were you?"

"Hell no, Will." But then, his eyes turning shifty, Hudson added, " 'Sides, it wouldn't be lootin'. We got the right, I hear."

"Who says?"

"One of Howard's men. We fought for this town street by street. So it's ours now by right of conquest. 'Sides, the way them whores in Warrenton treated us, I figure we ought pick ol' Virginny as clean as a bone."

Tyrrell said, "This ain't Warrenton."

"Jesus, Will—what's a couple trinkets compared to what these people done? Why, they stole half the goddamn Union." But then Hudson glanced back at the bodies and changed the subject. "They sure don't look like I thought they would." Bolder suddenly, he rolled another corpse onto its back. This boy was also fine-featured. Another shot to the heart. Again, virtually no blood. He was smiling, which made Tyrrell think of Annie for some reason. He didn't know why. The dead smile was nothing like hers. But it filled his mind with her face, her smell, her voice. He didn't like death and Annie all mixed up inside his head. "Let's go."

"Why?"

"What if the Johnnies came on right now? And got our colors?"

"There's a whole picket line 'cross town 'tween us'n them." Hudson went over to the last body, swaggering now, and flung it over. Once again, a shot to the upper breast. "One damn hunky rifleman got these Johnnies," he said, wiping his hands on the seat of his trousers. "I bet it was one of Berdan's sharp-shooters—don't you, Will?"

"I guess." Tyrrell peered over the fence. This is what the three Rebels had last seen: the middle pontoon bridge, the river purling past, gray-green under the winter sun. Ninth Corps was crossing it now. He shut his eyes, trying to see how much of the image survived the sudden black. But it faded after only a few moments.

"Where you suppose these Rebs were from?" Hudson asked.

"Mississippi," Tyrrell said. "That's what Mulholland said. We captured some of 'em yesterday evenin'." He had little idea what Mississippi was like. Hot, he supposed. Bugs and snakes. Cotton.

A shell thumped on the other side of town, and Tyrrell could hear bricks tumbling. The enemy batteries were blasting away at the crowded bridges again, but falling short of the river.

Hudson began prodding one of the corpses with a sharp stick off the trellis.

"Don't do that," Tyrrell snapped.

"Why not, Will? He don't feel nothin'."

"How d'you know?"

Hudson started to laugh, a grim and unhappy laugh, but then cut it short with a sucking sound as if he'd nicked himself shaving. "I'm gonna get drunk, Will," he said fiercely. "I'm gonna find me some tanglefoot and get blind."

3:17 P.M.
Colors Detail
On the Pike from Washington

The omnibus driver flicked his lines one last time, then gave up. The wheels were stuck fast. The pike had been a river of mud ever since Alexandria, but this stretch seemed bottomless. Any moment, McGee expected to see the team of horses sink down to the tips of their ears. He and the members of the brigade's executive committee had been met at the train station by Quartermaster Captain Martin, who'd been sent to Washington to buy food and drink for the banquet to receive the new flags. He'd hired this wagon, and McGee and the three Manhattanites had squeezed in among the crates for the long ride south.

"That's it, gentlemen," the driver now said, tying off his lines, "we're here till the night's freeze hardens up the road . . ." He then explained that the hamlet of Woodbridge was just around the next bend. There, the men might find something to eat, a warm woodstove.

"What do you say, Marty?" McGee asked.

Martin was a jovial man but vigilant when it came to the brigade's supplies. Every tin and bottle on his manifest would arrive in Fredericksburg unopened. "I'll stay and keep an eye on the goods. The flags too."

"Very well." McGee turned to the committeemen. "Gentlemen . . . ?" They were nabobs with large bellies and had no interest in exercise, so McGee offered to bring something back for them, if possible. He jumped down out of the back of the omnibus, and the mud immediately came over the tops of his boots.

"It's them ordnance trains what done it," the driver grumbled to his back. "That and this little thaw these past days. But somethin' big's happenin'."

McGee agreed as he set off down the road. He'd seen the signs himself. Train schedules in disarray all over the Mid-Atlantic states—he'd left New York Wednesday evening and was still traveling two days later. The roads had been so heavily trampled by supply wagons they were impassable. It was clear: Burnside was moving at long last. And McGee was half-sick with worry. The brigade had never gone into a fight without its green flags, and now they were miles behind the lines, furled and cased beneath the bench of an omnibus that was going nowhere.

He turned, looked back to see how far he'd gone. Only a few hundred feet. Martin waved. McGee doffed his hat, then slogged on. He wondered about the thing that was drawing him back to the brigade. It mystified him, this urgency to rejoin it. He'd even felt it at home, surrounded by those he loved most in the world. It had put a gulf between his wife and himself, clouded his joy as he held his children. His brother Lawrence, a sea captain, must have known something like it. He'd been drawn back to the ocean time and again until at last he was sucked down into its depths.

"A horse," McGee suddenly said out loud. He'd find one and go on alone with the flags.

He came to the relay station. There were a few exhausted-looking, mud-coated mounts on the horse-line, but the sergeant in charge refused to loan out any of them. "Sorry, Cap—riders changin' horses here is either comin' or goin' from Pennsylvania Avenue. So you can take it up with Mr. Lincoln."

One more sign.

Frowning, McGee turned for a nearby shed. Inside, a fire was roaring. The farrier barely had room in which to swing his hammer against the horseshoe he was shaping—for all the stranded officers hugging the billowed flames. McGee learned from them that there was no food to be had. As soon as his hands were warm, he started back for the omnibus, the bare trees throwing long shadows across the liquified pike.

4:04 P.M.
Water Street, Fredericksburg

Meagher wanted to see them all together one last time, see them drinking and laughing. He often wished that he'd had this chance before Antietam. One more good time with those all gone before the next sundown. But that final evening together had been spent in a rain-soaked bivouac, not in a comfortable house like this one.

It'd been ransacked by Howard's boys, but less so than the others Meagher had seen this afternoon. The silverware was missing. Bureau drawers had been rifled through, the portrait of a wigged colonial bayoneted in the nose, and some heathen had shat in the hall. But the main rooms were soon tidied up, candles lit to replace the broken gas fixtures. His orderlies found a cask of Madeira hidden in the cellar, and Meagher sent for his staff and colonels to pass the wait with him.

An hour before, a message from Hancock had ordered him to ready the brigade to march down this side of the river, cross Hazel Run and, with the rest of 2d Corps, join Franklin for an assault below town. Burnside, it appeared, had changed his mind. Fine. Meagher didn't care where the attack took place— as long as the brigade wasn't left in reserve. But then ten minutes ago, word came that the order had been revoked. Either Burnside had changed his mind once again or he had finally realized that it was getting too dark to give battle. At that moment, Meagher had resolved to enjoy the company of his men.

"Here they are," he said, rising with delight.

One by one, they came in from the cold—Nugent, Kelly, O'Neill, Heenan, Byrnes, and Father Corby, of course. Snow was dusting their shoulders. It was coming down again, on and off. There was a piano in a corner of the parlor, and young Johnny Flaherty was pounding the keys, his father accompanying him on the fiddle. "Take a smile off the tray, boys." Meagher, his own wineglass in hand, broke into a brief, clumsy jig that left him faintheaded. His knee now scarcely bent, but the dance amused the men. All but Nugent, who gloomed at the window, watching 9th Corps continue to quick-time across.

"When's that rascal Gosson due back?" Meagher asked. This gathering was in desperate need of Jack Gosson.

"End of the month, sir," Nugent said quietly. "Just got a letter from him. Says he's losing his touch. Couldn't persuade Jim McGee and Rich Emmet to get drunk with him."

"Well, Father," Meagher said to Corby, "may God protect the virtue of our wives. They're alone in New York City with Jack Gosson." He paused. "And we're in Virginia, sitting on our coffins." He swigged down the last of his Madeira, then screwed up his face in disgust. "No more wine. It poisons the Irish temperament. Turns it maudlin. Whiskey!" An orderly quickly appeared with a bottle from Meagher's own stores and uncorked it. "Whiskey mixes best with Celtic blood," Meagher went on. "One drop of the *rale ould* makes a ditchdigger a bard. Two turn him into warrior . . ." He hopped around the parlor, pouring into any glass that was half-empty.

"And three, General?" Nugent asked with a guarded look.

"He becomes a Fenian, dear Bob—Protestant or not." Meagher's knee suddenly buckled, and he slopped some liquor on Dennis Heenan's boots.

"No matter, sir," the 116th's colonel quickly said.

Meagher came close to saying something about his injury, but then decided to let everyone think he was just tipsy. "Of course it matters, Dennis. It's my father-in-law's best whiskey. And Mr. Townsend stores up some very fine whiskey."

"He does indeed, sir," Heenan said, forcing a smile.

An uncomfortable silence fell over the room, and at last Meagher dropped his cheery front. "What is it?" he demanded.

"What's wrong here . . . ?" Everyone averted his stung gaze. The newcomers, Heenan and Byrnes, seemed especially uneasy. "Pat, you've always been frank with me."

Kelly exhaled, then said, "I don't see a plan in the works, General. And I'm afraid we'll be tossed haphazardly into some business that's over our heads."

Meagher nodded, then swung toward O'Neill. "And do you feel the same, Joe?"

Straight as an arrow. "I do."

"Bob?"

"I felt better when it looked like Burnside would send us downriver to join Franklin," Nugent said. "That's where we should strike. Against Jackson. Not here behind town."

Meagher took a gulp of whiskey and held it until the roof of his mouth began to tingle, then swallowed. "I had my own worries about this operation," he said. "And I gave voice to them when it was still proper to do so. But this morning, we crossed the Rubicon. Anyone question that?"

Another silence.

"Good," Meagher said, annoyed, almost angry now. They were making the evening small. "Because personally," he went on, the words coming fast, "I take it as a compliment that this brigade is always given the heavy end of the stick. Don't you . . . ?" He started to smile but then found he had no time for it. "Let me tell you what I know about leading men—it's *style* that matters more than form. And if we officers put our breasts up to the attack, the men shall too. If not, we'd lose even if Bonaparte himself had crafted our plan—!"

A hiss flew over the roof of the house, followed by a loud explosion that rattled the windows. Meagher drained his glass, then limped for the front door. He stopped on the porch in a thin snowfall. Blossoming above the river was a chaos of flashes and little smoke-clouds. He could trace more shells coming over from Marye's Heights by the fiery tails of their fuses. The bursts were about a hundred yards north of the bridge at the lower end of town. Some division was in the process of crossing. The men knelt helplessly as the detonations came closer, ever closer, and then finally lit up the snowy air fifty feet above them. Several men dropped. The rest turned and ran back for the Stafford shore. Shrapnel pattered against the roof of the house, but Meagher saw none of his officers cower. The next salvo was mostly made up of duds, for the shells plunged unexploded into the river and sent up geysers of greenish foam. The troops on the far bridgehead began fleeing up the slope, even though the barrage seemed to be waning.

"Those boys'll wait for dark now," Kelly remarked.

"And that's where they differ from us," Meagher said. "We go when we're told. Wherever we're told." Then he noticed the flickering of a small fire down the street. "Whose men are those?"

"I believe they're mine, sir," Heenan said.

"No fires in town tonight." Had he forgotten to pass this word along? "General Burnside's orders."

Nugent said, "The men'll be uncomfortable, sir."

"Then they'll be uncomfortable," Meagher said. "Kindly make sure this order's enforced. Immediately." As the colonels went back inside for their coats, Meagher watched the shell smoke blend into the white sky. A lone rider was slowly coming down the street.

"General," Corby said, taking Meagher by surprise. He'd thought he was alone on the porch.

"Yes, Father."

The priest's expression was irritatingly grave. "One of the men came to me with a rumor that's making the rounds."

"What sort of rumor?"

"Well, he asked if he and his friends were going to be led in front of those guns he's seen the enemy placing for the past three weeks."

"And what'd you tell him?"

"Not to trouble himself. His generals knew better than that."

Corby waited a moment, then asked, "Did I give him the truth, sir?"

The horseman had stopped in front of the house. Slowly, he climbed out of the saddle and turned, showing his pallid face. A shivering Richard Emmet saluted. "Reporting, sir."

Inwardly, Meagher cursed the weak-minded army surgeon in Manhattan who'd cleared Emmet to return to the brigade. Anyone who'd been in the field would know at a glance that he was dying of the shakes. But then Meagher gave his aide-de-camp a bittersweet smile. Maybe it was fated that he spend this evening alone with the kin of a martyr. "Come inside, Rich," he said warmly, "and have a drink with me."

Twenty-One

◆

The streets were jammed with troops, tens of thousands of them. Corby threaded his halting way through the crush of bodies, the ammunition wagons and light cannon waiting to go forward. It set his teeth on edge: the crackling of broken glass and crockery underfoot. "Look at me play, Father!" a brogue from an Ohio regiment cried, his face bright and ruddy in the firelight of a shop that'd been hit by a shell. "And not a lesson to me name!" The private was dancing atop a rosewood piano, his heels crashing down on the keys.

"Get down, you peawit," Corby ordered, then was jostled aside by a pair of men running breathlessly toward the river, carrying a sewing machine between them. "You two there! Put that back right now before you burn in hell!"

He was ignored all around.

Permission hadn't been given to plunder, but neither had anyone with shoulder straps said no. Corby had meant to walk off his uneasy mind after the meeting with Meagher, but the streets of Fredericksburg were so filled with rowdy drunkenness he felt more stirred up than when he'd set out. The men sensed what tomorrow would be like; they were blotting it from their minds with liquor and stupid revels. And Meagher had given no answer to their suspicion that they'd be marched against the fortified heights now beaded with campfires as far as the eye could see.

Corby turned back for his old regiment, the 88th New York.

The advance units had taken over nearly all the houses not damaged by the barrages, and those left empty were then occupied by the officers of the late-arriving brigades. So one group of messmates in the 88th set up some furniture in a garden enclosed by a boxwood hedge. A kind of alfresco parlor, complete with a Brussels carpet spread over the mud. "Evenin' to you, Father," their corporal said, his head rocking unsteadily on his shoulders.

"Boys."

A glum silence followed. The men looked comically civilized, sitting under the stars, their drink-moistened eyes catching the light of their coal oil lamp. Corby saw no bottles in plain view, but was sure that they'd vanished as soon as he'd come into the bivouac. "Will you join us, Father?" the corporal asked without much enthusiasm, overshooting his knee as he tried to cross one leg casually over the other.

"Yes, Father Corby, will you now?"

"Don't mind if I do."

The men were obviously disappointed to be taken up on their invitation, but two of them made room for Corby on a settee. It was a squeeze, but he was done with strolling around town— *see no evil.* "I'm sure you'll put all these fine things back where they belong by morning," Corby said.

"Ah, this is nothin', Father," a cherub-faced private said, plucking a smoldering rolled tobacco leaf from between his lips. "You should see the Fifteenth Massachusetts. Laid out feather beds a block long, and they're all loungin' there like pagans."

"Pagans indeed, if they're taking what's not theirs." Corby buttoned up his coat. The temperature was plunging fast.

"Father, if I might ask somethin' . . ." This redheaded man

seemed less drunk than the others. His eyes had a sad, worried look.

"Yes, Private?"

"Is it entirely out of the question, you know, that we'll be goin' up these hills behind town with the comin' of the light?"

Corby said nothing for a moment. He could hear musket fire on the western edge of town. The sporadic Rebel shelling had let up at nightfall, but the sound of skirmishing came and went every few minutes. "No, boys," he finally admitted. No good would come from lying to them. "It's not out of the question."

The corporal sighed. "Well, that's that," he said fatalistically, reaching for the stone bottle he'd hidden behind his chair. "Let the dawn come." The rest followed his example and began drinking openly.

"What's that?" Corby asked.

"Scotch ale, Father. Have a drop?"

"No, thanks. Maybe later." Yes, that would be nice before trying to sleep. But where to bed down? A few fortunate men had torn away window shutters and doors to lie on. One fellow even had a feather tick in which he'd curled up. But most had simply unrolled their blankets on the muddy ground, which at last was firming up from the cold. Some regiments he'd passed, such as the 116th, had so little space the men could do no better than sit up all night, pressed shoulder to shoulder.

The corporal rose. "Well now, what harm tomorrow if it's all for the poor Old *Dairt?*"

"Sure," a private said from a garden bench half lost in the shadows, "and let's have some music again."

A concertina started up from the midst of some men crowded together on the steps of the house across the street. The corporal grabbed the cherub-faced private, pulled him to his feet, kissed his hand and asked, "Dance?" They staggered with every turn and once nearly capsized into Corby's lap.

Suddenly, there was a tinkle of glass, and a chamber pot flew through a big second-story window. It smashed against the sidewalk, scattering the men on the steps of the house. Above, the last shards were reamed out of the window frame with a musket barrel. Then astonishingly, a stout woman jumped up onto the windowsill.

Corby bolted to his feet.

She balanced herself precariously, grasping a champagne magnum in one hand and twirling a parasol over her shoulder with the other. The men were already twittering when Corby's first shock wore off enough for him to realize that it was a sergeant from the 88th. He was tricked out in a bonnet, lace chemise and hoop skirt. "Clear the way below!" he roared, almost tumbling over the edge.

"D'you mean to jump, Sergeant?"

"No, for chrissake. Where you from that your mind's so befuddled?"

"Banagher."

"Well," he harrumphed, "that explains it then."

"Explains what?"

"A backward town, I been there."

"Ah, but Banagher beats the Devil anytime."

"And Galway beats Banagher all the time," the sergeant came back at him, giving his parasol another spin. "Now make room for me coach and me niggur."

"Your *what?*"

"It's Friday night in hell, and I'm goin' out on the town."

"Kelly'll have your stripes for it," somebody warned.

"Won't be the first time," the sergeant said, stumbling back into the darkened room behind him.

A slow clop of hooves turned Corby's head. From an alleyway came a mule drawing a coach. The traces were held by a private in black-face. He wore a silk top hat and swallow-tailed coat. "Clear de way!" he bawled. "Make room for m'lady!"

Someone tugged at the priest's elbow, Colonel Kelly's orderly. "Father, I've heaped up some brush for you to sleep on. Sorry I can't do better."

Corby realized that the regiment was putting him to bed, whether or not he wanted to go. "Soon." First, he wanted a word with the sergeant, who came sashaying out the front door of the house at that moment, blowing kisses at the convulsed men. He used the parasol to bash hands trying to reach up under his skirt.

But Corby finally caught his eye.

"Father," the sergeant said quietly as the sniggering died away.

"I saw you take up the colors once." Corby could barely keep down his temper. "Why make a fool of yourself like this?"

The street went silent, except for the muskets sputtering in the distance. The sergeant scratched the powdered stubble on his cheeks. For a moment, Corby thought the man was on the brink of contrition, apology even, but then his heavily rouged mouth broke into a bitter grin. "Tonight's mine, Father, and I need to be the biggest fool in the world. Tomorrow belongs to the brigade." Then his eyes turned utterly humorless as he added, "The rest is God's, I fear."

With that, he stepped into his coach and was driven off to the roisterous cheers of the 88th.

9:09 P.M.
Marye's Heights

Lifting his head, Garnett McMillan watched his father pace along the line behind him. The old man's vest was unbuttoned, which usually meant that the pressure in his chest was bothering him. Most of "K" Company were already asleep, exhausted from last night's picket tour and kept awake all day by enemy sharpshooter fire. His father abruptly turned and came back to him. "Lieutenant," he said, his breath coming heavily.

Garnett rose, the small of his back sore. When standing during daylight, everyone had been forced by the pinging bullets to half-crouch. "Sir."

His father lowered his voice. "Go to the brow of the hill here, Garnett. Count the ammunition wagons for me." Then he walked on, his face turned toward the galaxy of campfires covering Stafford County. Burnside had filled Fredericksburg with troops, yet his reserves still across the river seemed as countless as ever.

Instead of tripping over the ankles of his resting men in the dark, Garnett decided to hike along the face of the slope. Fires weren't allowed behind the stone wall. Longstreet, no doubt, had seen what Garnett had while on picket below: the defenses along the sunken road would be virtually invisible to the advancing Federals until they were right on top of them. The wall was partially hidden by the dirt thrown from the roadbed.

He passed above the Widow Stevens's tiny house. General Cobb could be seen through a window, writing at the kitchen table, smiling to himself. A letter to his wife, then. Garnett had been fond of Mrs. Cobb, of all the family, really, including the general. He sometimes wished that the men in the regiment had known Tom Cobb in those days, as he himself had. The light from the same window fell out onto the road. Here, Phillips's Legion abutted against the 24th, and Sullivan was squatting in a circle with a dozen men from the neighboring regiment. "Eyes down," a brogue warned. Garnett chuckled. Fenians plotting, again.

He worked up the slope toward Marye's House, skirting the rifle pits, which showed as black circles in the starshine. He came to the first artillery pieces, a pair of Napoleons gleaming behind earthworks, their muzzles poking through embrasures. The ammunition chests had been taken off their limbers, and the crews were sitting on them, smoking, talking among themselves. Incredibly, it sounded as if they were discussing the explorations of Humboldt. Yes, that was definitely the topic. Washington Artillery, Garnett reminded himself. College boys and dandies from the best families of New Orleans. He crossed to the west side of the crest, halted and looked down on a small valley. The campfires of his division's reserves below heartened him, but he saw no ammunition wagons.

"May I help you find something?" a courtly voice asked from a copse of birches.

"The ammunition train, thank you."

A lieutenant of artillery sauntered out of the trees. "Back somewhere along the pike to Richmond, I hear. Old Pete's afraid the Yanks might touch it off with a lucky shot if the park's too close. Small chance of that. Every other shell we've fired these past days has been a dud. Might as well load river rocks." He offered his kid-gloved hand. "William Owen, battalion adjutant for the time being." They shook.

"Garnett McMillan, Twenty-fourth Georgia."

"Emory," Owen declared, taking a puff off his cheroot.

"I'm sorry?"

"You have the air of an Emory man."

"Close. Emory and Henry College here in Virginia."

"Same thing," Owen said indifferently. "Methodist, aren't they both?"

"Yes." Garnett paused. "Were you serious about your own ammunition?"

"Quite. What does explode pops off early, so keep your heads low. Our profoundest apologies."

"Well," Garnett said hopefully, "maybe things will stay quiet along here."

"I don't believe that's the expectation . . ."

"And what is?"

"Longstreet means to sustain the enemy's attacks here, repel them until they become exhausted, demoralized. After that, Jackson might go at them from the right. We'll advance if the chance arises to finish the philistines off. *If* they don't somehow finish us off first." Owen then asked, "Would you care for some punch, McMillan? Just brewed some inside the house. I don't believe we've ever had an Emory and Henry man for a guest."

Garnett was tempted, but then declined. "Thanks, can't tonight, I'm afraid. Colonel's waiting for my report."

"And his name?"

"Robert McMillan."

"Relation?"

"Father."

"Oh my," Owen said, "you have had a boring war, haven't you?"

Smiling, Garnett started back for the wall.

Yet, he lingered a moment midway down the slope, studying the enemy fires twinkling to the east. Talking to the artillerist had reminded him of John Brownlow, a friend at Emory and Henry. Friend and rival in one, something he'd not encountered in the regiment. Friends here were loved completely, without envy, and rivals wore blue. John had withdrawn from school the year before the war after accidentally shooting another student. But his younger brother, Jim, had still been enrolled during that hot-headed spring of 1861. Their father, the biggest Union man in Tennessee, came to take him home. There were no insults, no snubs as the old man helped his son pack, just a terrible feeling of awkwardness, an unexpected sense of shame that things had come to this. Garnett found himself looking for John and Jim whenever he and his men took prisoners, as they had this morning.

2:15 A.M., December 13
Bivouac of the 69th New York

Donovan lay on a pallet of broken hardtack boxes to keep him off the frozen mud of the street. Crowded all around him were the men of his company, wrapped in their blankets. Few were asleep, for there was little snoring. Snatches of whispered talk came and went. Too dank and cold to sleep, even though the temperature had risen slightly. In the last hour or so, the wind had died, but as it did a dense, suffocating fog returned. It curled

up from the river, drifted between the buildings and settled
over Fredericksburg like a shroud. Its moisture dripped off the
eaves and plopped against gum blankets. Donovan had thought
that the fog would muffle all sound. But it didn't. Again and
again, he listened to the creak and rumble of artillery trains.
Whose, he had no idea. So hard to tell the direction of noises
with much of his right ear torn away. From a house down the
block a piano was tinkling out "Hail Columbia," a drunken Irish
tenor stumbling through the lyrics.

A whisper caught his attention. "D'you remember that mad
old biddy up in Markham?"

Another voice, also barely audible, said, "The one who flew
into us so?"

"Aye . . ."

Donovan remembered too. Except the white-haired shrew
who'd run down from her porch to shriek at the brigade hadn't
been just any mad old biddy. She'd been mother to Turner
Ashby, Stonewall Jackson's cavalry commander, killed the June
before in the Shenandoah. She'd accused Meagher of murdering her son. Not true. The brigade had been a hundred miles
away at the time, murdering some other mothers' sons and getting murdered itself. The priests had tried to comfort her, but
it was no good. The old woman had put a curse on the brigade,
her eyes flashing in their dark sockets.

"You don't figure maybe she was the banshee?" the first voice
now asked. "Croonin' for us to die?"

"No, no. The banshee's young and beautiful."

"She can be a bloodless old hag," a new voice argued, "just
like that house-devil up in Fauquier County."

"Then somebody tell me for sure—was *she* the banshee . . . ?"

Donovan shut his eyes.

Twenty-Two

◆

6:02 A.M.
24th Georgia

McMillan could see twenty paces downslope into the fog. After that, there was nothing but a whirling gray. Straining into it made his already tired eyes ache. Somewhere out there were the brigade's pickets, stretched along a snake-rail fence between the Strattons' brick house and a millrace that coursed down the west side of town. This ditch had once channeled wastewater from a paper factory to a gristmill on the river, and still flowed hip-deep even after Burnside's engineers had tried to drain it yesterday.

Another crackle of musketry echoed against Marye's Hill, the second since the fog had brightened with dawn. At the sound of the first brush of the day with the enemy, McMillan had sent a corporal scrambling over the wall to check on the picket line.

The man had yet to come back.

McMillan stood up from where he'd slept for an hour, maybe less, and tried to walk along the road. He strained to swing his right foot forward, but the nerves refused to obey. He almost pitched over. Grunting angrily, he braced both hands on the ice-hard earth banked against the wall. Sullivan was quickly at his side, helping him up. "Ah sir, you shoulda spent the night with General Cobb at Mrs. Stevens's."

"No, no," McMillan said, fighting dizziness and that tireless wrenching in his chest. "It's just a cottage. Barely room there for his staff."

More musketry. Hotter. McMillan silently counted to fifteen before it died away. Waves. The pressure was coming from town in waves, a slow blue tide coming in.

"Here's the general now," Sullivan cautioned.

"Help me take a few steps, Michael. I want to meet him walking."

Sullivan held McMillan up under the arms and supported him long enough for some feeling to come into his legs. His blood seemed to start moving freely, but the surge of circulation was so painful he bit the inside of his cheek to keep from making a sound. In that instant, a terrible prayer flickered through his brain. He offered whatever health he had remaining in his life—just to make it through this day. This single day.

A raven cawed out in the mist.

Cobb came down the road from its north end, hands fisted. He paused briefly to chat with Tom Cook. The young commander of Phillips's Legion took a letter from his coat pocket and showed it to the brigadier, who scanned it, laughed, and gave the lieutenant colonel a pat on the arm before moving on. "Robert," Cobb said, approaching, "what's happening down there?"

"Not sure, sir. Sent a man out a wee bit ago."

Cobb was looking into the fog as if he expected the stars and stripes, thousands of bayonets to materialize out of it at any instant. Possible, McMillan realized. If the enemy made a quick, determined rush, they might capture the pickets before they could fall back. Hopefully, the weary, frost-nipped men out there would surrender their ground slowly, giving the brigade time to react. They were mountain boys from Rabun County on the North Carolina border. A little morning fog wouldn't rattle them. They wouldn't let themselves be driven in until it was the right thing to do.

"Your man got lost," Cobb said grumpily. It was how his nerves affected him sometimes.

McMillan half-turned. Of all the men along the road, his eyes fell on Sullivan.

As usual, the sergeant immediately knew what was wanted of him. "On me way, sir."

"Thank you, Michael."

Sullivan borrowed a musket, jumped over the wall and was swallowed by the murk.

"Is he a religious man, Robert?" Cobb asked.

"Oh, I think so, sir. In that peasanty Irish way. But it's half superstition."

Cobb nodded, then cocked his head to listen. The musket fire had stopped momentarily. Through this calm came the voice of an officer, far off, ordering his men under arms. Had to be Federal. It seemed a very young voice.

"I hope they didn't rise early," Cobb said.

McMillan agreed. Their 2d Corps could have been quietly roused hours before, the lines formed and already sent up the long plain from town. The skirmishers testing his pickets were but the fingertips of a massive horde. McMillan listened as keenly as he could for the sounds of tens of thousands of men moving toward the wall, the rustle of wool, the clink of canteens and cups, shoes scuffling the hard, icy fields. Now was the time for them to steal up to the heights, if Burnside had any sense. In the cloaking fog with Longstreet's corps benumbed by the night's chill, Alexander's artillery blind.

Cobb cleared his throat. McMillan thought he was going to say something about the enemy, but instead he chuckled. "Cook just showed me a letter from a friend back home in Dalton. Seems his fiancée recently went to a church social. Their minister asked all the girls what vocation they mean to follow. When her turn came, Tom's dark-eyed lovely said, 'I have no higher aim in life than to be a Cook.' " Cobb smiled over at him. "Remember those days, Robert?"

McMillan wasn't sure that he did. Not with the Army of the Potomac ready to burst upon this wall. He tried to recall something of his own courtship so long ago. But everything that had happened before this gray morning seemed not to have happened, and a fleeting image of Ruth Ann's teenage face, however sweet, struck him as nothing more than a figment of his imagination.

8:07 A.M.
116th Pennsylvania

The brigade stood waiting in column. Tyrrell held the national colors, Hudson the regiment's. Both flags were still cased to keep the fog from saturating the silk, making them too heavy to billow freely. Hudson, pasty-faced, said between hard swallows, "Gotta cast up accounts, Will."

"Don't. We're gonna march any second."

"Can't wait. Somebody take my flag." With that, the closest member of the guard grabbed the staff, and Hudson rushed for an alley. As promised over the frozen corpses of the Mississippians, he'd gotten blind drunk last night. He started off jolly enough, but then squatted down in the slush, Indian-fashion, and gaped emptily ahead. After an hour like this, he flopped over and started snoring. Tyrrell had rolled him up in his blankets.

Mulholland rode by, a brittle calm in his face.

"Sir," somebody asked, "when d'you think the regiment'll go into it?"

"Don't know, boys," Mulholland said absently, trotting on. "Keep yourselves ready."

Tyrrell had been doing that for two days now, and he felt as if he'd been holding his breath all that time. Unless something big happened soon, he'd burst. Last night had been intolerable, sleepless, the men of the regiment packed together in the street like herring on ice. In the midst of this misery, he'd suddenly realized that his letter to Annie was still in his coat pocket. The division's mail office had folded with the movement across the river, and now he had no idea how to get it to Philadelphia, save with a wounded officer headed home.

Hudson returned from the alley on wobbly legs. "I hope I'm shot dead right off," he said, taking his flag back.

"You don't know what you're wishin'," a paddy said from the ranks.

Tyrrell asked himself what he was wishing. Maybe for a ball to the legs, so he couldn't run when things turned hot. A wound that would guarantee to keep him on the line no matter what. He shook his head, trying to think of something else.

Musket fire sounded from across town.

Then it came to him—he wished to be like the New Yorkers. To go into this with a grin. But his face wasn't up to a grin, and his knees felt weak, like he'd just risen from a sickbed. He tried to hide the slight shaking of his left hand by hooking a thumb over the flag belt.

"I *am* gonna die," Hudson said quietly, earnestly.

"Stop that," Tyrrell whispered.

Finally, one of Hancock's riders galloped out of the fog, shouting for Meagher.

"Time to pay the butcher's bill," the same paddy said.

8:44 A.M.
Hancock's Field Headquarters

Meagher dismounted as quickly as he could, tossed his rein to the groom and glanced back down Water Street. His regimental commanders were still coming on at a brisk canter, but he didn't wait for them. Instead he hurried toward the steps of the house from which the 1st Division flag was flying. He wanted a word alone with Hancock, if possible, to find out what was planned for his brigade. And argue, if necessary. His knee had flared up by the time he reached the porch. He stopped at the open door and took a huge breath of cold, moist air. It lightened the pain a little but left him once again with the nauseating sensation that he was floating.

"You all right, Tom?"

Meagher hadn't realized that Zook was standing just inside the threshold.

"Fine, Sam," Meagher said, "just a touch of cramp."

"You sure?" the commander of the 3d Brigade said, lowering his clear-eyed gaze onto Meagher's stiffened knee.

"No matter. That's what horses are for." Meagher stepped past Zook into the foyer. Nugent, Kelly, O'Neill, Heenan, and Byrnes caught up with him there, and in file they went into the parlor. A darkly whiskered face turned toward the Irishmen, eyes uneasy. Meagher gave the man a cool nod in passing. John Caldwell, commander of the 1st Brigade, who could have outflanked the Confederates in the sunken road at Antietam had he not been so cautious. Or so absent. When General Richardson had gone to find out what had happened to any support for the hard-pressed Irish Brigade, he was told that Caldwell was somewhere to the rear. Behind a haystack.

Meagher thought that he was done with the man for the morning when Caldwell said drolly from behind, "Is that getup quite regulation, my dear General Meagher?"

Turning, Meagher said, "Why yes, my dear General Caldwell. What makes you think otherwise?"

Caldwell smirked at the dark green uniform, the yellow sash and the black shoulder straps, each glittering with a single silver star. "Then, is it on to Richmond this morning, sir . . . or Dublin?"

"Both," Meagher retorted, "and in that very order."

Laughter had just started up when Hancock said sharply, his breath misting, "Gentlemen . . ."

The unheated parlor fell silent.

The score of men, Hancock's brigade and regimental commanders, were all standing. Meagher looked around for a chair, but every last one had been slit open by Howard's revelers, and the cotton stuffing strewn over the carpet. Hancock, as always, was crisply dressed. Meagher searched his face for a hint of doubt. But there was none. The man had resigned himself to the day, whatever it brought, and Meagher now made up his mind to do the same.

"Gentlemen," Hancock went on, "General Couch has notified me that General French will attack the enemy on the heights in the rear of town, and we will support him . . ." He paused to let it sink in.

No one stirred for several long seconds, then Caldwell began to say something. He halted, shook his head, then started again. "Sir, yesterday—weren't orders received for us to march across Hazel Run and form up in the rear of Franklin?"

"Yes," Hancock said.

"Weren't small bridges constructed for that very purpose?"

"Yes."

"What I mean, sir—isn't this the first time a direct assault on Marye's Heights has been seriously entertained?"

"Yes." Hancock's voice had grown more strident with each reply. "Except, it's now been ordered, John. Not entertained."

Meagher asked, "What time do we push off, sir?"

Hancock smiled at him. "The movement won't start till the order comes from General Burnside."

Meagher couldn't recall a division forming into line of battle under much less than an hour. French would be first, then Hancock. Two hours then, at least, before the men of his own brigade set foot out of town and onto the plain. He knew that the fog would be an advantage for the attack, even though the formations might become confused in it. But he wanted the morning to clear. He wanted everything his men did to be *seen*. As it'd been at Antietam, where McClellan himself had glassed the green flags advancing.

"Formation's been prescribed," Hancock said. "Brigade front. Intervals between the brigade lines—two hundred paces. Zook, Meagher, then Caldwell . . . in that order. If one line stalls, the next must go over it. And the next over both, if need be. Till the works up there are carried."

A deep rumble turned all heads toward the window at the south end of the parlor. Artillery fire. About three miles off, Meagher estimated. Confederate shrapnel rounds. He could tell from the distinctive shriek made by their ragged leaden jackets passing through the air. Soon that sound would be plunging directly down on his head. No matter. Whatever the day brought. Mount the scaffold, eyes on the clouds.

"That's Franklin advancing against Jackson," Hancock explained. "Must hurry now, gentlemen. Get ourselves to the edge of town and be ready for word from General Burnside. Good luck. Ah, one more thing—" The officers who'd started for the door stopped. "All mounted officers go in on foot."

Meagher couldn't believe his ears. "Sir?"

"Tom?"

Meagher felt as if he were sinking through the floor. "I've *always* gone in mounted."

"Till now," Hancock said. "The fire will simply be too much."

"It was too much at Antietam. Malvern Hill."

Hancock glared, and Meagher forced himself to calm down. "I mean no disrespect to you or your wishes, sir, but if I go in on foot how will my men see me?"

"My God, Meagher," Caldwell exclaimed, gesturing at the green uniform, "they'd need blinders and sties in both eyes to miss you!"

The laughter grated. Meagher tried to smile, failed, then faced Hancock again. "I must ask you, sir . . . is this an order or only a suggestion?"

For the first time in memory, Hancock looked coldly at him. "Stay out of the saddle, Tom."

The conference broke up. The officers were saying good-bye to one another. Through his distraction, Meagher realized that, despite the joshing tone, they were doing this with an air of utter finality. Nugent took Colonel Cross of the 5th New Hampshire

252 ◆ *Kirk Mitchell*

by the hand and said, "We're going to have hot work today, Ed, but if you get into Richmond before I do, order dinner at Spottswood House."

Cross searched Nugent's eyes a long moment. Antietam had left a jagged scar on his bald pate. He looked sick today, chilled and feverish. But finally he grinned and said, "Goddammit, Bob, I will."

Meagher felt someone squeeze his arm. Hancock. "Tom," he asked, "care if I tag along while you inspirit your boys?"

9:22 A.M.
Lower Water Street

A Rebel shell came screaming down out of the fog as Rich Emmet rode up. Meagher's aide-de-camp jerked the rein to keep his horse from bolting. Corby, sitting beside Ouellette on the steamboat wharf, braced, eyes shut, for the impact. It came with the crunch of timbers being shattered—but toward the upper end of town. Relaxing again, the priest glanced down. His body was throwing a faint shadow on the waters below. The fog was beginning to lift.

"Fathers," Emmet said, his head tighter to his shoulders than before, "General Meagher's compliments. He begs you to come to a garden nearby and bless the boxwood."

Ouellette was as confused as Corby. "Bless some bushes?"

Two more shells. Midtown. Barely a second apart. Boom-boom.

"Yes," Emmet said after he'd flinched a little. " 'As a symbol of the Irish nation.' " He gave a wan smile. "That's what the general said."

"All right, Rich," Corby said, heaving himself to his feet, helping Ouellette up, "tell him we're coming." After this business, whatever it was, he meant to check on the hospital Surgeon Reynolds was setting up in the Episcopal Church. "Where's this boxwood?"

The lieutenant pointed as he wheeled and galloped away.

Corby saw that it was the same garden where the messmates of the 88th had laid out their parlor furniture yesterday evening.

Solid shot swished overhead. It fountained in the middle of the Rappahannock, about as far as the enemy batteries could reach today, having been driven back onto Marye's Heights by the Union skirmishers.

The priests began walking, arm-in-arm. "What is this box-wood custom, *Père* Guillaume?" Ouellette asked.

"I'm not sure."

"Christmas perhaps?"

"No," Corby said, far away for a few seconds. Yuletide at Notre Dame. High Mass, the choirs. But it brought something else back to him. He'd been Prefect of Discipline. Handing out Christmas amnesties to the young rogues he'd collared over the year. The intoxicating power of forgiveness. Nothing meek about it, he'd learned long ago. And that's what kept him here in the army, maybe, reconciling men to God as they knelt before him in their grave clothes. *Oh Father*, one boy had said after confession, with the skirmish fire crackling in the distance, *I feel so light.* And he himself had never felt so close to the divinity in men as he had at that big pile of straw that served as the brigade hospital along Antietam Creek—absolving dying Catholics, baptizing dying Protestants, sneezing half-blind from the straw dust.

The men were leaning on their muskets, waiting.

Ouellette and he slipped through the ranks of 28th Massachusetts to the garden. Corby was pleased: the boys from the 88th had put the furniture back, as told. Meagher's aides were going over the hedge like tea pickers, snapping off sprigs of boxwood, collecting them on a gum blanket. They stopped and looked up at the priests. One glimpse of their tight faces and Corby knew there'd be no march downriver to support Franklin. Second Corps was bound head-on for the heights behind town.

Ouellette asked, "Which blessing?"

Corby shrugged, unable to speak for the moment. Picking up a cluster of the teardrop-shaped leaves, he thought of the soldier who'd asked if his generals would be foolish enough to send him against all those guns on the heights.

"Maybe the blessing for vines?"

"Yes, good," Corby said, and together they fell into it. Yet, his mind was on that trusting face filled with relief to hear that his generals would never send him into a slaughter pen like a fatling.

They'd just finished the blessing when Meagher and Hancock trotted in front of the 69th. The brigadier was in a green uniform Corby had never seen before. He was sure it had raised eyebrows at division headquarters, but here it was received with a roaring cheer. Then the New Yorkers came to attention, but Meagher quickly put them at east again. He looked tired, yet his eyes were bright, his color up. Hancock was calmly stroking his imperial beard. "I'd like to address each regiment separately, sir," Meagher told him, and Hancock nodded. No wonder. At four abreast, the brigade was strung out along the street for more than three hundred yards.

Meagher's aides, each holding a corner of the gum blanket, carried the boxwood up to him. He reached down from the saddle and took a sprig, tucked it in his cap. Finally, he began. "Soldiers of the Sixty-ninth, for the first time we New Yorkers go into battle without our own beloved green. Our new flags are still on the way from Manhattan, so I'll ask each of you to place upon your hat or cap the color of our Fatherland. Do this in remembrance of the oppression and the oppressed we left behind." He paused. "Color guard . . ." The sergeant and his corporals snapped to just as a shell hit only a block away. "I ask you to make a wreath of evergreen and hang it upon the stars and stripes. Do this in honor of freedom, in gratitude for the opportunity to become free men in this land . . ." Another hit, close by. Roof tiles were spinning up into the air. "In a few moments, all of you will engage the enemy in a terrible battle. It may decide the fate of this country, the home of your adoption. This day you will strike a deadly blow to those wicked traitors who are now but a few hundred yards—!"

Corby didn't hear it hurtling down. Nor did he hear the shell detonate on contact with the street. He simply felt a gust of violently hot wind on the right side of his face. The ground lurched in the same split second, and he staggered a step before finding his balance again. Smoke boiled up, showing where the explosion had been. In the ranks of the 63d, but close enough to the 88th to have caused casualties in both regiments.

Incredibly, those unhurt remained standing in formation as if nothing had happened.

Corby ran for the 63d. The men parted for him, and he looked down on the remains, the shredded uniforms yet smoking. "How many were they?" he asked, unable to tell.

"Three, Father," a private said, clasping his bleeding forearm with his hand. Another man helped him tie a bandanna around the wound, then the private bent over and picked up his musket.

The 69th hurrahed Meagher as he and Hancock moved on toward the 88th.

$\mathcal{T}$wenty-Three

♦

"It's thinnin' out," a voice down the line said. The man could be barely heard over the crash and rattle of the fighting on the right. An hour old now. And every minute or so, the Washington Artillery on the crest behind the brigade blindly lobbed a shell into Fredericksburg.

Sullivan raised his head for a look over the wall.

No, the man had it wrong: the fog wasn't so much thinning as lifting slowly off the ground. Finally, Sullivan could see town, although the tops of the church spires were still spearing the low clouds. A few blue soldiers were visible here and there in the streets, but he was relieved to see no huge black boxes of infantry forming up at the bottom of the plain. Nor was there any sign of the Yankee skirmishers who'd driven the brigade's pickets back to the high board fence. Much of it had been torn down, but McMillan had ordered a few sections left standing to scramble the oncoming enemy lines.

From downriver came the sounds of the growing fight, but any glimpse of it was hidden by the fog.

"They're comin'," somebody said huskily.

A lone Federal horseman—no, Sullivan quickly saw—three

of them, strung out a hundred yards apart, were riding toward the wall, looking over the ground in advance of the formations that would surely follow now. The weight. He could feel them lurking in town, the many thousands. A great coiled spring. When the firing had started on the right, Dooley announced that Burnside, under cover of darkness, had pulled all his troops out of town and marched them downriver to take on Jackson this morning. But no, Sullivan was sure of it—an entire corps was still in town, avoiding the intersections with streets down which the Confederate batteries could sight their cannon.

The Yankee rider directly below the brigade came on without pause, holding his rein loosely, almost elegantly. No tension in the way he sat astride his charger.

A gunlock clicked in the sunken road.

"No, boys," a tired voice ordered, "none of that now." McMillan was standing nearby, leaning on his sword with one hand and gripping his field glasses with the other. His eyes were almost swollen shut by sleeplessness. "Let our pickets decide how troublous they are." Word was passed along, and the men mumbled their agreement. It'd only be murder. The three riders were now near enough for Sullivan to make out their shoulder boards. Young officers. On they rode through gaps in the snake-rail fence above the millrace. A wag called out from the picket line, "Y'all have breakfast yet?"

The closest rider tipped his cap. Sullivan believed that he was grinning, but the distance was too far to tell for sure. This man and his fellows finally halted. They seemed to focus on the brow of the hill, its artillery and rifle pits, rather than the stone wall. Invisible. Sullivan had the sensation that he and all the troops behind the dirt-banked wall were invisible—despite the colors Satterfield was clutching tightly to the staff, the flags of the rest of the regiments.

Then, as if one mind, the three enemy officers wheeled and started back down the slope at an unhurried trot. The brigade cheered them, and they waved with their caps before vanishing down a steeper part of the gently rising slope.

"Irish, I'm sure," Dooley suggested.

It'd seemed different out in the fog earlier this morning. No picket had probably felt that he was shooting at human beings, just warding off phantoms in the dank gloom. Sullivan had come back to Cobb and McMillan after ten minutes and told them that the Yankees were not yet making a serious attempt to drive in the picket line, although the men had withdrawn to the second fence because the first was too exposed to sharpshooter fire.

That drive would come anytime now.

Suddenly, off to the right, rifled cannon cracked to life. Sullivan could see the jets of muzzle flame pointing at a small wood below town. Enemy infantry were scurrying from the river toward these trees, antlike, almost comically tiny in the distance. The shells burst among them, and they flopped down in the snow-covered clearing, sprawled perfectly still for a few seconds, then picked themselves up—those who could—and ran back for the shelter of the bank.

No one along the wall rejoiced. It'd been too sudden, too small.

Over those brief seconds, it seemed as if every cannon in both armies had opened up.

Sullivan stared skyward.

The fog had gone, utterly. Yet, stretched between his eyes and the milky blue there seemed to be a vibrant membrane made of sound—of whistling and hissing and shrieking as the Rebel batteries took on Union troops, wherever their flags showed, and the farther-reaching enemy guns on Stafford Heights tried to silence those batteries. Turning, Sullivan watched a fuse trail curl down onto the ridgetop, and out of the white-hot blast a knapsack spun away into the hazy, smoky light. Ransom's and Cooke's North Carolinia brigades were up there, waiting in support. No stone wall to lie behind.

"Here we go, boys." Cobb appeared through the smoke wafting down off the artillery. Clapping his arm around McMillan's shoulders, he drew the colonel's attention about two miles distant to the plain below Deep Run. The fields there were sparkling as if they'd been sown with diamonds. Bayonets, Sullivan realized. Tens of thousands of troops were going forward, stars and stripes billowing before them. Farther to the south, streams of wounded were straggling rearward out of the smoke, away from the first action of the day.

"Well, Robert," Cobb said, shouting over the barrage, "Jackson gets the first dance!" Then something caught his eye, for he borrowed McMillan's binoculars. Turning, Sullivan fixed on what Cobb was glassing: a thick column of infantry halted on the Stafford shore, waiting to cross the bridges into town. It wound back into the Falmouth Hills and had no end that Sullivan could see. A human river with its tributaries flowing all the way down from Minnesota and New York and Maine, across from the Old World even.

The unkillable weight of them.

The cartridges had to last. If they didn't, and Burnside wasn't afraid to spill the blood of his men in buckets, the Army of the Potomac would crash through this wall, over these heights, and make its next headquarters in Richmond. Sullivan could tell that McMillan was growing steadily more nervous about the ammunition. No small worry. If it failed to come forward when needed, the dike would collapse and the blue sea would inundate northern Virginia.

"McLaws is right, then," Cobb said, handing the glasses back to McMillan. He began plucking at his lower lip with his fingers. For the first time in Sullivan's memory, the brigadier seemed nagged by doubt. "This is where their big assault will come. And suddenly too."

McMillan said nothing. He just studied the plain where it met the outskirts of town.

Rolling on his side, Sullivan watched along the road for the cooks' detail, Tully especially. They had yet to bring the day's rations. He wanted the boys to hurry, to come and be gone again before the blue people struck.

9:59 A.M.
69th New York

Donovan watched Zook's brigade hurriedly pass up the rocky lane above the wharf and deploy along the next street to the west, Caroline. His nostrils were filled with the lush, green scent of the boxwood he'd stuck in his cap. Father Ouellette, while blessing each man of the regiment, Catholic and Protestant alike, had paused a bit longer over Donovan than the others, and from that he'd been left wondering if there was something different about his own face today, something he himself had seen—or believed he'd seen—in the faces of men living their last hours.

Trying to shake off the thought, he ran his gloved fingers through his horse's mane, raked the tangles of coarse hair.

Father Ouellette's heavy glance had meant nothing. He'd just been his usual brusque Gallic self. Earlier, while the brigade stood in parade formation, Colonel Nugent had put some boxwood on the French-Canadian's priest's hat, making an honorary Irishman of him. Ouellette hadn't looked particularly honored, making the men laugh.

At last, down came the order—*shoulder arms, left face, forward . . . march*. The 69th led the column.

Donovan glanced back along the brigade. Meagher had used the intersections with the east-west streets as breaks between the regiments, for enemy artillery was bowling solid shot down toward the river when not raining shells on the town at large. The men crossed these shooting galleries at a dead run, then slowed when safely behind buildings again, making the column squeeze along like a blue caterpillar. A company of the 88th stopped a moment, the leading men holding back those behind them with outstretched arms. Two seconds later, an iron ball came bouncing through the intersection, a streak of black spraying mud, making a wicked sizzling sound. "God speed!" a paddy hollered as it plunged into the river.

"Was that the Fourth Avenue car?" another asked.

Donovan smiled, although his stomach had turned cold.

Thick smoke filled the street ahead. A cotton factory was still burning from yesterday's bombardment. He held his breath as he entered the choking dimness, the fires inside the tumbled walls warming the right side of his face. His horse nickered, snorted. Coming out, he looked up into the pall, saw fuses sparking through the dusky cloud, heard them hissing toward Marye's Heights.

Another brigade was blocking the intersection ahead.

Meagher, looking exasperated, trotted up to Nugent. His green uniform was already sooty. "It's Caldwell, as slow as ever," he said, then took a sip from his flask. "We'll have to halt again." The order went down, and Donovan sighed. Thankfully, the 69th was beyond the smoke from the burning factory, but the greenhorns from the 116th weren't so lucky. The fire had flared up again, and the heat was pressing them against the fronts of the houses across Water Street.

Donovan's mind wandered. Jimmy McGee. Where was he? Tom Leddy, acting major, just now recovered from a wound received at Malvern Hill, had arrived early yesterday morning from Washington and said that the pike was one continuous bog from Alexandria to Falmouth. Just as well. McGee had used up his luck at Antietam. Donovan shut his good eye. It felt parched from no sleep. Maybe the entire brigade had used up its luck at Antietam. *No use in dwelling on that.* He was almost dozing when the column moved again. The men began to march with the old swagger. Yet, they hadn't gone far when a second halt was ordered.

"Well, Bob," Meagher said to Nugent, even more agitated than before, "now we wait for French to attack!"

The shells kept coming down out of the western sky. After a while, Donovan climbed from the saddle. He stretched, yawned, checked his pocket watch. Joe Hogan, his first sergeant, ambled up, as chipper as ever. "Well, sir—here's hopin' French's boys open a gap for us."

"Yes," Donovan said, "here's to hope."

11:24 A.M.
24th Georgia

It seemed to happen in the same second, neither thing causing the other. The batteries on the crest behind McMillan went to rapid fire, the concussions drumming in his chest, and two lines of enemy infantry moved at the double-quick out of Fredericksburg. One sprinted from Hanover Street and the other from the lower end of town. Prussia Street, he believed. Briefly, the smoke from the cannon swirled down over the road, and he could see nothing. When it had cleared, he watched the artillery playing among the oncoming infantry. Stars burst over their heads. Solid shot skipped down the plain and into them.

The cannoneers across the river redoubled their own efforts, firing by files so that their white spurts of smoke crawled along Stafford Heights like a locomotive building speed. But then the Union gunners abruptly quit so as not to hit their own advancing troops.

McMillan trained his glasses below.

Men dropped at every pace, but on their infantry ran. The line from Prussia Street had already crossed the lower bridge over the millrace. The other was bunching up as it started to deal with the Hanover Street span. Longstreet had ordered its planks torn up, leaving only the stringer beams on which the enemy might file over, two at a time.

"They're coming in skirmish order, Colonel!" Captain Brewster shouted, pointing toward the canal. The pair of skirmish parties—three undersized regiments, counting their colors—had finished crossing. They angled toward each other, joined and became a single line before starting toward the stone wall. Yet they soon vanished behind the low bluff that lay just upslope of the canal, leaving their dead and wounded sprinkled behind them all the way back to the protection of town.

"Where are they?" somebody asked nervously.

"Waitin' for the rest of their brigade," Sullivan answered. "Suckin' breath."

McMillan agreed. His own men would be badly winded after such a dash. Now, their main brigade could be seen jogging by the flank past the railroad depot, the air over them peppered with deadly puffs. A shell flashed among them, and an entire company seemed to go down. He'd never seen a battle unfold so clearly. He realized that for once he'd have a godly view of the fight. The pain was still lodged in his chest, but he began to feel that his body could rise above the thunder and confusion—to see everything with absolute clarity. At last, after all these weeks, his mind felt sharp.

Hooves sounded behind him. Johnny Clark was charging up the hillside from Mrs. Stevens's house toward the Marye mansion. McMillan hoped the message the courier carried was for more ammunition. Now. Before it was too late.

"Up pops the Devil, boys!" an Irish voice cried.

McMillan spun around to see the enemy's heavy skirmish line spring up as if out of the ground itself. There was something weirdly inhuman, almost satanic about them. Like demons bolting their graves. They gave a huzzah that echoed above the roar of artillery. One of their color-bearers outran the front by at least twenty paces. He soon went down, and the guard scrambled forward to raise the flag again. McMillan took Sullivan by the arm. "Go along the line, Michael. Tell the officers to keep an eye on the newcomers. Our pickets will be coming in now, and I want no one seeing blue for gray."

"Aye, sir."

For a few seconds McMillan shut his eyes and prayed. For his men. For the men coming at him. For Garnett. Then he drew his sword. Ammunition. Must keep track of the ammunition. A mental ledger at all times.

Here came the pickets, loping up the slope, trailing their muskets. Each man looked jubilant as he leaped over the wall and into the safety of his friends. Must tell them later how well they did.

Adjutant Banks came huffing along the road. He started to ask something, but McMillan interrupted, "I want our fire held until the last possible second . . ." Nearly all of the regiment's muskets fired cartridges packed with a ball and two buckshot, ineffective at long ranges. "The last hundred yards. Only then. Tell the captains. And no gawking—have the men keep their heads down."

"Yes, sir." Banks was startled by a minié ball that glanced off the lip of the wall inches from his head, but then he began elbowing his way through the men. They were waiting at a semi-crouch, eager to begin shooting. "Steady there, boys," the adjutant implored, struggling with his own nerves. "Let them get close."

McMillan faced the plain again.

Their skirmishers had reached the snake fence. Some began knocking the split-rails down, most knelt to fire over them at the Strattons' place or the cluster of small houses along upper Hanover Street. They must have believed that these still hid sharpshooters. Below, the rest of their brigade could be seen threading over the millrace bridges. The Washington Artillery was mauling them, but there was no sign that they meant to do anything but keep coming on. His men *had* to make each shot count. Right behind the skirmishers, their main brigade was forming its line of battle in the cover of the swale. A brief lull, and then they too would set out for the wall.

Sullivan returned, went to his knees. "The tenderfoots are as calm as the old lags, sir."

McMillan nodded. His heart was going too fast. Must last the day. Must not falter. Must trust that God would never let him collapse. Bullets whisked overhead. Yards overhead. The blue skirmishers were approaching the second fence. Some aimed their pieces at the Washington Artillery, the North Carolinians supporting it. The Federal line had been badly thinned by now. Only three-quarters of the hundreds McMillan had seen break from town minutes ago. And the line could scarcely be called that, just a squiggle of men stretched unevenly over the rough and muddy ground. They were advancing as if they believed Longstreet's first defenses were along the crest of the heights. The big guns had captivated them.

McMillan took a deep breath, let it slowly out, then ordered the regiment to prepare to fire.

The men rose up and steadied their muskets atop the wall. Gunlocks snicked. McMillan tried not to focus on the faces. So young. So grave. Sweating in their overcoats from the warming of the day. "Fire!" he cried.

The first volley left a blinding pall of smoke in front of the wall. Through it came the clank of ramrods, a giddy laugh, a howling scream from below. He half-expected to see bayonets lunging at him through the acrid haze. But they didn't, and the smoke rolled away. The volley had completely prostrated the skirmishers. Those not killed or wounded had crawled forward to a slight swell of ground about a hundred yards below the sunken road, their chins pressed to the glazed mud. Here and there, muzzles dimly flamed. Through the ongoing cannonade, McMillan could hear bullets whining off the front of the wall or pelting the hillside behind him.

But he ordered the men to cease fire.

Half a minute passed before he was fully obeyed, due to the excitement and noise.

"Get down again!" he shouted. "Down!"

The bulk of the enemy's brigade could be seen advancing on the double. They never paused to shoot. They just surged on, a long midnight blue wave, heads bent against the canister and solid shot that were now scything huge gaps in their double line. Yet, these spaces were quickly closed. Fallen colors were picked up again and again. The alignment held. A thing of martial beauty. The flags and the bayonets. The fearless momentum.

McMillan glanced at his own men, squatting on their heels. Every face turned toward him. Black streaking their cheeks from the powder cartridges they'd bitten open. Lightheaded, he braced a hand against the wall. The stone was ice cold. Through it he felt the trembling of the earth from all the cannon. Only Confederate guns for the moment, he believed, for no shells were plowing into Marye's Heights and he could no longer make out the heavy reverberations of the enemy's long-range batteries.

Just as McMillan prepared to rise, Sullivan did it for him. "Brigade front a hundred and fifty paces below us."

"Thank you, Michael." McMillan forced himself to wait a few seconds more. Then he stood. Again, the Yankees were gazing up at the crest, the artillery and the smoke spouting from the rifle pits, as if these were their first obstacle, not the stone wall. They didn't even seem to see their own skirmishers lying on the ground in front of them.

"Fire, boys!"

This time, for an instant, McMillan saw the volley strike their line. The entire brigade seemed to freeze in place, then stagger. The smoke came too quickly for him to see how many of them had been hit and how many had simply dived for the ground. When it had cleared again, he watched the survivors rush ahead but go no farther than skirmish line, which they joined. The stands of colors were planted in the ground, and all the Federals went to their bellies to fire at the wall. From the corner of his eye, he saw one of his own men pitch backward, the top of his head bloodied, and come to rest with his arms open to the sky. Turning from this sight, he had the regiment fire at will. But his mind was still on the ammunition. "Careful aim, boys!"

He could see two more brigades on the way up from town.

Twenty-Four

◆

12:04 P.M.
116th Pennsylvania

The brigade stood in column, still waiting to go forward as enemy shot and shell went on falling into town. By chance, Tyrrell and the color guard had been halted in the chilly shade of a tall brick chimney. Just a few yards ahead lay a patch of sunlight, spreading over much of the 63d. The New Yorkers yawned and stretched in its golden warmth. A man played a reel on the tin whistle while another danced around him, his musket draped across his shoulders. By the looks of them, the old lags were in line to be paid. Tyrrell tried not to shiver. The day was becoming one of the warmest in weeks, but he was cold. And his grip felt week. He kept adjusting it on the flagstaff. Hudson, at his side, was staring blankly down at the muddy street. A few minutes ago, he'd stopped talking and from then on only nodded or shook his head in answer to questions put to him.

The sunshine suddenly dimmed.

A bank of gunsmoke had rolled down off the plain and was sifting among the houses. The air took on a sulphurous luster, the sun the dull glint of a brass disk. The Pennsylvanians faced the heights, listening to the musket fire swell. "That's the last of French's brigades going up," Lieutenant Foltz of "A" Company said in a conversational tone, although his upper lip was shining with sweat.

"When's our turn?" one of his men asked.

Heenan and Mulholland were nearby on horseback. "Steady, boys, steady," the lieutenant colonel said, lifting his hat to mop his brow on his coatsleeve. He too was perspiring. Was all the firing heating up the atmosphere? "You'll get forward soon."

Tyrrell wanted to steal a sip from his canteen, but knew that a dry mouth was a sign of nervousness. He felt as if every eye in the world was on him.

"What'd I tell you now?" a brogue said. "Here comes the butcher's bill."

The walking wounded from French's division began trickling through the ten-yard gap between the 116th and the 63d. Each man paused in the intersection, glassy-eyed, trying to recall which pontoon span was closer, either of the two at the upper end of town or the one below the ruined railroad bridge, before he made up his mind and staggered on. "How's your division faring, lads?" Heenan asked.

All ignored him, except a sergeant with his right arm slung in a bandanna. "Gettin' beat to hell."

Tyrrell bowed his head for a moment, then took a breath and looked up again. He hadn't expected to hear that.

Two privates were carrying a boyish-faced captain on a window shutter. He was out of his head with pain, rocking and thrashing on his hard stretcher, and many of the Pennsylvanians turned away when they saw why. His lower right leg was severed at the knee but for a white cord, a single tendon from which the limb dangled and swayed over the edge of the shutter. "For the love of God," a man yelled angrily from the midst of the 63d, "will you free the poor fella of it?"

The bearers made no sign that they'd heard the New Yorker, so a Pennsylvanian broke ranks and made them stop. Taking his penknife from his trouser pocket, he jerked his blade through the tendon, and the lower leg dropped into the mud with a soft thud. It was the worst sound Tyrrell had heard all morning, worse even that the screaming of the shells. The captain stopped writhing almost at once. "How very kind," he said, his voice hoarse and breathy. "Thank you." Then he was borne away.

Tyrrell realized that Hudson had watched none of this. His eyes were still downcast, his hands twisting the butt of his staff back and forth in the belt socket.

"Look out!"

A round shell bounded into the street just yards ahead of the regiment and rolled against the curb. Frozen, Tyrrell watched the fuse sputter down into the casing. He thought of neither God nor Annie. He just watched. The seconds ticked away, and nothing happened.

"S-s-steady, b-boys," Mac McCarter said. Everyone within earshot laughed, especially Mulholland, who apparently noticed the brigade clerk for the first time.

"Damn you, Mac," he said, "what're you doin' here?"

"Getting accustomed to those s-sparkly-tailed things, sir."

Tyrrell laughed again with the others. It felt like heaven to laugh.

More and more wounded were making their way toward the bridges, although surely their regiments had set up hospitals on this side of the river. A fair-haired private was being pushed along in a wheelbarrow. He was quietly puffing on his pipe even though his left foot had been shot off at the ankle. The stump was still bleeding. The soldier wheeling him was having trouble with the ungainly load, and when the barrow tipped nearly over the wounded man said with a German accent, "Ach, make right!"

"Ach, ach!" the men of the 63d hooted, finding this hilarious. Tyrrell heard from his own regiment a thin voice beseeching, "God between us and all harm."

Tyrrell tried to fill his mind with Annie's face. She smiled at him, but then vanished in a plunging screech. Smoke boiled up from the ranks ahead.

"Holy Mary," Heenan said, his horse skittering beneath him, "that hit right in the middle of the Eighty-eighth."

Hudson had shut his eyes and was breathing rapidly.

"Gettin' sick again?" Tyrrell asked.

The corporal gave a violent shake of his head, but then rested his brow against the staff.

General Meagher could be seen down the street, smoking a cigar. In between, Tyrrell glimpsed the green flag of the 28th Massachusetts. When the column formed brigade line, the Bostonians would have the center so all could see the Irish colors. He reached up with his left hand and made sure his sprig of boxwood was still stuck to his cap. Must write his father about this. The boxwood. Meagher's parting speech about doing credit to Ireland. Then he was reminded again of the letter to Annie that was yet in his pocket. He didn't really think he was going to die today, but doubt had begun to creep over him. He was afraid the letter might wind up buried with him. And if there was time, he would add a few lines. Back near the wharf, Father Corby had hurriedly gone through the ranks, blessing each man. One freethinker had asked, "And what if this don't take, Father?" Without batting an eye, the priest said, "Then try to die with God in mind." Impossible, Tyrrell had thought. He didn't know God's face. At least not the way he knew Annie's. It'd be easier to die with her in mind, her hair falling around his eyes. *Must add those lines, say more than I did with my first try.*

A big shadow passed him in the same second an ear-splitting shriek made him want to cringe. Then came a clatter of bricks, followed by a crunch as if timbers and boards were collapsing. Tyrrell was just starting to turn toward these sounds when a searing heat brushed the back of his neck.

His first thought was the colors. Had he dropped them?

No, his hands were still wrapped whitely around the pole. His ears were ringing, although he couldn't recall having heard the huge shell go off.

Irish Brigade Marches
Through Town to Plain
Midday, Dec. 13

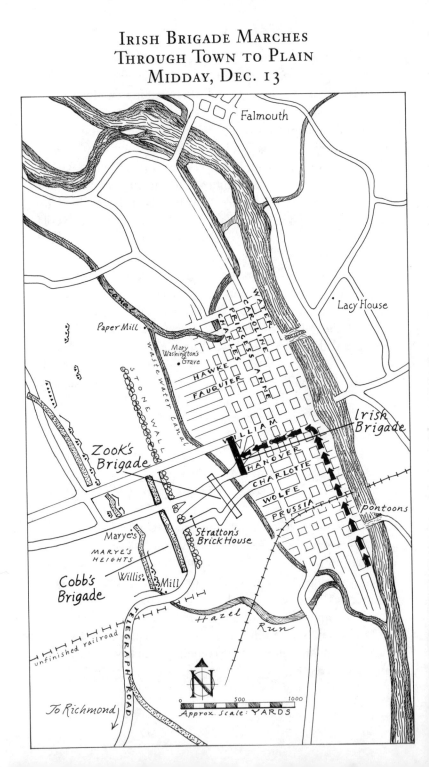

Falmouth

Lacy House

Paper Mill

Mary Washington's Grave

WATER

CAROLINE

PRINCESS

HAWKE

FAUQUIER

WILLIAM

Irish Brigade

Zook's Brigade

STONE WALL

Wastewater Canal

HANOVER

CHARLOTTE

WOLFE

PRUSSIA

Pontoons

Stratton's Brick House

Marye's

MARYE'S HEIGHTS

Willis' Mill

Cobb's Brigade

TELEGRAPH ROAD

Hazel Run

unfinished railroad

To Richmond

N

0   500   1000

Approx. Scale: YARDS

Heenan was snapping his fist in the air, the blood from it flecking his face. "Damn!" he howled. "Damn those bastards!"

Turning slowly, as if in a nightmare, Tyrrell saw that three men had been downed. For an instant he thought that a fourth man, a sergeant, was kneeling over them for signs of life, head bowed. But then his vision cleared a little and he realized that the sergeant's head was missing. He'd dropped to his knees, then stayed upright on his musket, which he'd been leaning on when hit.

"It's Marley," someone said.

"Should we look for his head?"

"No, let it go."

The corpse stirred with a baffling semblance of life, then pitched over.

Tyrrell locked gazes with McCarter. The clerk had an odd smile. Blood was pooling under his left shoe. "You're hurt, Mac."

"No."

"Look down."

McCarter glanced down but went on smiling. "No."

Mulholland whipped out his handkerchief and bandaged Heenan's hand for him. The order was passed from regiment to regiment, and the colonel picked it up, shouted, "Attention!" Ahead, Meagher tossed away his cigar and, drawing his sword, began turning the 69th up a street toward the plain. "Shoulder arms . . . forward . . . double-quick . . . do your duty . . ." Heenan's hand must have been throbbing badly, for he clenched it in an armpit. "March!"

Running had never felt so good. Tyrrell had to force himself not to race up on the heels of the 63d. One of his guards tapped him on the shoulder. "Look back, Will."

He quickly did. A man in "C" Company was lying spread-eagled in the street, the regiment flowing around him. "Hit?"

"Fainted," the guard said, "when that Dutchman come by in the wheelbarrow."

Tyrrell rolled his eyes.

"It's Billy Dehaven," someone added. "He's got grit enough, but it's his stomach . . . terrible weak stomach."

Meagher was no longer at the corner, but one of his aides had been left there to turn the 116th. "Looking proud, Pennsylvania," the feverish-faced lieutenant said over the slap of brogans. Tyrrell wasn't so sure. Not with a private passed out in the middle of Water Street. The lane climbed steeply up a terrace, and the column slowed at its top, winded. Another shell curved down into the 88th. Shrapnel whispered around Tyrrell's head. Again, Mulholland called on everyone to be steady. His mount's eyes were bulging with fear. Tyrrell jogged past the wounded from the blast. They were perched together on the low wall around a cemetery. One of them, cradling a mangled forearm in his lap, cried out to a private in the last company of the 63d, "What harm, Danny, if it's for the poor Old *Dairt?*"

"Well," the man replied, "I'd still rather be knobbin' down Broadway right now."

"Me too. Don't go and get yourself kilt."

"Not to worry. It's the Rebellers doin' all the killin'. I'll have no say in it."

A calico cat was sitting on a gate post, mewing at the column as it tramped past. The head of the brigade was nearing the houses that bordered on the plain. Ahead lay a slight rise topped by a long white fence. All at once, the noise was deafening, but between the roaring of the shells Tyrrell could hear spent bullets pelting roofs, shattering window glass. Smoke was billowing palely up into the sky. Scarves of it passed across the sun, making the light fade and brighten with a dizzying rapidity.

"Hurry, boys," Mulholland cried, "don't fall behind the Sixty-third!"

The street was strewn with dead and wounded. Every few paces, Tyrrell had to step over a body. He didn't look for faces. Nor did he answer a man who cried out wordlessly to him. Something tugged at the pole in his grasp, a sharp strike like a

hooked fish. He glanced up. The colors had taken their first tear.
The red-hot shell fragment that had done it sizzled as it cooled
in the slush.

Hancock galloped past on a large bay horse, trailed by his
aides. He waved his hat, urging the Pennsylvanians on.

"God between us and all harm," the same high voice begged
from the ranks behind Tyrrell.

A cheer went up from the regiment, quickly turned to laughter and whistling. Tyrrell looked around, confused until he saw
Private Dehaven. He'd recovered and was sprinting to catch up
with his company, the butt of his musket dragging in the mud
behind him.

12:22 P.M.
24th Georgia

At last, Sullivan had to stand. He'd been kneeling a few feet behind the colonel ever since McMillan had ordered the first volley, and his leg muscles were knotted by cramps. Grunting, he
eased up into the thick of the smoke. The whirring all around
told him that the enemy brigades were firing buck and ball, like
the 24th. He stamped his feet, trying to jar feeling back into
them. "Come, Michael." Suddenly, McMillan, who despite Sullivan's protests had yet to crouch since that first volley, had decided to prowl the line. The sergeant hobbled behind him, his
ears buzzing from the cannonade. He stole a peek over the wall.
The second wave of Federals had almost reached the survivors
of the first push. No officers. He saw no officers along their
ragged, stumbling line. Their swords and shoulder straps were
marking them for instant death as soon as they came into range.

McMillan paused behind "K" Company, and Sullivan caught
the old man checking on Garnett. Still up. Still unhurt. The
colonel permitted himself a faint smile.

Directly in front of Sullivan, a soldier rose and yanked his trigger. But then, instead of getting down as all the men had been

told, he gawked open-mouthed over the top of the wall at the approaching enemy. Sullivan grabbed him by the scruff of his light brown curly hair and wrenched him to the ground. "Did no one—?" He stopped, amazed. It was Tully. Sullivan felt an enormous anger boil out of him, and then it was done: he'd slapped the boy before he could think.

"I'm here on orders!" Tully cried, his tongue black from licking his powder-smeared lips.

Sullivan blinked at him, breathing thunderously. "Whose?"

"Sarn't Oliver. A letter come this mornin' from home."

"Give it to me."

"He's got it."

"Lie!"

Tully's underlip began twitching. "No, it ain't—Oliver gave me a message for Lieutenant McMillan!"

Sullivan eyed the boy a moment longer, then rushed down the line to Garnett's side. "Sir, in the matter of young Private Tully . . ."

The lieutenant shook his head. "Can't hear you!"

"Sir, is Tully there truly of age!"

"Oh yes." Garnett patted his coat pocket. "Oliver says he just received confirmation from an itinerant priest." Then the lieutenant noticed a prostrated man. He rolled him over—the top of the man's skull was gone—and ransacked his pockets for cartridges, gave them to another man.

Sullivan went back to Tully, who still lay slumped against the earthen bank. His cheeks were tarry from powder and tears. The sergeant tried to think of something to say, but nothing came to mind, and he felt little like apologizing. He'd slapped that other face after the last breath had gone out of it, hoping the sting of his hand would restore life. "Come on," he finally said, crossly, "recap, get loadin'!"

Suddenly, the volume of fire doubled.

Sullivan flopped on his back and gazed up. Marye's crest was lined with gray figures. A fresh brigade had come to its edge to lend support to Cobb: the North Carolinians, who'd been waiting in reserve just beyond the brow of the heights. Muzzles flaming, they let go a volley at the enemy that covered the sunken road with choking smoke.

"God bless the work!" Dooley shouted, then ran his fingertips over his lips. They were starting to crack and bleed from the dry, acrid stuff.

Hacking for air, Sullivan bolted upright, looked over the wall, then dropped down again. The second blue brigade, just battered by the North Carolinians, was finally getting ready to fire back. Sullivan grabbed Tully to make sure he wouldn't rise. A flurry of buck and ball hummed through the air. A man in "K" Company spun away from the wall, growling. Two of his fingers had been clipped off.

"That's it, boys!" McMillan hollered. "Now!"

"Use your potstick," Sullivan told Tully, rising again. "Get it over with!" The enemy's second brigade had been stopped short of the highwater mark of the first wave. It seemed as if a quarter of them had melted away in the last minute. Tough to march all that way up the open fields under shot and shell without being allowed to open fire. A regiment of Zouaves was among them, gaudy-looking. Fezzes and white leggings. But they'd come up the slope as if they were on parade. Hard men.

Working his ramrod, Tully struck Sullivan on the chin with a backstroke. "Mind your haste, boy!" he barked, then crawled over to Dooley, who'd just finished firing. "How many rounds have you left, Tommy?"

"Maybe fifteen."

"That's all?"

"Aye."

Sullivan scanned the crest, hoping to see an ammunition crate on the way down. If none came soon, McMillan would send him to McLaws to ask for one. The face of the slope was being raked with nearly every shot the blue infantry could loose.

"That's it, boys," McMillan's voice cut through the smoke. "You've got some of them turning back!" He was standing on the embankment, covered by the wall only waist-high. His chest was heaving, but his blood was up and he went on shouting at the top of his lungs, "Here they come again! Give it to them!"

Tully popped up, fired, then fell back on his buttocks in his rush to get down. Wide-eyed, he looked at Sullivan as if to ask how he'd done. His barrel had been inclined too high to hit anything short of Stafford Heights, but Sullivan's heart was softened by the quiet pleading in the boy's face. He nodded and said, "That's it, up and down. Just try not to bag old Abraham from here next time!"

"What d'you mean?"

"Lower your aim!"

A flight of shells shrilled overhead. They exploded behind the hill. The advancing Federal infantry was too close to the wall for their cannoneers to lob rounds into the sunken road, not without peppering their own men.

"Hurry now, boys!" McMillan hollered, his voice cracking as it rose above the din. "Pour it into them *now!*"

Dooley reared up and laid his barrel across the top of the wall. He hesitated. Nothing but smoke. But then it rolled on. Over the man's shoulder, Sullivan saw their third brigade line coming on at a flagging double-quick. Tired, so breathlessly tired. They fired, then immediately lay down. Sullivan watched as Dooley aimed for a head that was still uplifted. The white puff from the muzzle made it impossible to tell if anyone had been hit. Dimly below, a fourth brigade was forming into line of battle between the canal and the bluff. And behind it, just beginning to cross the upper bridge over the ditch, yet another brigade. And one more debouching from town.

The weight.

"You did it, boys," McMillan said in a more normal voice. "You stopped them."

The men gave him three cheers, and his face turned red as he lowered his sword.

Sullivan sensed movement behind him. Pivoting, he saw the line of gray uniforms sweep down off the crest into the road. A scrag of a private, an apple clenched between his front teeth, threw himself down behind the wall and began reloading. "Fired on the trip down," he explained around the apple. "Sure hated leavin' that orchard behind the house." He took a crunching bite, then tossed what remained to Sullivan and smoothly took a shot over the wall. "Have the rest, Sarn't. Compliments of the Forty-sixth North Carolina." John Cooke's brigade. That meant the 15th North Carolina, which had been Cobb's until last month, was lying in support on the crest. A comforting thought. Old friends. Pranksters but reliable men in a fight, those Tarheels.

The apple had been frozen, but Sullivan still found the mushy bite delicious. "What's it look like from the top of the hill?"

"No end to 'em."

"You bring any extra ammunition?"

"No, but we ain't fired much yet."

Sullivan handed the apple half to Tully, who gobbled it down, seeds and all. Rising slightly, the sergeant saw a carpet of blue bodies, living and dead, from one hundred to three hundred yards beyond the wall. The sight didn't cheer him. *No end to 'em*, as the Tarheel had just said.

Dooley shot at a stand of colors, the clot of men kneeling around it.

Dropping once more, Sullivan listened to the balls and bullets passing above the road, the sharp zings of strikes against the exposed face of the wall. But this fusillade was slackening off. Pinned down, the Yanks in the shallow depression below the Strattons' fence were mostly resting on their arms, awaiting the brigades that were still putting themselves together below.

McMillan ordered the regiment to cease firing.

Jesse, Cobb's manservant, came walking tall along the line with a bucket of water and a dipper. His master refused to stoop under fire, so he wouldn't. Cobb himself wasn't far off. He was standing in Mrs. Stevens's yard, talking to Captain Brewster and Tom Cook of Phillips's Legion. "Obliged, Jesse." Sullivan drank, then gave back the tin dipper and glanced over the wall.

"What's for?" Tully asked.

"Stay down," Sullivan ordered, then sat. The thawed mud of the embankment was becoming slippery under all the exertions of the men. "They're rollin' out the field batteries on the upper edge of town," he said, then went over to McMillan, who was upright beside Satterfield and the colors. "Colonel—" He paused for a distant series of thumps. Just what he'd expected. The Union artillery had been waiting for a chance to open up, and now with the first three brigades flat on their bellies their cannon could pound the sunken road. "Sir, I don't suppose you might lower yourself behind this fine, stout wall."

"Not today, I think, Michael." McMillan's eyes brightened slightly. "Besides, I'm safe up to the *oxters.*" Armpits, in Ulster.

"I'm sure, sir, but you do all your commandin' from the *oxters* up."

A smile tugged at the corner of McMillan's mouth, but then he jammed the heel of his hand against the side of his ribcage. "Michael," he said when the moment had passed, "kindly ask the North Carolinians to share their rounds with our men."

Twenty-Five

◆

Meagher handed his rein over to an orderly. The man had found a sheltered garden for the officers' horses among the last houses of town. "Help me down," the general said. "Quickly." The column was unraveling into brigade front, two long ranks of jogging men, in the open field just beyond a whitewashed fence, and he didn't want to fall behind. *Must keep in the lead. Must see how much this damnable leg will bear.* He'd go all the way to the heights, if only his knee didn't buckle.

Hancock was across the street, sitting on his tall bay, of course, despite the order he'd given his command to stay out of the saddle. He was herding some stragglers from French's division back toward the plain with the flat of his sword when he noticed Meagher limping up the boardwalk toward his brigade. "Tom," he cried, pointing with his blade, "keep to the left of that big brick house!"

He couldn't see it, but nodded anyway, and Hancock dashed off. Then, for the moment, Meagher was alone in the milky light, walking toward the heart of the roar. Rich Emmet was still dismounting. The aide gave his charger a parting swat on the rump, then broke into a feeble run to catch up. Grimacing,

Meagher slowed. Lightning was flashing behind his eyes with each stride. Emmet fell in beside him, smiled even though his breath was rattling in his throat. They found a gap in the white fence, then paused on its far side. Meagher looked for the brick house Hancock had been talking about. The smoke parted, revealing a cove in the pall that sparkled with shrapnel bursts. Ahead, off to the left, troops were jammed up in a mass, waiting to cross some kind of bridge by twos. That'd be Zook's outfit. Hancock had said nothing about a bridge. No one had said anything about what terrain and obstacles lay in front of the attack.

"General Meagher," a major said, approaching him out of the west. He was soaked to the waist. Division engineer. "Sir—"

"What's the delay ahead?" Meagher asked.

"Bridge over a twenty-foot-wide canal. Johnnies ripped up the planks, and we're left with only the stringers."

"How deep?"

The major gestured at his wet trousers, then said, "I'll try to find some bridging material," and set off for town.

Meagher took his field glasses from his coat pocket and scanned through the broken patches of smoke for the brick house. Marye's Heights were enshrouded, but at last he located the two-story structure. The lawn seemed to be blue. He imagined it to be some trick of the light until he realized that hundreds of French's men were cowering behind the house. No wonder Hancock wanted the Irish Brigade to advance to the left of it, clear of this groveling mob. *Must not let the men lie down. Must keep them moving.*

He limped on, Emmet at his side, but an overhead burst stopped them again. Hot iron fragments pelted the ground all around. A quick inventory of his own body parts, then Meagher asked, "You all right, Rich?"

Emmet just smiled. His eyes shone with fever, and at their pits Meagher saw something, an airy calm perhaps, that told him the boy knew he would be dead soon, one way or another. Canister shot whistled just to the right of them, but looking at his aide Meagher could imagine the iron marbles to have been hummingbirds. He felt, as he had last evening, that Robert Emmet was with him, ghostly pale and silent—but with him. Yet, loneliness still dogged him, and he needed to talk. "As my old dear mother used to advise, Rich," he said brightly, although the pain was nauseating him now, "say your prayers and don't fasten the Devil." He paused. "I saw the Beast this morning in the flesh."

"Sir?"

"Charles Mackay." The New York correspondent of the London *Times*, a turncoat Irishman who made no secret that his sympathies lay with both the crown and the Confederacy. Charles Lawley, the Richmond correspondent and an Englishman, was only slightly more detested for his skewed reporting.

Mangled dead lay all about, a few from the brigade but most from French's division. Emmet seemed to glide over them. "Then let's give Mr. Mackay something to write home about, sir," he said, smiling again, shivering.

12:51 P.M.
24th Georgia

Most of the percussion shells struck the crest around the Marye mansion, but one landed near Mrs. Stevens's little house. McMillan wouldn't have noticed the impact but for the winter-browned leaves of the widow's oak trees. They came down in a shower. The Washington Artillery flew back at the Union field batteries lined up on the edge of town, where after a few minutes a black pillar suddenly shot high into the sky. A caisson had been hit, McMillan noted with satisfaction.

He could hear his name being passed man-to-man down the road toward him.

"What is it?" he asked.

"General Cobb wants you," Garnett said.

McMillan started toward the widow's house, skirting his Georgians and their North Carolinian reinforcements by keeping to the upslope side of the road. The men, weary of elbowing through one another to find space to shoot, had begun passing loaded muskets to the men already at the wall. For the moment, the small-arms fire coming from the plain had eased off, so the men rested, wiped their powder-darkened faces on their sleeves and passed canteens around.

McMillan realized that Sullivan was following him, moving at a simian crouch. "We stopped them, Michael."

"Yes, sir . . . so far."

"A division, I'm sure."

"Aye, a whole division."

Beyond the sergeant, McMillan could see a regiment running down off the heights, doubling up with Phillips's Legion along the wall. The 2d South Carolina, he believed. The more the better as long as the men found ways to keep up a smooth, workmanlike fire. Coming into Mrs. Stevens's crowded dooryard, he searched for Cobb.

"Here, Robert . . ." The brigadier was lying on a stretcher in the middle of the road only yards from McMillan. A silk handkerchief had been tied as a tourniquet around his thigh, but his trouser leg was sticking to the limb with fresh blood. And the bottom of the litter was saturated. An artery had been blown, and the handkerchief was doing little to stem the flow. "Robert," he went on with a sleepy smile, "I seem to have ruined my new coat." His face was like candle wax, making his teeth look yellowish. "Poor Marion. Went through such trouble to get me this one."

McMillan knelt, and an assistant surgeon immediately told him, "Be brief, sir. We have to get him back to our hospital right away."

McMillan nodded.

"The brigade's yours, Robert." Cobb then appeared to grow confused. "How are the others?"

"Others, sir?"

Cobb's gaze shifted across the road, where the surgeon and Mrs. Stevens were tending to three men in a row, all flat on their backs. Sullivan, who'd been helping them, said urgently, "Colonel, when you have a moment."

"Go," Cobb said.

McMillan rose and went over.

He couldn't believe that a single shell had done so much. Tom Cook of Phillips's Legion was dead. A piece of the shell had caved in his right temple. That brown-eyed girl in Dalton. *I have no higher aim in life than to be a Cook.* Beside him lay Cobb's adjutant, Herring, delirious from a gaping hole in his hip. And last, Walter Brewster lifted his heavy, swaying head and stared at McMillan as if he didn't recognize him. He'd been hit just above the knee, although the wound looked more from a minié ball than a shell fragment. "I saw the general fall," the young captain carefully explained. "I was going to see if I might help when . . ." He glanced down toward his leg.

"I'm sure you did the best you could, Walter," McMillan said. It grieved him to see how much his words seemed to reassure Brewster.

Sullivan was at his elbow again. "Sir, they're movin' the general now. Down the road to keep off the slope."

McMillan gripped Brewster's flaccid hand. "I'll check on you as soon as I can . . ."

But the captain had passed out.

Jesse and Johnny Clark carried the stretcher at a half-trot, but the general groggily begged them to slow down. Driblets of blood were leaking through the canvas. He craned his head backward and gazed through slitted eyelids at McMillan. "Robert?" he said with a quizzical tone, that of someone calling into a darkened room.

McMillan then realized that his sight was going. "Here, sir."

"You've got the brigade."

"I know, Thomas." The name, once so familiar, sounded odd

after all these months of subordination, but McMillan had felt a powerful need to say it now.

Cobb closed his eyes.

They had to halt. The enemy shelling forced them to lie low for a few minutes. All but McMillan stooped. Still standing, he leaned over Cobb for fear that the man would be struck again.

12:55 P.M.
69th New York

Once across the millrace, Donovan saw that the rush up to the heights wouldn't be a clear sweep. There were buildings, gardens, and fences in the way. A small shop lay straight ahead along the pike, and off to the left a brick house with a wooden outbuilding. These were the obstacles—if the brigade ever got over the plankless bridge into the plowed field just beyond. So far, it was mostly stacked up on the town side of the canal, with only the 69th across, waiting in battle line under heavy fire.

There was a loud thwack somewhere behind Donovan. Lead striking bone. He didn't turn to see who'd been hit. He was standing at his proper place, to the rear center of his company, and from now on would leave the dressing of the thinned ranks to his file closers. With each casualty, these men would help shift the lines toward the colors, keeping the formation tight.

The men suddenly cheered.

Meagher was approaching the bridge on foot. His knee seemed to be locking like a rusty hinge. Stopping, he gazed down into the dark green water, the surface chopped every few seconds by shrapnel. Bodies floating. Pieces of bodies too. The general didn't seem eager to thread the narrow beam, and Rich Emmet, at his back, was too frail to help. A pair of privates, each with a wounded arm, were wading back toward Surgeon Reynolds's hospital in town when they saw Meagher poised on the bank. "Strike hands, sir," one of them said, extending his uninjured arm up to the general. The other soldier ducked under the stringer and did the same from the opposite side.

"Thanks, boys," Meagher said, going heel-to-toe over the beam, which was slick in places with blood. Letting go, the two privates looked pleased to have had a touch of the great man.

Nugent was waiting for him. "Hell of a place to dawdle. They've got the perfect range of this damned bridge!"

"I know, Bob." Meagher looked no less impatient than the 69th's colonel. Donovan realized that the brigadier was now using his sword as a cane. A loud splashing turned heads. One of Hancock's aides was urging his horse through the ditch water toward Meagher. A shell strike foamed to the side of him, but he ignored the sudden shower and spurred his mount up onto the bank. "General Meagher—" The horse shook, splattering everyone within twenty feet, and the droplets felt like ice on Donovan's face. "Sir, General Hancock asks you to throw out two companies to the right of your line—skirmishers."

"Where exactly?" Meagher asked, flexing his knee.

The rider pointed at a small knoll before wheeling and thrashing back across the canal.

The general began talking low with Nugent. Donovan didn't want his company to be saddled with some sideshow. Not on the afternoon that might end the war.

A voice yelled, sounding almost jolly, "Comin' through!"

Something big and fast whisked past Donovan's ear, raising the hair on his nape. The round shot bounded over the ditch and into the ranks of the 28th Massachusetts, which had just begun to cross. It cut a swath, nearly taking out the color guard. But the green flag went on rippling in the rising breeze.

Sweat was collecting behind Donovan's eyepatch. He lifted it and dabbed the socket with his coatsleeve.

Nugent called for the commanders of "C" and "I" Companies. They came at a run, holding their scabbards steady against their sides. Donovan exhaled with relief. Good. His own men wouldn't spend the afternoon as skirmishers. If the rumor was right, at this very hour, all over Virginia, Federal armies were screwing shut the vise on Richmond. He wouldn't miss this for the world.

Meagher had taken out his pocket watch. "That's it," he fumed, snapping shut the case. "That's bloody it. Can't spend the rest of the day here!" He then ordered the remaining men to ford the ditch, all but officers and color guards. "Jump, boys!"

1:12 P.M.

116th Pennsylvania

The 63d suddenly rushed for the ditch, leaving the 116th behind. "What's happening?" Hudson asked anxiously. Tyrrell was afraid that the enemy were counterattacking through the smoke, but then he had no time to think about this: Mulholland was bawling for the regiment to wade the canal and re-form on the far bank. The lieutenant colonel added something more, but his words were lost under the deafening clap of a shell, the screams of the wounded that followed. Tyrrell coiled the trailing end of the flag around his forearm and ran. He tripped over a body, but two men of the guard took hold of him from behind, kept him from falling.

"Hurry!" Meagher's voice could be heard under and over the artillery. "Zook's ready to go!"

As Tyrrell neared the ditch, a New York major, a short man, ordered him and the guard to cross the stringers. "What, sir?" he asked, not understanding at first.

"Walk the beam, son!"

Lieutenant Montgomery of "I" Company darted in front of Tyrrell, but the officer had taken no more than a few steps along the bridge beam when his body jerked and he tumbled over. Tyrrell tried to see if he was still alive, but the canal was a chaos of foam and rushing men, a sound like hungry fish boiling the surface of a pond. He and the color guard wound up on the far bank in the midst of the 69th. A captain with an eyepatch motioned toward the left and said cordially, "The line forms that way, gentlemen."

Tyrrell trotted past the other regiments, already arrayed, toward Colonel Heenan, who was waving his bandaged hand for the Pennsylvanians to gather on him. Hudson and the rest of the guard fell behind, so he slowed for them. Must not outrun the line when the advance came. That'd be bravura, and it might ruin the alignment of the entire brigade front.

Between the booming of the cannon, a soft fluttering could be heard: the air being strummed by balls and bullets and canister. Tyrrell coughed. The taste of sulphur was clinging to the back of his throat.

"Oh God," someone said, sounding terribly surprised.

Tyrrell glanced over his shoulder: one of his guards was down on all fours, his neck splashed with blood. "Keep on," Tyrrell told the others. Dead and wounded were littering the plowed field everywhere. The big, half-frozen clods grabbed at his feet, threatened to turn his ankles.

"Stand there, Sergeant!" Mulholland pointed at the spot with his sword. Tyrrell halted. Hudson and the guard fell in around him, and then the regiment, given a center once again, its two flags, swiftly formed the left end of the quarter-mile-long battle line. A few hundred feet forward, Zook's brigade was lying just below the brow of the slight rise, bayonets fixed.

1:19 P.M.
24th Georgia

Garnett McMillan squeezed shut his eyes. They were burning from the bad air, the salt of his sweat, the strain of peering into the shifting veils of smoke for human figures. His spittle had a black taste to it, and there was an itch in his chest no amount of coughing would relieve. He opened his eyes, studied the enemy line just below the wall. A few muzzles blazed along the length of it, giving off puffs of white that ran away with the stiffening breeze. The three stands of Union colors were still planted in the ground, tantalizingly close, their bearers either dead or hugging the ground like the rest of the survivors. Several of Garnett's men had volunteered to try to capture the flags. But the colonel had said no before going off to check on Phillips's Legion, leaderless now that Tom Cook was dead.

Garnett saw that one of the North Carolinians, a boy, was sobbing, twisting his felt hat in his hands. "What is it?" he asked him.

"Mrs. Stuart's sure gonna take this hard."

Garnett looked away in confusion. Mrs. Stuart? Then, after a second, it hit him. The young Tarheel thought his brigadier, John Cooke, Jeb Stuart's brother-in-law, had been killed by the shell that had wounded Cobb and Wally Brewster. Adjutant Banks, in spreading the word, had said simply, "Cook's dead."

"Listen, North Carolina," Garnett raised his voice over the Washington Artillery, which was going to rapid fire again, "it was Tom Cook of Phillips's Legion who died. Not your general, not Johnny Cooke. Do you understand?"

Most did, all but the boy, who wiped his nose in his hat and went on crying.

Garnett tensed. Something was coming this way, another push. He could tell from the cannoneers. High on the crest, they saw everything first. He looked for his father. Not back from the north end of the road. The old man had said nothing as he'd walked behind Cobb's litter, but Garnett had known with a glance that the brigadier was dying. He'd never seen a face so bloodless. Like white marble. And he alone of all the Georgians could tell how distraught his father was—by the steely frost that had fallen over his eyes. They'd been the same when he buried James and then Emma.

The cannon smoke wafted down into the road, and Garnett began hacking again. Lungs on fire. He wiped some warmth off his lips with his handkerchief, then gaped in amazement at the cloth. Blood.

"Here they come ag'in," somebody warned.

Garnett saw the next brigade break over the rise below, heard their hurrah echo against the heights. Again, the enemy seemed to swell out of the very earth. "Hold your fire," he said.

"Yes, wait for my word, boys," his father's voice cried from behind, "and then shoot low!"

The breeze was clearing the smoke, opening the view all the way to Stafford Heights. There, a giant balloon was floating above Lacy House. They were clever, these people coming at the wall. But there was something wicked about their cleverness, a devilish genius for machines and amassing worldly goods. Cobb had once said something like that. And now he was dying. Hard to absorb. So vigorous just an hour ago, pacing the line with his hands balled up in fists. Yet, Garnett knew that the men were relieved to have Robert McMillan over them. No bombast, just a rock steadiness, orders coming in that unflappable burr.

The enemy shelling got even heavier. Garnett could see a battery section posted at the outlet to each street. Glints of brass. Shellbursts walked up to the wall. One flashed among the 18th Georgia, and another ricocheted off the slope and soared over the crest to tear the crown out of a pine.

"Wait now, wait," his father insisted.

For a moment, Garnett felt sorry for the approaching brigade. It was awful to come on like that, not allowed to return fire, feeling your chances slip away with each passing instant. He'd done what they were doing and hated the thought of it, even though his own artillery was gouging wide holes in their line. The living sidestepped over the dead and maimed, and the gaps vanished along the ever-thinning front. Dropped flags were picked up by new hands.

"Soon, boys, soon," his father promised.

They were midway between the snake-rail fence and the Strattons' house.

Garnett found himself confused that they were attacking again. Was it simply to cover the withdrawal of the division that had already failed? He glanced at his father. Sharpshooter bullets were spalling bark off the locust tree behind him. Garnett could hear the 24th's colors flapping.

"Now!" the colonel shouted.

For the first time, Garnett saw a volley land against their line. Men were swatted off their feet, hurled to the ground, but most came on, shooting now, leveling their bayonets toward the wall. Survivors from the first division got up and joined them. Garnett rose so he could keep track of this onslaught. Seventy yards and closing. His men quit passing loaded pieces forward and instead delivered shots from wherever they stood. The enemy line staggered, began to slow. A muzzle blast left Garnett's right ear ringing. He was rubbing it when he realized that men other than his own or the North Carolinians were jostling forward to pour fire into the faces of the Yankees. He turned. Another regiment had come down out of reserve. He shouted to a middle-aged sergeant major, "Who are you people!" He had to ask once again before the man heard him.

"Eighth South Carolina!"

Garnett braced, tightened his grip on his sword. Several blue-coated men were only forty yards from the wall. Their lips were clean of powder. They had yet to reload but seemed determined to take the wall with their bayonets. On they came. But then Garnett blinked, and they were gone. Those a short way behind them stopped, then crawled back to the main line and went prone. A squad here and there tried to get the attack going again, but these men were cut down almost as soon as they reared their heads.

Garnett looked for his father. Still standing unhunched. Turning, he took the sergeant major from the 8th South Carolina by the sleeve. "We've got to organize this throng!"

"I agree, Lieutenant."

Garnett pulled his men back from the wall, mostly to let their muskets cool while they reloaded for the new arrivals. But the South Carolinians must have been firing for some time too—a flash went off only feet from Garnett. A burly Georgian stumbled out of the smoke cloud, cursing. His eyebrows had been singed off and his beard crisped. He'd rammed a round down a hot barrel only to have the musket discharge prematurely in his face.

"Give me a canteen," Garnett ordered. Tossed one, he poured water over the man's quivering eyelids. "Can you see, Hezekiah?"

"Not worth a damn," the private answered. "But I can reload in the dark." Then he told his messmates to go on handing him muskets.

Garnett picked his way through men six-deep to a portion of the wall with less earth heaped against it. The sergeant major was already there, leaning his forearms against the capstones. "Well, Lieutenant, here come the next gang of 'em," he said, sighing.

Garnett could see no troops, but the sunlit golden eagles atop the stars and stripes were just showing above the swale hiding the next brigade. "What's going on with Jackson?" he asked. Impossible to distinguish any firing from that wing of the army.

"Not much," the South Carolinian said, shifting a plug of tobacco to his other cheek. "About over down there, what I hear. But we're in for it now."

"What do you mean?"

"Ol' Kershaw sent us down here with orders to hold to the last man." The sergeant spat over the wall.

1:24 P.M.
Irish Brigade

Meagher stood atop the small bluff, glassing the progress of Zook's brigade through the drifting smoke. It was approaching a partly torn-down board fence on the far side of the brick house. That, he had decided, was the signal for his own men to set out. About-facing, he raised his sword. Seeing this, his five regimental commanders cried, nearly as one, "Attention!" The men got up off their stomachs, although many couldn't rise. Ten minutes of lying under the hammering cannonade had taken their toll. Scores stayed down in the muddy field, motionless among the dead of the previous brigades, and a few wounded were dragging themselves toward the Hanover Street bridge, which was now jamming up Caldwell's brigade. *Fix bayonets.* Little clinking sounds ran up and down the line. Chilling.

"Irish Brigade, advance!" Meagher tried to roar above the head-jangling thunder. He feared that his voice had been lost in it.

But his colonels put the order into motion—*right shoulder, shift arms, battalion forward, guide center . . . march.* The line started up the gentle slope toward him, green flag at its center, the boxwood in the men's caps vivid against the dun colors of the winter-fallow field. Behind the brigade remained the dead and wounded, piles of blankets and haversacks. Ahead, the enemy musketry rose to a clamor like hail pounding a tin roof, then a seamless, crackly roar that was like nothing else. Meagher stopped hobbling long enough to focus his glasses on Zook's men. He could pick out no sky blue of trouser legs, only the darker blue of overcoats. That meant Zook's brigade had gone prone. It too was stalled near the foot of the heights. He'd never let his own men do that. Once down, they were down for good. *Must not allow that.* His commanders—Nugent, Kelly, Byrnes, O'Neill, and Heenan—were all forward of their men, and then even the captains trotted to the front centers of their companies.

Twenty-Six

◆

1:31 P.M.
Irish Brigade Colors Detail

McGee had heard the strange whispery rumble of the battle all morning, yet what little news he learned along the muddy pike was bewildering and contradictory. Each passing courier had it differently. General Franklin had outflanked Jackson: Lee's army was skedaddling for Richmond, and the war was won. And then a hurried shout that the Left Grand Division was actually stymied midway between the river and the heights south of town. And now, as Captain Martin, the brigade committeemen, and McGee rode up to Lacy House in the omnibus, a sentry reported that Franklin had given up for the day and everything depended on Sumner. "But how's Second Corps doing?" McGee asked.

The man shrugged, cocked his bored eyes toward the unbroken roar of cannon and musketry from across the Rappahannock.

The troops of 5th Corps were massed on both sides of the lane, waiting around their coffee fires. The omnibus driver slowed his team through them, then halted behind the mansion. At last, the crated bottles of champagne and whiskey stopped clicking, and McGee could hear himself think. "I'll try to find

out where our boys are," he told the others as he climbed down
from the wagon.

"Do you suppose they're already engaged?" one of the nabobs
asked eagerly.

"Don't know, sir," McGee said, his politeness strained. He'd
wearied of their self-satisfied company over the long miles.

Nearby, an observation balloon was spinning on its tether a
few feet off the ground, basket empty. He went around the
house, saw some officers in a bunch at the Signal Corps's telescope. He was afraid Burnside might be among them, but a
quick check of shoulder straps showed Colonel Teall, Sumner's
son-in-law, to be the highest rank. He was working the scope
over Marye's Heights, frowning. Suddenly, he backed away
from the eyepiece, jotted a quick note and handed it to the closest lieutenant. "Take this to General Burnside right away."

"Where is he, sir?"

"Upstairs, the big bedroom." Teall noticed McGee and offered a smile that had no feeling in it. His mind was obviously
elsewhere. "You look lost, Captain."

"No, sir . . . but I'm wondering about my brigade."

"Meagher's, I'm sure."

McGee nodded, given away by his accent. "I have the new colors from New York. I was hoping—"

"Too late." Teall gestured for him to have a look.

Taking off his hat, McGee stepped up to the telescope.
Whitish smoke was sheeting up behind town, but through it he
could see a heavy skirmish line, lying down, with a narrow strip
of field between it and the base of the heights. No sign of the
28th Massachusetts' green banner among the implanted stands
of colors. "May I adjust the view, sir?"

"Help yourself," Teall said.

McGee shifted to a brick house with second-story curtains
dangling out an open window. The yard facing town was blan-
keted with hundreds of blue troops, flattened to the ground. A
little lower on the plain, a sergeant was crawling through the

dead and wounded toward the rear, his head bandaged. He was clasping the stars and stripes to his chest. So things were that bad. The color-bearers were bringing back their flags, if they could. "I don't see my brigade, sir," McGee said. "Come down to that Virginia fence just above the millrace."

1:32 P.M.
116th Pennsylvania

Tyrrell and Hudson slowed to half-steps for a section of snake-rail fence that hadn't been torn down. The rest of the guard, joined by men from "A" Company, ran forward to clear the way for the flags. A big shell barreled just overhead, leaving a hot, turbulent wake that bleared Tyrrell's eyes. He could hear screams all around, as well as the officers ordering the gaps in the line closed. The litany never stopped, screams and shouts. Black fragments whirred through the smoke toward him. Like bats winging out of a cave at dusk.

"Damn!" Two of his guards had a ten-foot rail swatted out of their hands by a small solid shot. The force of the strike must have broken their fingers, for they couldn't pick up their muskets again. Almost at the same time, a mass of men went down on Tyrrell's right. They were blown back off their feet, leaving nothing but a patch of smoking earth where they'd been ripping down rails. A soldier's tin cup rolled in front of him. It came to rest against a blue cap that was still burning.

"Guide center!" Heenan cried from the front, the cords standing out in his neck. "Show the colors, boys!"

Tyrrell and Hudson hurried on into the breach in the fence, waving the flags. A Zouave captain was draped over one of the bottom rails. Tyrrell thought he was alive, but then realized that the twitching of his arms and legs was from the impacts of balls. The ground before the line seemed to be jumping as if covered with grasshoppers. Every little spurt was a piece of lead furrowing into the earth.

"Where the shit is Zook's brigade?" someone asked from the second rank, sounding furious and confused.

Tyrrell had no idea. Vanished. All the troops he saw were down. One man, bleeding from both thighs, was calmly writing in what appeared to be his pocket diary. Another, gutshot, asked for water. Red meat was scattered everywhere. Humps and ridges of dead men began slowing the advance. "Oh my Jesus," Hudson gasped as an enemy battery found the brigade, and a long series of explosions thundered up and down the line. Tyrrell shut his eyes against the heat and flying dirt. He tried to crawl deep within his own mind, cocoon himself against the blasts, but it was no good. He was alive to every sensation, every warm puff of air in his face that was a passing fragment. He'd sweated through both his shirt and coat, and these wet patches now felt like ice. Just when he thought most of the artillery fire was coming from the left, a storm of iron broke from the right and pummeled the line.

"Close up, dammit!" Mulholland's voice competed with the shrieking of the shells.

There was a loud click, a crunch, and Hudson groaned.

"You hit, Joe?" Tyrrell asked.

The corporal looked down. The socket had been shot off his flag belt, plus the butt of the staff. No blood, but he said, his voice shaking, "I don't know, Will. I just don't know."

"You'll know," a white-faced man said from the ground as Hudson and Tyrrell split to pass around him. He was lying on his back, holding his intestines in with both hands.

"Guide center!" Lieutenant Foltz cried. He was only feet from the colors, hatless, his eyes big and wild.

While checking the alignment, Tyrrell noticed McCarter. The bill to the clerk's cap had been shot off and was dangling by a curlicued thread. Blood was flowing over the top of his left brogan. Yet, he limped along in the first rank, the new musket Meagher had given him tucked against his shoulder. He'd kept his blanket, although the order had come down in the swale to unsling gear.

IRISH BRIGADE ENTERS THE WRECKAGE
OF FRENCH'S AND ZOOK'S ASSAULTS
1:30 P.M., DEC. 13

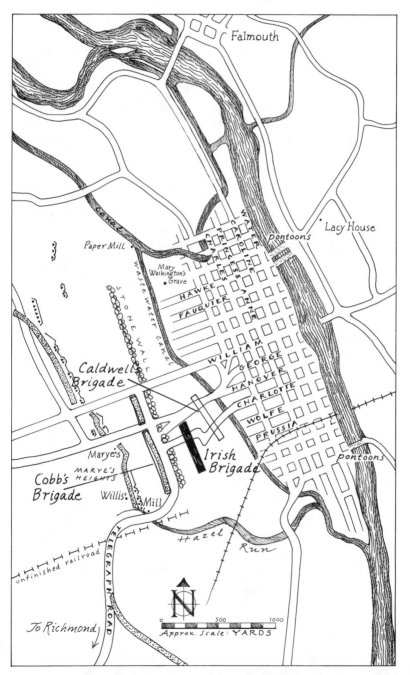

Falmouth

Lacy House

pontoons

Paper Mill

Mary Washington's Grave

WATER
CAROLINE
PRINCESS
PRINCE
CHARLES

HAWKE
FAUQUIER

Waste-water Canal

Canal

STONE WALL

Caldwell's Brigade

WILLIAM
GEORGE
HANOVER
CHARLOTTE
WOLFE
PRUSSIA

Irish Brigade

pontoons

Marye's

Cobb's Brigade

MARYE'S HEIGHTS

Willis. Mill

Hazel Run

unfinished railroad

TELEGRAPH ROAD

To Richmond

N

0   500   1000
Approx. scale: YARDS

A twelve-pound ball came through the line, leaping and slapping the mud. It looked deceptively slow as it bounced over the lower plain.

"Heenan's down," somebody said.

Tyrrell looked for the colonel, noticed the long sweep of the advancing line instead. Only now, under all this fire, was it beginning to sway a bit at its middle. The 69th, on the far right, and his own 116th, holding down the left, were only a few yards ahead of the 28th Massachusetts. More dead passed underfoot. Their faces looked as if they'd been bleached. The flag began jerking wildly in his hands. He glanced up. The silk was being lacerated, slowly shredded.

Staring forward again, he found it hard to swallow, harder yet to get air. Pressure in his chest seemed to toss each breath up his raw throat before it could reach his lungs.

"I only hope I go fast." Hudson sounded almost giddy now.

"Don't open your grave with your gob," a brogue said off to the side, contemptuously. "Don't—" Then a blast of fire cut it off.

A stout, green figure hobbled in front of Tyrrell. "Boys," General Meagher shouted, "I'm still with you! Come on, Pennsylvania!"

1:35 P.M.
24th Georgia

McMillan watched two of his men go down at once. The first was struck through the mouth; the second gashed along the arm when a ball glanced off the forestock of his musket. That was enough. He turned to Sullivan. "Michael, find Mr. Banks. Tell him I want the men down behind the wall during these lulls. All the men, the whole brigade!"

"Aye, sir."

The sergeant rushed off, and McMillan glassed the oncoming line. Green flag at its center. These men knew how to march

under fire. In their caps were snippets of foliage. Richard Montgomery, his granduncle, had had his Continentals wear sprigs
of hemlock in their hats that snowy New Year's eve they at-
tacked Quebec. To set them apart from the enemy because they
were wearing captured British uniforms. Montgomery had died
that night, cut down by grapeshot.

"Down, down!" Banks was screaming above the tumult.

The men stooped behind the wall but griped about it.

McMillan understood. It was entrancing to watch the arrival
of the next brigade into the wreckage of those that had floun-
dered before it. And this new line, of all he'd seen today, came
on as if it wouldn't be blown back like thistledown. Holes were
closed almost as quickly as they were blasted open. Flags bobbed
on toward the second fence at the same irresistible pace. Again
and again, officers marching in advance of their commands were
felled, but others darted out of the ranks to replace them. The
two huge Parrott guns were mauling them, yet McMillan knew
this only because their front, originally more than a thousand
feet wide, had shrunk toward the center by at least a third.

Sullivan returned, but at a distracted, shuffling walk now as
he fastened his eyes on the green flag. He stopped short of
McMillan and absently gripped the shoulders of his young
charge, Tully, who with fumbling hands was trying to seat a
fresh cap on the nipple of his musket's firing mechanism. The
sergeant's gaze never left the approaching flag. Tully stopped
recapping and looked back at him in worry.

"That's Meagher's brigade—ain't it, Sarn't?" one of the native Georgians asked, half-smiling.

Sullivan didn't reply, but Dooley said, "That's them, all right.
I can see the harp on their colors." Then the private crossed
himself, which made McMillan grit his teeth. In truth, this wall
was as thin as an eggshell. It was the resolve of the men behind
it that mattered, and he couldn't have them blessing an enemy
who was attacking at the double-quick. He feared hesitation
more than anything, a mindless pause in the firing just when it

was most needed. Rage, exaltation, or sympathy, sympathy especially, could slow the rate of fire.

"Get ready," he said. He'd faced this brigade before, but knew little of Meagher himself. A line from a New York newspaper article had stuck in his mind all these years: *God just made him to step off a scaffold with a big speech in his mouth.*

"Damn," a Georgian said admiringly, "but don't they come on dapper?"

Meagher's troops gave a sudden cheer. McMillan didn't recognize the words but knew them to be Gaelic.

Letting go of the boy, Sullivan turned away with a stony look and sank slowly down onto his heels. He seemed to be staring right through the hillside. He picked up a cartridge someone had dropped, began rubbing it between his palms.

"Michael . . ."

No answer. The sergeant went on rolling the cartridge in his broad hands.

McMillan peered down the line toward the 18th Georgia's position. The entire brigade was his. He'd told Cobb that he knew this, but only now did it really hit him. He had four times the distance to cover on foot, four times the men to watch over. Ruff of the 18th was a steady man. He'd know to conserve the ammunition, know that resupply was never a given in this army. And the 27th North Carolina had reinforced him. Still, McMillan felt that he should go to that part of the sunken road, even though the jumble of troops behind the wall looked impossible to negotiate.

Some kind of disturbance began off to his left.

An entire company in Phillips's Legion had stood upright, and the men were hurrahing, shaking their muskets over their heads, tossing up their hats. "Lochrane Guards," Garnett explained, smiling. McMillan wondered if Lee or Longstreet had come down to the line. The outcry swept on toward the 24th, picked up by individual men. His Irish-born, he realized. They were applauding the advance of Meagher's brigade, now nearly to the bared posts and rails of the Strattons' fence, green flag tilting forward.

Only Sullivan kept out of it. He remained squatting in the slimy road with his back to the wall. The cartridge twist had come apart in his palms, smearing them black.

Dooley and the Haddock brothers were bellowing as loudly as they could, calling out to the Irish in blue.

McMillan nodded to himself. Understandable. And dangerous. The slightest wavering, and those onrushing bayonets would be over the wall, inside the wall. The thousands hugging the earth down there, resting on their muskets, needed only that spark to rise and charge. "Yes, that's Meagher's brigade," McMillan announced. "Give it to them, boys!"

1:36 P.M.
69th New York

Donovan felt as if he'd waded into a sea of blue-coated men. Wherever he stepped there seemed to be a body underfoot. Some reacted to his tread, curses, hands drawn into chests. Most did not. Dark clouds billowed overhead, and pools of smoky, golden light drifted over the garden below the brick house. Uprooted beets lay everywhere among the men, the greens trampled. Faces were pressed in profile to the mud, single eyes gaping in terror. The line was far too winded now to keep up the double-quick.

Major James Cavanagh grabbed Donovan by the cuff. "John," he said as if apologizing, "command's devolved on me."

"Where's the colonel?"

The little major pointed back down the slope. "Shot in the breast." Two men had formed a chair from their muskets and were taking Nugent off the field in it. The colonel's head was lolling against his shoulder.

"Major," someone pleaded, "let's get to blazin' away at 'em!"

"Soon, soon. Come on." With that, Cavanagh stumbled

ahead over French's and Zook's men, led the regiment around the house and toward the final fence. Most of the boards had been stripped away, but a blizzard of splinters was flying off the standing sections—bullets and balls chipping away at the wood.

A hand reared up, groped for the hem of Donovan's overcoat. "Don't try," a voice wailed, "it's a bad fix!"

He jerked his coat out of the man's grasp and scrambled on, looking askance, left along line. What remained of the brigade was bowed like a crescent moon. The air was whishing with minié balls. They were coming down at an angle from rifle pits pocking the facing slope of the heights. He could hear them smacking against the ground, into the corpses on every side. Many of his men were turning their faces as if walking against sleet or hail.

Cavanagh slowed the regiment with a wave of his sword, explaining, "Give the Twenty-eighth time to catch up!"

A long, low stone wall lay beyond the final fence, enemy battle flags behind it. Donovan heard hurrahing. Not those unearthly Rebel yells, but shouts almost like the Union huzzah were coming from behind the wall. Donovan glanced back. Most of the file closers were down, but the men were sidestepping over the fallen, closing ranks on their own. Hogan, his first sergeant, grinned at him.

"Guide center!" he cried, although he wasn't sure if any sound had escaped his dry mouth. Not far to the wall now. He was thinking about how he'd climb over it, whether he'd stand atop it to urge his men on—when hundreds of gray infantry sprang up, squinting over their musket barrels. Everything came apart in that instant, yet he kept moving as if an invisible hand were pushing at his back. He felt as light as a dry leaf. Flame erupted all along the wall, and then smoke blinded him. He could hear bones being smashed by buck and ball. Definitely buck and ball. He looked down at his boots. No longer moving. He could recall making no decision to halt. But he had. He expected a respite between enemy volleys while they reloaded, yet there was none. They went on firing at an unbelievably rapid rate.

Major Cavanagh came out of the stinging murk, slipped past him like a ghost. "No extended order like this, John," he said, breathing explosively. Enemy shot and shell had left a man every six feet, not any order the captains had given. "General Meagher wants the line massed close together!"

"Can we fire?" a voice begged, almost sobbing.

Donovan relayed the major's order, but then glimpsed only a few men shifting toward the green flag, now thrust into the earth by its bearer. Stepping back out of the line of fire, Donovan nearly stumbled over Lieutenant Burke from his company, who was sitting down, holding his left shoulder with a bloody hand and thoughtfully pursing his lips as if he were trying to remember something vital.

"How bad, David?" Donovan asked.

Burke removed his hand. The ball had carried a wad of blue material all the way down to the bone.

"Go back," Donovan ordered.

"As soon as I find the son of a bitch who did this." The lieutenant rose, began seeing to his platoon.

At last, Cavanagh hollered, "Blaze away and stand to it, boys!"

The sound of the brigade's volley was lost in the crackle of the continuous fire from behind the wall. A few of the men had gone to a knee to shoot, but most were on their bellies. They rolled onto their backs to reload. Donovan remained upright. He saw Bernie O'Neill, the lieutenant commanding "D" Company, pick up a musket and squeeze off a shot at the wall.

A voice from the left cried, "Fire at will!" Meagher's, Donovan believed. Nugent was gone, but the general was still with them. He felt a little better.

"Cap," a prone man said while taking a cartridge from his pouch, "you're wounded."

Donovan felt nothing. "Where?"

"In the head!"

He doffed his hat, ran his hand over his scalp and came away with no color, no gore. Then he noticed two holes in the crown of his hat. "I daresay—" The quip he had in mind was forgotten as something struck his left shoulder, hard. He dropped to his knees, forced himself to look. His metal shoulder strap had deflected a ball down through his coat front. He took a deep, exploratory breath, waiting for frigid pain to follow. None did. He patted himself for the ball, found it jammed up in his underwear. Finally, he stood once more, focused on the wall, the endless volleys coming from it. "Aim for their hats!" he cried. Turnabout was only fair play. A few of his men were making breastworks from the bodies of French's men. Reeling from this sight, he hailed O'Neill. "Bernie!"

The lieutenant was preparing to flash powder again. "What, John?"

"Do you have a dispensation for that?" Officers weren't allowed to fire muskets.

"Damn the dispensation," O'Neill said. "I'm showin' Caldwell's brigade we're not all dead up here!"

Then a violent blow dropped him.

Twenty-Seven

◆

The brigade had stopped advancing.

Meagher's men were down among the wreckage of French's division and Zook's brigade. All the colors had been stuck in the ground like beanpoles, and the troops seemed to be melting into the mud. Meagher himself choked on the smoke, almost gagged as it gusted thicker over him. He felt as if he were floundering through a nightmare, too slow either to face the danger or escape it. Too small as well. He felt so small without his horse. A roar like a waterfall filled his ears, punctuated by the swish of solid shot flying overhead. Only Heenan's Pennsylvanians were within hailing distance. Turning, he cried for them to get up, to run for the stone wall again. *Attaque à outrance.* Attack excessively. Caldwell's brigade was just down the slope, coming on with a throaty hurrah. Line after line at the double-quick, like wave after wave hitting a beach. Keep throwing in the attacks no matter what. Shock after shock after shock. "Boys," he begged "don't die on your bellies!"

The eyes of the world.

He hobbled behind the firing line. Wounded men were passing their muskets forward. He'd never harangued his brigade before, nor could he bring himself to do it now, but he began to feel a hard, slow anger. "Up . . . on your feet!"

The color sergeant of the 116th was down on his left knee, waving the stars and stripes. His right leg was stretched out before him, the trouser wool soaked with blood from mid-thigh down. The regimental flag was missing.

Meagher ordered the line to attention.

Only those men within a few yards of him heard. Two of them stood, muskets braced against their hips, but went down again at once, riddled by bullets. Meagher looked for Heenan to help him get the regiment up and moving again. If the New Yorkers saw these Philadelphia greenhorns grabbing the hot end of the poker, they'd stop hugging the field and race for the wall. But Heenan was nowhere to be found. "Colonel Mulholland . . . ?"

"Hit, sir," a lieutenant answered, rising guiltily to a crouch. "Off to hospital."

Suddenly, Meagher was down on his side. He thought for a second that he'd been struck by a ball. But there were no rips in his uniform. His knee had simply given out for the moment. He peered back down the rolling sweep of the plain. Hancock was galloping across the field below the millrace, using his sword to urge little groups of men to turn around and go back.

"Look at that," Meagher said bitterly.

"Sir?" the lieutenant asked, offering a hand and pulling him up again.

"You can see Hancock at a quarter mile!" With that, the decision was made. *Damn the consequences.* Meagher started back for his mount on the edge of town. If his men could see him, as they had at Antietam, at all the other battles, they'd go forward. Afoot, he was too small to be seen, so small he'd become separated even from his own aide-de-camp, Emmet. Caldwell's brigade flowed around him, the eyes of the men fixed dazedly on the heights as shells clapped the air over them.

1:41 P.M.
116th Pennsylvania

Tyrrell didn't know when Hudson and the rest of the guard had gone down. He just knew that no one was standing beside him. He clenched the staff, hands palsied. A ball from the enemy's surprise volley had caught him in the right thigh. The bone had been either clipped or broken, for he couldn't put any weight on the leg. For a few seconds after the impact, he'd felt nothing, but then a chill had gone through him like lightning, making him feel as if he'd been jolted off the ground. His wish had been granted: he'd taken a wound that made running away impossible. He now wondered if he'd cursed himself. He shouldn't have been so careless with his prayers.

Glancing aside, he saw McCarter sprawled on his back, biting off the end of a cartridge. Spitting paper, the clerk winked at Tyrrell. He'd just started to drive the rammer when his right arm was flung bloodily down to his side. He didn't know that he'd been hurt, for he went on trying to tamp with his suddenly useless hand.

"Mac, get out of here!" Tyrrell cried. "You're hit!"

The man continued fumbling with his ramrod.

Lieutenant Foltz appeared, blowing from running up and down the line. "You're doing fine, Will," he said, then moved on.

Tyrrell checked the colors. Shredded but still billowing off the pole. Must find someone trustworthy to take them, should he pass out. His vision had turned gray, and his thigh was beginning to throb with breathtaking pain, keeping time with the runaway beats of his heart. He was slipping under, he realized. Dying even. Frantically, he thought of McCarter as the man to take the flag, and he looked that way again. But the clerk now appeared to be dead or unconscious, jaw slack, face soft and childlike. He'd bunched his blanket against the top of his head as if to deflect enemy balls. The breeze lifted his cape over his cap, then smoothed it down again.

Tyrrell felt the staff break in two.

The colors began floating down, spreading over him like a striped canopy. He was reaching out to catch the flag when he was knocked backward. Still clawing for the tumbling silk as he fell, he saw a red mist envelop his left hand. He tried to raise his right arm, but it refused to move. Blackness sifted down around him. He saw nothing but could still hear the cannon and musketry as clearly as ever. Indians. He could also hear Indians whooping.

1:42 P.M.
24th Georgia

His eyes blank, Sullivan watched a loaded piece being shuttled carefully forward by four pairs of hands. Just as it reached Dooley at the wall, the sergeant realized that its wooden forestock was smoldering. "Tommy—" Too late. Dooley winced as he took hold of the overheated barrel, leaving skin from his palms on it. But then the man calmly aimed and fired at the next brigade to clear the snake-rail fence. How many had it been now? Six? It felt as if the whole Army of the Potomac had already come this way. Dooley turned from the wall, letting the Tarheel behind him shoot for a while. He stooped next to Sullivan in the cool shadows of the men, his face a dark blue. He wiped his sweaty eyes with a burnt, trembling hand, then looked up sadly. "Mike . . . ?"

"Aye."

"I won't flash powder at that green flag," Dooley said.

Sullivan had already seen. Each time, the private had swung his muzzle away from the emerald colors at the center of their line. Sullivan didn't know what to say. He had no will to say anything. He felt apart from Dooley, from all the men tussling with one other to reload and fire. Smoke curdled over the line. When

it cleared a moment later, Sullivan was a little surprised that
Dooley was still across from him, that all the others along the
sunken road hadn't been dissolved by the corrosive pall. If not
quite that, he felt that this valley should have shuddered apart
by now, leaving only sulphury clouds beneath his feet.

Dooley was rubbing his shoulder. "Sore as a blister. How
many rounds we fired so far, d'you figure?"

Sullivan shook his head. Too many, given the number of blue
troops still pouring out of town.

"Did you hear the cry they raised, Mike?"

Sullivan rubbed his nose. *Clear the Way.* In the mother tongue.
Dooley started to say something more, but the sergeant abruptly
crawled away through the thicket of legs. He stood again only
when he was near the colors. There, McMillan and a courier
from General Kershaw were shouting back and forth over the
racket. The rider's beard was encrusted with mud and powder.
Sullivan had no interest in what was being said. The Washington Artillery had broken into rapid fire again. He watched the
Louisianans shooting double canister, their cannon leaping off
the ground from the dangerously big powder loads. Keep that
up much longer and they wouldn't have two canister balls to rattle together when Burnside threw in another corps. There was
at least another Yankee corps waiting on the fringes of the
smoke.

"Get down!" McMillan shouted.

A boy, out of his head with excitement, had jumped atop the
wall. He whipped off his hat and, wildly waving it, gave three
Rebel yells to the exploding sky. Briefly, Sullivan thought that
it might be Tully. But he was another child, Jimmie Williams
from Nachoochee Valley. His friends pulled him down, pinned
him to the embankment.

"Steady," McMillan warned.

Farther down the wall, a limp body was being passed to the
rear, dragged and shoved out of the way by as many hands as
could take hold of it. Sullivan paid no mind until Dooley called

with a queer edge to his voice, "Mike?" Then Sullivan knew. He began jostling a path through the men, batting aside muskets with his hands. From behind, McMillan ordered, "Michael, a message to Colonel Bryan . . ." But Sullivan kept going until he was leaning over the downed private. Then, after a moment in which all sound faded, he dropped heavily to his knees.

Dooley had Sullivan by the arm, trying to tug him to his feet again. "It's done, Mike."

Sullivan shook off his grasp and began unbuttoning Tully's shirt to have a look at the wound. Upper breast. He must plug the hole with something. A bit of moss. Mud, even. The boy's upper right arm was the deep purple of a ripe plum. From all the firing. "He's still with us," Sullivan said, pointing at what seemed to be new blood spilling from the corners of Tully's lips.

"Touch an eye, man," Dooley said.

Sullivan wiped a gritty thumb on his jacket, then pressed it to one of Tully's eyeballs. The tissue didn't spring back. He was trying again when a shadow fell over him. He twisted around, saw McMillan's face looming over him. The man's mouth was shaping words, but Sullivan could make little sense of them. His ears felt as if they were stuffed with cotton, and they were aching. ". . . Sixteenth's in reserve at the mill, Michael . . ." He looked down at the boy again, held the back of his hand up to the breathless nostrils. ". . . far side of Willis' Hill here . . ." He paused, trying to think of some other test, but finally admitted to himself that Dooley was right. Tully's eyes were so lusterless Sullivan turned down the lids. Then, out of habit alone, he patted the boy's trouser pockets for cartridges, took them out, handed them to Dooley. "Go round by the road," McMillan was saying all the while, "carefully now, Michael, and tell Colonel Bryan to place his regiment on our brigade's right . . ." Sullivan began to see McMillan's words in pictures, the 16th filing into place beside the 18th. The view they would have of Hazel Run. "Watch for the enemy to come out of the railroad cut. Repeat the message."

But Sullivan just began plodding up the slope, dead leaves crunching underfoot.

"By the road, Michael!" McMillan hollered after him.

1:46 P.M.
69th New York

One sound, of all those jarring Donovan's head, made him smile. War whoops from the 5th New Hampshire. He'd last heard their almost comical battle cry at Antietam. And now, once again, they were coming on like Mohawks. Last chance, he told himself, to clear this maze of death, as going forward seemed only slightly more dangerous than going back. He was about to appeal to his men, the able-bodied few who remained, when the same notion was picked up by a major of the 88th, Bill Horgan, who was standing with his pale fists propped on the hilt of his sword. "Irish Brigade," he shouted, voice breaking from the strain to be heard, "let's give Caldwell's boys a hand!"

The 88th's adjutant, Johnny Young, jumped up, grinning. "What's the harm now?" he implored. A lieutenant joined the twosome, and then anyone who could was rising and helping fill the gaps in Caldwell's brigade line. Donovan stumbled forward, waving on a handful of men from his company. He fell in beside a New Hampshire sergeant, who kept saying, "Thank you, thank you ever so much." Donovan tripped over some dead piled before him. Once again, he quickly checked to make sure he hadn't been hit. No use bleeding to death. Wrenching and hammering noises made him glance up: the line was grappling with the last fence, the men pounding out boards with the butts of their muskets. Shells found them, and shards of wood cartwheeled through the advance, slowing it. But Horgan and Young had found an opening in the fence and were already halfway to the stone wall.

Rising, Donovan was running for the same gap when something hot and flat glanced off the left side of his chest. He kept moving, but he felt as if he'd passed into a stretch of ground that was dark and silent. Then he began to sink into the earth itself.

1:51 P.M.
Cobb's Brigade

The blue major sprinted toward the wall. He was leading a squad of men, young officers mostly, swords wagging. He wore a green sprig in his hat, as did the man just behind him. His eyes looked mild, even though his mouth was wide and round with a shout. McMillan traded fleeting gazes with him. But by then his mix of Georgians and Carolinians had hurried enough loaded muskets to the front rank to let go a volley. Smoke spread from the muzzles. When it had rolled away, no enemy was still on his feet, and scorched lint from the expended cartridges drifted among the corpses like snow.

His men cheered, but McMillan rasped for them to get down again. Ever closer. Despite the slaughter, the tireless blue tide was breaking ever closer. And taking its toll on his own line. A row of dead at the foot of the slope was growing longer by the minute. The earth thrown before the wall looked like a shingled beach, spent balls and bullets heaped several inches deep after striking the stones. His mouth was hot and dry. He borrowed a canteen from a private, took a swallow which gave him his voice back. "Thank you."

"Pa!" Garnett called to him.

McMillan looked to his son, who was pointing over his shoulder at the sun. It seemed locked in the sky, no farther along toward dusk than it'd been at noon, a sluggish red fire marking the death of time.

"Joshua," Garnett said solemnly, then turned and tended to his company. Some of the men were beginning to sway on their feet from exhaustion.

"Again, Colonel!" Banks said.

Below, the Hanover Street bridge stringers were thronged with blue once more. No end to them. McMillan took off his hat, felt the sunlight on the back of his neck. Instantly, the warmth made him drowsy. No end to these people. His mind was clouded. What had Garnett meant by *Joshua?* How marvelous some coffee would be right now. Or better yet, his mother's strong breakfast tea.

He lifted his glasses to his burning eyes.

Another of their regiments had formed battle line in the plowed field and was angling toward the Strattons' house. He frowned. Just a regiment this time, not a brigade. Did that mean something? Yes—another regiment was now working up the left side of Hanover, toward the rifle pits on the north end of the heights. Finally, Burnside might be shifting his main thrust away from the stone wall. McMillan prayed that it was so. The smell of blood in the air reminded him of sucking on an English penny as a boy.

He was putting his hat back on when it came to him. Joshua. Garnett had a preacher's instinct for scripture. *The Lord gave the Amorites over to the men of Israel, and Joshua said in the sight of Israel, "Sun, stand thou still . . ." And the sun stood still until the nation took vengeance on their enemies.* The day would never end as long as graceful blue lines pushed up out of Fredericksburg. It was beyond the will of man. And this sickening gift wasn't McMillan's to decline even if the millrace ran red with blood, even if all the human masses of the North piled up before his eyes. The horror Joshua must have felt as that unnatural day dragged on. And more the strain from not being able to express it, lest God find him ungrateful.

A bullet streaked by, a thread of sound seemingly hanging in the air after it.

"That one almost got you, sir," a private said, stopping mid-stroke with his clanking rod.

"Ram your piece, boy, and pass it forward."

Must check on the other regiments. Especially Phillips's Legion now that Tom Cook was dead. McMillan had just taken a stride toward Mrs. Stevens's house when the inside of his head went white. He grunted as he spun around, clasping his hand to a fiery spot on his neck. A spent ball, still hot, dropped from his hand to the road.

Garnett was rushing toward him. "Pa, are you hurt!"

"Hit, but not hurt," McMillan said, stopping him. "Back to your company."

Garnett stared in worry a moment longer, then obeyed.

McMillan bent stiffly over, found the ball and dropped it into his vest pocket. A memento. Not to remind him of this near miss, but rather of the desperate, fearful love he'd just seen in his son's eyes.

2:11 P.M.
Irish Brigade

Meagher reached his horse, seized the rein from the orderly and climbed into the saddle. He sat a moment, winded from his tortured hike down through the carnage. Good. Done. Now he'd ride back to his stalled line, although to the right side this time. Nothing against the Pennsylvanians, who were standing up to the fire well enough, but he meant to find the 69th near the brick house and rally it. His old regiment would get the rest of brigade moving again. "Orderly, mount and follow me," he said over his shoulder. He wanted a second charger handy should his own be cut down.

Spurring, he trotted up the rubble-littered street toward the heights. Men crawled and limped down it toward the hospitals in mid-town. French's men mostly, thank God. He looked for the two companies of the 69th that Hancock had ordered him to throw out as skirmishers. Fresh and unblooded today, they might do the trick, get the others up, running, cheering. Break that stony gray line in the center just when everyone thought it impregnable.

All at once, Meagher slowed the gait and leaned over the pommel. He couldn't believe his eyes. The 63d's regimental colors were coming back toward him, borne by a gaggle of muddy, powder-stained men. Leading them was a giant of a man, John Gleeson of Tipperary. The towering captain had served with the Papal Brigade, had saved a green flag at Antietam—this made no sense. Gleeson had always gone forward. "What's happened, John?" Meagher asked, his heart pounding.

The captain averted his eyes. They were red-rimmed. "The order to retire was passed down, sir."

"Who gave it?"

"I don't know."

Meagher now noticed a few men of the 69th straggling along. "Where's Colonel Nugent?"

"Shot, sir," one of them answered, blood on his face, his sprig of boxwood.

"Cavanagh?"

"Shot too. All shot."

"Where's your regiment, boys?"

"Winked out, sir," another said.

$\mathcal{T}$wenty-Eight

◆

2:59 P.M.
69th New York

Slowly, Donovan opened his eye.

He could see a brick house wrapped in stringers of smoke. But just when he thought he'd claimed himself again, he saw something unbelievable. A woman was hovering outside an open window, floating ten feet off the ground. She spread her flowing white arms as if they were wings, then closed them as if enfolding the world. Her face was a luminous blur one moment, a shadow the next, although Donovan was sure he could make out the faint suggestion of a smile. Below her, thousands of blue crabs were scuttling up the plain, inching along, eyes terrified, claws chattering.

A shell exploded nearby. It rocked the earth, spewed mud and clumps of grass roots over him.

"My God!" His mind cleared like the wooden slide in a confessional snapping open. He started to rise but a hand held him down. "Don't, Cap," a voice cautioned. "The bastards are sure to shoot you. Anybody who gets up. Anybody who runs." Joe Hogan, his first sergeant.

Still, Donovan raised his head a few inches.

He was among a great sprawl of men, all lying as close to the brick house as they could. Lace curtains, the kind used to screen out bugs in summer, were dangling from a second-story window, shifting on the foul breeze. So much for his lovely banshee. He licked his cracked lips. They felt papery to his tongue. "Where's Cavanagh?"

"Carried off the field," Hogan said.

"Dead or wounded?"

"I had no time to ask, sir."

"Who commands?"

Looking away, the sergeant plucked a leaf stalk from a beet still in the ground. Answer enough.

The shadow off the heights crept over them. Instantly, Donovan felt cold. His coat and trousers were damp from the mud, and he tried not to shiver. Smoke hid the stone wall, but just above it a dusty orange sun was sliding behind the enemy breastworks, limning a cannon crew at work. Donovan believed that the batteries up there had slowed their rate of fire over the last few minutes.

The men around him gave a weak hurrah. He asked Hogan what it meant.

"Ah, sir—we figured the sun would never go down."

The smell of offal drew his eye to pieces of men scattered among the living. *Mustn't look too closely.* Those who could move their arms had fashioned little shelters against the fusillades: thin parapets from fence boards, pathetically shallow pits gouged out with bayonets, the bodies of their friends. The dead, the wounded, and the survivors were jammed elbow-to-elbow, head-to-toe from the board fence nearly all the way down to the snake-rail fence. It looked as if the entire army had blundered here and was now trapped forever. "Have we been relieved by another brigade, Joe?"

"No." Hogan, face still pressed to the mud, was chewing on the beet green stalk. His teeth were stained red. "Same as when you got clobbered an hour ago. Us, the Eighty-eighth, and the New Hampshire fellas."

Donovan glanced down at his aching chest. Nothing had pierced his coat, but his left arm was powerless. "What got me?"

"Don't know, Cap. But it came bouncin' along like a plowshare. A lump of railroad, maybe."

Donovan flinched for an airburst. A canteen rolled past his face, dribbling water from several holes. Seventh New York was inscribed on the cover. A German regiment. In his outlandish dreams of the past hour, there had been a soft undercurrent of whispered German. "What d'you mean—a lump of railroad?"

The sergeant, staying low, reached over and picked up a chunk of iron. "Like this." A six-inch-long section of rail, scorched black by powder.

"It's an insult, if you ask me," a man from another company piped up, "beltin' junk our way." His beard was clotted with dried blood. "Might as well fire chamberpots at us."

Donovan smiled. There was life here yet. He reared up as far as he dared. Chest pain seized his breath for a second. Only a few of the men around him were shooting at the stone wall. A big volume of musketry was coming from just down the plain, some brigade in late support, hanging back, afraid of entering the vast unburied graveyard. Easing down again, he asked Hogan, "Were we ordered to retire?"

"I'm not sure, sir. Word like it was passed along 'bout an hour ago. God knows there's no hearin' drums or bugles in all this."

"Why didn't you go then, Joe?"

"I saw no future in it."

Yards ahead, a private gasped and stiffened, then went still. A messmate crawled over to him, inspected the bullet wound in the man's back. "Stop!" he cried toward the rear. "You're layin' out your own!"

Other men cussed in agreement, and from that Donovan got an idea of how many had survived in his immediate area. Less than twenty. His spirits sank, and he began shivering uncontrollably. In the space of two hours, victory had gone from a grand push on Richmond, with Banks pressing Fortress Monroe and Sigel pouring across the upper Rappahannock, to saving twenty men. Still, he said, "Dusk, Joe."

"Cap . . . ?"

"I'm taking us out at dusk."

3:22 P.M.
116th Pennsylvania

Tyrrell lay blind, his body numb from the shoulders down. He was very cold, and he missed his blanket, which he'd left in the swale below. Between the explosions and musketry, he heard the rustle of uniform cloth. Canteens were sloshing, banging against hipbones. Shoes beat the earth. Officers shouted for their men to close gaps, guide center. All this commotion, he sensed, was downslope from him, approaching fast. Just when he thought the line would pass over him, trample him, the fire from behind the stone wall swelled into a big sputtering crackle like flames finding the pitch in a pine log. Then, without warning, Tyrrell's sight returned, although at first it was dim and gray around the edges. Dark, angry things were winging over him, but he was too weak to move his head and track their flight. A yellowish burst came and went. Its round cloud of smoke drifted away on the breeze. The officers, still some yards below Tyrrell, were now screaming for their men to shoot at will. "Show the goddamned colors!" one of them bawled.

The colors.

"Hudson?" Tyrrell asked. His own voice frightened him. It sounded old and gravelly, like his father's. He called out other names from the guard. There was no answer, just a low, anguished moaning like the mewing of a cat. Tyrrell fell silent, watched the blue of the sky deepen. He realized that he didn't know how to die. Pain was flaring up in his arms and legs, yet he had no idea how to escape it.

"Tyrrell?" someone asked as if it hurt terribly to breathe.

"Yes . . . who . . . ?"

322 ◆ *Kirk Mitchell*

"Frank . . . Frank Missimer."

Strangely, Tyrrell saw not Missimer's face but Davey Major's that day when Frank and the others had swaddled him in all those overcoats alongside the Warrenton pike. Davey's last day. "How are you, Frank?"

"Shot all over."

"I'm sorry," Tyrrell said. He tried to view the man, but moving even slightly was impossible. "Can you see the colors?"

"No."

"What?"

"Gone."

Tyrrell groaned. Captured. Lost forever. He should have fought harder for consciousness, tucked the flag inside his coat. There was so much he could've done if only he'd kept his head.

"Quinlan took 'em," Missimer added.

"What?"

"The lieutenant ran up . . . took the colors back down the hill."

"Thank God." Tyrrell shut his eyes. Annie. He didn't see the girl, but rather an old woman with Annie's eyes. How would she make it without his pay? He was glimpsing the future, not the past, and there was a bottomless hole in it. He was that dark hole, he realized, and shame filled him. "Anybody comin' back for us?"

"No, Will." A pause. "I'm goin' to go now."

"All right, Frank." Tyrrell heard no movement. After a few minutes, he understood.

3:44 P.M.
24th Georgia

Garnett McMillan had no felt anger toward the Federals until now. Several times, watching them fall by the hundreds, he'd come as close to remorse as his fear of them would allow. And the inexhaustible courage of their color guards and officers had moved him. Flags tumbled but seemed to levitate right back up.

Officers fell along the brigade fronts, yet there were always others to replace them. But moments ago, in another lull between attacks, one of the South Carolinians had pitched back dead into the arms of his friends, shot through the skull.

Whist. Another minié now came over the wall. By this time, all the men had taken cover, and it splatted harmlessly against the hillside.

"I can see 'em proper, Lieutenant," Billy Haddock said, pointing at the railroad cut.

Garnett picked out a string of black dots—the heads of sharpshooters lying side-by-side on the lip of the defile. He was momentarily distracted. To the left of the tracks another blue line was setting out from town no less cautiously than those that had come up before. Surely, the men could see the melee that awaited them, the fugitives streaming back against them for the safety of town. "Bring me a rifled musket," he ordered. The regiment had a number of them, taken from the enemy.

Whist.

"Message for Howell Cobb," somebody quipped.

Waiting for the rifle, Garnett glanced up at the Washington Artillery. What was wrong? The guns were spewing only a few shells every minute, scarcely enough to keep the heads of the enemy down. Squads of them were getting up, surging through the shoals of dead toward the board fence. He had the uneasy feeling that, given the slightest encouragement, all of them might spring up suddenly and take the wall in a single, howling rush. His own men were lifting their arms questioningly toward the gunners. As if in answer, one of them stood in his embrasure and pulled his trouser pockets inside out. Empty. He was saying that their ammunition chests were empty.

Garnett turned to the nearest private, Dooley, and asked, "How many rounds left, Tom?"

Hands trembling with fatigue, the man rummaged through his clothes and came up with four cartridges. "I could use a power more of 'em, sir."

Garnett raised his voice to his company, the Carolinians among them. "Go through the pockets of the dead and wounded. Make every shot count from now on." He could see his father gazing south, the direction from which an ordnance train would come. There was no sign of wagons.

At last, a rifle was handed to him. "Primed and ready, sir."

"Thank you." Garnett rested the forestock atop the wall, squinted down the barrel at the onrushing brigade. Running now, flags slanting forward. He was tempted to fire on the color guard, to try to slow this latest wave. Death was his to dole out at will. But then he swiveled around on the railroad cut. He sucked in a shallow breath and squeezed the trigger. When the smoke had cleared, he suspected that one less black dot was visible. But wasn't sure. He coughed. His lungs felt as if they were stuffed with cockleburs.

"I'd get down if I was you, sir," somebody drawled.

"Flash below!"

"Down!" Dooley yelled as he pulled Garnett to the ground. The lieutenant landed on his scabbard. *Whist.* The bullet sang through the air just where his head had been the instant before.

The men were silent a moment, then laughed uneasily, no doubt wondering how an Emory and Henry man would take being yanked down on his buttocks. All eyes on him, Garnett rose and brushed off the seat of his trousers. "How might I express my gratitude, Private Dooley?"

"How 'bout champagne for everybody, sir?" another man blurted.

"Well," Dooley said, his tired eyes twinkling, "it's the only kind of pain we ain't had since answerin' Gov'nor Brown's call."

Adjutant Banks, who'd been working his way along the line, murmuring something every few paces, came to Garnett and his men. "General Cobb," he said quietly, "died a few minutes after he got to the hospital."

Garnett turned to check on his father. The old man lowered his head for a few moments, prayed perhaps, then looked south again for ordnance wagons.

4:01 P.M.
Willis' Hill

Sullivan sat on a low wall. It enclosed a cemetery plot just big enough for a single family, a dozen stone monuments scabby with lichen. A little snow was banked up on its north side. He reached down for a handful, ran it over his parched lips as his gaze traced the limits of the Yankee advance, the undulating blue swatch below the sunken road. Even now, white smoke spurted from it: prone infantry trying to help the next brigade to come into the slaughter pen. It was already forming down by the railroad depot, officers flitting around to make sure the march would be pretty, even though the plain awaiting them was an inferno: geysers of smoke, demons cackling and hissing through the air, yellow fire poxing the sky.

"One hell for another," Sullivan said, eating some snow, chewing it into a slurry.

Bullets were clicking in the bare branches of the trees. One pinged off the wall a few feet from him. He didn't budge. Ever since leaving McMillan, he'd felt as if he were already dead. He'd lost track of time. The world had shifted round, and the setting sun was the rising one; shadows were frozen to the ground. And from this timeless height, he saw his folly, and it made him weep. Refuge. He'd left home on the promise of refuge, convinced that Ireland was the only hell in the universe. He'd come to believe this because of the hunger, the soup kitchen lines, that hole he'd cobbed out of the earth along the road to Cashel and covered with a scrap of canvas for his wife and children while they were yet alive, a grave for the living.

Yet, what had he escaped to? A valley stinking of brimstone. A new hell, raucous and flowing with Irish blood.

Suddenly, horses, a limber and a Napoleon streamed past.

He stood, drying his eyes.

The Washington Artillery was pulling out, dashing south toward Telegraph Road. He clasped his left hand to the side of his face, shading out the dazzle of lowering sun. What was going on? He could see all the signs of another onslaught: rectangles of men backed up in the streets of Fredericksburg, once more the pontoon bridges choked with blue. That leviathan weight. It was stirring again, yet six, seven . . . nine Napoleons were being dragged off the heights toward the rear. The very cannon that had kept the enemy from making those last running steps up to the wall all afternoon.

And then he knew what still mattered: the brigade. It was all he had left. Everything else was food for worms. "Sir!"

An artillery captain slowed from a gallop to a canter, held his hand behind his ear.

"Where you off to—if I might ask?"

"Out of ammunition," the captain replied. "So's the infantry, I hear. Sent a detail out an hour ago to find the ordnance train." He finished with a hapless shrug, spurred his horse on.

A shell flew through the branches, striking a pine behind the cemetery. The crown lazily bent over and crashed to earth. Needles showered the gravestones, trickled down Sullivan's shirt collar. Reeling, he scanned below for the enemy's field batteries. A section had come halfway up the pike to punish the stone wall, the rifle pits. And blue apparitions, encouraged perhaps by the skirring off of the Washington Artillery, were getting up again, leapfrogging forward, firing on the run.

Sullivan took to his feet.

He headed for Telegraph Road, the point where it curved around the nose of Willis' Hill and started winding southwest toward Spotsylvania. He slid down an overgrown bank, his heels leaving a furrow in the matted leaves. Here, the sunlight was already gone, and a chill hugged the evergreen foliage. The slope bottomed out in a grassy hollow. Wounded from the 16th had crawled into it, a quiet place to agonize, to die. Closer to the line, a surgeon was working in a dry ditch. His saw glinted from the lantern his orderly had just lit against the gloom.

Halting, chest heaving, Sullivan peered up the road to where it became a tunnel through the woods. He was sure that the ordnance trains were parked in the fields just beyond, out of the range of the Union guns. Yet, instead of wagons, artillery was on the roll toward him. Horses were rearing against the lash, caissons bouncing so heavily over the shell-pocked road the men riding them could barely hang on. The two officers guiding the fresh battery were crouching low over the necks of their mounts. Sullivan then saw why—fuses were waffling through the heavy air of dusk. The enemy shells began bursting around the old mill as the gray battery streaked past Sullivan. A confusion of legs and wheels. A horse screamed, went down, its withers bloody. The limbered twelve-pounder skidded to a stop, spraying mud over the tangled team. The driver leaped off his perch and began cutting the dying beast out of the traces.

"Where you bound with these guns?" Sullivan asked, helping him.

"Marye's House," he said.

Sullivan glanced up the road again. "Have you seen an ordnance train or two?"

4:20 P.M.
Cobb's Brigade

McMillan muttered a little prayer of thankfulness. He saw the shell fragment as Providence. It had sliced through his left coatsleeve and started a warm trickle of blood winding around his wrist. Before, he'd been drifting off. It'd been impossible to concentrate, focus on what counted at this minute. The ammunition. It was almost spent. The little wound cleared this fog, got him turning the possibilities over in his mind now that the Washington Artillery was gone. Bayonets. Blunt the next enemy charge with steel, unless reinforced in the meantime.

What would Cobb think of that? No matter. Thomas would have done anything to hold this wall.

"Michael!" McMillan shouted along the crowded line. No reply. He frowned. How long since Sullivan had gone off with that message to the 16th? No idea. Time had lost its measure. He felt as if he'd been born and reared behind this stone wall; his first memory was of an enemy brigade scurrying from the streets below. He had no wife other than the colors. No children other than the son in "K" Company, who banged away at sharpshooters between the never-ending assaults. And he'd still be standing among these lank, stark-faced men when the east dawned red with final judgment. "Mr. Banks!"

The adjutant's head was slumped. He gazed up in momentary confusion, then came over. "Sir."

"Kindly see that another message is sent concerning the ammunition." McMillan lowered his voice. It hurt to speak, his throat was so raw from the smoke. "I'll hold, but I don't fancy doing it with empty muskets."

"Colonel, you're bleeding."

"The message, Mr. Banks."

The adjutant went off, looking for a courier. Stuporous. He seemed to be only half-conscious, as did the men as they reloaded at a snail's pace, sloppily now, some scarcely able to lift their arms. They drunkenly bit open their cartridges and spat away the scraps of paper, overshot the barrels with their ramrods.

"Cease fire!" McMillan ordered, sheathing his sword.

He stumbled forward, realizing for the first time that his legs and feet were so swollen his boots would never come off tonight. Two men parted for him, and he rested on his arms against the wall. The injured one was no longer bleeding. The men were staring at him with dull, bloodshot eyes. He struggled to think of something to say. "The enemy will try one more time, hard, before nightfall. Another division at least, I'm sure."

"Yes, sir," a man said.

The rest had no reaction.

A frenzied hurrah reverberated from below. Up and down the wall, hammers clicked back.

"Wait," McMillan said.

Through a hole in the smoke, he could see the next Federal line. It was midway between the fences. The blue figures began to double-quick, knees pumping, but then were slowed by the windrows of dead and wounded heaped in front of them. The survivors had made parapets of bodies to hide behind, and these were turning the fresh attack into a steeplechase. The officers in the lead looked as if they were wading through seaweed.

"Let them get close." Fighting dizziness, McMillan took a deep breath, let it out slowly. "Closer."

Now that the light was going, the plain seemed even more terrible to the eye. The dark splotches of individual soldiers melded into a single organism that was creeping over the land, sending tentacles forward to explore, jerking back others when bitten by the cannon still firing from Telegraph and Howison's Hills, as well as the north spur of Marye's Heights. Yet, all the while, this creature sparkled with menace: musket bores hurling lead toward the wall, into McMillan's men.

"Colors!" somebody hollered.

McMillan turned toward the flag. It had gone down briefly, but was now up again, waving. A dozen hands had reached for it. Fred Satterfield, the color-bearer, was dead, shot through the face, although his expression was curiously alive. Glowering, McMillan watched him being passed to the rear. Satterfield's friends from White County gathered around him for a few moments, talked quietly among themselves, then went back to the ranks. Seeing this, some of the lightly wounded who'd been binding themselves asked for muskets so they could reload.

Commands rang out: the enemy officers closing the gaps in

330 · Kirk Mitchell

their line. They sounded near, looked even nearer. McMillan pivoted from the sight, afraid that his strained nerves would make him give the order too soon. He saw that the slope behind the wall was spattered with the blood of his men. Yelping, a boy flew out of the bunched-up ranks, squeezing his shoulder with a hand. He ran first one way, then the other before a corporal grabbed him by a suspender, pointed him off toward Mrs. Stevens's house, where everyone had last seen the assistant surgeon.

The men chuckled, but McMillan said, "Down—or there'll just be more of that."

A concussion jolted him, showered the line with clods.

Recovering, he listened carefully to the din on the left. In that way, he soon located the offending field guns. Most of this section's horses were dead, but the blue cannoneers went on loading and firing from upper Hanover Street. Brave men, but he wanted them killed, quickly. A flood of smoke was coming off the rifle pits to the north of Phillips's Legion. The Tarheel sharpshooters there were thinning the enemy gunners, forcing officers to help with the loading. Another horse went down, gnawing at its wounded haunch.

One of McMillan's men tripped backward from the wall, sat with a bounce and explored his face with his hands. His lower jaw had been peeled down and to the side by a bullet. Calmly, he got up and ambled along the road.

McMillan heard the creak of wheels above him on the crest. At last, a battery was arriving to relieve the Washington Artillery. Sighing, he waited for the tightness in his chest to ease, but it didn't. His heart knew the truth. There was only enough ammunition for one more good volley. And he dreaded the coming darkness, when his men would be blind.

The men behind the wall cheered the artillerymen. Virginians: they planted the blue flag of Virginia. Lathered teams pulled the guns into line. Crews jumped down, unhitched the pieces, handwheeled them into the empty redoubts and prepared to fire.

The twilight was stitched with red streamers from the enemy shells. Roaring bursts blossomed along the summit. Horses fell before they could be led away. A limber was burning, and in its light McMillan could see an officer being carried off toward the mansion, his hands dragging the lawn.

He looked below.

The advancing brigade line looked like an ocean swell as it built momentum over the prostrated thousands. Their colors were now black. The sun was gone, its last light just a blush in the west. *Raise the black flag and give no quarter to any scoundrel who crosses the river.* Poor Cobb. Somehow, had he been shown what the day of his death would be like? McMillan's eyes narrowed. How close was their line? And was another angling toward him from the direction of Hazel Run? The men were inching up for a look over the wall. He decided to trust their younger eyes. He'd gauge the nearness of the Federals by the growing restlessness along his own line.

One good volley.

What if the enemy refused to lie down this time? What if they kept coming on? Union shells were falling short, speckling down onto the plain two hundred yards short of the wall, yet the blue line refused to stagger.

McMillan got out of the way, withdrew to the far side of the road. A bullet sang by, pushing hot air against his eyes. Providence. It whistled and shrieked and exploded all around. He'd never felt so tiny in the grip of Omnipotence. Ducking was more than cowardice. It was faithlessness. A courier from Ruff was at his elbow, asking for more ammunition, nearly crying he was so frustrated. The 18th was fixing bayonets in expectation of being rushed at any moment.

McMillan ignored him, drew his sword. Garnett glanced back, offered a nervous smile that told him it was time. "Give it to them!" the old man cried.

The flashes illuminated the faces behind the wall, made them look ghoulish, sinister. Again, empty muskets were passed back, but no reloaded ones came forward. "That's it," a man in the rear said.

Ruff's messenger was still standing there, waiting for a reply. And now a man from Phillips's Legion, his neck bandaged. "Sir, we beg you—"

"A moment." Something made McMillan turn. Two figures were toiling down the slope, lugging an ammunition chest between them. The man in front was Sullivan. He avoided McMillan's gaze. All along the hillside, stores of ammunition were coming down into the sunken road.

McMillan looked to the couriers again. "You must understand," he said slowly, "it wasn't mine to say when we'd be resupplied. From now on, make your pleas to God Almighty, not Robert McMillan."

Twenty-Nine

◆

Yet another brigade was coming up from the lower end of town. Donovan heard their cheer but couldn't see the line through the smoky twilight. Nor could he make out the U.S. on the cartridge box of the dead man lying open-eyed to his right. Minutes ago, he'd decided this would be the sign that darkness was deep enough. Now, he wanted the musketry to fade too. But it was peaking again, the rattle drowning out the banging of a loose shutter against the side of the brick house. Despite all these sounds, there was a ghostly stillness to the ocean of men surrounding him, and he felt as if he were talking to himself as he readied the survivors within earshot to fall back. "On *march*, boys," he said. The hair went up on the back of his neck when nobody answered. He looked left at Hogan, but the sergeant's face was turned away.

At last, the musket fire began to ebb.

Donovan cried, "March!" Forgetting his injury in the excitement, he tried to push himself off the ground with his left arm and went down on that shoulder. The impact almost made him vomit, but he quickly rose on his good arm. About a dozen men—black silhouettes—were sprinting in front of him, among them Hogan and a few others from the brigade still marked by the boxwood in their caps. Donovan chased after them, leaping over corpses, trampling hands and brogans and discarded muskets. His left arm flopped painfully against his side, and he cradled it with his right. Other silhouettes rose from the dead. One had a wounded man on his back. Grimacing, Donovan tried to run faster. He knew that he and all the other upright figures were sticking out against the grayish smoke sifting over the field. Flights of musket balls kept buzzing past like swarms of bees. Men fell, but others got up to test their luck.

"Fly!" a stridently merry voice bellowed from the ground. "Fly away, children!"

A few lights were twinkling in town. Donovan had no idea where Hogan and the others were now, so he swerved for these faint beacons. He was getting sick to his stomach again: the slaughterhouse smells all around. A man just ahead stopped, clasped his throat with both hands and tumbled into the murk. A shell burst, making a circle of daylight in the nightfall. The flash was so brief, Donovan nearly tripped in the rush of blackness that followed it.

Then he was too breathless and nauseated to go on.

He collapsed to his knees, braced his hands against the earth. The cold was hardening it again.

From below, shouts echoed up. "Fourteenth Connecticut . . . anybody from the Fourteenth?" "Second Delaware, sing out, boys, and we'll find you!" Parties of survivors were braving the fire once again to rescue their own from the field. "*Kameraden,* Seven New York!" He listened hopefully for any of the brigade's regiments, but a minute passed in which the only sounds were those of balls thudding into dead flesh. He staggered to his feet. Just as he set out again, his hat was swatted off his head. He grabbed for it, too late, then ran his fingers over his scalp. The skin hadn't been broken.

He stumbled on toward the lights.

The faster he tried to run, the longer the slope seemed to stretch before him, a desert with bodies for dunes. His sore chest made deep breaths impossible. He was wheezing. The toe of his boot struck skull bone, but there was no protest. A man off to his left kicked a drum.

Reaching the snake-rail fence, he had to rest again.

In the swale just below, a regiment lay prone, heads raised apprehensively. "Don't shoot!" he gasped, afraid the men would let go a volley in his face.

"What was that now?" a brogue asked.

"He said don't shoot," another voice answered. "All that's left of him is here, and he don't want to lose no more."

"Who are you?"

"Captain Donovan, Irish Brigade." Letting go of a rail, he came dizzily down the slope and into the regiment, weaving among the men. "Eighth Ohio?"

"No, sir," someone said, rising. A warm, peasanty voice. "They're all used up, I hear. We're the Sixty-ninth Pennsylvania. We was waitin' to go forward again when the night come first. Let me help you across the bridge, Cap."

"Oh, don't endanger yourself, man." Miniés were whizzing through the darkness. Wherever Donovan went, they seemed to follow.

"God should make you a general, sir." The soldier took hold of Donovan under the arms. "Is your poor wing all shot up?"

"Broken maybe, not shot." Donovan began fighting tears. In all his battles, he'd never come close to this. But now, as the faceless paddy helped him sidestep over the bridge stringer, he didn't trust himself to speak. The town was finally so near. He could see ambulances in the streets, candle lanterns set before the doors of makeshift hospitals. The dead were receding behind him, the living awaited him. Life awaited him. Home. Below, bodies were floating in the canal, the gleaming surface pricked by bullets and shrapnel. He'd had no idea how thickly the lead was still flying until he saw the water.

"A shame to see a fine gentleman like yourself . . . on his own, hurt, in the middle of a fight."

"No gentleman."

"Well then, you're proof it's better to be born lucky than rich . . . what, sir? God speed."

Before Donovan could thank him, a voice hailed him from the far bank. "John!" It took him a moment to recognize the man in the darkness. Charlie Clarke, a captain from the 88th. He was sitting on a broken gun carriage, his left boot stripped off and his ankle bandaged. "John Donovan!"

"Yes." Donovan turned, looking for the soldier, but he was already halfway back across the bridge, and a field battery had started up nearby, its three-inch rifled guns barking, disgorging fountains of sparks. He plodded the last yards over to Clarke. "Where the brigade?"

"What?"

"The brigade . . . where is it?"

"No idea. Just got here myself." Clarke broke out his flask, offered it to Donovan.

He declined, despite his thirst. He was afraid he'd drain it just to dull the agony his chest was now giving him. All the muscles were stiffening, forming a vise around his lungs. "Have you seen many of us go by?"

"No," Clarke admitted. "Been busy, John." His flask glinted as he tipped it toward a wounded man lying nearby. "Barely got poor Horgan off the field."

"*Major* Horgan?" Donovan asked, incredulous. The last he'd seen of the major he'd been streaking toward the wall, sword over his head. It gladdened him to think that the man had somehow made it.

"No, the other—Captain Horgan. The major's dead." Clarke exhaled. He tried to pull up his stocking, but was too weak to give it anything more than a little tug. "It's a conspiracy, you know, John."

"Conspiracy," Donovan repeated hollowly.

"Sure," Clarke went on, "the whole affair. Washington's way of getting rid of all our best generals. Replace them with radicals, abolitionists and such. Burnside was in on it from the start."

Donovan was too tired to digest this. He stood. "Think I'll find Surgeon Reynolds. Throw an arm around my neck and come with me, Charlie."

"Not quite yet," Clarke said with mild insistence. "I'll wait a while for the rest of my boys to show. Night's young, and most of them will be along, I'm sure."

"Of course," Donovan lied. Nothing left now but the solace of lies. "See you in camp." He shuffled down the street toward the middle of town. The dead here had been tidied up into rows, if only to give the ambulances room to pass. Shadows danced from the light of a burning house, and the flitting glow itself made the bodies seem to quiver as if in restless sleep. Donovan began to cry. Life was so sweet—and ugly. He felt a strange joy, but knew even at that moment that he'd never remember it as being joy.

5:00 P.M.
Lacy House

Meagher drew rein beside the porch overlooking the river. He looked around the garden for Sumner, anybody from the grand division commander's staff. But the horse-line was practically deserted, and only the grooms remained, crowding a small fire they'd set behind some shrubbery. Dismounting, he asked one of them, "Who's here?"

"Nobody, sir. General Sumner went 'cross the river earlier. Want your mount fed?"

Meagher stood a moment, gazing past the house and down

into the hollow where he'd left them. All of his brigade who'd come off that killing plain. Less than three hundred. The slightly maimed had helped the more severely wounded across the swaying pontoon bridge.

"Sir . . . ?"

"What's that?" Meagher's ears were still ringing.

"You want your horse fed?"

"Please." He reached inside his green overcoat, patted his vest pockets for tip money. "I'm sorry. I have nothing on me."

"No matter, sir." The groom led the white charger away, a ghost horse in a dying country. Surely, the Confederacy had won more than a battle today.

Meagher climbed the porch steps, grunting softly. Yet, damnably, the pain was less, not worse, and the knee more pliable after the exertions of the day. Or perhaps he felt nothing at this point. Yes, that was it. Body and mind felt nothing.

He stared out over Fredericksburg.

The rising breeze had revealed stars above the ground-hugging smoke. Beyond the church spires, a thin sheet of flame erupted along the base of the heights. That unassailable stone wall, still flaring, still spewing death. No force in the world could rush those last one hundred yards. The Atlantic might as well lie between the board fence and Richmond. And in that the future had made itself known to him. He shut his eyes against the loss. He didn't see his brigade's flags, his father-in-law's Fifth Avenue mansion, not even Elizabeth. Proud and handsome Elizabeth Townsend. He saw Ireland as he'd last spied it from the ship taking him off to exile. *Will no one come out to hail me from Dunmore? I pass by, and my own people know nothing of it.* He watched it all fade by: the estuary of the Suir, river of his boyhood, and then the rocky coast from Bunmahon to Clonea, and finally Knockmeldown Peak lowering into the swells.

"I see," he simply said.

He'd never return now. The men who would have made that possible were lying dead or crippled between the Rappahannock

and that distant squiggle of musket flame. Liberation. This afternoon, the cup had been passed to another, perhaps yet un-
born. In a blast of muskets, the shuttles had stopped flying and
ambition had become an idle loom. He wanted only to sleep.
Again, he saw Catherine's grave. A love that hadn't known how
to criticize. A love he'd underestimated in his heady, selfish
youth.

"Tom Meagher, is that you?"

He opened his eyes, unaware that Burnside and his staff had
ridden up. The commanding general climbed out of the saddle,
took the steps with a surprising vigor. "It is you, by God."

"Yes, sir."

"How's your brigade?"

Wiped out. No other phrase came to mind. But he couldn't
make himself say that. Instead, he found himself going on about
something he thought he'd put out of mind. "Sir, there's been
some sort of misunderstanding."

"How's that?" Incredibly, Burnside sounded cheerful. Did he
have any idea what that long slope had looked like under the last
light?

"Earlier, I was under an erroneous impression that General
Hancock wanted me to bring what's left of my brigade across
the river."

"Didn't he?"

"I'm not sure, sir. That's why I wanted some clarification
from General Sumner . . ."

Burnside just quietly looked at Meagher, the light from the
grooms' fire in his pupils.

"My wounded were dangerously exposed, sir. Fatally exposed.
I wanted to save what I could, you see. Save as many of my boys
as I could. Those not in hospital. Bring them across the river to
safety . . ." Across the sea. Catherine's grave, its greenery dewy.
"And so I misunderstood a message to that effect."

"To what effect?" Burnside asked remotely.

"Authorizing me to withdraw my brigade. Procure rations and

ammunition for my men. Both exhausted." Meagher felt as if his voice were getting smaller and smaller. He knew that he sounded slumberous, almost drunk, but he couldn't stop talking. "And I accept full responsibility, sir. That's why I came here to the house. To report myself to General Sumner. My action in this matter to him."

Burnside said, "I'm sure you did what was best for your command, Tom."

"I have no command left, sir."

With that, Burnside glared.

Meagher felt as if he'd spurned a kindness. "General, may I volunteer my services as an aide to you . . ." The glare softened. ". . . to whomever you choose."

"I'll keep it in mind, Tom. Thanks." Then, astonishingly, Burnside grinned. "Did you hear the good news . . . ?"

"Sir?"

"Sturgis reports his men are only eighty paces from the crest and holding on like hell."

Meagher said nothing. He'd watched this brigade melt before the stone wall like all the others. Yet, he couldn't bring himself to tell Burnside that the Right Grand Division had failed. He'd leave it to Sumner.

After a moment of awkward silence, Burnside went through the front door.

6:19 P.M.
Episcopal Church

Lightheaded, Corby drifted toward the door of the lecture room. The chloroform fumes were starting to overwhelm him. The surgeons were splashing it onto paper cones, then clasping these little masks to the faces of the sufferers. Eight tables were going, and the floor was filled from wall to wall with those awaiting the knife, the saw. Every twenty minutes or so the orderlies had to carry off the severed limbs. Larry Reynolds was showing his Crimean War experience as he calmly supervised the other surgeons.

Corby reached the entryway. It too was packed with men lying quietly in their agony. No screams. No shouts. Just hands reaching up to stop him for absolution. *I offer all my sufferings in atonement for the sins by which I have crucified Thee.* . . .

But the priest needed air.

Turning, he waved at Father Ouellette, who was working the nave, where the pews had been pushed against the altar to make room for at least two hundred wounded. The French Canadian nodded, understanding at once Corby's need for relief, and started for the breathless lecture room.

Fearing now that he might pass out, Corby hiked the hem of his cassock and rushed for the night. Even the front steps were jammed with wounded. And dead. Men were dying as they waited for one of those blood-washed tables to open up. Without protest. "Father . . . Father Corby, please . . ."

"In a moment." He went into the street, almost reeling now. The dangerous street where only a few hours ago he'd met up with young Captain Sullivan of the 63d. The man had no sooner said how happy his aged parents in Albany would be to learn that he'd survived the massacre than a round shot came down the street and carried away one of his legs. Corby had heard his dying confession. How many since then? No idea.

Finding a garden that was almost empty, he leaned his back against a tree and rested his eyes for a moment. A shell burst somewhere in the neighborhood, and falling bricks clinked.

A voice begged, "Over there, please, for this poor fella."

Corby opened his eyes. Two men were depositing a wounded sergeant at the priest's feet. Leaving him, they turned and plodded back up the street toward the plain, nameless angels going under fire again and again to save what could be saved of the brigade. Corby tried to tell them that God knew their names, but he was out of words. He looked down. They'd just brought in the color sergeant from the 116th. The boy had that terrible, glorious calm in his face.

Corby hesitated out of weariness, his mind barely cleared of the chloroform fumes, but then knelt.

The boy's right hand fumbled inside his coat and came out with a crumpled envelope. It was covered with dried blood, which he clumsily tried to wipe off on his bullet-torn left sleeve.

Corby accepted it, read the address. *Mrs. Annie Tyrrell, 310 So. 7th Street, Philadelphia, Penna.* "Is your Annie pretty?" The question so visibly tortured the boy, so flooded his eyes, Corby regretted having asked it. He quickly stuffed the letter in a pocket already bulging with them, then took out his small oil stock and wetted his thumb.

The sergeant's eyeballs fluttered up as he began convulsing.

9:28 P.M.
Cobb's Brigade

Word came down. Longstreet wanted more rifle pits dug, all the earthen fortifications on Marye's Heights strengthened during the night. McMillan realized that this could only mean that the corps commander expected the Federals to renew the attack first thing in the morning. He was turning to see that the work was started when the ground came up to him. He blacked out for a moment, then saw that he was down on his left hip, his be-numbed legs and his scabbarded sword tangled under him.

Garnett ran across the road, helped him sit up.

"I'm fine," McMillan said, content for a moment to let his son's arm support him. Only a single rank at the wall was fir-ing. Sensing occasional movement inching up the plain, he wanted to send scouts over, but it'd be too perilous for them. Most of his men were squatting in the mud, nerves dead with fatigue, hands dangling limply into their laps.

He felt Garnett clasp him harder. "You did it, Pa. You stopped them. Somebody says even Lee thought for a while they'd break us."

"Who . . . ?"

"Just a rumor."

"We mustn't pass along rumors, Garnett." McMillan saw his son run a tired hand through his thick hair. A boy. His own boy, still alive. Yet, in the midst of his thanks he felt no warmth for Providence. He was too much in awe of It. Too powerless. It had taken James and Emma from him, but not once had a mutinous hatred filled his heart. He was only a man. So impotent. And today he'd seen that same Infinite Power smash the long dark waves rising toward this wall. Tomorrow It might find his own men wanting—and smash them just as completely.

A murmur ran among the men. They were rising. For an instant, he thought that some new conflagration had ignited in town. But this light was burning greenly. Skirts of green and now violet.

"The northern lights, Pa."

McMillan believed that he'd glimpsed them through the smoke earlier. "Saw them often when I was a lad. Help me up." He threaded his arm over his son's shoulders. Glancing aside, he saw by the glow of the celestial blaze that Garnett's face was bleeding from a small wound below the right eye. But McMillan said nothing about it. They both knew how close death had come today. Red now, the polar lights wavered over Stafford Heights, changed shape in intricate ways that were never repeated. This day would never be repeated in quite the same way, and for that McMillan was grateful. He'd been Joshua for one eternal afternoon—and had taken no sense of vindication from it.

"Hell," one of the men exulted, "heaven's kickin' up its heels for us!"

"No," McMillan snapped, "don't say such a thing." Yet, he knew that Cobb would have seen it that way. Dropping his arm off Garnett's shoulders, he said quietly, "Write your mother—

we'll give new hymnals to the church in Emma's memory. She loved music so." Then, before his son could say anything, he turned and shouted, "Michael!"

The sergeant stood from beside the row of dead, his pitted face expressionless, dark with spent powder.

"Michael, kindly find some picks and shovels for us."

Thirty

◆

McGee watched the surface of the water in his glass start to ripple. The long table at which he sat trembled and then went still again. The men around him paid no mind to the little disturbance, as if the enemy cannon were lobbing afterthoughts into Fredericksburg instead of shot and shell, echoes of a day everyone had tucked away. A scarlet autumn leaf pressed between the musty pages of an old book. The brigade officers packing the small theater were the few to have survived. The guests, twenty generals and the three committeemen who'd helped McGee bring the new colors from Manhattan, flanked Meagher on the stage. The brigadier wore a simple uniform and smoked a cigar with the distracted air of an actor going over his lines in the wings. The rafters above him were decked with boxwood. The swirling tobacco smoke and hum of conversation made McGee feel as if he were back in New York, attending another semi-conspiratorial banquet to advance the cause. *No surrender.*

But the purpose of this gathering was to receive the colors, baptize them with the bottles of champagne and whiskey that had clinked so irritatingly in the omnibus all the way from Washington. The reception had been planned for the thirteenth, two days ago. After Bloody Saturday, as it was now called, McGee thought it'd be postponed at least until the shock eased. He'd been there in the mist of yesterday morning, listening to the captains and lieutenants counting heads. Only 280 of the brigade's 1,300 men were present and fit for duty. And, until noon, Sunday, these survivors believed that they'd been brought back across the river to be thrown against the heights in support of 9th Corps. A bayonet charge, this time. McGee heard no complaint from them, no bitterness, and he prepared himself to lead his company up into the heavy skirmish fire that had started at dawn. But then word came that Sumner had talked Burnside out of one last attack. Some of the men wept upon hearing this, and in that McGee glimpsed the despair they'd hidden behind the usual banter and joking.

Rousing himself, he took a bite of canned salmon. The feel of cold flesh between his teeth revolted him, but he chewed and swallowed.

Yesterday, he'd crept up to the western edge of town and seen the remains of the disaster. He hadn't stayed long. The wounded not carried off the field under cover of darkness were once again trapped beneath the enemy's guns. He couldn't stand to hear their cries for help, for water. Even the Regulars who'd pushed up the slope the midnight before to relieve 2d Corps found themselves pinned down until nightfall.

Donovan.

A witness had him dead, shot to pieces while rushing the wall beside Major Horgan of the 88th. McGee knew enough to put off his grief. He'd been through other aftermaths and knew that early reports weren't to be trusted. And so he felt scant surprise when one of the 69th's surgeons told him that Donovan had been put on a northbound ambulance Sunday afternoon. His chest had been massively bruised, but he would live. Other than

Donovan, the news hadn't been good. Sixteen of the regiment's nineteen officers had been killed or wounded. It was much the same with the rest of the brigade, and even worse with other units of 2d Corps. The list of the dead numbed the mind, so the living went on as if it didn't exist. They smoked, codded one another, and hid an enormous gratitude that felt more like shame than anything else.

The chatter fell away to a murmur.

General Meagher had stood. McGee studied his face for a hint of the man who'd wept in the hospitals Saturday night, gone down the aisles clasping the hands of the brigade's wounded, his breath coming in sobbing gasps. He and the others had never seen the general, any general, so unstrung. Yet today, that anguish was under wraps, and Meagher smiled as a shell landed somewhere down the street. "Generals, brother officers, and comrades of the Army of the Potomac," he said with a steady voice, "fill your glasses to the brim . . ."

All came to their feet, and the waiters poured.

McGee had the vague sense that none of this was happening. Not really. He either was sleeping on the train from New York or had died with the colors at Antietam, and this reception was some grotesque, purgatorial rite. His brother d'Arcy would think so. How predictable it was, he'd say—the failure of Irish arms followed by a swaggering demonstration that all was not lost. It'd be lost only when the last paddy was put under the sod. d'Arcy had turned his back on that. Gone to Canada.

Yet, McGee found himself hoisting his glass along with the others.

"I have the honor and pleasure," Meagher went on, "to ask you to drink to the health of my esteemed friend on my left, General Alfred Sully . . ." Of Irish parents, of course. "And I want you to understand, gentlemen, that he's not one of your political generals, but a brave and accomplished soldier—who attracted his star by the electricity of his sword!"

The men cheered, but somehow, McGee couldn't join in. It was no time for recrimination. That could wait for later. The brigade's dead were still lying unburied above town, stripped white by the clothes-hungry Rebels.

A captain from the 63d leaned over and whispered, "Are you all right, Jim?"

"Sure."

"Well, why the long face?"

McGee hesitated, but then went ahead and said quietly, "I just don't see the point to this sort of talk."

"Mackay's the point," the captain said, eyebrows arched.

"What?"

"The bastard's been around, inquirin' about the spirit of the brigade."

McGee slowly smiled. So that was it. This was a performance for the benefit of the London *Times*. He downed his drink in a single gulp. Everything became clear. It was all for the eyes of the Beast, the *Times*, whose readers would remark over tea how mercurial and savage the Celtic heart was—swinging like an ape through the trees: from despair to revels in less than forty-eight hours. And the doubt would be fanned that civilized men could ever be made from the likes of those who'd stormed the heights behind Fredericksburg. So let the barbarians go their own way. Let them go. He held out his glass as his waiter poured again.

Next, Meagher praised Hancock, who coolly slid a hand into the parting of his coat as the Irish roared and pounded the tables with the butts of their bottles. "The general," Meagher cried above the tumult, "we should have had at Ballingarry!"

When the toasting was finally done, he called for the commanders of the New York regiments to receive the flags. But only Pat Kelly of the 88th went all the way up onto the stage. The deputies for Nugent and O'Neill—both colonels were in hospital—hung back like altar boys. A shell hit close, a building or two away, and plaster dust drifted down over the tables. McGee sneezed.

"General Meagher," Kelly said somewhat awkwardly, his soft eyes watering up on him, "we gratefully acknowledge the arrival of these hallowed flags from the people of New York City, but . . ." He paused, either out of unease or by plan— McGee wasn't quite sure, although his suspicion was growing. ". . . in conscience, we can't accept them."

The committeemen gave no reaction, and Meagher asked a bit too quickly, "Why not, Colonel?"

"Our numbers are so . . ." A blast interrupted, and then a brick wall could be heard tumbling down across the street. ". . . so reduced we can never hope to defend them."

Meagher stared a long moment, then said, "I understand, Colonel Kelly."

And so did McGee now. But the drift was lost on the non-Irish generals, Couch especially, who turned grumpily to Hancock and asked so all could hear, "What's this rot about?" Hancock probably knew, but he just hiked a shoulder. Meagher meant to recruit the brigade back up to full strength. That's what he was saying by this gesture.

"I do so understand," Meagher repeated, and as if on cue the survivors rose once more with glasses lifted toward him. Like the tragic heroes of old, his life was fixed on a single course, no matter what. They drank to that as much as to the man himself.

Meagher's cook came in from a side door and carried a silver service up to the brigadier. "Yes, Joseph?"

"Message for the gen'ral."

Looking confused, Meagher removed the cover, revealing a twelve-pound solid shot.

"Just flew into me mess chest," Joseph added sourly.

Meagher turned to the hall. "I believe I've just been told these proceedings are adjourned."

11:48 P.M.
Ambulance train

Tyrrell awakened with a start. The ambulance had begun to
rock and pitch as if it were crossing a choppy sea. He tried to
raise himself up a little. His head was spinning, and he was
hemmed in by the other wounded, as many as the bed of the
cart would hold. But he lifted up and saw water on both sides
of him, glistening under the waning moon. They were going
over one of the upper pontoon bridges, and Lacy House appeared above the ears of the horses. The wheels made almost
no sound over the planks. Another man, his right arm gone
from the elbow, also found this curious, for he sat up and looked
over the tailgate. "Straw," he explained, "they put straw on the
bridge."

"Quiet, boys," the driver said low. "Whole army's pullin'
back across the river tonight, and there's no use lettin' Johnny
know about it."

"Pullin' back where?" someone asked.

"Our old camps. Hush now, for godsake."

Tyrrell eased back down. He tried not to move, although he
felt little pain. A hospital steward had given him a big round pill
just before the train had clattered away from the Episcopal
Church. It brought on a quick, dreamless sleep which obviously
hadn't lasted long. He was wide-eyed now, although his head
was thick and his stomach raw. Five wounds, the surgeon had
said before putting him under, caused by four musket balls. The
sawbones believed that one of them had done double service,
piercing both Tyrrell's left hand and arm.

The moonlight dimmed, and he saw that clouds were the
cause. Thunder. He could hear thunder. It sounded clean, oddly
innocent to him, now that he'd spent most of a day under the
man-made kind. The wind was out of the south. It was driving
small waves into the hulls of the pontoons, and the backwash
chuckled under the planking. Another rumbly peal made an

Irish voice say, "The Lord's bringin' home the turf." Just what Tyrrell's father said whenever he heard thunder.

A man sprang upright and vomited over the side.

"Goddamn opium pills," the driver said sympathetically.

The ambulance reached the Stafford shore and started up a steep lane. All the wounded slid back toward the tailgate in a bunch. One man groaned, "Oh my God . . . oh my God."

"Can I help?" Tyrrell asked.

"You can't," he answered.

"Are you pinned?"

Silence.

Tyrrell squirmed forward on his back as the jumble of men tried to get comfortable once more. A horse snorted, hooves clopped out an easier rhythm. He began to feel sleepy again. The fringes of the clouds turned to mother-of-pearl as they drifted over the moon. He heard a fat drop hit the canvas top. Then another. And suddenly it was raining a torrent. He could hear waves of it coming over the river, bending the tall grass on the bank.

"Farewell, stone wall," a man said. "You can keep this god-forsaken country."

No one else wanted to talk about Saturday afternoon.

Tyrrell thought he knew why. He'd never expected to feel so afraid, so humiliated by his own terror, so alone. Yet, he'd gone down with the colors. The thing he had feared the most, a complete loss of nerve, hadn't come to pass. It had taken four balls to loosen his grip on the staff. But Burnside had failed. That much was clear now. He prayed there was some wisdom beyond his own small understanding for the army to come back across the river, some great plan that would be revealed to everyone, even the dead. Something to compensate Hudson and the rest of his color guard, who'd been swallowed by that muddy slope, something to give Davey Major a reason for being left alone in a graveyard so far from the Walnut Street Theater.

"Where we bound?" somebody asked the driver.

"Aquia Landin'. From there by steamer to Washington."

Washington. It came to Tyrrell. Annie and his parents could take the train down from Philadelphia to see him. Annie would wear a bonnet and his mother would bring a wickerwork basket filled with foods from home. On this, he slept.

Thirty-One

◆

Sullivan sat beside McMillan's fire in a Water Street garden, polishing his new sword with spit and wood ashes. Most everyone in Longstreet's corps had one now, if the regulations allowed. Hundreds of them had been left on the plain. But it'd been impossible to find a scabbard that hadn't been dented by balls or shell fragments, so Sullivan had to make do without one. He tilted the blade in his hands, and it shone with the light of a moon that was almost full. An hour ago, the colonel had gone off with Garnett to Methodist services in the middle of town, leaving the brigade along the waterfront. Nobody expected trouble, although in late January Burnside had marched much of his army upriver in the hope of outflanking Lee. The blue people never had a chance: rain and sleet fell by the buckets, flooding the fords and turning the pikes into brown seas. Their plans were being frustrated by Providence, or so said McMillan, and the Army of Northern Virginia could expect the same if ever it fell from God's favor through wickedness.

Sullivan stopped rubbing his gritty fingertips over the sword for a moment, thinking.

He had no idea why some causes were blessed, others cursed,

some men raised up and others laid low. The Yankee pickets said that Burnside had been sacked and Hooker put in charge. Colonel Wofford of the 18th Georgia had come back from sick furlough, been promoted to general and made commander of Cobb's Brigade. Over McMillan, who couldn't hide his disappointment, although he said nothing of it and deferred to the younger man as if things had always been that way.

Sullivan went on polishing. He knew nothing. Nothing was knowable.

By last Friday, the Union army had settled once again into its Stafford camps. Now fires blazed up and down the Rappahannock as far as the eye could see. Opposing pickets stood in full sight of one another, day and night, with little fear of being murdered—as if that Saturday in mid-December had never been.

"Mike," Dooley said, stepping out of the darkness. "The fellas over there . . . they're askin' for you."

"Ah, they don't know what they're askin' for."

Dooley neared the flames, hands outstretched. "I think you oughta go, have a word with 'em. As our captain." He paused. "Did you hear the singin'?"

Yes, Sullivan had heard it. All the old rebel songs. The Lochrane boys and the Georgians had joined in. But these past weeks, he'd had no taste for songs. For words either. Many times he'd tried to pen a few of them to Mrs. Tully, but they'd turned empty on the back of the piece of wallpaper he was using. *Hugh died for Southern rights. For Irish freedom. Forever. He died forever, and all the generals, who can move men in the thousands like cattle, can't make him stir a single finger ever again. . . .* The townspeople had given over a plot of land for the Confederate dead. Sullivan had dug the boy's grave there. His blanket had been stolen, so there was nothing to wrap him in, but he framed Tully's head with sprigs of boxwood taken from that long, shallow depression in which Meagher's brigade had been slaughtered.

"Mike . . . ?" Dooley asked again.

"I have no heart for it." Sullivan began wiping the sword on a rag. "Let the hare lie, Tommy."

"Then go for the boy's sake."

Sullivan glowered up at him. "What kind of thing is that to say?"

"Go for all the boys, Mike. Here and across the sea."

Sullivan was quiet a few seconds, then he suddenly snapped the blade in two across his knee. He tossed the pieces away. "Feel like a bloody fool wearin' a sword," he said, rising from the fire and starting north along the riverbank.

Dooley fell in beside him.

The water was glazed with ice, all but the middle of the stream, which showed light riffling. Yesterday, before this latest freeze, a message had come over on a flat piece of pine bark with a handkerchief for a sail. It was from the Fenians of the 69th New York. They wanted to know if on that awful night, with the northern lights festering, the commander of Cobb's Brigade had sent an Irish sergeant over the wall to where he'd seen the 69th's national ensign go down. Rather than see this flag become a trophy in Richmond, the sergeant had hid it inside the coat of the dead Federal color-bearer, who was found the next day by his companions propped against a tree. Was the Rebel sergeant actually Captain Michael Sullivan of the Circle of the Army of Northern Virginia?

Ridiculous.

As far as Sullivan knew, only one Rebel had gone over the stone wall, a sergeant from the 2d South Carolina, who'd disobeyed orders when he could no longer stomach the cries of his wounded enemies for water.

Sullivan and Dooley came into that part of the picket line manned by the Lochrane Guards. A bonfire crackled every thirty feet. The Macon men were standing openly on the bank, muskets stacked behind them. Across the river, a large tent came into view, canvas glowing from within. It'd been pitched in a ravine just upstream of Lacy House. Below it, a score of blue figures stood along the shoreline without muskets. "That's him, I'm sure. That's Sullivan," one of them said, his voice carrying across the still night.

A graybearded man came through the tent flaps, gripping a lantern. He stopped at the river's edge, peered out, his candle throwing a shimmer of gold across the dark waters. "Captain Sullivan?"

"I'm Mike Sullivan of Savannah." Then he forced himself to sound more cordial. "It's been some years, Doctor Reynolds."

"It has indeed. And are you still a friend?"

Sullivan wanted to walk away. The darkness would be a comfort. He could feel Dooley and the others growing restless, but no words sprang to mind. He should've gone west years ago, right off the boat. There was no war on the frontier, except with the Indians. There was no division.

"I understand we owe you a debt," Reynolds went on.

"Oh, I don't know about that."

"General Cobb involved you in an errand . . ."

Sullivan smiled up at the stars. Yes. An odd errand. McMillan had taken him to a house down along the road to Spotsylvania. There, Jesse and he had washed that bloodless shell of a corpse for shipment home to Georgia. Already, Cobb seemed to have turned to marble. The people of Athens would just have to open the box, take him out and hoist him onto a pedestal in the city square. "No, sir," Sullivan corrected the enemy surgeon, "General Cobb got his mortal wound early that afternoon. Me own colonel, Robert McMillan of County Antrim, commanded the brigade."

Reynolds nodded. "Then it was this colonel who sent you over the wall?"

Sullivan bit the inside of his cheek to keep from laughing. Again, McMillan was watching Jesse and him wash the corpse, the old man's eyes dry with envy. The secret cruelty of that Saturday was that few of those men had been old enough to long for the grave. Life had had them beguiled, yet.

"Say somethin', Mike," Dooley pleaded.

"What kind of people are we?" Sullivan whispered. "Is the truth too much?"

"Yes."

"Then where does that leave us?"

"With a river between us," Dooley said grimly.

Sullivan shook his head. A people starved for nationhood, getting by on a gruel of legends, fashioning little visions of heaven from the wreckage of hell. And he was so very tired of fighting Irish to free Ireland. His enemies should have horns and tails, not brogues and the faces of home. This valley had gotten the better of him, of everyone who'd somehow survived. He had no words, just weariness—and a deathless loyalty to things that seemed so remote tonight.

"Are you a friend, Captain Sullivan?" Reynolds asked once more.

"I am a friend," Sullivan finally answered.

An Afterword

◆

Brigadier General Thomas Francis Meagher, Irish Brigade
In May 1863, he resigned his command after the War Department refused to let the brigade withdraw from campaigning for rest and recruitment. A year later, he returned to duty and served on General Sherman's staff in Tennessee. After the war, he looked west rather than ally himself with Fenian schemes that led to an ill-fated raid on Canada in 1865. Perhaps the war had made him appreciate the human cost of armed revolt. He was appointed acting governor of the Montana Territory. On the night of July 1, 1867, he vanished off the stern of a steamboat and was presumed drowned in the Missouri River. As with most chapters of his life, the final one is shrouded in controversy. One report has him drunk at the time of his death, another sober but in fear of assassination by former Rebels in the territory. Whatever, the world wouldn't see an Irish-American public figure of his dash, wit, and charisma for nearly a century. His widow, Elizabeth, spent some months searching in vain along the banks of the Missouri for his body, but finally returned to Manhattan, where she lived alone until her death in 1906.

Colonel Robert McMillan, 24th Georgia

He continued to lead the regiment until his health completely deteriorated in January 1864, forcing his resignation. His surgeons' certificates strongly indicate that he suffered from congestive heart failure throughout the war. He died in 1868 and is buried with his wife and children in the Clarkesville Cemetery.

Chaplain William Corby, 88th New York

Two bronze statues—one at the University of Notre Dame and one on the battlefield—commemorate his most famous hour: the general absolution he gave under fire at Gettysburg. By that time, all the regiments of the brigade, except the 28th Massachusetts, were down from ten to two companies each. After the war, he was twice president of Notre Dame. He died in 1897.

Sergeant William H. Tyrrell, 116th Pennsylvania

Promoted to second lieutenant, he received his sixth wound while on provost guard duty in Washington. He was shot in the neck by a drunk and disorderly Union officer he was attempting to arrest. He was officer of the day in the capital on April 14, 1865, and submitted one of the first reports on President Lincoln's assassination. He was married twice and had four children. His injuries left him disabled the rest of his life, even for silversmithing. He spent his last years in Atlantic City, New Jersey, and then died penniless at the Pennsylvania Soldiers' and Sailors' Home in 1916 at age seventy-six. His body lies in Philadelphia's Central Laurel Hill Cemetery.

Sergeant Michael Sullivan, 24th Georgia

He emerges from obscurity and vanishes into legend. A dubious anecdote in a history of the 69th New York has him swimming the Rappahannock and taking a picket's bullet—all to return the 28th Massachusetts' green flag, which was never reported lost, to his brother Fenians. The same source has him ferried back to the Rebel line, duly promoted to captain in a Georgia regiment, taking part in the Fenian raid on Canada, and finally becoming a prosperous citizen of Savannah. None of these assertions could be verified. Still, there were hundreds like him, refugees of the Great Hunger who built the South's railroads and served in its armies.

Captain John H. Donovan, 69th New York
Like Sullivan, he left little behind for historians. He has no pension record on file with the National Archives.

Lieutenant Garnett McMillan, 24th Georgia
Cited in dispatches for gallantry at Chancellorsville, Spotsylvania, and the Wilderness, he was transferred to the 3d Georgia Battalion of Sharpshooters and promoted to captain. After the war, he married, had four children, and studied law under his ailing father. In 1874, he was elected to the U.S. House of Representatives but died at age thirty-two of tuberculosis a few months before Congress convened. He was widely held to be one of the rising political stars of the postwar South.

Captain James E. McGee, 69th New York
He later commanded the remnants of the brigade, but was discharged after wounds received at Petersburg in 1864.

Captain Walter Scott Brewster, 24th Georgia
His leg was amputated the evening of the battle, but he died the next day. His body lies in Alta Vista Cemetery in Gainesville, Georgia.

Private William McCarter, 116th Pennsylvania
He was carried off the field by friends and survived a severe wound to the right shoulder and upper arm, which disabled him for life. For three years in the 1880s, he made his home in Fred-

ericksburg, perhaps to come to grips with the experience of his one and only battle. It was his belief that Lieutenant Christian Foltz was killed while trying to rescue him.

Private Thomas J. Dooley, 24th Georgia
He fought with the regiment at Chancellorsville, Chickamauga, Gettysburg, the Wilderness, Spotsylvania, Cold Harbor, Winchester, Cedar Creek, and Petersburg—then deserted in January 1865.

Colonel Robert Nugent, 69th New York
He was shot through the hips and lower abdomen, contrary to the belief on the field that he'd been wounded in the chest. While recovering at home, he was made acting assistant provost marshal general of New York City. In July, Irish anger over the draft and labor competition from free blacks erupted into five days of rioting and murder. Nugent's house and belongings were destroyed by the mob for his part in trying to suppress the disturbance. After the war he served in the Regular Army until his retirement in 1879. He kept faith with his late brigade commander by leading efforts to see that Elizabeth Meagher, who'd fallen on hard times, was given a widow's pension. He died in 1901.

Major Robert Emmett McMillan, 24th Georgia
He survived the leg wound he received at Sharpsburg and died in 1890.

Lieutenant Richard Riker Emmet, 88th New York
He died of complications from his recurrent malaria shortly after the battle.

Private John H. Haddock, 24th Georgia
He rose to first sergeant and surrendered with the regiment at Appomattox.

Colonel Patrick Kelly, 88th New York
He later commanded the brigade and was killed in action at Petersburg in June 1864.

Private William B. Haddock, 24th Georgia
Promoted to first lieutenant, he was on sick furlough at the time of the surrender.

Lieutenant Colonel St. Clair A. Mulholland, 116th Pennsylvania
Wounded at Fredericksburg, he was back in action at Chancellorsville, for which he was awarded the Medal of Honor. After the war, he became the Philadelphia commissioner of police.

Major General Edwin Vose Sumner, Right Grand Division
After Burnside was ousted, Sumner was relieved by his own request and transferred to the Missouri Department. On the way to his new command in March 1863, he suddenly died, allegedly of a broken heart.

Corporal Joseph Hudson, 116th Pennsylvania
Like so many men of color guards on both sides that Saturday, he was killed in action.

Major General Ambrose Everett Burnside
He was given lesser commands after Fredericksburg, including that of his old 9th Corps during Grant's Virginia campaign of 1864. After the war, he was governor of Rhode Island from 1866 to 1869 and died a U.S. senator from that state in 1881.

Correspondent Charles Lawley, the London Times
The former member of parliament continued his newspaper career, covering the Franco-Prussian War next. His reports on the battle of Fredericksburg included, rather surprisingly: "To the Irish division, commanded by General Meagher, was prin-

cipally committed the desperate task of bursting out of the town of Fredericksburg, and forming, under the withering fire of the Confederate batteries, to attack Marye's Heights, towering immediately in their front. Never at Fontenoy, Albuera, or at Waterloo, was more undaunted courage displayed by the sons of Erin than during those six frantic dashes which they directed against the almost impregnable position of their foe. . . ."